BOOKS BY AVA MARIE SALINGER

FALLEN MESSENGERS

Fractured Souls - 1

Spellbound - 2

Edge Lines - 3

Oathbreaker - 4

Harbinger - 5

Crimson Skies - 6

Wicked - Fallen Messengers Short Story Collection

THE MAGE AND HIS BRUTE

Arcane Entanglement - 1

∾

CONTEMPORARY ROMANCE WRITTEN

AS A.M. SALINGER

NIGHTS

One Night - 1

The Escort - 2

Tokyo Heat - 3

Sweet Obsession - 4

Sweet Possession - 5

The Proposition - 6

AVA MARIE SALINGER

ARCANE ENTANGLEMENT

THE MAGE AND HIS BRUTE

BOOK 1

COPYRIGHT

NOTE TO READERS

This book is written in British English, as befits the story and its characters.

APPENDIX

Welcome to the world of *The Mage and His Brute*. To help you navigate this complex and fascinating realm, we've compiled this appendix of key terms, concepts, and institutions.

This guide is designed to enhance your reading experience, providing quick references to the rich tapestry of magical and social elements that make up our alternate London. Feel free to consult this appendix whenever you encounter an unfamiliar term or want to delve deeper into the intricacies of this world. It's our hope that this resource will enrich your journey through the streets of magical London alongside Evander and Viggo in the fascinating, arcane world of *The Mage and His Brute*.

Magic and Magic Users

1. Mage: The most powerful and versatile of magic users, able to manipulate the fundamental elements of water, wind, earth, and fire. More rarely, there are mages who can manipulate light and dark magic. The latter two are referred to as Light Mages and Dark Mages.

2. Archmage: An extremely rare and powerful mage who can wield at least four elements and perform complex, large-scale magical feats. Some Archmages can temporarily lend their magic to other mages.

3. Charm Weaver: A specialist who creates enchanted objects and imbues items with magical properties. Artisans and crafters who spend long hours weaving intricate spells into their creations, their magic is more subtle and indirect than that of mages, but can be just as powerful in its own way.

4. Enchanter: A magic user who can influence the minds and emotions of others. Enchanters are often diplomats, negotiators, or even spies, using their magic to smooth social interactions and gather information. However, their powers can also be used for manipulation and control, making them potentially dangerous.

5. Alchemist: A specialist who deals with magical potions, elixirs, and substances. Their creations can be used for medicine, magical enhancement, or even as weapons in the right circumstances.

6. Healer: A rare magic user who can perform healing magic. The strongest ones are considered on a par with mages. They can command high fees for their services, with most attending only to nobles. There are few healers among the poor social classes and none among thralls.

7. Caster: The lowest rank of magic users, specialising in simple, formulaic spells.

8. Light Mage: A rare mage who can use light-based powers and possesses the ability to foretell the future.

9. Dark Mage: A rare mage who practices forbidden dark magic.

Important Terms

10. Thrall: The lowest class in society, consisting of magicless individuals who are often treated as property.

11. Brute: A rare breed of magicless individuals with extraordinary strength and resistance to magic.

12. Blood Magic: A forbidden form of magic that manipulates life force and vitality.

13. Sanguine Subjugation: A form of Blood Magic allowing complete domination over another person.

Artefacts and Devices

14. Illusion Amulet: A magical item used to alter one's appearance.

15. Disruptor Rod: An anti-magic artefact used to interfere with spell casting.

16. Anti-Magic Marbles: Artefacts that create a thick fog that obscures vision and disrupts magical targeting.

17. Blood Siphon: A device created to absorb and store the life force of magicless individuals.

18. Midnight Obsidian: A rare substance that can absorb and amplify magical energy.

Organisations and Institutions

19. Royal Institute for the Arcane: A prestigious magical academy for training gifted magic users.

20. Mage Council: The governing body for mages.

21. Arcane Division: A department of the Metropolitan Police dealing with magical crimes.

22. Arcane Forensics Division (AFD): A specialised unit within the Arcane Division for magical crime scene investigation.

23. Nightshade: An information guild run by Viggo Stonewall.

Historical Events

24. War of Subjugation 1825-1830: A historical conflict between magic users and the magicless.

Magical Techniques & Abilities

25. Shadow Imprint: A magical technique used by Archmages to reveal where a soul recently left the world.

26. Shadow Manipulation: A dark magic ability that allows the user to control and shape shadows. It can be used for concealment, creating illusions, or even as a means of transportation.

27. Shadow Creatures: Monstrous entities created from pure darkness through potent dark magic. These beings can interact with the physical world and are often used to attack enemies. Only the most powerful dark mages can create and control shadow creatures.

CHAPTER 1

THE BODY OF THE DEAD MAN LAY AT A STRANGE ANGLE, HIS broken arms and legs spread out where he'd landed awkwardly on his front, as if he had been attempting to take flight to escape his fate. His neck was twisted in a way that would not have been possible in life, his dilated pupils staring unseeingly at a brown brick wall.

A gaping wound in the left side of his torso exposed his ribs and innards.

A sliver of unease skittered down Evander Ravenwood's spine as he observed the injury. Pale bones and gristle gleamed under the dull sunshine attempting to pierce the overcast sky above the East End of London, the perpetual clouds of smoke that shrouded the district casting it in a near permanent twilight that reflected its sombre mood.

The wound looked too clean to have been made by an animal. More to the point, the victim's heart was missing.

As a Special Investigator for the Arcane Division of the

1

Metropolitan Police, Evander had seen his fair share of horrific things over the years. Though this case might appear to be a straightforward murder, the fact that someone had deliberately removed an organ from the victim made it more chilling than a bloodied crime scene littered with corpses.

He was distracted from his grave musings by Lyra Shaw's low mutter.

"That's interesting."

The forensic mage squatted beside him and gently poked a gloved finger inside the corpse's chest cavity, heedless of the filthy water soaking into the hem of her department-issued coat. Her button nose wrinkled not so much from distaste at what she was doing or the stench of rotting refuse and horse piss rising in the cool autumn air, as it did from being deep in thought.

A rising star in the Arcane Forensics Division, Shaw was an earth mage known not just for her razor-sharp intelligence, but her meticulous attention to detail and her ability to spot clues others might miss. She could also drink most Met officers under the table.

"His arteries look to have been drained of blood," the mage commented, as if giving her opinion of what shade of ribbon would best suit a friend's new dress. Her keen gaze swept the ground around the dead man. "Probably explains why he didn't make more of a splashdown."

A young constable who looked too green around the ears to be wearing his black badge heaved at her comment.

Shaw ignored him and furrowed her delicate brow. "I wonder what kind of magic did this."

"What makes you think this was magic rather than a physical weapon of some sort?" Evander asked lightly.

He was watching an alchemical analyst carefully collect a lump of the unfortunate victim's brain where it had in fact splashed rather messily in a puddle some ten feet away. It was a moment before Evander became aware of Shaw's silence. He turned his head and met her pointed stare.

"Is that a trick question, your Grace?" the forensic mage voiced with her usual no-nonsense frankness.

"Humour me."

Shaw pursed her lips at his request.

"Because the wound bears evidence of magic cauterisation, your Grace," she said in the tone of one addressing a fool. She pointed at the barely visible burn marks lining the hole in the dead man's chest.

They both overlooked the disapproving scowl Sergeant Griffiths shot at Shaw for her discourteous manner. Though many would be forgiven for not knowing Evander's station as a Duke, one need only examine his clothes and bearing to know he was of high nobility.

Evander paid no heed to such formalities among colleagues. He gave Shaw a rare half smile.

"Just making sure you noticed."

The forensic mage blinked. Evander's aloofness was legendary not only in the Met but in the whole of London society. The expression that flashed across her face for a split second before she looked away showed she was pleased by the compliment. She prodded around the corpse's innards some more.

Evander grimaced. "How about you stop doing that? You know what Inspector Grayson will say if he finds out you interfered with the body." He looked over his shoulder at the figure at the opening of the alley.

Rufus Grayson, the man in charge of this sorry affair and a good friend of Evander's, had his back to them and was taking notes while he interviewed the poor shopkeeper who'd discovered the dead man behind his establishment that afternoon.

Rufus's magic quill danced over the yellow papers of his notebook as they conversed in hushed tones, his black hair curling where it brushed the collar of his dark blue coat. The silver aiguillette on his left shoulder flashed faintly in a rare ray of sunlight.

It denoted his rank as an inspector.

Evander carried a similar insignia on his official winter coat and summer jacket. Except his was silver and gold, a symbol of his status as a Special Arcane Investigator. His aiguillette also bore blue threads. He was the only officer in the Met to possess them.

They signified an additional station that had nothing to do with his role in the Arcane Division.

A temporary cordon rose a short distance beyond Rufus and the witness, the translucent barrier issuing from the magical device sitting on the ground catching the light here and there as it held back the crowd of curious onlookers who'd gathered at the mouth of the alleyway to gawk at the crime scene. Unfortunately, the projection did little to block out the noise of the slum sandwiched between Hackney Road and Bethnal Green.

The cries of street sellers, hawkers, and barrow boys

mingled with the clip-clop of horseshoes striking cobblestone and the jarring rumble of wheels rising from carts and carriages trundling through the thoroughfare.

The East End was a noisy, messy place on the best of days. Market Day made it ten times worse.

"What Inspector Grayson doesn't see won't hurt him," Shaw muttered presently.

Evander traded a resigned glance with Vincent Brown, the alchemist who'd just gathered another piece of the victim's brain and was tucking it inside a secure slot in his evidence box. A rotund man with a bushy red beard, Brown wore a constant glint of curiosity in his eyes.

"Look here, Shaw," the alchemist started, "how about you stop mucking around and—"

Something went "squelch" under the mage's probing finger.

Blood and a sticky black substance spurted out of the dead man's chest cavity, flew an inch past Shaw's left cheek, and landed on one of Evander's expensive, lace-up boots with a wet splat.

They stared, horrified.

Evander swallowed a groan.

Jasper is going to kill me.

Jasper Hargrove was his manservant. A caster and former Navy man, he prided himself on making sure Evander was smartly dressed whatever the occasion. Evander suspected if he ever had an appointment with Death, Hargrove would make sure he was perfectly presentable for the deadly rendezvous.

The constable who'd barely recovered his composure gagged, twisted around, and vomited noisily against a wall. Griffiths patted him on the back and directed a dark look at Shaw.

The forensic mage was too busy chewing her lip to pay attention, her eyes locked on the unsightly blob presently sinking into the exquisite leather of Evander's boot.

"Oh, you've gone and done it now, Shaw," Brown grumbled. He threw his hands up in the air. "His Grace's boots are bound to be worth at least half a year's salary!"

Evander didn't bother correcting the man. His boots had cost far more than that. He knew because he'd seen the receipt from Greystoke & Co, the fine leather goods shop in Pall Mall Hargrove purchased his dress shoes and boots from.

Shaw paled, her expression a mixture of remorse at what she'd done and shock at the idea that someone would wear boots equivalent to half her annual wage.

Evander reconciled himself to getting an earful from his manservant and sighed.

"Would you be so kind as to lend me one of your specimen vials, Mr. Brown?"

The alchemist had just passed him a glass tube and a scooping stick when a voice made them flinch.

"What the devil happened here?!" Rufus snapped.

The inspector had joined them.

He took one look at the bloodied end of Shaw's gloved finger and the grim evidence Evander was patiently scraping off his footwear before clenching his jaw so hard they heard his teeth grind.

"Miss Shaw," Rufus grated out, "what have I told you about sticking those fickle hands of yours where they don't belong?"

Shaw recovered and flashed a smile at the inspector, undeterred. "Look on the bright side, sir. I just saved Dr. Mortimer the trouble of discovering that black substance, whatever it is." She waved at the stygian lump on the scooping stick Evander was holding.

Ambrose Mortimer was the chief physical examiner of the Arcane Forensics Division. Despite his morbid sense of humour and his unsettling habit of talking to the corpses he examined, Mortimer was a stickler for following procedure.

Rufus closed his eyes and pinched the bridge of his nose. Brown heaved a weary sigh and shook his head.

Evander didn't blame them.

Mortimer was going to have an apoplexy when he found out what Shaw had done to his precious body.

Rufus frowned at the constable who was still hurling his breakfast and, by the looks of it, yesterday's dinner, before observing Evander candidly.

"What do you make of this, your Grace?"

CHAPTER 2

EVANDER MET THE INSPECTOR'S GAZE STEADILY. HE HAD been on his way back from a business luncheon when he'd received an urgent message from Rufus requesting his assistance. Since he knew his friend was more than capable of handling a murder, Evander had gathered something about the case was unusual enough to warrant his involvement, even on his official rest day.

He'd proceeded to the address Rufus had given him without stopping at his townhouse to change clothes, something Hargrove would no doubt grouse about when he returned to his home in Mayfair.

One look at the scene of the crime had made it instantly clear why Rufus had sought him out.

The victim had arcane symbols carved into the back of his neck.

Evander frowned as he studied the cryptic marks once more. Judging from the appearance of the skin, they had been made postmortem.

His immediate reaction upon seeing them had been a near visceral response to the foul energy they emitted.

The symbols reeked of dark magic.

Few people could detect its presence. He wasn't sure whether it was a gift or a curse that he was particularly sensitive to the dratted thing.

The power the marks emitted was akin to a vile and insidious heaviness, one that pressed in on all sides, leeching the warmth from the air and leaving an oily residue in its wake he could almost feel on his skin.

That a dark mage was involved in this crime was undeniable.

And dealing with rogue mages, especially those who went around killing people and engraving runes into their flesh, fell squarely under Evander's duties as a Special Arcane Investigator. It might not be official yet, but Evander had little doubt Rufus would soon be handing the case over to him.

"All I can tell you is this was definitely the work of a dark mage. Beyond that, these symbols…don't really make any sense."

Confusion clouded Rufus's slate-blue eyes. "What do you mean, your Grace?"

"It is just as I say." Evander gestured at the marks. "This is either a coded message of some sort, or whoever engraved them into his skin was in a rush." He paused. "I am pretty certain I am correct in my conjecture, but we should ask Mr. Inkwell to take a look, just in case."

Quentin Inkwell was the chief Occult Researcher in the AFD. He was, in fact, the *only* Occult Researcher in the division.

It was, unsurprisingly, a field of study few pursued with academic enthusiasm.

A muscle jumped in Rufus's cheek as he observed the dead man's remains. "The shopkeeper doesn't recognise him. Neither do the proprietors of the businesses that back onto this alley." He glanced at the few worn-out doors lining the derelict passage. They were being guarded by constables to prevent the owners of the establishments from spying on the crime scene. "Whoever he is, he wasn't from around here."

Evander furrowed his brow.

Yet another mystery to add to the bag it seems.

Something about this case was already giving him a bad feeling. It had started when he'd walked into the alleyway and gotten his first hint that it involved dark magic. His misgivings had only gotten worse after he'd examined the scene of the crime with his associates from the AFD.

Evander couldn't quite put a finger on the why. Murder was never straightforward. There was an entire library full of cold cases in Scotland Yard that attested to its complexity.

It was just that his instincts were warning him to be extra vigilant. And Evander's instincts had saved his skin one too many times for him to ignore them.

He locked eyes with Rufus. "There's something you should know." Evander rose to his feet and scrutinised the roofline of the shop beside them. "I am almost certain he wasn't killed here. And he wasn't pushed off that building."

Rufus startled. Brown lowered his brows.

Shaw straightened to her full five foot three. The mage was frowning. "Is it the lack of splashdown that makes you say that, your Grace?"

"For God's sake Miss Shaw, will you stop using that damn word?!" Griffiths groaned while the constable under his wing turned a nasty shade of green once more.

"Sorry," Shaw muttered as the young man was led stumbling towards the mouth of the alley by another colleague. She turned to Evander, her expression keen and her role in the poor man's unfortunate state all but forgotten. "So?" She fidgeted from foot to foot, her excitement clear. "Go on, spill it, your Grace."

Evander saw Rufus's cheeks flush with ire at her tone. He replied before the inspector could utter a cutting remark.

"It's not just the lack of—blood around the body. A fall from that height would have broken his bones for sure, but it would not have splattered his brain in a fifteen-foot radius around the point of impact."

Rufus, Shaw, Brown, and even Griffiths stared up and down the alley at the small red flags the alchemist had planted in the ground to indicate where he had collected the various fragments of the contents of the victim's skull.

Shaw's face cleared. She slammed a fist into her palm. "By Jove, you're right, your Grace!" She beamed at Evander like he'd performed a miracle.

"Wait." Rufus cut his eyes to the roofline before aiming a probing stare at Evander. "If he wasn't pushed off that building, then how did he get here and in such a state too?"

Evander faltered before voicing the words that had

been at the forefront of his mind for the past ten minutes. The words that had raised goosebumps on his skin when he'd first thought them.

"He was dropped from at least a hundred feet above the ground."

Shock widened Rufus's eyes. Brown drew a sharp breath.

Shaw crossed her arms and started pacing the alley, her face focused. "That makes sense. Which means our dark mage…" She trailed off, realisation striking her like lightning and drawing a gasp from her lips. Her head tilted jerkily as she met Evander's steadfast gaze.

"The murderer may be able to wield wind magic too."

Rufus licked his lips in the tense hush that followed Evander's statement. "So, we could be dealing with a dual elemental mage?"

Evander could hazard a guess as to what everyone was thinking from the unease growing on their faces.

Mages were powerful enough as it was, ranking highest in the hierarchy of magic users above healers, Charm Weavers, enchanters, alchemists, and casters. A dual elemental mage was rare, a tri-elemental mage rarer still. As for a quadri-elemental mage, that was the stuff of legends.

Because a mage who could wield four elements or more qualified for the title of Archmage. And of those, a mere handful were born each century.

Formidable figures that had shaped mankind's history since magic flourished in the mid-1500s, Archmages had enjoyed vast privileges and power over the centuries, putting them on par with royalty.

Evander masked a frown.

Or at least they used to.

Though still glorified and revered the world over by nobles as symbols of the purest form of magic, the reputation of Archmages suffered a severe setback after the War of Subjugation. They came to be feared and reviled by the common man and the masses, especially the magicless thralls who formed the lowest class of society and who were often treated as little more than property. Many thralls who survived the war and the illegal purges that followed still bore ugly marks that had been branded into their flesh to denote their status as quasi slaves. Cattle to be used and disposed of at the will of those possessing magic.

An all too familiar wave of bitterness swept through Evander at the thought of the thousands of innocent men, women, and children who perished during the misbegotten conflict that ripped through the British Empire and the continent in the first quarter of this century.

Though the war began and ended well before his birth, he could not allay the anger, shame, and remorse he'd carried deep inside him ever since the day his brother John first told him the true facts of the matter.

It was never a war to begin with. It was genocide.

Evander clenched his jaw. Now was not the time to dwell on a subject that had long haunted his thoughts and dreams.

Rufus's voice brought him back to the present moment.

"Wouldn't such an individual have to be registered with the Mage Council?"

The Mage Council was the governing body for mages in the British Empire. All mages, regardless of their status in society, had to be on their official records, their powers carefully documented so as to satisfy the rules and regulations set by the council.

Similar guilds existed for other types of magic users.

"Not if he is a rogue mage who chooses to hide his abilities," Evander muttered.

Shaw and Brown traded a troubled look.

A loud crash made them all jump. Evander's shoulders knotted as they stared towards the mouth of the alley. Cuss words and shouts clouded the air somewhere on the thoroughfare.

"What in the blazes?" Rufus mumbled.

The crowd beyond the cordon began dispersing, a swarm migrating towards the next source of gruesome entertainment. A constable rushed into the passage a moment later.

Evander stiffened at the sight of the crimson stains on his clothes.

CHAPTER 3

GRIFFITHS SWORE AND RUSHED FORWARD, RUFUS ON HIS heels.

"Good God man, are you quite alright?!" the sergeant barked.

"Yes, Sir," the constable replied hastily. "But—it's a disaster!"

Shaw moved past the inspector and the sergeant, and picked some kind of seed off the constable's uniform. To everyone's horror, she brought it to her mouth and licked it.

"Jesus wept, Miss Shaw!" Griffiths rasped.

Shaw arched a quizzical eyebrow at the constable. "Melon?"

The young man nodded jerkily, colour staining his ears a little at Shaw's proximity. "Yes, Miss. A cart full of melons bound for Covent Garden crashed into a wagon of berries and pomegranates headed to Kensington Market."

Relief shot through Evander. Rufus visibly relaxed.

Brown's lips twitched. "My, it sounds like a veritable—"

"Don't say it," Evander warned.

"—fruit salad out there, eh?"

Everyone groaned, including the constable with melon stains all over his uniform.

Brown beamed at Evander's sharp stare. "What's life without a good pun now and then, your Grace?"

Evander sighed. "It's less irritating, Mr. Brown."

Another constable dashed into the alley. "Sarge, we could use some help out here! A fight's broken out!"

As if to underscore his words, an enchanted whistle pierced the rowdy air.

"Bloody hell!" Griffiths cursed.

He hastily gathered his men and headed towards the thoroughfare, the runes on his truncheon coming to life as he removed the weapon from his waistband. The Met's preferred mode of dispelling rabble-rousers these days was to use defensive magic before inflicting bodily harm.

Rufus hesitated and looked over at Evander.

"Go." Evander jerked his head after Griffiths's disappearing figure. "We'll be alright."

Rufus nodded and headed after the sergeant, leaving Evander in the alley with the forensic mage and the alchemist. Evander knew he was keen to make sure things didn't get out of hand out there.

Tensions between the magicless and those who ruled over them were on the rise, a result of the stark and growing disparity in wealth that existed at either end of the societal class. The East End, with its squalid districts rampant with poverty, crime, and desperation, was a simmering cauldron of resentment and loathing just waiting for the perfect spark to kindle a fresh conflict. One Evander feared could lead to another War of Subjugation.

Shaw watched Rufus leave with a conflicted expression.

"What's the matter?" Brown asked.

"I'm wondering if I should go out there and secure one of those lost melons."

Brown squinted. "They ain't lost, Shaw. And what you're describing is theft." The alchemist glanced at Evander. "Help me out here, your Grace."

"Mr. Brown is right, Miss Shaw," Evander said as he wandered deeper into the alley. "You'll get in trouble with the law." He paused and arched an eyebrow at the forensic mage. "I'll bring you a melon next time my cook buys some, so please refrain from accidentally nicking one of those unfortunate cantaloupes on your way out of here."

Shaw brightened and fist-pumped the air. Brown muttered under his breath.

Something clinked against Evander's boot. He frowned and lifted his foot out of the puddle he'd just stepped into. Water dripped into the dirty spill, spreading ripples across the brown surface.

A faint blue light flashed weakly beneath it.

Evander's pulse quickened. He squatted and carefully moved aside the rock his boot had dislodged, exposing a small object.

Shaw and Brown joined him as he picked it up and brought it to eye level.

"What is that, your Grace?" the alchemist asked curiously.

Evander stared at the small crystal vial. It had a slim body and two tapering ends, fitting easily in the palm of his hand. A clear, sparkling azure liquid filled the hollow chamber within.

It didn't look like the sort of thing you'd find in the East End.

Evander's heart slammed against his ribs.

His intuition was telling him the object was a magical item. One linked to the victim.

His gaze shifted to the dead man, gauging the distance between the body's point of impact and the location of the vial.

Was it on him when he fell?

The hairs lifted on the back of Evander's neck in the next instant.

The air in the alley thickened with a suddenness that made his ears pop. Dread chilled him when his breath misted in front of his face.

Dark magic!

Shaw and Brown doubled over before he could shout a warning. Their hands rose to clutch their temples even as their faces contorted in expressions of pure agony, the suddenness of the invisible attack robbing them of breath and stealing their cries before they could form.

The only thing that protected Evander from the debilitating effect of the spell that incapacitated his associates was his powers.

Coolness bloomed in the centre of his chest and filled his veins as he drew on his water magic, the tingling flow matching the rhythm of his heart. The sensation changed to a sharp, biting cold when he shifted its focus from liquid to ice.

Fire magic would have been more useful under the circumstances, its purification effect capable of burning away dark energies and spells from the air.

Sinister black trails coiled through the frigid atmosphere out of the corner of Evander's right eye just as a two-foot long icicle materialised in his left hand.

He twisted sharply on his heels and hurled it at the gap in a doorway that should have been sealed. The weapon flew straight and true, its trajectory guided by his powers.

The hooded figure lurking in the shadows of the building jumped back and cursed. Wind whipped violently into life around him, shifting the icicle's path at the last moment.

It slashed a cut in the man's right thigh, pierced his cloak, and smashed into the wall behind him. Glittering fragments peppered his clothes as he whirled around and vanished from sight.

Evander scowled. He jumped to his feet and gave chase.

Shaw and Brown gasped and wheezed behind him, the dark mage's fading spell removing the constraints binding them in place.

"Wait, your Grace!" Brown shouted weakly.

Shaw started running after Evander, earth magic blossoming on her fingertips.

He darted inside the building without waiting for her. The enchanted folding cane strapped to the inside of his right forearm snapped out of the sleeve of his frock coat with a flick of his wrist.

Stairs appeared at the end of a gloomy passage. A startled shout rose from somewhere up them. It was followed by a cut off, gurgled scream.

Evander gritted his teeth.

Blast it!

He took the stairs two steps at a time.

Movement above him sent his pulse skittering.

Evander smashed aside the dark magic bolts raining down on the staircase with his cane. The projectiles raised clouds of brick dust where they impacted the walls.

The first landing came in sight around a corner. A man lay on the floor, body limp where he'd fallen on his front. Blood trickled from a fresh wound on his temple.

Evander paused long enough to make sure he was breathing before leaning over the banister.

"We need a doctor!" he shouted at Shaw.

The forensic mage nodded briskly at the bottom of the staircase, a stone truncheon in hand. She spun around and retraced her steps, her chest heaving with her breaths.

Evander looked up and narrowed his eyes.

Their assailant was on the second landing and moving fast.

He resumed the chase, his body growing light as he called upon his wind magic. Currents formed under his feet. They carried him up the staircase, nearly doubling his pace.

A vicious oath somewhere above told him his attacker had clocked his new speed. Evander had no doubt the man had picked up on the fact that he could wield both water and wind magic.

By the time he reached the attic room the dark mage had run into, the man had disappeared through an open window under the rafters. A breeze carrying the sour reek and noise of the slums ruffled the thin curtains framing it.

Evander crossed the rickety floor and hooked a leg over the windowsill. A loose tile shifted under his foot. His gaze found the cloaked figure running nimbly along the ridge of the building.

Evander climbed out onto the pitched roof, stabilised his body with a buffer of wind magic, and went after him.

The dark mage accelerated as he neared the end of the ridge. He leapt across the fifteen-foot gap to the next building and landed in a low crouch on the roof, magic cushioning his fall. He rose and broke into a run, a smirk stretching his mouth under his hood as he glanced back at Evander.

His expression froze in the next instant, shock rounding his pale eyes and causing his steps to falter.

The icicle left Evander's hand at the same time he jumped across the drop, wind magic beneath his feet and at his back.

The dark mage veered desperately to avoid the attack. He cried out and stumbled when the weapon found his left flank.

Evander touched down lightly on the roof and bolted after him.

The wounded mage gained momentum. Shadows misted the air around him as he called upon his dark powers.

Evander lowered his brows.

This bastard has no intention of stopping!

He accelerated, the tiles trembling under his footsteps.

The dark mage didn't slow down when he reached the roofline. Instead, he twisted his body, spread his arms, and fell backward off the building, his cloak fluttering wildly around him and his eyes burning with hate as he glared up at Evander.

Evander's heart leapt in his throat as he skidded to a stop on the brink of the drop, velocity tilted his body perilously forward. He pinwheeled his arms, slammed his cane in a groove in the roof, and stepped back, his boots knocking a couple of tiles off the building.

The clay slabs tumbled through the air before smashing noisily into the street below, narrowly missing a barrow boy and a butcher's stall. The pair startled and swore loudly, the boy's curse words painting the air blue.

"Evander!" Rufus yelled somewhere behind him. The inspector's voice was full of fear.

He'd dropped all formal address in the heat of the moment.

"I'm alright," Evander shouted back.

He panted, gaze sweeping the busy market lane.

There was no sign of the mage, nor could he sense any trace of the dark magic he had used against them.

Evander frowned as the shrill sound of enchanted whistles splintered the neighbourhood, the crystal vial he'd been hanging on to throughout the chase digging into his palm.

CHAPTER 4

IT WAS NEARING SUNDOWN BY THE TIME EVANDER MADE IT back to his townhouse in Mayfair. His manservant took one look at the state of his attire when he stepped inside the foyer and said something rude.

This earned Hargrove a disapproving stare from Cordelia Sinclair, Evander's former nanny and the current housekeeper of the Ravenwood estates.

"What the devil have you been up to, my Lord?" Hargrove fussed as he divested Evander of his coat.

"I had to visit a crime scene."

Hargrove took a sniff of the coat and curled a lip. "Was it in a cesspit, my Lord?"

"Mr. Hargrove," Mrs. Sinclair warned in a stern voice.

Hargrove shrugged, unrepentant. "What, Mrs. S? I'm sure you can smell our Lordship's new *Eau de Latrine* from where you're standing."

Mrs. Sinclair narrowed her eyes behind her wire-rimmed spectacles.

Evander swallowed a sigh and tugged on his cravat as his housekeeper and manservant launched into one of their daily squabbles. He was halfway to the grand staircase dominating the entrance hall when Mrs. Sinclair addressed him in a sharp tone.

"I hope you haven't forgotten about your engagement tonight, my Lord."

Evander mouthed a silent curse under his breath. The fact that he was meant to be attending a ball that evening had completely slipped his mind after this afternoon's events.

He turned and directed an apologetic look at the housekeeper.

"Thank you for reminding me, Mrs. Sinclair. I'm afraid I'd forgotten about it."

The housekeeper's expression softened at his contrite mien. "You best make haste, my Lord. The hour is late and your partner for the ball is not known for her patience."

Hargrove headed for Evander, a worrying glint in his eye. "Do not fret, Mrs. S. I'll make sure he's spick-and-span for the lady."

Evander resigned himself to his fate as his manservant shepherded him towards his private quarters on the first floor.

Night had fallen by the time his carriage pulled up outside a magnificent, white stucco townhouse in Eaton Square. The ornate magic lamps framing the glossy, black double doors cast an enchanted light on polished brassware and the irritated expression of the beautiful, green-eyed blonde who stood waiting at the top of the flight of steps leading to the entrance.

"You're late, your Grace," Lady Genevieve "Ginny" Hartley snapped as Evander's footman alighted and opened the carriage door.

Evander ducked his head and stepped out to greet her. "It couldn't be helped, my Lady."

Ginny's resplendent peacock-blue gown shimmered when she descended the stairs, diamond and sapphire glinting in her ears and at her throat. Her piqued expression faded as she greeted the footman.

"Hello, Samuel."

The young lad bobbed his head mutely, his ears flushing a delicate pink.

Ginny's gaze shifted to the coachman. "I'm glad to see you've recovered from your cold, Graham."

The older man tipped his top hat with a faint smile where he sat in the box seat. "Thank you, my Lady."

"It appears the Duke's help is getting more respect than the Duke himself tonight," Evander said drily. He took Ginny's white, silk-gloved hand and pressed a kiss to her knuckles.

"That's because the Duke often forgets the concept of time," Ginny retorted. She perused his outfit with a shrewd stare. "You look nice."

Evander smiled faintly. "So do you." He waited until she'd gathered the skirt of her gown before handing her inside the carriage. "I'm sure I'll be the envy of every gentleman at tonight's ball."

Ginny preened a little as she sank into the dark green velvet upholstery covering the bench seats. "And I'm certain I shall be the envy of all the ladies, your Grace."

After being forced to listen to Hargrove's nagging for

25

the state of his clothes and shoes, Evander had submitted to a long, hot bath followed by an hour of his manservant fussing as he fitted him out for the ball.

Even he had to admit the end result was rather spectacular.

The dress coat and trousers he wore had been crafted from the finest wool by his personal tailor at Blackthorne & Sons, the lapels and cuffs adorned with intricate, silver embroidery and the subtle pinstripe in his perfectly pressed trousers shimmering faintly in the light. His white dress shirt was fastened with custom-made onyx cufflinks from Madame Elise's Enchanted Emporium on New Burlington Street and his black silk cravat was held in place by a silver pin from the same exclusive boutique. Not only did they bear his family crest, a raven perched on a crescent moon, they were enchanted with protective charms and could serve as small explosive devices if needed. As for his polished, black Oxfords, they were from the same place in Pall Mall Hargrove would be sending his expensive, stained lace-up boots back to come morning.

They waited until the footman had closed the door and they were underway before relaxing. The sleek, black four-wheeler was enchanted not only to provide a perfect environment and riding experience for its passengers, it was also equipped with a privacy spell that prevented anyone outside from spying on the conversation taking place within. There was even a button that could render the windows opaque, adding another layer of intimacy to the interior.

"I heard about the incident this afternoon," Ginny said as the elegant townhouses and leafy streets of Eaton Square flitted past the window. She frowned. "Is that why you're late?"

Evander dipped his head.

Ginny was a secret informant for the Met Police and the Arcane Division, her connections in high society as well as her contacts in the London underworld affording her access to crucial intelligence that had helped him and his colleagues foil many a serious crime.

It was a rare and unexpected occupation for a woman born the eldest daughter of a viscount.

When her father died after squandering the last of the Hartley family fortune to gambling debts eight years ago, a then seventeen-year old Ginny begged an aunt to help her debut in London high society in a bid to support her young siblings. Instead of putting herself on the marriage mart like many had assumed she would, she defied convention by becoming the most sought after courtesan in the city within a couple of years, her beauty, intelligence, and sharp wit attracting wealthy and influential men who sought a suitable companion to share their evenings with during the London season.

Life as a high-end courtesan offered Ginny a far more opulent and freer lifestyle than marriage ever could. Not only did her profession allow her to follow her many intellectual and physical interests, including business ventures that made her a pretty enough sum to make sure her family would never be in need of money, they also granted her access to a world that was the exclusive privilege of aristocratic men. It was why she was loathe to marry, despite the many proposals that had graced her doorstep.

They'd met five years ago, when Evander had been forced to seek a high born lady with whom to attend a mandatory royal banquet, shortly after taking on the title of Duke of Ravenwood. He had been leery of the introduction by an acquaintance at first, convinced he would have to fight off the advances of a cunning young woman who would no doubt see him as the proverbial golden goose that he was.

The reality had turned out to be the complete opposite of what he'd expected and he'd been shocked by how much fun he'd had in Ginny's company. They'd attended several gatherings over that summer and, once it became clear they shared many common interests, had become fast friends.

One of those passions was their ambition to bring about justice for the magicless, a mission Ginny was as devoted to as Evander, so much so they were in the minority of nobles in London who counted thralls among their household staff and in their business holdings.

"Is it true that a dark mage attacked you?"

Ginny's voice stirred Evander from his contemplations.

He met her steady gaze. "Yes. Rufus and I suspect he's the murderer."

Ginny frowned. "Why on earth would the perpetrator return to the scene of the crime?"

It was a question that had occupied Evander's thoughts on his way home that afternoon. He suspected he wasn't going to like the answer when he finally figured it out. Lights outside drew his gaze, distracting him for a moment.

They had passed Knightsbridge and were approaching Hyde Park Corner. The coachman guided the horses onto Piccadilly.

With its brightly illuminated shops, restaurants, and clubs, it was London's most fashionable street and a beacon of aristocratic privilege. Magic crystals bobbed inside the glass orbs atop the street lamps, providing ample lighting for the nobles enjoying the evening air.

It was a far contrast to the cheap gas lamps and oil lanterns in the slums a few miles away.

"Things will hopefully become clearer once we know the identity of the victim," Evander told Ginny quietly.

He didn't mention the vial he'd discovered in the alley. With everything that had happened that afternoon, he'd forgotten to hand it over to the Arcane Forensics Division.

Evander frowned.

Hopefully, Brown and the other alchemists might have an idea what's inside it after I meet with Rufus to take over the case tomorrow morning.

The carriage veered south on St. James's Street and entered the heart of aristocratic London. The grand facade of Ashbrooke House soon came into view, the tall, multi-paned windows of the magnificent Georgian mansion glowing prettily in the night where it overlooked St. James's Square.

The queue of carriages bringing guests to the ball had all but died down. Evander and Ginny were greeted by a score of footmen in Ashbrooke livery as they pulled up in front of the grand portico over the main entrance.

Muted sounds of revelry reached them when they disembarked and proceeded up the steps.

"Ready to brave the lion's den?" Evander said as the doors started swinging open.

CHAPTER 5

"Fear not, your Grace." Ginny removed a delicate mother-of-pearl fan that matched her gown from her silk reticule and snapped it open. "I shall do my best to keep you from getting ambushed by madames keen to marry off their young charges to one of London's most eligible bachelors."

Evander groaned at her teasing tone. "And I shall endeavour to stop any unwanted suitors from making advances towards you, my Lady."

They shared a small, secretive smile.

It was an arrangement they'd come to a few years ago, when they realised they could help each other avoid getting pestered by all sorts of unsavoury individuals keen to gain their favours at social events. It was a pact that had proven to be especially helpful in their line of work, when they'd used their rumoured status as lovers to infiltrate gatherings so as to spy on suspects or approach potential business partners.

They entered a marble foyer lit by a grand, crystal chandelier and were greeted by their hosts.

"Duke Ravenwood, Lady Hartley. What a pleasure it is to see the two of you," Lady Ashbrooke said with a warm smile as she came forward. She kissed Ginny affectionately on the cheek.

Ginny beamed. "You look lovely, Lady Ashbrooke."

Lady Ashbrooke's eyes twinkled. "So do you, Lady Hartley. That dress is simply ravishing."

Emmeline Ashbrooke carried herself with a beauty and grace that belied her fifty odd years. She was a renowned enchantress, famous for her ability to create stunning illusions, and could charm any room she entered with her wit and presence.

The distinguished gentleman beside her kissed Ginny's knuckles and shook Evander's hand.

"You look well, Ravenwood."

Evander bobbed his head. "Thank you for the invitation, my Lord."

Percival Ashbrooke was as tall as Evander and had a stately bearing that matched his high-ranking position in the Ministry of Arcane Affairs. With a keen intellect and a strategic mind, he was a powerful earth magic mage and a trusted advisor to the Queen.

A faint frown wrinkled the older man's brow.

"Terrible affair in the slums last week, eh?"

Evander knew he was referring to the riot that had recently rocked Whitechapel. It was one of several incidents to have taken place since the summer and was yet another sign of the growing hostility thralls felt towards the powerful nobles who ruled over them, yet knew nothing of their daily plight.

Lady Ashbrooke gave her husband a sharp look.

"You promised not to discuss work tonight, my dear."

"I'm sorry, dearest," Lord Ashbrooke said sheepishly.

Lady Ashbrooke's expression eased fractionally. She turned to talk to Ginny.

"See you in the smoking room later?" Lord Ashbrooke took the opportunity to whisper to Evander out of the corner of his mouth.

Evander nodded as the Ashbrookes' next guests arrived.

Lord Ashbrooke was bound to question him about the current affairs of the Arcane Division when they were in private, especially the disturbances involving the slums. Evander's mission tonight was to subtly gauge the waters in turn and see if his suspicions about the House of Lords were correct.

He and Ginny left their hosts and moved past portraits of long dead Ashbrookes as they proceeded to the ballroom.

It was a magnificent space that occupied the entire rear of the house. The gilded mirrors lining the walls reflected the light from the numerous chandeliers dotting the coffered ceiling. Magical fireflies danced above the guests' heads, producing a sparkling radiance that bathed the room and the assembled nobles milling around the polished parquet floor in a golden glow.

A piano quartet played quietly in a corner.

At the far end of the room, tall French windows

opened onto a terrace overlooking mature gardens, a space for guests to cool off and take in the night air.

And for some to venture into the grounds to engage in illicit encounters under arbors and behind bushes.

Evander's mouth twisted at the wry thought. Alas, his role as Special Arcane Investigator kept him so busy these days he'd all but forgotten the last time he'd engaged in a tryst. Not that he could do so in present company.

His taste in lovers was different from most men.

They took the champagne flutes a footman offered them and began navigating the ballroom, Ginny's hand resting lightly on his arm.

"Who's your mark tonight?" Evander murmured.

He nodded at several distant acquaintances with the polite, detached expression that had earned him his reputation as the Ice Mage.

"Lord Aldous Fairfax." Ginny smiled coquettishly at one of her many admirers and blissfully ignored the glower directed at her by his wife. "We met at a business gathering last week. I intend to approach him about my new venture."

Evander had missed the meeting at the mercantile guild. He'd been up in Yorkshire, busy consulting on a case involving a cursed artefact.

He took a sip of his drink. "Does this concern your enchanted soap factory idea?"

"Yes. Fairfax owns a few enterprises that can source the raw materials I will need." Ginny's eyes gleamed. "He is rumoured to be a skilled alchemist himself. He will make a good partner."

Evander was conscious of the avid stares they were

drawing as they meandered to a table laden with roast meats, oysters, truffled pâté, and various other expensive delicacies. They'd been the subject of many an extravagant rumour over the years. It seemed that unless something especially scandalous happened at tonight's ball, they would be the subject of fresh gossip fodder come morning.

Ginny's mouth curved in a beatific smile as they helped themselves to some entrées. "If looks could kill, I would be as dead as a doornail right now."

Evander gave her a quizzical look.

"Our favourite rumourmongers are in attendance," Ginny said wryly. "Twenty feet. Your seven o'clock." She turned so Evander would have a reason to look in that direction.

He picked out the couple glaring at them straightaway.

Hector Thompkins was a young nobleman with a reputation for dark proclivities and for wasting his family's fortunes in gaming houses and dens. Standing beside him was Lady Amanda Vane, a woman who had used scandal and strife to climb the social ladder.

Having each been respectively spurned by Ginny and Evander when they'd sought to make romantic advances towards them during the previous season, the pair were now seemingly hellbent on bringing them down in the eyes of the aristocracy.

In a society where gossip and scandal still counted as powerful weapons and where even the most baseless rumours could ruin lives and reputations, it was a dangerous game to play indeed.

Unfortunately for them, Ginny was more skilled at it.

"Lord Thompkins and Lady Vane appear to be in a particularly murderous mood tonight," Evander said lightly. "What did you do to them?"

"Oh, nothing much."

Evander arched an eyebrow, not in the least bit fooled by her innocent tone. "Really?"

Ginny finished the last bite of her roast beef and horseradish finger sandwich and dabbed her mouth delicately with a lace handkerchief.

"I may have inferred that Lord Thompkins has developed the pox on his genitals and that Lady Vane is partial to riding well-hung horses."

A man on the other side of the table choked on a canapé.

Evander gave Ginny a stern look. "That's low, even for you."

Ginny shrugged. "They started it first."

Evander couldn't help but smile faintly at her unabashed mien. An evening with Ginny was never boring.

They filled up on more finger food before heading into the crowd.

Ginny brightened a few minutes later. "Ah. There is Lord Fairfax."

Evander followed her gaze to a tall man with silver-streaked hair standing next to a potted plant.

"Oh hell and tarnation!" Ginny cursed with her next breath. She grasped Evander's arm and pulled him behind a column, startling a portly, middle-aged couple.

Ginny eyeballed them until they moved away. She

scowled in the direction of Lord Fairfax. "He's been cornered by that Wentworth shrew."

Evander had already spotted the cause of her concern. Lord Fairfax was currently engaged in conversation with a stout matron with steely grey hair who'd been hidden from view by the leafy fronds of the fern.

Lady Agnes Wentworth was one of London's most notorious matchmakers.

Evander had fallen victim to one of her matrimonial snares in the past and was keen not to experience such unpleasantness any time soon. The older woman wasn't a fan of Ginny and had been at the source of the vicious rumours that had branded the young woman as little more than a glorified prostitute when she first gained a reputation as a high end courtesan.

Evander was one of a small number of people who knew that Ginny was incredibly particular about who she allowed in her bed chambers. No amount of money could convince her to sleep with someone she wasn't attracted to. And the odd men who had tried to be forceful in their amorous advances soon discovered that Ginny's physical interests lay beyond horseback riding and a game of croquet.

"Judging from Fairfax's glazed expression, the subject matter Lady Wentworth is currently discussing is boring him out of his mind," Evander observed warily. "Maybe we should leave them a moment. Lady Wentworth is bound to lose interest soon."

Ginny's expression darkened behind her fan. "Care to bet?"

Evander's stomach sank.

CHAPTER 6

LADY WENTWORTH WAS INTRODUCING A BEAUTIFUL brunette with large, doe-like blue eyes and perfect porcelain skin who'd been standing demurely a short distance away to Lord Fairfax.

"The man buried his wife two summers ago," Ginny said between gritted teeth. "Now that witch wants to pawn the Miller girl off to him?!"

Ophelia Miller was the daughter of Baron Edward Miller, a member of the House of Lords known for his philanthropic work. Though it was her first season, Evander had no doubt it would be her last. She was without a doubt the current belle of London society.

He'd even heard of a wager at several clubs betting she would be off the marriage mart come the end of autumn.

"Surely there are gentlemen of more consequence that she could be introducing Miss Miller to?" Evander murmured.

"A rumour reached my ear last week," Ginny said

darkly. "Lord Fairfax will soon be coming into a considerable inheritance, courtesy of a dead aunt in Scotland. It seems that old hag heard it too."

Evander swallowed a sigh. Old hag seemed a harsh, if appropriate term for Lady Wentworth. He glanced at his companion.

"Is that why you chose Fairfax as a potential business partner?"

"It wasn't the only reason." Ginny furrowed her brow. "I have it from a reliable source that he makes regular contributions to charities that offer aid to thralls. I believe he is someone who could be of benefit to our cause." She stiffened, another unladylike curse tumbling from her lips.

The centre of the ballroom was clearing, the piano quartet preparing to perform the first of the evening's dance music. Lady Wentworth was urging a beleaguered Lord Fairfax and an awkward-looking Miss Miller towards the emptying floor.

Ginny snapped her fan closed and shoved it in her reticule. "Time to save my future business partner." She grabbed Evander's hand and dragged him towards the battlefield, her face full of a single-minded determination he had seen far too many times before and that made him bite back a groan. "You take the girl." She side-eyed Evander like he was the worst rake in London. "And do try not to break her heart, will you?"

Horror rounded Lady Wentworth's eyes when Ginny barged into the middle of her attempts to browbeat Lord Fairfax onto the dance floor.

"Ah. There you are, Lord Fairfax." Ginny placed herself

squarely between her nemesis and her mark for the night. "I believe you promised me a dance." She offered Fairfax her gloved hand.

Lord Fairfax blinked owlishly. Relief and gratitude filled his eyes in the next instant. "Indeed I did, Lady Hartley." He murmured an apology to Lady Wentworth and Miss Miller, before whisking Ginny onto the dance floor.

Lady Wentworth opened and closed her mouth soundlessly, her face so puce Evander feared she would bust a blood vessel. The matchmaker twisted around and glowered at him like he was the one who'd stolen away Lord Fairfax.

Evander dipped his head politely. "Lady Wentworth. A pleasure as always." He turned to the young woman beside her and bowed. "Miss Miller, Duke Evander Ravenwood at your service. Would you do me the honour of this dance?"

Miss Miller hesitated. She shot a worried look at her livid chaperone, came to a decision, and bobbed gracefully. "Of course, your Grace."

Evander took her gloved hand and guided her expertly into a waltz under Lady Wentworth's death stare and the hungry gazes of the assembled nobility.

Miss Miller slowly relaxed when her chaperone disappeared from view.

"You are very light on your feet, Miss Miller," Evander said when they reached the other side of the ballroom.

Miss Miller blushed slightly. "So are you, your Grace." Her gaze flitted to Ginny where she and Lord Fairfax were already engaged in a lively conversation as they spun around the dance floor. "Won't Lady Hartley mind you dancing with me? I hear she is quite the fearsome woman."

Evander blinked, surprised at her forthrightness. He studied the young woman in his arms with fresh eyes.

There was a glint in Ophelia Miller's eyes and a certain set to her jawline that looked strangely familiar. He smiled when he recognised who she reminded him of.

"Lady Hartley and I are good friends." He paused. "I believe the pair of you should get to know one another."

It was Miss Miller's turn to look astonished. "You do?"

Evander's smile widened. "I think you may find that you have certain…things in common."

"Oh." Miss Miller blinked. Faint lines wrinkled her delicate brow. "I thought you were deliberately avoiding the marriage mart, your Grace."

Evander tensed a little. "I am, Miss Miller."

Miss Miller pursed her lips. "Then you should avoid flashing that smile at impressionable young ladies like myself. It is bad for our hearts, your Grace."

Evander couldn't help burst out laughing, the sound shocking Miss Miller as much as it seemed Ginny and the rest of the aristocrats who witnessed it.

Miss Miller recovered, giving Evander further grounds to believe she was not quite the innocent damsel she pretended to be.

"That laughter isn't any better, your Grace."

Evander chuckled at her chastising tone. "You and Ginny will most certainly hit it off. I pray you heed my advice." He glanced around the ballroom before fixing his dance partner with a steady stare. "I apologise if this comes across as bold, but I daresay you may discover that there is more to life than this farce of a marriage mart."

Miss Miller's expression turned thoughtful.

"You are an interesting man, your Grace."

"Pray, do not lose your heart to me, Miss Miller," Evander teased, his mouth curving. "Or else my dear friend Lady Hartley will most definitely have my guts for garters."

Miss Miller sighed. "There's that lethal smile again, your Grace."

The dance finished all too soon and Evander returned a reluctant Miss Miller to her near apoplectic chaperone. Ginny lifted a pair of drinks from a footman's tray and whisked him towards the French windows before her archenemy could launch into a diatribe.

They stepped out into the cool evening air, the terrace empty but for the two of them. A muffled giggle came from the direction of the gardens as they rested against the stone balustrade.

Whoever was out there was likely engaged in an activity more interesting than eavesdropping.

"What was that about?" Ginny took a sip of her drink, her curious gaze on Evander's face.

"Nothing much." He turned and looked at the couples swirling around the ballroom. To his utter lack of surprise, Miss Miller had already found another partner. "Let's just say Ophelia Miller is a much more fascinating young lady than she appears to be at first glance."

Ginny raised an eyebrow. "Fascinating enough for you to develop an attraction for the fairer sex?"

"Gods no," Evander protested. He faltered. "I hope you

don't mind, but I advised her to get in touch with you. I believe the two of you could become friends."

Ginny's mouth flattened to a thin line.

Her reputation precluded many close friendships in London high society. Bar Lady Ashbrooke and a handful of mutual acquaintances who knew better than to judge her from appearances, she didn't have many female companions she could confide in.

"You have a nasty habit of sticking that pretty nose of yours where it doesn't belong, your Grace," Ginny said sourly.

Evander's lips twitched. "You think my nose is pretty?"

Ginny rolled her eyes. "You are a delight from the top of your head to your toes. If it weren't for your interest in lovers, I would have gobbled you up years ago." She propped her back against the ledge and stared at him shrewdly over the rim of her glass. "So, how long has it been since you've had a nice, thick cock inside you?"

Evander almost spat out the mouthful of champagne he'd just taken. "Jesus, Ginny!" He looked around warily.

"Relax," Ginny drawled. "The only one who heard us is that stone cherub over there. His mouth has failed to round in horror and his eyes have yet to fall out of his head." Concern clouded her face. "Seriously though, you look like you could do with blowing off some steam."

CHAPTER 7

EVANDER RUBBED THE BACK OF HIS NECK AWKWARDLY.

Ginny was one of a handful of people who knew of his sexual preferences.

Though no longer a punishable crime since the turn of the century, homosexuality was still frowned upon in England and the wider British Empire, particularly by nobles who relied on marriage to maintain their lineage and social standing. Attitudes were more relaxed among the middle class and the magicless, where there was a much greater acceptance of diversity in relationships. The act however still carried a deep level of social stigma among those of a religious ilk, this despite the fact that the practice was known to be rife among the clergy.

Evander first became aware of his interest in men when he was fifteen years old. He was at the Ravenwood estate at the time, on break from the elite, magic boarding school he attended in London. He'd found his gaze following the new stable boy, a strapping young man called William who was three years his senior and freshly arrived from Ireland. A hard working and guileless soul, it hadn't taken William long to become a well-liked figure on the estate and one the maids often sighed over.

Judging from the way he'd sneaked glances at Evander whenever their paths crossed, the attraction Evander had felt had been mutual.

After procuring several foreign books on the art of sex between men from an obscure shop in London, Evander finally convinced William to teach him the pleasures of the act a year later. Initially reluctant to cross the line that defined their relationship as master and servant, William eventually succumbed to temptation.

Their first attempt at sex was a fumbling affair in one of the barns late one night. Evander had felt more pain than pleasure as William pierced him clumsily with his cock, his grunts and groans echoing in Evander's ear where he'd bent him over a bale of hay, his hand busy on Evander's trembling manhood.

The nights that followed and the afternoons in the hunting lodge where Evander had the stable boy accompany him when he went horseback riding brought more delightful experiences, William proving as keen a student as Evander.

Soon, they'd mastered every sinful act a man could perform with another man, thrilled time and time again by the devastating pleasure it brought them.

Evander would forever remember that first enchanting summer when he lost his virginity. The long hours spent exploring his own body and his burgeoning sexuality with a willing partner. The heady feeling of being pinned to a bed by a man, his legs spread wide and his heels propped on his lover's shoulders as the latter pounded him ruthlessly into the mattress. Performing fellatio and having it performed on him. Being bent over a table or a chair or lifted up against a wall and fucked within an inch of his life. Straddling his lover's body so he could bounce on the thick cock impaling him to his heart's content.

The smell of sweat and sex had made Evander's senses swim as they'd rutted wildly, seeking and taking gratification from one another with a frenzied, almost insatiable hunger, the sounds they uttered animal-like in their intensity.

Their affair lasted three summers and ended when William returned to Ireland. Though they never exchanged words of a romantic nature, Evander still recalled his first lover with fondness. From what he later learned, William went on to marry a woman from his village and was now the proud father of three children.

It wasn't until Evander attended the Royal Institute for the Arcane that he met a man with whom he entered into a serious relationship. One that lasted until the year before he was forced to take on the mantle of Duke of Ravenwood due to his father's premature death and became a Special Arcane Investigator.

His sexual encounters since had been few and far between and mostly confined to an exclusive club in Bloomsbury where guests' identities were masked by illusions and they could indulge their wildest fantasies in sumptuous private rooms equipped with all sorts of wicked restraints and enchanted toys.

Evander ended up procuring one such device for those nights when his needs could not be satisfied with just his hand.

"A penny for your dirty thoughts?"

Ginny's teasing words brought him back to the present. His ears grew warm at her sly look.

"You know, you really shouldn't make fun of—"

Evander froze, his scalp prickling. He'd just caught a whiff of an unsettling magic from the direction of the gardens. His head snapped around, his pulse speeding up.

"Evander?" Ginny asked warily.

He stared into the shadows, trying to pin-point where it had come from. But the scent was already fading on a breeze that carried the fragrance of roses.

"What's wrong?" Ginny moved closer to him, tension radiating off her as she followed his gaze.

"I—" Evander stopped, not sure if he'd imagined the whole thing. "I thought I sensed something."

Ginny frowned. She knew better than anyone not to question his instincts.

They were distracted by an "Aha!"

Lord Ashbrooke had appeared on the terrace. "There you are, Ravenwood. Care for a port in the smoking room?" His eyes gleamed with a light that said they had much to converse about.

"Of course, my Lord," Evander murmured.

He took one last look at the gardens and escorted Ginny into the ballroom.

It was midnight when they thanked the Ashbrookes and prepared to leave. Though the party was still in full swing, they both had commitments in the morning that could not be put off.

By then, Evander had all but forgotten about the incident in the gardens, his mind concerned with the grave matters he'd learned from his host.

Just as he'd suspected, the House of Lords was getting ready to petition the government for the Arcane Division to become a separate entity from the Metropolitan Police. Evander was aware the motion had been gaining grounds in the halls of power, at the behest of a group of elitists who wanted the Arcane Division to become the exclusive remit of the aristocracy.

A department of magic run by nobles for nobles.

It was a dangerous idea and one he feared would make relations even more strained between thralls and those gifted with magic. Worse, it could lead to another war between the two factions. A war the nobles no doubt wanted.

Evander firmly believed the Arcane Division belonged in the Met and that the department needed all types of magic users and even thralls in its workforce. It was the only way to deliver true justice at every level of society, rather than enforce powers that would prove disadvantageous to many. To his relief, it seemed Lord Ashbrooke agreed with his views.

He and Ginny were almost out the front doors when someone called out to him breathlessly.

"Duke Ravenwood!"

Surprise jolted Evander when he turned.

Miss Miller was rushing towards them, her face pale and her eyes strangely glassy. He stiffened when she walked right up to him and grasped his arm, her hold surprisingly strong for someone so slender.

"What the—?!" Ginny mumbled.

Magic warmed Evander's flesh even through his clothes. He shivered, awed by its purity and power. Ginny drew a sharp breath beside him.

White sparks danced like stars in the depths of Miss Miller's pupils.

"*Be careful, mage,*" she warned Evander, her voice low and grave. "*You are in danger. You must put your faith in the purple flower. It is the only way you will survive all that is to come!*"

A figure loomed behind Miss Miller in the next instant.

"*Ophelia Miller!*" Lady Wentworth hissed. "Please comport yourself!" The older woman was huffing and puffing, having evidently dashed after her young charge.

Her chaperone's voice snapped Miss Miller out of her daze. She blinked, awareness returning to her face on a rush of colour.

"I'm—I'm so sorry, your Grace!" She snatched her hand away, mortified. "I don't know what came over me." She avoided Evander and Ginny's eyes, curtsied stiffly, and headed back towards the ballroom.

Lady Wentworth groaned and gathered her skirts before following at a fast shuffle.

CHAPTER 8

EVANDER AND GINNY STARED AFTER THEIR DISAPPEARING figures.

"What was that about?" Ginny muttered.

Evander swallowed, his skin still hot where Miss Miller had touched him. He had a feeling he knew the magic he'd just felt in the young woman's touch and glimpsed in her eyes.

"Evander?"

Ginny's voice made him flinch. She was studying him with a troubled expression. "You've gone as white as a ghost."

Evander registered the curious stares they were drawing from the nearby footmen and the few couples in the foyer.

"I'm alright," he murmured. "We should leave."

Ginny shot furtive glances his way as they navigated the front steps of Ashbrooke House. They were inside their carriage and out of St. James's Square in minutes.

"All in all, that was quite a strange evening," Ginny said after a while. She dropped her head against the padded back of the carriage seat and closed her eyes.

Evander dragged his gaze from the street lights outside. Piccadilly was quieter than it had been earlier that evening, the only people about late night revellers emerging from clubs and hotels.

"Did you have a satisfactory meeting with Lord Fairfax?"

"I did." Ginny opened her eyes and pinned him with a knowing stare. "Did your talk with Lord Ashbrooke confirm your speculations?"

Evander nodded grimly.

"Those old coots." Ginny furrowed her brow. "Do they not realise what kind of godawful misfortunes their actions might engender?"

The carriage approached Hyde Park Corner, the clip-clop of the horses' hooves and the gentle rattle of the wheels the only sounds in the still night.

"You know as well as I do that they think only of themselves." Evander's face tightened. "I won't let that petition go through. Even if I have to convince Her Majesty—"

A horrid stench filled his nostrils at the same time a bitter taste danced across his tongue, freezing his words. There was motion out of the corner of his eye.

Shadows bolted from beneath some trees on the left side of the road.

Instinct had Evander reaching for Ginny and yanking her onto his lap. Her shocked gasp was drowned out by the noise of something large smashing violently into her side of the carriage.

The only reason the door didn't break was because of the wards protecting the vehicle. They could not however stop the carriage from being physically moved.

The alarmed neighs of the horses and the startled shouts of the coachman and footman reached Evander as they were shoved across the street, wheels scraping across granite cobbles in a shower of sparks.

His eyes rounded in horror where he had his arms wrapped tightly around Ginny and a leg braced against the opposite seat.

They were headed straight for a ditch.

Evander's stomach plummeted when the right wheel dropped into the muddy trench, jolting them violently. He clenched his jaw, pressed a hand to the roof, and channelled wind magic through wood and metal.

A storm detonated at the side of the carriage as it began to tilt precariously, drawing a gargled scream from young Samuel in the box seat.

There was a shocking moment of stillness, as if the whole world was holding its breath. Ginny swore colourfully when the carriage slammed back down on the road with a torturous creak, the bouncing motion jostling them all over again.

Glass exploded next to Evander, peppering him and Ginny in glittering shards. A massive arm reached through the carriage window, snatched him by the front of his shirt, and dragged him out before he could react.

"Evander!" Ginny screamed. She grappled at his clothes in vain.

Evander got a glimpse of a dispassionate face as he was hoisted into the air. He clutched the wrist of his attacker and kicked out viciously when the latter started squeezing his windpipe.

He might as well have struck an iron wall for all the difference it made.

Air rasped through Evander's throat as he got his first look at his assailant.

The man who'd attacked the carriage was a colossus.

Bar throttling Evander, he stood deathly still, his features devoid of emotion.

What the devil is a Brute doing here?!

Ginny's shout reached him. "Use your magic, dammit!"

Evander scowled. Coldness flooded his veins.

Frost formed on the giant's fingers. He flung Evander across the street.

A sky full of stars whirled across Evander's vision.

He barely had time to cover his head with his arms before he landed hard on his side and rolled, the protective charms built into his cravat pin and cufflinks activating to minimise injury. The impact knocked the breath out of him despite the buffer of wind magic he'd manifested at the penultimate moment to cushion his fall.

"Your Grace!" Graham shouted, alarmed.

Evander looked up from where he'd come to rest on his front, knuckles scraped and heart racing. The coachman was climbing down the box seat, Samuel's petrified face round and pale behind him.

Evander's eyes widened.

The Brute was accompanied by three cloaked, masked figures who stank of dark magic. Evander's stomach curdled when one of them turned towards Graham, shadows coalescing around his fingers.

No!

He scrambled to his feet, fear and fury causing a violent burst of ice magic to fill his body on a rush of power. Evander's breath fogged in front of his face as he drew his arm back and hurled the weapon that had come to life in his hand with all his might.

The icicle impaled the dark mage's shoulder just as the crack of a firearm shattered the night. The man jerked twice. Light flashed around the projectile that had smashed into his left flank and latched onto him with spider-like legs.

A cry left the mage's throat as he was enveloped in dazzling static. His entire body went rigid before he convulsed and dropped to the ground, muscles spasming and back contorting uncontrollably.

The magic sparking across his clothes faded as he lost consciousness.

Everyone's gaze shifted to the smoking pistol in Ginny's right hand.

She'd kicked the carriage door open and was leaning out of the vehicle, her arm steady and a scowl darkening her pretty face as she aimed her enchanted derringer.

A mage lunged for her, a nasty blade in hand.

Ginny jerked out of the way, grabbed the top of the door frame, and shoved herself out of the vehicle. Her stockinged leg moved in a graceful arc as she twisted and back kicked the man in the face with her left foot.

Bone crunched under the heel of her delicate silver slipper.

The mage staggered sideways on a colourful curse, blood spurting from his broken nose. Ginny landed lightly in front of him, took hold of his shoulders, and kneed him violently in the groin.

Samuel sucked in air, horrified delight dawning on his young face.

The mage's eyes crossed.

"That's what you get for making me ruin this dress, you swine!" Ginny hissed as he groaned and slumped to the ground before her. She knocked him out with a blow from the handle of her pistol.

Dark magic bloomed around the third mage's fingers.

Graham moved to intercept him as he raised his hand towards Ginny.

"Stay back!" Evander barked.

The coachman froze.

The mage stiffened when he sensed Evander's wind magic. He tried to avoid the attack.

"Too late," Evander growled.

The mage gasped as an invisible lasso wrapped around his throat. He clutched at bands of nothingness, his fingers sinking impotently through tightening loops of wind magic. His toe caps scraped the cobbles as he rose from the ground.

Evander moved his hand and sent him flying into a tree fifteen feet away.

CHAPTER 9

THE MAGE SMASHED INTO THE TRUNK WITH A HARSH GRUNT. Leaves rained down on him as he slid to the ground, his head lolling forward, chin on chest.

Evander started across the street, the power humming in his blood making the hairs on his skin stand on end.

"Take Samuel and go find help."

He removed his Arcane Division issued enchanted whistle from a pocket in his waistcoat and lobed it at Graham.

The coachman caught it.

Evander kept his eyes on the Brute as he sent ice racing along the harness shackling the horses to the carriage. The straps snapped at a flick of his fingers, freeing the nervous beasts.

The giant stared at them but did not move. Evander frowned heavily.

Why is he working for mages? And dark mages at that?!

Graham's anxious gaze shifted from Evander and Ginny, to their attackers.

"We will be alright," Evander reassured the nervous coachman. "You know as well as I do that Lady Hartley and I are more than capable of looking after ourselves."

"We'll catch up in no time, Graham," Ginny added briskly. She ripped the side of her skirt open from the mid-thigh down and removed the knife strapped to her stockinged leg before flashing an encouraging look at Samuel. "Take care of the old man, will you?"

Samuel jumped down from the box seat and bobbed his head jerkily.

"Alright, my Lady," Graham said reluctantly. He cast a final, regretful look at Evander. "Stay safe, your Grace."

The coachman climbed on one of the horses and pulled Samuel up behind him. The clatter of hooves faded in the direction of Piccadilly as they set off at a gallop.

The shrill blast of the whistle came a moment later, a signal to nearby Met officers to offer assistance.

"Kill…them…"

Evander's head whipped around. The third mage had roused at the base of the tree. He extended a hand towards the Brute, an ugly expression twisting his features. Crimson light flared inside the dark stone crowning the ring on his middle finger.

The same light flashed in the Brute's pupils, bringing him to life. The giant turned towards his closest target.

Evander's gut twisted. "*Ginny!*"

Ginny backed away from the figure closing on her, her face tight. She dodged the Brute's fist by mere inches and sliced his underarm as she dove to the side.

The giant did not even flinch at the cut.

He turned and lumbered towards Ginny.

A warm weight settled in Evander's legs, rooting him to the third element he could wield. Magic grounded his body as he called upon the power of the rich loam beneath the cobbles.

The ground trembled, startling the Brute.

A wall of dirt rose between him and Ginny.

The mage's eyes rounded behind his mask. He climbed unsteadily to his feet and glared at Evander.

"You're a tri-elemental mage?!"

Evander ignored him and finished surrounding Ginny with a protective barricade of earth. The Brute had stopped moving, confused by the apparition of a wall that hadn't been there a moment ago.

"Let me out of here!" Ginny's angry voice was muffled by the thick layer of dirt and rock. "Goddammit, Evander! You can't take them on your own!" She started pounding on the wall.

The third mage approached Evander just as his two companions stirred.

Evander narrowed his eyes.

"What do you want? And don't pretend this is a robbery. Dark mages don't make a habit of looting nobles' carriages."

The mage stopped a short distance away. He glanced at his associates where they were rising from the ground before observing Evander shrewdly. "You seem to know a lot about our kind, Ice Mage." He jerked chin, signalling to his men to surround Evander. "Now, where is the vial you stole from the alley? We know you have it on you."

Evander blinked as he met the mage's piercing stare.

Wait. They're after the vial? His scalp prickled as understanding dawned. *They must be working for the mage who attacked us in the alley!*

A chilling cold seeped into his bones. His shoulders knotted.

A sinister energy was pooling around the three men. Their dark magic turned the shadows to a thick, oily fog that made it hard to breathe and sent an unpleasant buzzing through his ears.

Evander braced his legs and drew on his elemental powers. They pulsed through and out of him, clearing the air on a violent, sparkling haze that shook the leaves in the nearby trees and made the ground quake.

The mages hesitated on the verge of launching their next attack, their nerves showing at this absolute show of force.

It was all the time Evander needed to act.

A dozen icicles bloomed around him, the weapons moving even as they formed. The first and second mages tried to jump out of the way, only to find their feet yanked out from under them by shackles of dirt. Gargled cries left them as Evander's ice attack pierced their clothes and pinned them to the street.

Evander deflected the dark magic wreathed blade the third mage threw at him with the folding cane that sprung out from inside his sleeve. He sidestepped the man as he charged at him and whacked him in a flurry of lightning-fast strikes.

The mage shook his head dazedly. He tottered about and fell clumsily onto a knee, as if intoxicated.

"What the hell did you do to me, you bastard?!" he snarled. He tried to get up, to no avail.

Evander straightened and propped the cane on his shoulder. "I hit your pressure points." He cocked his head. "Learned it from the same man who taught Lady Hartley how to fight like a street thug."

"I heard that!" Ginny snapped from behind the dirt wall.

Evander smiled coldly at the mage. "You won't be able to get up for a while, so I suggest you and your associates sit tight and wait for the police to—"

An evil smirk twisted the mage's mouth.

Air shifted behind Evander. Pain exploded inside his skull before he could react. His breath locked in his throat, the agony of the attack dulling his senses and sending his ears ringing. It took him a moment to figure out what had happened.

The Brute had slammed his giant hands on either side of his head. He squeezed.

Black spots blossomed in front of Evander's eyes.

Ginny screamed his name.

Something jolted the Brute as he began crushing Evander's skull. The motion loosened his hold for a fraction of a second.

Evander grabbed the back of the giant's hands and let loose his ice magic, his head throbbing and his stomach roiling.

The Brute released him.

Evander whirled around.

Ginny had climbed over the wall of her barricade and jumped onto the giant's shoulders. She wrapped her legs around his throat in a choke hold and pressed her gun to the base of his skull, a scowl darkening her face.

"Wait!" Evander warned. "Magic doesn't work against them!"

"We'll see about that," Ginny said grimly. She squeezed the trigger.

The pistol cracked. Once. Twice.

The Brute remained unfazed by the projectiles that fastened on his flesh and tried to stun him. He looked at the ice fading fast on his fingers and reached up to grab Ginny.

Evander ripped his cufflinks off his sleeves, engaged the explosive magic they contained, and lobed them at the Brute's face.

"*Jump!*" he yelled at Ginny.

She pushed off the giant and somersaulted into the air.

The Brute brought his arms up as the enchanted devices detonated in front of him. He grunted at the blast, staggered back half a dozen steps, and shook his head. His expression cleared for a moment.

Confusion clouded his face.

The Brute's pupils flashed red. He pinned Evander with a blank gaze once more.

Evander's throat tightened.

Those explosions would have incapacitated a small mob!

There was only one thing left for him to do. Though it was magic, its effect would be more physically devastating than anything else he'd tried so far.

Heat burst to life inside Evander's chest. It filled his

body and warmed his blood, bringing with it the fourth element he could wield. The air around him shimmered on a warm haze.

The Brute blinked when Evander walked up to him and pressed a hand to his chest. Flames burst into life around his fingers.

Ginny's eyes rounded where she'd landed a short distance away.

She had only seen him use this power once before.

The fire magic Evander manifested knocked the Brute off his feet and carried him clear across the street. He slammed into a brick wall, the impact leaving a ten foot crater that sent fracture lines racing across the surface.

Thick droplets of water coalesced from thin air at Evander's command. They doused the flames engulfing the Brute's clothes. The giant moved sluggishly amidst the rising steam and pushed himself off the wall, only to stop dead when ice encased his feet.

He stared at the glittering prison racing up his body. The Brute looked up and met Evander's eyes seconds before his expression froze behind a thick, pale wall that chilled the air with a faint, white, swirling mist.

Evander's heart thumped painfully as he stared at the icebound Brute.

He flinched when Ginny fired her pistol.

The dark mages were disappearing in the direction of Hyde Park.

"Shit." She lowered the gun, her jaw clenched tight.

Footsteps pounded the street behind them as constables from the Met arrived.

CHAPTER 10

"Dammit all to Hell, Evander! Why didn't you tell me about the bloody vial?!" Rufus snarled.

He raked his hair with a hand where he paced the floor before the fireplace, the flames in the hearth casting an orange glow on the sharp angles of his face and his untidy locks.

"I completely forgot about it," Evander admitted guiltily.

He hissed when Hargrove dabbed some ointment on his knuckles. The manservant ignored his sound of protest and carried on tending to him where they sat at his desk, in the formal study of the townhouse in Mayfair.

It was gone three in the morning.

One of the night duty sergeants at the Met had sent a message to Rufus's home about the incident near Hyde Park Corner after the Brute was taken into custody. Despite the lateness of the hour, the inspector met up with Evander and Ginny as they were leaving police headquarters and insisted on escorting them to the townhouse.

"Honestly, Mrs. S, it is but a scratch," Ginny protested. "You should see to Evander's wounds."

Evander's housekeeper tsk-tsked. She was perched next to Ginny on a mahogany, button-back sofa upholstered in gold and green damask. "I will get to Master Evander in a moment. A lady must take care of her face, Lady Hartley." Faint green light shimmered around Mrs. Sinclair's fingertips as she healed the shallow cut on Ginny's cheek.

"We all know she ain't a lady," Rufus muttered distractedly.

Ginny narrowed her eyes. "You asking for an ass-whooping, Grayson?"

Hargrove snorted. Mrs. Sinclair's expression grew pinched.

"Sorry, Mrs. S," Ginny mumbled. She shot a glare at Rufus from under her lashes.

Rufus smirked.

Evander swallowed a sigh. He'd wondered if the pair might develop amorous feelings towards one another when he'd first introduced them. Alas, Rufus saw Ginny as nothing more than an irritating younger sister he needed to keep in line, while Ginny considered Rufus a maddening older brother in serious need of removing the stick permanently wedged up his arse.

Ginny frowned at Evander as Mrs. Sinclair finished her ministration.

"Look, I know you got us out of a pickle tonight, but

what you did was reckless. Those mages saw you use all your elemental powers."

Mrs. Sinclair froze. "He never did," she mumbled hoarsely.

"Bloody hellfire, my Lord!" Hargrove cursed.

"You mean there are dark mages running around London right now who know what you are?!" Rufus said, horrified.

Evander met their accusing stares with a contrite expression. "It couldn't be helped."

Less than ten people in the world knew of his status as an Archmage. Considering Archmages were considered de facto property of the state because of their dangerous powers, it wasn't something he was keen to make public.

Mrs. Sinclair's gaze held a healthy dose of concern mixed with incrimination.

Evander suspected she was thinking of one person in particular who would be most vexed that he'd accidentally revealed his true nature. The person he ultimately answered to and who'd kept him in a gilded cage for the last six years.

Ginny sighed. "So, what's this about a vial?"

Evander removed the enchanted cane strapped to his forearm and twisted the top end, exposing a hollow metal compartment. It was short and narrow, just the right size to take a rolled-up note or a miniature magical device.

The crystal vial fell out into his palm when he tipped the stick, the blue liquid inside it shining faintly.

Hargrove whistled softly under his breath. "Now, that's a thing of beauty. You can tell the Charm Weaver who made this put a lot of work into it."

Evander and Rufus stared at the manservant.

"What makes you think this is the work of a Charm Weaver?" Evander said, puzzled. "They are normally metal crafters."

"That goes to show how much you know about Charm Weavers, my Lord," Hargrove scoffed. "The best artisans can work with any material." The manservant closed the medicine box and ignored Mrs. Sinclair's disapproving look as she took the seat he'd vacated.

Rufus came over to the desk and carefully picked up the object Evander had recovered from the alley.

"You found this near the dead man?"

He held it between two fingers and examined it against the light.

"Yes." Healing magic warmed Evander's hands as Mrs. Sinclair began treating his scrapes. "I think it was on the body of the victim when he fell. And I believe the mage who attacked us in the alley sent those men to retrieve it tonight."

It had been a moment's distraction that had made Evander slip the evidence he'd collected from the East End inside the cane before he'd left the townhouse to go pick up Ginny. The act had turned out to be providence of the most dangerous kind. One Evander hoped would lead them to the killer.

"Do you know what it is?" Rufus asked curiously.

"No. But I hope Mr. Brown and his associates will be able to decipher the substance it contains and its function." Evander hesitated. "Whatever it is, there's some kind of magic tracer on it. They knew I had it on me."

Ginny lowered her brows where she'd joined them at

the desk to study the vial Rufus held. "That strange magic you sensed in the gardens at Ashbrooke House." She glanced at Evander. "You think that was them sniffing this out?"

Evander dipped his head. Ginny was sharper than many of the Met inspectors he knew.

"What happened at Ashbrooke House?" Rufus asked guardedly.

They gave him a shortened version of the events at the ball.

"You danced with the season's belle?" Rufus said incredulously.

Even Hargrove stared at Evander like he'd grown a second head.

"Just because I'm not interested in matrimony doesn't mean I can't enjoy a dance once in a while," Evander said, barely masking his irritation.

"Pardon the crudeness my Lord, but everyone in this room knows you prefer bollocks to tits," Hargrove said bluntly.

Mrs. Sinclair dropped the cup she'd been gathering from the tea table. It hit the Persian rug and bounced.

Evander groaned.

Ginny bit her lip hard, shoulders quaking.

"I mean, not that we even know what kind of bollocks you like, since you never bring them home," Hargrove prattled on, oblivious to the unhealthy shade of red rising in Mrs. Sinclair's face. The manservant rubbed his chin thoughtfully as he observed Evander. "You should visit that club soon, my Lord. You could do with blowing off some steam."

"That's what I said!" Ginny exclaimed in a vindicated tone.

"Jesus," Rufus muttered under his breath.

"*That's it!*" Mrs. Sinclair roared. She pointed imperiously at the door. "Mr. Hargrove, *out!* Inspector Grayson, please be so kind as to take Lady Hartley home. Master Evander, to bed with you."

Rufus and Ginny protested as she shooed them towards the exit, Hargrove wearing a martyred expression ahead of them.

"Mrs. Sinclair," Evander called out as the housekeeper prepared to step out of the room.

She paused on the threshold and turned. "Yes, my Lord?"

"How are Samuel and Graham?"

Her expression softened at his concerned tone. "They are not any worse for the wear, my Lord. Young Samuel was all fired up after witnessing Lady Hartley in…action," she said diplomatically. "I gave him a toddy and sent him to bed."

Relief loosened Evander's shoulders. "Good. Please grant them the day off. I shall get a hansom cab in the morning."

Mrs. Sinclair dipped her head. "As you wish, my Lord."

It wasn't until Evander was slipping under the plush, goose-down comforter of his four-poster mahogany bed that the Brute the Met had arrested came to his mind.

The man had appeared utterly terrified and befuddled when he'd emerged from the melting ice block he'd been encased in. The blood had drained from his face upon realising his whereabouts and seeing the officers surrounding him, truncheons at the ready in case he made an attempt to escape. No one had been more shocked than Evander when he'd fallen to his knees instead and begged them not to kill him.

Evander frowned at the underside of the green velvet canopy.

He was like a different creature altogether from when he attacked us.

Brutes were a rare breed among the magicless. Gifted with Herculean builds and extraordinary strength, they were renowned for their remarkable resilience, their immunity to pain, and their resistance to all but the strongest magic. Though the first mention of a Brute was made in historical records in the late 1600s, their origins were still unclear to this day. Only one thing was certain about them. They were exclusively men.

After Evander learned of the War of Subjugation and the Brutes who played a crucial role against the zealot mages howling for the blood of innocents, he'd thought their existence a miracle borne of nature.

Like he'd said to his brother John before the latter's untimely death, it was as if the world had decided to lend a helping hand to the powerless thralls by granting them monstrous beings who could defend them.

Brutes considered mages their archenemy. Which made the situation Evander had found himself in tonight the more puzzling.

His last thought before sleep claimed him was the mysterious message Ophelia Miller had imparted to him before he'd left Ashbrooke House. One that seemed even more prophetic now than it had appeared at the time.

CHAPTER 11

"HIS NAME IS ALASTAIR MILLBROOK," RUFUS SAID sombrely. "He was a talented Charm Weaver and renowned craftsman known for his ability to create powerful magical artefacts."

Evander frowned at the body of the dead man on the examination block of the morgue. He had heard of Millbrook.

Heavy rain drops struck the imposing arched windows of the special wing of Scotland Yard that housed the Arcane Division. Even the dreary daylight seeping inside the chamber could not mask the marked lividity of Millbrook's body.

A tall, gaunt man with a pale complexion and a shock of white hair was deftly incising the corpse, scalpel slicing through skin and fat with a proficiency that spoke of years of experience.

Dr. Ambrose Mortimer put the knife down and

reached for the bone saw. "You might want to step back for this, gentlemen."

Rufus and Evander moved away from the table.

"Did the Charm Weavers Guild mention anything else of interest about Millbrook?" Evander asked above the shrill whirr of the device. "Something that might give us a clue as to why he was murdered?"

Rufus pressed a handkerchief to his nose, his face pale at the sight of Mortimer retracting the two halves of the dead man's breastbone and exposing the contents of his chest.

He'd never been a fan of necropsies.

"The guild master mentioned the victim hadn't attended the last two guild meetings."

Evander filed this information for future consideration. Rufus had officially handed the case over to him when he'd arrived at Scotland Yard at noon that day. The inspector would be staying on to assist him, as per the recommendation of the head of the Homicide Unit and Evander's own commander.

"Did Millbrook specialise in a particular kind of magical artefact?"

"The guild master didn't specify. All he said was that Millbrook's clients tended to be aristocrats interested in having items with peculiar functions made for them."

The image of the crystal vial danced before Evander's eyes. He'd given the object to the Artificers' department an hour ago.

Mortimer's eyes narrowed behind his goggles a moment later. "It appears Miss Shaw was correct. Our friend's arteries have indeed been drained of blood." He poked around the thoracic cavity with a metal probe before looking up and meeting Evander and Rufus's stares. "Whoever removed the heart did so with a precision that can only be attributed to a highly skilled magic practitioner."

Evander exchanged a startled glance with Rufus.

"Do you mean to say the murderer has committed this kind of crime before?" the inspector said sharply.

Mortimer shrugged. "If he has, he's either done a good job of burying the bodies or practiced on plenty of animals. I have never observed this calibre of magical excision before and I've done plenty of necropsies in my time." The physical examiner paused. "Oh, and I noted something interesting when I examined the skull. He had suffered some kind of blow to his head before his death."

Unease chilled Evander's skin.

He'd been right about this case giving him a bad feeling.

He walked over to a worktop and picked up the specimen vial containing the black substance they'd recovered at the scene of the crime.

"What of this? Any idea what it could be?"

"Oh. You mean this thing?"

Rufus gagged a little when Mortimer pulled out a long, stringy, dark clot from one of Millbrook's main blood vessels. It was identical to the blob in the vial.

The physical examiner studied it under the light of his head lamp, his eyes gleaming with fascination.

"I am not certain yet, but I am willing to bet it is some kind of breakdown product of the magic that was used to perform this heinous act."

Evander lowered his brows. "Do you believe it could be dark magic?"

Mortimer dropped the congealed mass in a bowl. "It is difficult to be certain. All I know is I've never seen the likes of it. Fascinating, isn't it, your Grace?" He beamed at Evander, his entire face transforming with an expression akin to an excited child unwrapping his birthday presents. "Why, nothing gets the mental juices going like a good old mystery."

Rufus looked like he was ready to bring up his breakfast at the mention of juices in the context of a necropsy.

Mortimer ignored the inspector's sweaty complexion, picked up his scalpel, and leaned over the body. "Now, Mr. Millbrook, what shall your intestinal organs reveal to us?" He cackled under his breath.

Evander swallowed a sigh. There were days when he worried about his associates in the AFD. He and Rufus left Mortimer muttering to the corpse and exited the morgue.

They bumped into Shaw in the corridor.

"Ah, there you are, your Grace," the forensic mage said brightly. "I was just coming to see you. I've finished examining the scene of the attack near Hyde Park Corner."

Evander straightened. "I can tell from your smile that you found something."

Shaw rocked back on her heels. "I did indeed," she beamed.

Rufus eyed her suspiciously. "Please tell me those wayward fingers of yours went nowhere near whatever evidence you unearthed?"

Shaw rolled her eyes. "Honestly, you should place a bit more faith in your juniors, Inspector." She exhaled noisily at Rufus's doubtful stare. "I promise I did nothing untoward."

"What is it you found?" Evander said.

"Some kind of purple powder," Shaw replied as they started down the passage. "There was a trace of it on the tree suspect number three made contact with, as per your report. I've handed it to Mr. Brown."

They made their way to the fourth floor of the south wing, where the holding cells designed to handle criminals and objects of a magical nature were situated. Like the rest of the imposing Gothic fortress that housed the headquarters of the Metropolitan Police, the rooms were heavily warded to protect against physical and magical attacks.

"How's the prisoner, Sergeant Dwyer?" Evander said when they entered the anteroom.

The officer supervising the lockup that day rose from his desk, his expression weary. "I'm afraid he's still refusing to talk, your Grace. Had he not begged for mercy like he did last night, I would have wagered he was a mute."

Dwyer led them into the area with the holding cells. He inserted an enchanted key in the lock of the fortified room where the prisoner was being held, removed the wards on the bolts with the Met issued ring on his finger, and opened the door.

The Brute jumped up from the stone bench he'd been sitting on when they entered the cell, his foot rattling the tray containing his untouched food. He backed away until he struck the far wall and hunched down so as to make himself a smaller target, his eyes wide with fear behind the arms he'd raised to defend himself.

Surprise jolted Evander. He could see bruises on the Brute's chest through his torn shirt. He cut his eyes to Dwyer.

"Did someone beat him?"

Dwyer shook his head vehemently at his cold tone. "No, your Grace. No one has touched the man. He wouldn't allow a doctor to examine his wounds, let alone a healer."

Evander pursed his lips and studied the Brute with a frown. Now that he saw him in the light of day, he was amazed he'd managed to stop him in his tracks last night.

The man was a hulking six foot eight, with a broad muscular frame and thick, trunk-like legs. His skin was a rich olive and his thick, black hair curled over his ears, framing soulful brown eyes that seemed to carry the weight of a troubled past. A thin, white scar ran from his left eyebrow to his cheek and a fresh cut scored the underside of his forearm, courtesy of Ginny's blade.

"Who did that to you?" Evander asked curtly. He pointed at the injuries on the Brute's body.

The Brute blinked. He unfroze after a moment and slowly straightened, as if the slightest wrong movement might bring about his downfall. He hesitated before indicating Evander with a trembling finger.

Evander blinked. "Oh."

Remorse knotted his stomach. He found himself the focus of stares and rubbed the back of his neck awkwardly.

"It must be from last night, when I fought him."

Shaw wrinkled her nose. "What did you use, your Grace? A battering ram?"

Evander caught Rufus's narrow-eyed look.

"We mean you no harm," he told the Brute, injecting some warmth into his voice. "All we want to know is who you are and why you attacked my carriage last night."

The Brute was silent for so long Evander began to wonder if they should get an enchanter to influence his mind and have him comply with their questions. It was a method he loathed using and had only ever done so a couple of times in the past, and as a last resort at that.

"I—" The Brute stopped and swallowed heavily. "I will talk. But only if you bring Viggo here."

Evander's pulse quickened at the name. Dwyer cursed. Shaw's eyes rounded.

"Viggo?" Rufus asked harshly. "As in Viggo Stonewall?!"

The Brute licked his lips and nodded.

CHAPTER 12

THE NIGHT MIST RISING FROM THE NARROW, WET STREETS Evander and Ginny treaded carried the unpleasant smell of stagnant water from the nearby river and the acrid stink of chemical and dye runoffs from the numerous factories and workshops lining the embankment.

Ginny cast a tense look at him from under her hood.

"There is no guarantee he will agree to meet you," she said for the umpteenth time.

"I know. But this is the only way I'm going to get that Brute to talk."

She furrowed her brow and accelerated her pace. Mud churned under Evander's feet as he kept up with her.

They were in an area of Stepney sandwiched between Limehouse and London Docks. Though nowhere near as squalid as the East End, it was still a deprived district, the roads and buildings a sharp contrast to the elegant squares and fashionable streets frequented by the wealthy, magical elite a mere handful of miles away.

Evander glanced at the shadowy figures lurking in the side alleys they passed.

Who knew Nightshade *was located here.*

The man they were going to see was a mysterious figure linked to an elusive guild of which even less was known. Though many suspected *Nightshade* to be involved in illegal activities, no one had been able to provide evidence to support the rumours, hence why it had avoided raids by the Met. Said to be frequented by crime lords and royalty alike, the guild quickly gained a reputation as London's most notorious information network after first appearing on the scene some fifteen years ago.

Just as infamous was the man behind the organisation. Viggo Stonewall, AKA the Ironfist Brute. Rumoured to be one of the strongest of his kind in all of Europe, he was said to have once stopped a train with his bare hands.

Evander couldn't help but feel a deep spark of interest concerning Stonewall. The man was revered as a legend by thralls all over England. Having never had reason to cross his path in his role as a Special Arcane Investigator, he was curious to finally be meeting him.

Of course, he hadn't told Ginny any of this when he'd visited her townhouse that afternoon. If anyone in his circle knew how to get in touch with *Nightshade* and its enigmatic owner, he'd been certain it would be her.

"How is it you know the man again?" Evander enquired as they navigated a labyrinth of filthy alleys, the hems of their cloaks brushing their cheap boots.

Ginny hesitated. "I don't know him personally. He wasn't present on the occasions I availed myself of the services of his organisation." She met his wary stare and sighed. "I needed to investigate some potential business partners. *Nightshade* is quicker and more efficient than any other information guild out there."

Fifteen minutes after being dropped off at the junction of Commercial Road and Cannon Street by a hansom cab, they reached a building bearing a neat sign that said *Ironclad Shipping* above its front door.

It was identical to any of the dozens of merchant companies in the area.

Ginny ducked into a side alley that led to the back. She ignored the rear exit and headed for a nondescript door tucked at the corner of the establishment. A flame sizzled inside the oil lantern next to it.

The feeble glow washed across a metal symbol in the shape of a small purple flower nailed above the lintel.

Evander's scalp prickled as he stared at it, Ophelia Miller's warning ringing in his ears.

Ginny glanced at him. "That's why I agreed to bring you here without making a fuss." She frowned. "It crossed my mind that the purple flower Miss Miller alluded to was *Nightshade,* but it wasn't until you mentioned wanting to see Viggo Stonewall that I became certain of the connection."

She walked up to the door and knocked on a small window at eye level. It slid open immediately. A baleful gaze swept them from head to toe from behind a row of metal bars.

"What do you want?" the figure asked in a hostile tone.

"*Solana,*" Ginny said, unfazed.

The figure narrowed his eyes. The window banged closed.

"He's pleasant," Evander observed.

"Best get used to it," Ginny said in a thin voice. "This isn't going to be like your gentleman's club in Pall Mall."

There was the sound of multiple bolts sliding.

"Is *Solana* a code?" Evander asked curiously.

"Yes. I am told it comes from *Solanaceae*, the plant family the nightshade flower belongs to."

Evander raised an eyebrow. It seemed whoever came up with the password was well versed in botany.

The door opened, revealing a gloomy stone passage lined with wooden trunks and crates stacked haphazardly atop one another. A heavy, wrought-iron door was visible at the opposite end. It was being guarded by a shadowy figure.

They were about to start down the corridor when the portly doorman with the ruddy face and gimlet eyes who'd let them inside the building stepped in their path.

"You forgot the entrance fee," he said gruffly.

Ginny sighed, fished inside the pocket of her dress, and dropped a shilling in his hand.

The man didn't budge. "Fee's gone up, love." He flashed tobacco-stained teeth at them.

Ginny wrinkled her forehead. "Since when?"

"Since I said so." The man leered and reached for her. "You're a pretty little thing. I can forego your entrance fees if you let me kiss—"

The rest of his words disappeared on a high-pitched wheeze.

Evander winced.

Ginny had twisted the doorman's wrist and grabbed him by the balls.

"Would you care to complete that sentence?!" she hissed in his face.

The man shook his head jerkily, legs crossed and tears pooling in his eyes.

"Good." She released him and started down the passage.

The doorman gasped and crouched, hands covering his privates. An incoherent sound of protest left him when Ginny retraced her steps and swiped her shilling back.

"That's for being a prick," she said coldly.

"Wait," the doorman protested. "I need to pat you down for weapons."

Ginny arched an arrogant eyebrow.

The doorman sagged. "Just tell them I did so if they ask, will ya?"

The man guarding the next door knew better than to challenge her. His gaze moved curiously over Evander as they passed him, no doubt wondering what their relationship was.

Considering the outfits he and Ginny were wearing, it would be difficult for anyone to guess they were nobles.

"Henry will be proud," Evander drawled as they negotiated the passage beyond the second door. "You'll have to report that you turned yet another man's genitals black and blue and not in a nice way."

Ginny rolled her eyes.

Henry "Jab" Flintlock was a retired Navy man who owned a training club in the East End. There, he taught anyone willing to learn the fighting skills he'd picked up from his time in the military and the years he'd spent traveling through the Far East studying under various masters of Kung Fu, Karate, and Jujutsu. It was Hargrove who'd introduced Evander, Ginny, and Rufus to Flintlock after Ginny had requested an instructor to teach her the art of street fighting. Being a high-end courtesan came with its own risks and she'd been determined to be ready for any situation she encountered.

Though Evander and Rufus had initially tagged along to make sure she was safe, they'd soon found themselves swept up by the atmosphere of sweat, determination, and camaraderie that characterised Henry's club and soon became his students. There were no ranks or titles on the training floor. No differentiation between magic users and thralls, between nobles and slum dwellers. Everyone was equal in Henry's club and he treated them as such.

The corridor branched off after some twenty feet. Ginny turned left, crossed two doors, and stopped in front of an opening leading to a stone staircase.

The steps spiralled beneath the building. She started down them.

Evander followed.

A low murmur of voices reached him when they arrived at the first landing. He frowned when they got to the third landing with no visible end in sight.

"How far does this go?"

"This place was built over a network of limestone caves," Ginny said guardedly. "It's deep."

The noise swelled to a brouhaha that soon filled Evander's ears, the raucous sound of chanting and whooping making the air buzz with an energy that made his skin tingle.

His breath caught when they emerged on a mezzanine overlooking a giant space that could easily accommodate two ballrooms.

A labyrinth of chambers, galleries, and passages opened off both levels, offering glimpses into the world of the information guild. He spotted a dining hall, a library, and numerous offices with walls lined with cabinets and nebulous figures crouched over tables strewn with paperwork even at this late hour, their faces etched with eldritch shadows by the light of oil lanterns.

Evander perused the fat candles crowding the chandeliers dotting the ceiling and wall lights gracing the exposed limestone, before focusing on the expansive floor below.

Most of it was taken up by chairs and tables where guild members could sit and talk, as well as some card and billiard tables where they could try their hand at a game of chance and skill. Fireplaces and pits were arranged around the vast chamber, their flames keeping away the chill while the smoke they produced filtered through vents in the ceiling.

His gaze landed on an arena at the far end, where the noise was coming from. It resembled a Roman colosseum, with giant stone pillars demarcating the corners of the sunken floor. A crowd was gathered around it.

Evander frowned. "Is this a fight club?"

"No," Ginny said. "It's more a training ground for thralls."

Evander was aware of dozens of piercing stares as he and Ginny descended the steps leading to the lower floor.

They made their way towards the source of tonight's attraction and stopped on the edge of the mass of men and women cheering for the two giants fighting in the middle of the colosseum.

"That must be Stonewall," Ginny murmured.

Evander's stomach tightened on a flutter of awareness.

CHAPTER 13

AT SIX FOOT FOUR, THE BRUTE WHO HAD DRAWN HIS attention was slightly shorter than his opponent, with broad shoulders and a muscular build toned to perfection. His cropped hair and beard were dark and his ebony eyes burned with an animal-like intensity in a chiselled face currently set in a grim expression of determination. Blue ink covered his chest, back, and arms in fascinating swirls, the patterns tracing his sun-kissed skin reminiscent of the motifs belonging to the indigenous tribes inhabiting remote islands in the Pacific.

Evander swallowed. The Brute was mesmerising.

Judging from the delicious tension filtering through his groin, his body very much liked the raw masculinity on display.

"What makes you think that's Stonewall and not the other man?"

Ginny gave him an incredulous look. "Are you serious?" She indicated the tattooed Brute like Evander was an idiot. "Everyone's eyes are on him. And it's plain to see why. His presence is simply—"

"—magnetic," Evander mumbled.

Ginny stared at him. She was distracted by the noise swelling around them.

The fight was nearing its inevitable end.

Viggo Stonewall ended it in three blisteringly quick moves, his gloved fists striking his opponent with enough force to make the air tremble. The other Brute fell on his back, the impact sending a tremor through the ground.

The crowd went mad.

"*Viggo! Viggo! Viggo!*" they chanted, their claps echoing their shouts.

Instead of strutting around the ring, the Brute squatted and said something to the stunned man on the floor. The latter nodded weakly before taking his hand, a smile dawning on his bloodied face.

The Brute pulled the defeated man to his feet and tugged him in a quick bear hug. They climbed out of the colosseum and disappeared towards the back of the guild.

"And what have we here?" someone said behind Evander and Ginny.

They turned.

A lean, wiry man with red hair, sea-green eyes, and a cocky grin that spelled trouble was watching them curiously over his crossed arms where he sat straddling the back of a chair.

"Mr. Callaghan," Ginny greeted politely.

The man's grin widened. "You're hurting my feelings, Lady Hartley."

He rose, came over, and took Ginny's gloved hand. His

smile turned seductive as he leaned down and pressed a gallant kiss to her knuckles, the hooded look he gave her from beneath his lashes full of sensuous Irish charm.

"I told you to call me Finn the last time we—*ow! Ow! Ow!*"

Ginny had grabbed his hand and was bending it backward.

The low murmurs around them told Evander they were drawing unwanted attention.

"Hmm, Ginny—" he started.

She ignored him, her voice low and hard as she fixed the redhead with a cutting stare. "Mr. Callaghan, our transactions have and always will be purely business. Please stop insinuating otherwise."

"I was just jest—" Finn started, chagrined.

"What's going on, Razor?"

A dark man with intelligent sable eyes was approaching from the left. His quiet, watchful demeanour was reminiscent of a panther, while his sinewy build suggested he was a seasoned street fighter.

Evander could tell he was the more dangerous of the pair.

Ginny released Finn's wrist.

The Irishman gave her a wounded look before addressing the newcomer.

"Nothing special, Sly. I was just greeting the lady, is all."

The man frowned at his associate before studying Ginny and Evander.

"I've not seen you before." Ginny was studying the stranger with a glint in her eye that made Evander uneasy.

If the man registered her burgeoning interest, he did not show it. "Solomon Barden at your service. How may we be of assistance?"

Evander traded a vigilant look with Ginny. He stepped forward.

"I would like to request a meeting with Mr. Stonewall."

A wary stillness came over the two men.

Solomon's gaze burned into Evander's face, like he could see behind his facade. He cut his eyes to Ginny.

"Lady Hartley, are you aware that you're breaking the rules of the guild by bringing someone who hasn't been vetted here?" he said thinly. "It's clear this man is an aristocrat."

Ginny met Solomon's irritated glare unflinchingly. "It's an emergency."

"Your employer is going to want to hear this," Evander added quietly.

Solomon observed them for a moment longer before cocking his head, a trace of arrogance flitting across his handsome face.

"And whom shall I say wants to meet him?"

Ginny's shoulders knotted a fraction.

This was the part they'd been uncertain about.

Even though he had never had any dealings with *Nightshade* in either a personal or business capacity, Evander's identity as a Special Arcane Investigator was bound to be a sore point for members of the guild. After all, thralls and slum dwellers distrusted the Met and viewed most police officers as their enemy.

He could hardly blame them.

Recent changes in the laws of the empire may have

meant no one could throw a thrall in lockup without just cause anymore, but the damage done by centuries of violent oppression and forced servitude could not be unravelled in a matter of years.

Evander took a shallow breath.

Magic swirled inside his chest, warming his blood and filling his body with a subtle flow of power. He was fairly confident he and Ginny could take on the men in the room. He wasn't sure if they could do that *and* deal with the two Brutes present on the premises at the same time.

Ah, well. In for a penny, in for a pound.

"Tell Mr. Stonewall Evander Ravenwood is here to see him."

The silence that spread out from where they stood was so sudden and deep Evander could have heard a pin drop. A muscle jumped in Ginny's cheek when she registered the immediate hostility on Finn and Solomon's faces.

Finn's eyes shrank to slits.

"You brought the *Ice Mage* here?!" he spat at Ginny.

He made to lunge for her.

"Razor, wait—!" Solomon started.

The soft click of the derringer sounded like a bomb in the hush.

Finn stared unblinkingly into the barrel of Ginny's pistol, feet rooted to the floor.

"Stand down," Evander warned, his cane in hand where he'd flicked it out from his sleeve. His gaze swept the room and the mass of angry faces turning towards them. He raised his voice. "We did not come here to fight."

"What's all this ruckus?"

Evander looked around.

A burly man in his late fifties with greying hair and a weathered face was crossing the chamber towards them. His sharp gaze skimmed Ginny and the gun.

"How about you put that down, miss? Nothing is going to happen to you." He stopped and lowered his brows at Solomon and Finn. "Am I right?"

Solomon and Finn traded a morose look.

"Yes, sir," they muttered.

Ginny hesitated before lowering the derringer. She grimaced. "What are you, their keeper?"

"No," the man grunted. "I just happen to have known them since they were snot-nosed little brats." He offered his hand to Ginny and Evander. "Jack Stonewall. I own *Ironclad Shipping.*"

Surprise jolted Evander as he shook the older man's strong, rough fingers. "You are related to Viggo Stonewall?"

"I am his uncle." Jack eyed the sea of onlookers. "I suggest everyone get back to their own business," he said sharply. "Ain't nothing like sticking your nose where it doesn't belong to lose it."

"We're an information guild, sir," someone said sullenly. "Sticking our nose where it doesn't belong is our calling card."

Jack's frown deepened. The crowd dispersed.

Evander slowly relaxed. Viggo's uncle didn't look like the kind of man who'd stand by and let the guild members do whatever they wanted to him and Ginny.

"Care to explain why my two boys here looked like they wanted to tear your heart out a moment ago?" Jack asked Evander lightly.

Finn jutted his chin out.

"This posh nob says he's Evander Ravenwood," he said in a peeved tone.

Jack stiffened. Surprise rounded his eyes for a fleeting moment before his face turned carefully blank.

"You're Duke Ravenwood? The Ice Mage?"

Finn's jaw dropped. "Wait. The toff is a *Duke* to boot?!" he squeaked.

Solomon hushed him as ears pricked around them.

"Look, the faster he sees your nephew, the faster we'll be out of your hair," Ginny told Jack.

The older man studied them broodingly. "Why do you wish to see Viggo?"

"I have some information he will want to hear." Evander faltered. "If I'm being completely honest, I need his help."

The three men almost did a double take at that.

Jack appraised Evander with fresh eyes.

"You are different from the rumours, your Grace," he finally murmured.

"In what way?" Evander said carefully.

"You are not the unfeeling monster the gossip seems to suggest you are." Jack's expression turned wry. "One thing is true though."

Evander met his steady gaze warily. "And that is?"

"They did not exaggerate your beauty."

Evander's mouth parted on a flummoxed, "Oh."

Finn made gagging noises.

"And you, Lady Hartley, are as ravishing as Finn raved you were," Jack said with a gallant half bow.

"Oh, please." A flirtatious smile danced on Ginny's lips.

Jack offered his arm to her. "Shall we? Viggo's office is this way."

Evander followed alongside Solomon and Finn as they made for the direction in which Viggo had disappeared.

"How come Jack gets a smile and I get my wrist twisted?" Finn complained to Solomon in a low voice.

"It's all in the delivery." Solomon's tone hardened. "By the way, who is manning the main door tonight?"

"George is."

"Well, George deserves a kick in the bollocks for letting these two in with weapons," Solomon said thinly.

"I wouldn't blame George," Evander said. "And his balls are already bruised. Before you ask, it wasn't me."

Finn's expression turned from shocked to dreamy as he gazed at Ginny.

"Is it wrong that I find that terribly attractive?" he mumbled.

"If you want your balls crushed that badly, I'll do it for you," Solomon muttered.

Finn shuddered. "No, thanks. My dick will shrivel up and die if you so much as look its way."

CHAPTER 14

Viggo's office was at the end of a gallery lined with desks and chairs. The soft glow of candle lanterns and oil lamps washed across heaps of paperwork stacked upon the surfaces and loaded bookshelves on the walls.

It was becoming increasingly clear to Evander why *Nightshade* was so successful. Viggo Stonewall not only ran a tight ship, it seemed he'd made sure his guild members received more than just a basic education.

The door was slightly ajar when they reached the room.

Jack rapped his knuckles on the wood. "It's me."

"Come in. I'm almost done cleaning up."

Viggo's voice was deep and gravelly and did all kinds of unseemly things to Evander's pulse.

Jack pushed the door open.

Evander's first impression of Viggo's modest office was of books.

He blinked. They were everywhere.

On the solid oak shelves and cases lining all the walls bar one. On the weathered walnut desk buried under piles of ledgers. On the floor, stacked in haphazard towers that threatened to tumble at the mere whisper of a breeze.

It took a moment for his startled gaze to find the man he'd come to see.

Viggo stood with his back to them to the left of the room. He was splashing his face and neck with cold water from a basin, rinsing away the sweat and grime from the fight. He reached for a flannel hanging on a hook and started wiping his face as he straightened.

Their eyes met in the mirror above the basin. Viggo froze.

Evander wasn't quite sure how to describe the feeling that swept through him in that moment. It was like being struck by lightning, his body tingling and sparking from dozens of blistering shocks. He felt dizzy and breathless, as if he'd run a considerable distance.

One thing he did recognise, much to his chagrin.

The sharp punch to the gut he was experiencing could only be sexual attraction. It was immediate and so wonderfully and terrifyingly strong, Evander found it a miracle he wasn't sporting an erection.

Viggo turned.

"Who is this?" he asked, his expression cryptic.

His gaze flitted to Ginny before locking on Evander once more, like he couldn't look away from him either.

Jack introduced them. "This is Lady Hartley." He paused, wariness creeping into his voice. "And this is Duke Evander Ravenwood."

The change that came over the Brute was sudden and spine-chilling.

One moment he was on the other side of the room, the next he'd crossed the floor, lifted Evander up by the collar of his cloak, and slammed him into the bookcase on the opposite wall.

"Evander!" Ginny cried out.

Evander grunted and grabbed Viggo's wrist, books spilling out around him. His heels found purchase on a shelf.

Viggo's eyes burned with the rage of a thousand suns as he glared at him.

"Don't!" Evander snapped when he saw Ginny reach for her pistol out of the corner of his eye.

He dared not look away from the Brute.

Evander's heart raced as he met Viggo's livid gaze. It was taking all of his will power to fight his body's instinct to unleash his magic and defend himself.

Solomon and Finn framed Ginny, their expressions vacillating between concern for their boss and open hostility towards him.

Jack approached and placed a hand on Viggo's shoulder.

"Stop," he told his nephew firmly. "He came here to talk. Says he has some information for you."

Viggo clenched his jaw, his hand hot against Evander's skin. He could no doubt feel the pulse drumming frantically at the base of his throat.

For a moment, Evander thought he would not listen to his uncle.

The fury blazing in Viggo's pupils slowly abated.

He let go of him abruptly and retreated to his desk, wiping his hands on the flannel he held like he wanted to clean any trace of Evander from his flesh.

Evander swallowed, mouth dry where he'd braced his back against the bookcase. Though his knees were shaking, he couldn't let it show.

He could sense the tension vibrating through the Brute all the way from behind the table. Showing any sign of weakness in front of this man would be akin to a lamb exposing its throat to an apex predator.

"What do you want, Ice Mage?" Viggo ground out. He grabbed the shirt on the back of his chair and shrugged into it.

Evander wondered at the ability of his libido to note the enticing way the Brute's muscles moved as he angrily buttoned the item of clothing, while still in the midst of a rather precarious situation. He swallowed a curse.

Jasper and Ginny were right. I need to blow off some steam.

"May we sit?" he said after he'd recovered his breath. He indicated the book-laden chairs in front of the desk.

Viggo looked at him as if he'd lost his mind.

Evander sighed. "This may take a while."

Viggo scowled, sat down, and crossed his heels on the table, his boots striking the wood like death knells.

Evander took this as a sign the Brute wasn't bothered what he chose to do with himself and headed over to the chairs. Ginny joined him as he carefully moved the books to the floor.

Jack came over to stand by Viggo while Solomon and Finn took up position by the door. Evander noted this with interest.

Looks like they've been in this kind of situation plenty of times before.

From Ginny's guarded expression, she too had clocked the way the men had positioned themselves. It was an arrangement meant to intimidate their guests.

Unfortunately, Evander and Ginny had navigated far worse waters at the society balls and dinner parties they attended to be cowered by such a display.

"You are being rather tight-lipped for someone who wanted to talk, *mage*," Viggo said sullenly, the last word uttered on a tone of pure contempt.

His gaze dropped briefly to Evander's mouth. He removed a cigar from a drawer, clipped it expertly, and lit it on the candle lantern on the desk.

"I see you like Homer."

Viggo blinked, nonplussed.

Evander indicated the worn copy of *The Iliad* on the shelf behind the Brute. "That tome looks rather well used."

"I got it from a second-hand book stall in Spitalfields market," Viggo grunted.

He seemed surprised by his own answer in the next moment, as did Jack.

Evander suppressed a smile. He suspected he'd just discovered one of Viggo Stonewall's weaknesses.

The Brute furrowed his brow, like he could guess what Evander was thinking right now.

"If you came here to discuss our mutual tastes in books, I think you'll find you have far more in common with those posh nobs you mingle with at *The Prestige*."

Ginny barely managed to mask a gasp. Evander's body grew cold.

The Prestige was the name of the gentleman's club he frequented.

"How do you know I attend that place?" he asked tightly.

"This is an information guild, Duke Ravenwood. We gather—" Viggo exhaled a cloud of smoke in Evander's direction and sneered, "—information."

Finn snorted by the door. Solomon elbowed him in the ribs.

Evander clenched his jaw, the faces of the dark mages rising before his eyes.

"Does this mean someone asked you to investigate my movements?"

Viggo's expression grew shuttered at his angry tone. "*Nightshade* is the best information guild in the whole of England. I do not state this as a matter of pride. It is a fact. And no information guild worth their salt would divulge details about their work or their clients."

Evander exchanged a tense glance with Ginny.

Have we walked into the lion's den? He fisted his hands as he met the stony gaze of the Brute across the desk. *No. However much animosity I can feel from this man, I don't think he or his guild would associate with dark mages. Not willingly anyway.*

"The night isn't getting any younger, mage," Viggo grunted. "State your business and be gone with—"

"Last night, my carriage was attacked by a Brute and three dark mages."

CHAPTER 15

THE STILLNESS THAT CAME OVER VIGGO WOULD HAVE MADE most men nervous.

Evander Ravenwood's bewitchingly handsome face remained as calm as his voice, his ice-blue gaze never faltering as he met Viggo's stare.

"Lady Hartley and I managed to fend them off," he continued, as if he were describing a tea party where the worst thing that happened was someone broke a cup. "The Brute was taken into custody by the Met. He is currently in one of our holding cells in Scotland Yard." He paused. "He refuses to speak to anyone unless you're present."

Viggo felt a vein throb in his temple. He suspected the only reason the Brute was still in Scotland Yard and not locked up in Coldbath Fields or worse, Irongate Prison, was thanks largely to the man sitting opposite him.

Not that long ago, attacking a mage, let alone one of

Evander's noble status, would have been a crime punishable by death.

"Were you and Lady Hartley injured?" he said brusquely.

The question made Evander's eyes widen a little. "No."

"We know how to defend ourselves," Ginny said curtly.

"I can vouch for that," Solomon murmured.

Viggo clenched his jaw. "Then, was the Brute injured?"

It seemed a stupid thing to ask. After all, not many people in the world could physically hurt a Brute.

He knew Evander Ravenwood could.

A dual elemental mage able to wield ice and wind magic, he had used his powers to defuse many a potentially explosive situation involving the Met and thralls over the years, all without injuring anyone. So Viggo had read in various reports. Now that he was in the presence of the man, he wondered if he too might struggle to win a fight against the mage.

He'd sensed it all too well a moment ago, when he'd held him up against the wall.

He'd seen the potent magic swirling in the depths of Evander's arresting blue eyes. Smelled it in the sweet breath that had washed across his fingers. Felt it in the skin his knuckles had brushed. The skin he'd wanted to expose and touch to see if it was as hot and supple everywhere else.

Viggo's groin swelled as he imagined that sinfully delightful sight. He shifted, lifting his feet off the desk and leaning his elbows upon it to mask his arousal.

Evander Ravenwood was dangerous to him in more ways than one.

He realised the mage hadn't answered his question. "Well?"

"He has some bruises and cuts," Evander confessed. "He refuses to see a doctor or healer," he added at Viggo's scowl. "He won't even tell us his name."

"Describe him," Viggo said coldly.

"Six foot eight, curly dark hair, brown eyes."

A name danced immediately through Viggo's mind.

"He has a scar running from his left eyebrow to his cheek," Ginny gestured.

Jack froze. So did Solomon and Finn.

Viggo's stomach knotted on a wave of dread, his suspicion solidifying into certainty.

"Magnus Graveoak." He exchanged a stunned look with his uncle and his two right-hand men.

Evander straightened. "So, he *is* an acquaintance of yours?" he said sharply.

"He disappeared two years ago," Viggo said slowly, frustration underscoring his voice. "Used to work on the docks. His employer turned up one day, looking for him. Owed him a whole month's wage." He fisted his hands.

He and Magnus had met shortly after he'd fled to London following the incident that had seen his entire village and his family massacred in a single night of terrifying violence by a group of magic zealots led by an Archmage. It was in the slums that Viggo first befriended Solomon and Finn, the two boys similarly orphaned by the dire circumstances of their birth.

As children growing up in the poorest districts of the capital, they'd had each other's back and quickly bonded over their shared struggles and their hatred for the magic society that ruled their lives and fates.

Magnus had matured before all of them, his rapid physical growth a sign of the Brute he would become. As such, he was often their protector and used his size and strength to defend Viggo, Solomon, Finn, and other weaker children from bullies and predators. Yet, despite his intimidating size and appearance, Magnus harboured the most gentle of souls.

Viggo closed his eyes briefly.

Thank God he's alive!

Jack pressed a gentle hand on his shoulder.

"*Nightshade* has been searching for Magnus," the older man told Evander and Ginny quietly. "He's a good friend of Viggo's from their days growing up in London."

"We couldn't find any traces of him." Viggo rubbed his hands down his face, relief and remorse tightening his throat in equal measure. "Now you're telling me he's been working with dark mages?!"

"I find that hard to believe." Solomon frowned. "The Magnus we know wouldn't hurt a fly."

"We thought for sure he was at the bottom of the river," Finn muttered.

Everyone looked at him.

The Irishman shrugged. "What?"

Viggo took a deep breath and finally met Evander's gaze. Determination hardened his voice when he spoke.

"Take me to him."

Eight hours later saw Viggo standing across the road from the fortified walls enclosing the grounds and daunting fortress that housed the headquarters of the Met.

A nightmarish construction of black stone and reinforced glass and steel windows said to be resistant to brute force and magic attacks, the Gothic stronghold overlooked Victoria Embankment and the river.

"You sure about this, boss?" Solomon said warily as he gazed at the imposing buildings rising out of the early morning mist.

They were already earning suspicious stares from the constables trickling through the gates for the shift change.

Solomon might have been able to blend in the background, but there was no hiding Viggo's stature or his true nature.

"Yes, I'm sure."

They'd left Finn in charge of the guild's affairs that morning. The Irishman might have a mischievous streak a mile long, but he had a remarkably good head on his shoulders when it came to running the show in Viggo and Solomon's absence.

Jack had wanted to accompany them. Alas, with fresh ships arrived in the docks that morning, he would be too busy tending to cargo manifests and taking ownership of the wares he'd arranged to distribute. Hidden among them would be secret messages and reports from guild members currently on the continent.

Viggo glanced at the weathered watch hanging off the inside breast pocket of his coat. It was seven, the time they'd arranged to meet Evander. He frowned.

Where is that damn mage?

He was distracted by the sound of an approaching carriage.

A sleek, black four-wheeler drawn by a pair of magnificent horses turned the corner and approached Scotland Yard. The body of the vehicle was made of polished ebony and bore beautiful silver inlays forming the crest of a raven perched on a crescent moon on its doors.

Viggo had no doubt the carriage was heavily warded since it appeared to belong to someone of import. He blinked, a sudden suspicion blasting through his mind.

*Wait. Don't tell me that's—*his *carriage?!*

As if to confirm his worse fears, the vehicle pulled to a stop in front of where he and Solomon stood. A young lad in livery jumped down from the box seat and opened the door. His curious gaze flitted to Viggo. He froze, eyes rounding and jaw dropping on a shocked inhale.

Viggo's heart sank when Evander stepped out of the carriage. He was dressed in his formal Met uniform, the silver buttons on his dark blue coat and the aiguillette on his left shoulder gleaming in the insipid sunshine piercing the morning mist, his blue eyes as clear and as cool as they had been when they'd met last night.

Viggo could tell the quality of the mage's clothing was superior to the other inspectors in the Met. And it confirmed once more the bleak thought he'd had after the Ice Mage had left *Nightshade*.

He and Evander Ravenwood came from diametrically opposite worlds.

Worlds that were as different from one another as night was from day.

Which meant Viggo could never explore whatever the…*feeling* was he'd experienced in the presence of the man last night. The same feeling currently quickening his pulse and hastening his breath despite his will. The feeling that was compelling him to touch and kiss this man.

Viggo swallowed, his nails digging into his palms.

Mages were his sworn enemy. And there was no way in the nine Hells he would ever sleep with one.

CHAPTER 16

BUTTERFLIES SWARMED EVANDER'S STOMACH AT THE SIGHT of Viggo.

His breath caught when he glimpsed the array of emotions that flashed in the other man's eyes.

Surprise. Dismay. A smouldering heat that sent his heart aflutter and made him forget his resolution to ignore the burn of attraction between them. A resolution he'd come to after several sleepless hours last night.

Viggo's jaw set in a hard line, expression growing shuttered.

Evander could practically feel the invisible wall he'd just put up. He swallowed his disappointment.

This is a good thing. The more distance there is between us, the better it is for the both of us.

He became aware of young Samuel fidgeting beside him.

"Yes?"

"My—my Lord," the footman squeaked, "is this—is this gentleman *Viggo Stonewall?!*"

Evander's face relaxed at the excitement in his eyes. Young Samuel was acting like he'd just met his idol.

"Yes, it is."

Samuel almost swooned. "Oh."

An idea came to Evander. "Would you like his autograph?"

Viggo furrowed his brow. Samuel blinked.

"You mean," the footman's voice quavered, "like his *signature?!*"

Evander removed his notebook from the pocket of his coat, tore out a page, and presented it to Viggo along with a magic quill.

"Would you be so kind as to oblige? It appears my footman is one of your ardent admirers."

Viggo looked at the paper and quill like they were poison.

Solomon pressed a fist to his mouth and turned away slightly, shoulders quaking.

Viggo glared at his associate.

Evander bit his lip, similarly struck by a sudden urge to laugh at the Brute's outraged look.

"I promise, they don't bite," he managed in a strangled voice.

Viggo clenched his jaw. He eyed Samuel's breathlessly expectant expression, snatched the page and quill from Evander, and scribbled his name.

"There." He thrust the autograph to Samuel. "Though I do not know why a magic user would want the signature of a Brute of all things."

"I'm not a magic user, sir," Samuel said distractedly, staring at the treasure in his hands.

Evander had no doubt he'd be sleeping with it under his pillow tonight. He clocked Viggo's surprised look.

Solomon's pensive gaze swung from the footman to Evander.

"So, the rumours are true? You employ thralls?"

"Yes," Samuel chirped enthusiastically before Evander could reply. "My sister and cousins work as maids for his Grace. My other sister and uncle work at Lady Hartley's townhouse. There are thralls working on their country estates too."

"Come now, Samuel," Graham murmured from the box seat in the awkward silence. "We should let his Grace get on with his business." He dipped his head courteously at Evander. "We shall see you this afternoon, my Lord." The coachman smiled faintly and tipped his hat off to Viggo as the footman reluctantly climbed into the seat beside him. "Young Samuel here has long talked about your exploits, Mr. Stonewall. It is a pleasure to finally put a face to the name."

Viggo stared after the disappearing carriage.

"Are all your employees like that?" he murmured.

"You mean, the opposite of a cold, unfeeling bastard who distrusts everyone he meets at first sight?" Evander said mildly.

Solomon made a choked sound.

Viggo narrowed his eyes. "You think I'm a cold unfeeling bastard who distrusts everyone he meets at first sight?"

Evander arched an eyebrow, not in the least bit intimidated. "Do you deny it?"

The question seemed to startle the Brute.

Remorse flashed through Evander. He sighed.

"Forgive me. I am being rude despite the fact that I'm the one in need of your assistance. Come, let us go in."

Viggo and Solomon signed the visitors' logbook with the kind of expression that suggested they were being made to donate a limb. The eyes of the sergeant and two constables manning the gates bulged as Solomon divested himself of his many weapons.

Evander frowned at the pistol, two knives, leather sap, and knuckle duster in the tray.

Where the devil was he keeping all that?!

The sergeant handed Solomon a receipt and gazed expectantly at Viggo.

"Do I look like I need a weapon?" the Brute said coolly.

The sergeant swallowed, gaze darting to Evander.

Evander sighed. "I shall vouch for him."

"Alright, your Grace." The sergeant nodded at Viggo and Solomon. "You, er, may proceed."

The pair followed Evander through the gates and into the grounds.

There was a drill going on in the yard, the sergeant leading it barking orders at the young constables running briskly in the cold morning air. Dozens of curious eyes followed Viggo and Solomon's progress as they headed for the iron clad doors at the top of the steps fronting the main entrance of Scotland Yard.

A couple of sergeants came out of the building.

They stopped and greeted Evander with deference before going about their business.

"You appear to carry a lot of weight around here," Viggo observed. "Is it because you're a Duke?"

"No." Evander met his guarded gaze. "It's because I'm a Special Arcane Investigator."

"Is it true that only dual elemental mages are allowed to be Special Arcane Investigators?" Solomon asked curiously.

"That is correct."

Viggo frowned at the aiguillette on Evander's uniform. "Is that the reason yours has gold and blue threads?"

"The gold, yes."

"What of the blue?" Viggo asked doggedly.

Evander smiled faintly. "That's a secret."

This answer seemed to annoy the Brute.

Then they were inside the foyer and amidst the morning rush of officers and staff swarming the administrative block of the Met.

Evander saw Viggo's shoulders subtly knot as they navigated the crowded space in front of the ornate, imperial staircase rising towards the upper levels of the building. The movement would be invisible to most but the keenest of observers.

"You have quite a varied taste in literature," he told the Brute in a conversational tone. "I spotted books pertaining to subjects other than philosophy on your shelves last night."

Viggo's stiff gaze shifted from the dozens of constables and sergeants milling about the marble-floored lobby.

"You want to talk about books?" he asked Evander leadenly. "*Now?!*"

Solomon was similarly looking at Evander like he'd lost his marbles.

Understanding dawned belatedly on Viggo's face. He lowered his brows. "If this is an attempt to distract me—"

"It is," Evander said briskly. "I'd rather we reach our destination without you accidentally," he waved a hand, "—killing anyone with your death glare." His face softened at Viggo's scowl. He wasn't sure why he'd ever been afraid of this man. "Humour me. I am genuinely interested."

Viggo hesitated for so long Evander thought he might avoid the topic entirely.

"I've always enjoyed reading," the Brute finally confessed. "I like…learning new things."

"Did your uncle teach you to read and write?"

Viggo shook his head. "My ma did. There was a school in the village where I was born. She was the teacher." A haunted expression clouded his face. "She died a long time ago."

Evander could tell the Brute was recalling the tragic circumstances surrounding his mother's death.

The War of Subjugation began in 1825 and lasted five years. Since those with magic were afforded advantages that those without never received, the unequal society where rich mages and magic users routinely abused the poor magicless masses created a festering resentment that finally exploded into a conflict that swept not just across England but across half the continent.

The war was triggered by a single incident.

A family of thralls was unjustly accused of crimes they

never committed and burned at the stake by a mage before a formal investigation was carried out. Six children and two adults died that night while their neighbours and friends were forcibly held back and made to watch.

Though the real criminal, a caster, was caught the very next morning and punished, no apology was ever offered to the relatives of the dead family.

Like the crack in a dam, one thrall rebelled. Then another. Then half a dozen. By the end of that first week, riots had broken out across the south of England and began spreading north.

Appalled by the actions of people they considered nothing more than cattle, the magic users retaliated with a brutality that far exceeded what the thralls did.

The war that followed was led by the five most powerful Archmages in England and became a period of history that would forever be tainted with the terrible tragedy that was the deaths of thousands of innocent magicless. Thralls who perished at the hands of organised mobs of mages who swept through capitals, towns, and countryside villages on a misbegotten mission to rid themselves of the enemy amidst them.

It was as if those who'd inherited their powers by the simple virtue of their births had decided to purge the world of those who hadn't been as lucky as them. To cleanse humanity of the defective bloodlines that could never birth magic. To "rid the world of dirty thralls."

Evander had felt sick to his stomach when he'd learned that that had been the motto and the objective of the war in its last year, the real reason behind why the conflict started in the first place lost amidst a sea of spite and venom.

It was the protests of the highest born nobles of the land, among them Evander's father, and their European counterparts that finally drove an ill King William IV to rise from his bed and persuade his niece Queen Victoria to put an end to the awful war. Queen Victoria eventually threatened to divest the Archmages of all their titles and lands and restrain their magic, the royal family having in its possession a secret artefact that could do this.

Though the war officially ended in 1830, the persecution of the thralls did not. It was another two decades before the zealots who, fuelled by a twisted ideology of magical supremacy stemming from the Archmages who led the War of Subjugation, had subjected dozens of thrall communities and villages to campaigns of terror were finally arrested and their leader sent to Irongate Prison. Stripped of his powers by Queen Victoria, the Archmage was ironically set upon and murdered by a mob of thralls a few years later. His body was buried in a nameless grave and his once powerful family lost their seat in the House of Lords.

Evander had heard rumours concerning Viggo's origins. The Brute was said to be the sole survivor of the last terrifying purge led by the Archmage. One where he had seen his entire village massacred before his eyes when he was but a boy. Remorse knotted Evander's insides at having inadvertently caused Viggo to recall his painful past.

CHAPTER 17

"I'm sorry."

Evander's voice dragged Viggo from the dark turn his thoughts had taken.

"Whatever for?"

"For making you remember something unpleasant," the mage said quietly. There was no conceit in his voice or expression.

"How strange," Viggo said.

Evander glanced at him quizzically. "What is?"

"That a mage cares so much about thralls. And a Brute at that."

Evander stopped walking abruptly, causing Viggo and Solomon to nearly bump into him. The look in the mage's eyes made Viggo's breath catch when he turned to face them.

Evander's ice-blue gaze had shifted to the colours of a storm-tossed sea.

"The only thing that differentiates us is the

circumstances of our birth, Mr. Stonewall," he said in a voice that would have quaked with anger had he not had such a tight rein over his emotions. "And that is nothing but a stroke of luck. It is simply fortune, or misfortune, that neither of us had any control over. At the end of the day, we're all made of flesh, bone, and blood."

An awkward silence fell between them. Evander twisted around and resumed walking at a brisk pace, evidently not caring if they followed or not.

Viggo and Solomon fell into step behind him.

"I like history and science too," Viggo volunteered gruffly after a moment. He ignored Solomon's side stare. "And botany. I very much like botany."

Evander's shoulders slowly unknotted as he accepted this tentative olive branch. "I also saw books on commerce and law in your office."

Viggo's chest loosened. He didn't know why, but he didn't like seeing this man upset. By the time they reached the west wing of the fortress and the Arcane Division, Viggo learned that they shared many a reading interest.

A man with dark hair and slate-blue eyes was waiting for them inside Evander's office.

"Thank goodness you're alright!" he started in a voice full of relief as Evander entered the room. He rose from his chair. "I got your message late last night. Is Mr. Stonewall really joining—?" He stopped at the sight of Viggo and Solomon, surprise flitting across his face before he carefully schooled his expression. "Oh. My apologies, your Grace. I didn't know you had company."

The silver aiguillette on the stranger's uniform indicated he was an inspector in the Met. And the way he'd quickly shifted from a casual to a formal address told Viggo he and Evander were close acquaintances in private.

Evander waived honorific as he made the introductions. "Rufus, this is Viggo Stonewall and his associate, Solomon Barden." He indicated the inspector. "This is Inspector Rufus Grayson. He's assisting me on this case."

Viggo's stomach sank. "The case? I didn't realise Magnus was being formally investigated."

"Oh." Evander's expression turned contrite. "I apologise for the misunderstanding. We are not investigating Mr. Graveoak. The attack on my carriage is related to a case Rufus and I are working on."

Relief shot through Viggo at that.

"Magnus Graveoak is the name of our Brute in the holding cell," Evander explained at Rufus's inquisitive look.

"Can I ask what your case relates to?" Viggo said curiously.

Rufus frowned. "I'm afraid that's—"

"It's a murder," Evander said.

The inspector gave the Ice Mage a chagrined look.

Unease prickled Viggo's scalp. He exchanged a cautious glance with Solomon.

"You mean the man who was found dead in Bethnal Green two days ago?"

Full blown suspicion clouded Rufus's face. Viggo could tell the inspector trusted him as far as he could throw him.

Evander met Viggo's stare levelly.

"Do you know something about the murder victim?"

Viggo shook his head. "Only that magic was involved in his death."

"Everything that happens in the slums eventually reaches *Nightshade*'s ears," Solomon explained at Evander and Grayson's guarded expressions.

The two men shared a look.

"Then we may have need to call upon your guild for future assistance on this matter," Evander said. "Is that something you would be willing to entertain?"

Viggo lowered his brows. "You want *Nightshade* to help the Met?"

He couldn't mask the disbelief in his voice.

"Yes."

Solomon's expression turned shrewd. "It will cost you."

Rufus bristled. "I hope you're not intending to rip off the Met, sir!"

Solomon's eyes shrank to slits. "The last time someone called me sir, he had to look for his teeth in a ditch."

Rufus scowled.

Evander sighed. "How about we go see Mr. Graveoak for now?"

Tension oozed through Viggo as Evander and Rufus led the way to the south wing of the complex. He could sense dozens of cool stares upon him and Solomon the farther they ventured inside the fortress.

It was clear not everyone appreciated seeing thralls in the hallowed halls of the Met. If Evander registered the veiled distaste being projected by his associates, he did not show it.

"Wait, your Grace!" someone shouted behind them.

They stopped and turned.

A petite young woman with dark hair and bright eyes was running to catch up with them, a ream of paper in hand.

"Miss Shaw," Evander said warily. "What's wrong?"

Shaw came to a stop and bent over, hands on her knees. "Just—give me a moment!" she wheezed. "Blimey, I'm getting too old to be running around like this!"

"You're three and twenty, Miss Shaw," Rufus remarked. "You're hardly past your prime."

"Miss Shaw is a forensic mage working the case with us," Evander explained to Viggo and Solomon while the colour in the mage's face slowly settled.

Shaw straightened and waved her paperwork with a triumphant expression. "Mr. Brown sent a message. He believes he has identified the powder I discovered at the scene!"

Evander's expression cleared. "He has?"

"Yes," Shaw gushed, practically hopping from foot to foot.

Viggo furrowed his brow. *Powder?*

Shaw was about to say more when she belatedly registered Viggo and Solomon's presence. She studied them with an astute look far beyond her years.

"By the way, your Grace. Who might these two gentlemen be?"

Evander reluctantly made the introductions.

"Bloody hell!" Shaw's eyes rounded with awe. "You're the Ironfist Brute?!"

Her squeal echoed down the corridor, drawing several disapproving frowns.

"What did I say about keeping your voice down when you're out and about, Miss Shaw?" Rufus said glacially.

"But—" Shaw cocked a thumb at Viggo, her tone dropping to a conspiratorial hiss, "it's the *Ironfist Brute*, sir! Like, *in the flesh!*"

Rufus groaned. Solomon's mouth pressed to a thin line, shoulders quaking with barely suppressed mirth.

"I think you have another admirer," Evander told Viggo in a resigned voice.

"She's not gonna want an autograph, is she?" Viggo asked uneasily.

Shaw brightened. "You're offering autographs?"

Evander distracted the forensic mage before she could harass the Brute for his signature and allowed her to tag along as they made their way to the holding cells. Sergeant Griffiths was in charge of the lockup that morning. He observed Viggo and Solomon guardedly while Evander briefly made introductions, before guiding them to Magnus's prison.

Relief made Viggo dizzy when he saw the Brute sitting comfortably on a bench reading a book.

"Magnus," he breathed, his voice trembling ever so slightly at the sight of the man he thought he would never see again.

Magnus froze. His head snapped around.

"Viggo?" His face crumpled. He jumped to his feet and dropped the book as he dashed across the cell. "*Viggo!*"

A gentle breeze stirred Viggo's clothes as Magnus ran into his arms crying. It caught the tome inches from the ground and silently returned it to the bench.

Evander's finger twitched. The breeze disappeared.

The speed and control the mage demonstrated over his wind magic in that split second sent a shiver down Viggo's spine as he hugged Magnus. He wasn't sure whether it was fear or admiration he was experiencing in that moment. One thing he was certain of.

Evander was one of the strongest mages he'd ever crossed paths with.

It was a while before Magnus calmed down enough for Viggo to get any sense out of him. What he went on to tell them sent a chill through Viggo that had little to do with the powerful ice mage in the room and everything to do with the blood curdling tale the Brute recounted.

CHAPTER 18

"I DON'T REMEMBER MUCH ABOUT THE EVENTS OF THE LAST two years," Magnus said in a harrowing voice. "It all feels like a nightmare. One with no end in sight." He swallowed. "I have a dim memory of being approached by a man while I was working the docks one night. He offered me a temporary job as a bodyguard and said I had to leave with him there and then. I—" The Brute stopped and licked his lips, his face full of regret. "I knew the money would come in handy for the kids at the orphanage, so I agreed despite my misgivings. The last thing I recall is following him into an alley."

Evander studied Magnus with a faint frown. He knew the Brute was telling the truth about what had happened to him. The way his shoulders hunched and the terror making his voice tremble could not be easily feigned.

"You fool." A muscle worked in Viggo's jawline. "You should have come to me if you needed money!"

Magnus shook his head. "You've already done so much

for us, Viggo. Almost every penny *Nightshade* can spare goes into supporting us thralls so that we have a better life."

Surprise jolted Evander at that revelation.

Judging from Solomon's stiff expression, he didn't like this fact being made common knowledge.

Rufus's gaze reflected Evander's growing unease. Magnus's statement made it clear this case wasn't just about the murder of a reputable Charm Weaver.

There's a darker plot afoot. Evander frowned. *And whatever that crystal vial is, it's at the heart of it.*

"Do you remember attacking my carriage two nights ago?" he asked Magnus.

The Brute flinched at his question.

"It's alright," Viggo reassured. "The Ice—" he stopped and glanced at Evander, "I mean, his Grace means you no harm."

"Please, call me Evander."

Solomon sucked in air. Rufus and Shaw's eyes rounded. Sergeant Griffiths went slack-jawed.

Viggo stared, his face unreadable. "I don't think that's a good idea."

"And I will be terribly offended if you keep calling me your Grace," Evander said mildly.

Magnus looked between them, confused.

"Alright," Viggo finally grunted.

"Now that you ask, your face does look vaguely familiar your, er—your Grace," Magnus mumbled. "I get the feeling I recently glimpsed it for a brief instance."

Evander's pulse quickened. "Oh."

"Evander?" Rufus said warily.

"When my cufflinks detonated." Evander's mouth had gone dry. "I think he regained control of his senses for a moment!"

Viggo froze. "Regained control of his senses?" His expression grew thunderous. "What do you mean by that?!"

"He has exploding cufflinks?" Solomon hissed to Rufus.

Evander's mind raced as he finally connected the pieces of the puzzle.

Magnus can't remember anything for the simple reason that he was not in control of his own mind and actions.

He realised everyone was staring at him, Viggo with a look that said he'd better speak up and fast.

"The dark mage who was leading them had a ring with a black gem," Evander explained. "I believe that's how he and his associates have been controlling Magnus. The gem lit up with a red light when he gave Magnus the order to kill me and Ginny. Magnus's pupils glowed the same shade of crimson before he attacked us."

Magnus blanched. "I—I tried to kill you?!" His voice broke.

Evander crossed the floor and dropped to his knee in front of the startled Brute before anyone could react. He touched the man's trembling hand gently.

"It wasn't your fault, Magnus. I doubt anyone could have resisted that spell."

Magnus's chin quivered. "Do you really mean that, your Grace?!" he choked.

"Yes. I shall convince my Commander to release you."

"Evander," Rufus warned, "you know that might not be possible."

Evander jutted his chin out. "The man is innocent, Rufus. You and I both know it. I will not have him rot in prison while we finish solving this case. I'll speak to Winterbourne. Hell, I will get him out even if I have to see the Commissioner himself!"

Viggo drew a sharp breath. Even Solomon looked stunned at Evander's declaration.

"You best not argue with him, sir," Shaw told Rufus. "You know what his Grace is like once he makes up his mind. He's as stubborn as the son of a mule."

"I hardly want to hear that from you, Miss Shaw," Evander muttered.

Magnus sniffed and wiped his gleaming eyes. "But—I must have hurt you."

Evander grimaced. "Having my head nearly crushed was not the most pleasant experience." He paused. "To be fair, Lady Hartley did shoot you in the back of your skull. Twice."

Magnus startled. "She did?!"

"Yes. If it wasn't for the fact that you're a Brute, you would have been in trouble."

"Oh." Magnus touched the back of his head. "My ma always said I had a hard skull—" He froze, brow wrinkling. "What's that?"

"What do you mean?" Viggo said.

Magnus twisted on the bench. "There's something there. Can you see it?!" His voice rose, panic setting in at whatever it was he was feeling.

Something glinted about an inch above his hairline.

Goosebumps broke out on Evander's skin, his instincts as an Archmage warning him of imminent danger.

Viggo scowled. "What the devil?!" He reached for it.

"*No!*" Evander made to grab his hand. "Don't touch—!"

Viggo's fingers grazed the object buried at the base of Magnus's skull just as Evander grasped his wrist.

The force that whomped out of it knocked Viggo off the bench and sent Evander crashing onto the floor. Viggo flew across the cell and smashed into a wall with a grunt, the impact cracking the surface.

A bellow of pain left Magnus.

Evander's heart raced as he pushed up on his elbows and watched the Brute clutch his head, his face a mask of agony. Magnus's roar cut off just as abruptly as it'd started. He collapsed to the ground and began convulsing.

It's a cursed artefact!

Magic warmed Evander's blood as he jumped to his feet.

"Sergeant Griffiths, evacuate the other cells and isolate this floor!" he barked. "Miss Shaw, go get Mrs. Scarborough! Rufus, guard the door with Solomon!"

The room's occupants unfroze, his rapid-fire orders bringing them to life. Shaw and Griffiths ran out of the cell.

Magnus's eyes rolled into the back of his head. His back arched and his heels drummed the stone floor, his laboured gasps loud in the stunned hush.

Viggo straightened from the wall.

"What's happening to him?!" he said numbly.

"I'll explain later." Evander shrugged out of his coat and undid his cravat hastily, his chest tight with dread.

"You have to pin him down and stop him from biting his tongue!"

Determination filled Viggo's face. He removed his trouser belt and joined Evander. They pried Magnus's jaws open so he could slip the leather band between the jerking man's teeth.

"Help me get him on his front!" Evander snapped.

Viggo cursed. Magnus was turning blue.

He obeyed Evander nonetheless.

"I don't care what you do but try and keep him still," Evander ordered in a hard voice as he took up position by Magnus's head. "Sit on him if you must!"

Wind magic lightened his body. He used it to carefully part Magnus's hair, exposing what was buried in the man's flesh.

Viggo stiffened where he was holding Magnus down. "What in the name of Hades is that?!"

Rufus swore when he saw the object.

Evander's stomach knotted. He could sense the malevolence contained within the gemstone embedded in Magnus's head. It reeked of dark magic.

"I think this is how they've been forcing him to follow their orders." Evander met Viggo's grim stare, his pulse pounding. "It must be connected to the ring that mage was wearing!"

A muscle jumped in the Brute's jawline. "Can you get rid of it?"

Evander hesitated. "You saw what happened when you touched it."

Despair darkened Viggo's eyes. He glanced at Magnus

where the latter thrashed beneath him. "There's nothing we can do for him?!"

"I didn't say that."

Shaw returned before Viggo could ask more questions. She was dragging a tall woman with dark skin, golden eyes, and wire-rimmed spectacles that were currently askew by the hand.

"What on Earth is going on, your Grace?!" Philippa Scarborough adjusted her glasses, her chest heaving with her breaths. "Sergeant Griffiths has sealed off this floor. And Miss Shaw here tells me I—"

"I don't have time to explain, Mrs. Scarborough," Evander interrupted. "Can you remove the curse on this gem?!"

Mrs. Scarborough stared from Evander, to Viggo and the Brute on the ground. Her expression grew focused when she saw the dark stone. She approached briskly, the protective amulet on her necklace swinging against her dress.

"Don't worry," Evander reassured a tense Viggo. "Mrs. Scarborough is the best curse-breaker in the Met. In fact, she is one of the best curse-breakers in the whole of England."

"You flatter me your Grace." Mrs. Scarborough knelt beside Evander and studied the jewel buried in the back of Magnus's head intently. "Was this triggered by someone touching it?"

Viggo flinched.

"I see." Purple light lit up the curse-breaker's pupils and danced on the tips of her fingers. "We'll just have to do our best then, won't we?"

A breeze that smelled faintly of violets danced across Evander as she unleashed her magic and attempted to shatter the curse on the gemstone.

Sweat broke out on Mrs. Scarborough's forehead after a minute.

"This sure is something else, your Grace!" she grunted.

Evander looked from Magnus's puce face to the curse-breaker's flushed expression. The fact that she was struggling to break the spell made his stomach knot all over again. He fisted his hands.

Whoever created this cursed gem must be an incredibly powerful mage!

"Is there something I can do to help?!" he asked harshly.

"We need to cool him down." Mrs. Scarborough winced. "His body temperature is rising and making things worse!"

Coldness flowed through and out of Evander, lowering the room's temperature by several degrees.

"Will this do?"

"Yes!" Mrs. Scarborough panted.

"We're running out of time!" Viggo snarled, his breath misting in front of his face.

"And I'm—" Mrs. Scarborough gasped, "running… out…of magic!"

The curse-breaker shuddered. Evander knew she wasn't lying.

He could feel her power being drained by the gemstone. Her amulet trembled violently where it hung around her neck, its powers clashing with that contained within the cursed object as it tried to protect its owner.

Evander's mouth flattened to a thin line.

Dammit! Is that *the only option left?*

A guttural rasp left Magnus.

Evander knew the Brute would draw his last breath within the next minute if he didn't act now. He clenched his jaw and pressed a hand to Mrs. Scarborough's back, aware that what he was about to do would expose the secret he had kept all of his life.

"Brace yourself!" he warned the curse-breaker.

"Evander!" Rufus took a step forward, his face full of alarm. "You can't!"

Mrs. Scarborough looked between the two of them, confused.

"I must," Evander ground out. "Or Magnus will die!"

His fingers grew hot as he focused his powers into them. He gritted his teeth and poured a controlled wave of magic into the curse-breaker's body.

Mrs. Scarborough gasped and stiffened. Searing purple brightened her pupils and hands, the light so bright Evander had to squint.

The gemstone cracked under her revived magic.

Magnus went limp.

Viggo paled. "Is he—is he—?!"

"No." Evander held a hand out towards Solomon. "Mr. Barden, if you would be so kind as to lend me the knife strapped to your left calf please!" he said urgently.

Solomon flinched. "How did you—?!"

"Solomon, the knife!" Viggo barked.

Solomon removed the weapon from the sheath on his leg and tossed it to Evander.

Evander cooled Magnus's flesh with a layer of ice

magic and cut out the cracked gemstone. The wound oozed a little. He pressed his cravat to it.

"Get a healer," he told Shaw grimly.

The forensic mage hesitated before nodding jerkily and running out of the room, her face ashen.

Viggo climbed off Magnus and fell on his backside, his chest shuddering with his breaths. He gave Evander a grateful look.

Evander's nails dug into his palms. He knew Viggo's gratitude would be short-lived once he realised what had just happened.

Tremors racked Mrs. Scarborough's frame. She stared at Evander, her eyes dark with dread. The same dread he'd glimpsed on Shaw's face before she'd left the cell.

"That power." The curse-breaker gulped. "Your Grace, are you—an *Archmage*?!"

CHAPTER 19

Viggo stared blindly at Magnus's washed-out face, his mind a jumbled mess.

The unconscious Brute was lying in a bed in the Met's infirmary.

"I can't believe Ravenwood is an Archmage," Solomon muttered darkly where he sat opposite Viggo.

Viggo clenched his jaw. If mages were his sworn enemy, then Archmages were the devils he'd promised he would eradicate from all of England. His kind had lost too much to them.

He had lost too much to them.

Memories of the day when he had learned the true meaning of the word terror, when he had been made to watch as his entire family and village were slaughtered before his eyes, scorched his inner vision. The rage and hate that forever simmered in his heart tightened his chest until he could barely breathe.

Concern clouded Solomon's face as he eyed Viggo's

whitening knuckles where he gripped the armrests of his chair.

"Steady there," he warned in a low voice. "You shouldn't go breaking things in this place. I'm sure they're looking for any old reason to put us behind bars." He sneaked a look around.

Contrary to Solomon's assertion, the few staff in the ward were staying well clear of them. It was Evander who had instructed they be given some privacy after Magnus had been treated by one of the Met's healers. The expression on the Ice Mage's face when he and Rufus had left a short while ago rose before Viggo's eyes.

Resignation. A smidgen of dread.

There had even been defiance in Evander's ice-blue gaze.

What had been lacking was remorse.

Evander did not appear to regret inadvertently revealing his status as an Archmage. That he had disclosed such a staggering secret to save Magnus's life was the only reason Viggo hadn't gone for his throat in that cell.

And what would I have done? Throttle him to death?!

The tension knotting his stomach and groin told him killing the mage would have been the last thing on his mind had he gotten his hands on him.

Evander Ravenwood was a much bigger threat to his sanity than he had originally anticipated. Because the thoughts and feelings he was entertaining about the man were as far removed from loathing as the sun was from the moon.

There were other facts about Evander that continued to puzzle him.

His status as a Duke meant he had scarce need for a profession. From what Viggo recalled hearing about his estates and business ventures, the man's wealth likely surpassed that of the combined riches of half the nobles in the capital.

Yet, Evander had chosen to be a Special Arcane Investigator. Not only that, he had peacefully mediated many a dispute between the police and thralls since he had taken up that position. In fact, bar the incident with Magnus, Viggo could not recall a single instance where the mage had harmed a thrall.

There was only one thing he wished to ask Evander.

Why was he working for the Met?

Frustration gnawed at Viggo's insides.

Maybe if I know the answer to that question, I might understand why I feel this way about him.

It dawned on Viggo that he was blatantly disregarding his own steadfast resolve that morning to stay away from the mage. Judging from Solomon's troubled expression, he'd caught on to that fact and didn't like it one bit.

"We should take Magnus and leave as soon as he wakes up."

"They may not let him go." Viggo rubbed the back of his neck and sighed at Solomon's mutinous expression. "Look, it's not as if we have a choice in the matter. Magnus's involvement in the case Evander and Rufus are investigating means we can't just walk away from this." He lowered his brows. "Besides, I want to catch the bastards who did this to Magnus. And I know you do too."

Solomon's mouth flattened to a thin line.

"Promise you won't get involved with him," he said brusquely.

Viggo startled. "What?"

"I see the way you look at him." He pinned Viggo with an accusing gaze. "Promise me you won't fuck the mage, Viggo. It will lead to no end of trouble if you do."

Motion caught Viggo's eye before he could come up with a suitable denial.

Shaw had entered the infirmary. She exchanged brief words with the healer who had taken care of Magnus before approaching the bed.

"Commander Winterbourne requests your presence," she told Viggo. "If you could please follow me."

Viggo tensed. Reginald Winterbourne was the commander of the Arcane Division and Evander's chief. Judging from Shaw's nervous expression, it seemed Evander's discussion with his superior was not progressing as he'd wanted it to.

He got up and fell in step behind the mage as she started across the room.

Solomon rose from his seat to accompany him.

Viggo paused. "Stay with Magnus. He'll be scared if he wakes up in here on his own."

Solomon hesitated before nodding and slowly sitting down.

Viggo caught Shaw's curious glance as they exited the infirmary.

"What?"

"Are you upset with him?" The forensic mage scratched her cheek. "His Grace, I mean?"

"Why would I be upset with him?"

"You hate mages," Shaw said bluntly. "And he's the pinnacle of magehood."

Viggo grimaced. "Is that even a word?"

Shaw sniffed. "I'm making it so."

Viggo bit back an involuntary smile. He couldn't help but like the spunky mage.

They passed a group of officers. If Shaw noted the wary looks Viggo earned, she showed no sign of it. Low murmurs followed them as they navigated the corridors of the Arcane Division, Viggo's skin prickling at scores of vigilant stares.

It seemed news of the incident in the lockup had spread throughout the Met.

"Did you know?" Viggo said after a moment. "That he was an Archmage?"

Shaw pursed her lips. "None of us knew." Her brow wrinkled. "Except maybe Inspector Grayson. He didn't seem that shocked by what happened in that cell."

Viggo recalled Rufus's warning to Evander. He frowned.

He knew alright.

"How likely is it that the Met will keep his secret?" he grunted.

Shaw seemed as surprised by the question as he was for uttering it.

"Wait. Are you worried about his Grace?"

"It's our fault he had to reveal his status as an Archmage," Viggo said awkwardly.

Shaw watched him for a moment before smiling. "You truly are a gentleman, Mr. Stonewall."

"Please, call me Viggo." He made a face. "Also, I don't

know what to make of that statement. I feel I should be insulted rather than flattered."

Shaw laughed. "I wouldn't worry too much about his Grace. He has a way of...getting himself out of the most ridiculous situations with nary a hair harmed on his pretty head." Her smile faded. She sighed. "As for your question, do bears shit in the woods?"

Viggo blinked. "Pardon?"

Shaw wrinkled her nose. "What I mean is, there ain't a bigger bunch of gossipmongers than Met officers. So, no. I'm afraid Duke Ravenwood's secret will be common knowledge in all of London come evening."

Viggo's heart sank at that.

Time away from Evander had made him realise one thing. There had to be a good reason for him not to have revealed his status as an Archmage.

After all, that title would have earned him even greater wealth and power than he already has. So why keep it a secret?

Winterbourne's office was on the fifth floor, dead bang in the middle of the administrative offices of the Arcane Division. The location of the commander's office made it clear he was a man who liked to be in the heat of the action.

Raised voices reached them as they crossed an open space crowded with dozens of desks where men and women sat pretending not to be listening to the vociferous row taking place behind the double doors at the far end.

Shaw stopped and looked at the man sitting at the table closest to Winterbourne's office.

"Should we give them a moment?"

Winterbourne's secretary took on the air of someone who'd been asked if he wanted to juggle with knives.

Shaw rolled her eyes and knocked politely. The sound was lost in the noise of the altercation. She squared her shoulders and opened the door just as Evander growled,

"—and you can take that threat and shove it where the sun does not shine, *sir!*"

CHAPTER 20

"EVANDER," RUFUS GROANED.

"What?" Evander snapped.

His nails bit into his palms as he glared at the lean, wiry man seated behind the impressive oak desk dominating the office.

Reginald Winterbourne watched him with a flinty expression. The older man's face was lined with the marks of years of service, the thin white scar running along his left jaw a memento from a fight in his younger days. One of the most formidable magical duellists of his generation, Winterbourne hailed from a long line of law enforcement officers. He joined the Met after graduating with distinction from the Royal Institute for the Arcane and rose rapidly through the ranks of the force, his involvement in several high-profile cases catapulting him to fame.

But it was his legendary battle with the rogue necromancer behind the "Crimson Fog Murders" of 1842 that sent him on a fast-track to a leadership role in the Met, making him the youngest commander to ever grace its halls.

Though a fair and demanding leader with an unwavering commitment to justice, Winterbourne was a traditionalist who favoured tried and tested methods for crime investigation and law enforcement. This often put him at odds with progressive officers like Evander and Rufus, who favoured a more experimental approach to their line of work. It also meant Winterbourne could be terribly intransigent when it came to breaking protocol.

Like right now.

Frustration churned Evander's stomach as he studied the man he'd long considered his mentor.

"It is not a threat, Ravenwood," Winterbourne said in a glacial tone. "It's a hard, cold fact. Magnus Graveoak will be remanded to Coldfield Baths as soon as I sign the edict. He will await trial there for his crimes—"

"Like hell he will!" someone snarled.

Evander's head whipped around.

Viggo stood framed in the doorway, his hands curled into fists and his expression thunderous.

Shaw peered sheepishly around his powerful frame.

"I brought Mr. Stonewall as instructed, sir."

"Thank you, Miss Shaw." Winterbourne ignored Viggo's scowl and indicated the chair next to Evander. "Take a seat, Mr. Stonewall."

For a moment, Evander thought Viggo would refuse the order.

A muscle twitched in the Brute's cheek as he met Evander's gaze.

139

Evander braced himself for the accusation and loathing he expected to read in his eyes. But all he saw was annoyance towards Winterbourne. Surprise and something that felt fleetingly like hope quickened Evander's pulse.

Does he not hate me?

Viggo crossed the floor and sat beside him, the chair creaking under his weight as he settled into it. Though they were separated by a couple of feet, Evander could feel the heat radiating off his body. It sent a shiver down his spine that had little to do with their current precarious situation.

Winterbourne steepled his hands under his chin and observed Viggo broodingly, blissfully unaware of the errant turn Evander's thoughts had just taken.

"I'll get straight to the point, Mr. Stonewall. Your friend committed a serious felony. Not only did he attack a noble, he laid his hands on an officer of the Met. As such—"

"And like I've said a dozen times already Commander Winterbourne, Magnus was not in control of his faculties!" Evander interrupted harshly, his focus squarely on the situation at hand once more. "Rufus witnessed what happened in that cell. And you only need ask Mrs. Scarborough about the cursed gem she destroyed."

Winterbourne lowered his brows. "Unfortunately, Mrs. Scarborough is not in a position to talk right now. The shock of witnessing—or rather shall I say, *experiencing* the powers of an Archmage appears to have overwhelmed her. I sent her home."

Guilt tightened Evander's throat. "Is Philippa alright?"

Winterbourne watched him for a moment before sighing heavily, the fight visibly draining out of him. "She will be." He sat back and pinched the bridge of his nose. "Hell and damnation, Ravenwood." His tone softened as he gazed at him. "Do you even realise what you've done? What *she* will say when she hears of this? You know I have no choice but to inform her."

Viggo shot a puzzled glance at Evander.

A sour taste filled Evander's mouth at Winterbourne's pitying look.

He'd been doing his best to ignore the full ramifications of his actions in the cell that morning. After all, there were more pressing matters at hand. Like stopping an innocent man from going to prison and finding out the identity of the mage who'd killed Alastair Millbrook and orchestrated the attack on his carriage.

And let's not forget the vial I discovered in the alley.

"You may lose those blue threads in your aiguillette," Winterbourne said tiredly. "Her Majesty would be well within her rights to strip you of your role as a Royal Arcane Liaison after the trick you pulled this morning. Heavens man, she may even demand you quit being a Special Arcane Investigator and leave the Met!"

Rufus cursed under his breath. Viggo froze.

Someone sucked in air in the deadly hush.

They all looked towards the door.

Shaw stood there, eyes bulging and mouth round behind the fingers she was pressing to her lips.

"Miss Shaw, what are you still doing here?" Winterbourne said thinly.

"Being a fly on the wall, sir," Shaw confessed unashamedly.

"Go be a fly on someone else's wall."

"I promise I'll be as quiet as a mouse in a church," Shaw protested. "You won't even notice—"

"Now, Miss Shaw!" Winterbourne snapped.

The mage's shoulders slumped. She turned and shuffled out of the room. The door closed quietly behind her.

"You work for the Queen?"

Blood pounded inside Evander's veins as he met Viggo's accusing stare.

Dammit. I didn't want him to find out this way!

"Not as such," Evander admitted reluctantly.

Viggo's eyes flitted to his uniform. "So, those blue threads *don't* represent the Royal Family?"

Evander shifted awkwardly in his chair. "They do."

"Then, that makes you her loyal dog, does it not?"

Viggo's vicious words stabbed through Evander, leaving him breathless in the face of the revulsion he could no longer hide. The revulsion that was turning his eyes to dark gems full of loathing.

Evander could hardly blame the Brute. After all, it had been within the royal family's powers to stop the War of Subjugation and its cruel aftermath had they so desired. Still, he could not stop the painful feeling choking his chest.

He'd wanted Viggo to trust him.

Rufus shot to his feet.

"How dare you?!" he hissed at Viggo. "You know nothing of Evander's circumstances!"

"That statement could earn you time behind bars, Stonewall," Winterbourne warned. "Be grateful I'm willing to keep it off the record."

Evander paid no heed to his friend and his commander.

"I do not deny that my allegiance lies with Her Majesty Queen Victoria," he told Viggo quietly. His nails carved grooves into his palms as he struggled to maintain a steady voice, the tumultuous emotions he'd kept on a tight leash for the last six years threatening to burst from behind the dam where he kept them. "But I am nobody's dog." He straightened, his face so stiff his jaw hurt. "I may live in a gilded cage of Her Majesty's making, but that is only because I choose to let her do so. She knows there is a line I will never cross, whatever she may order me to do."

Viggo curled a lip. "And that line is?"

Rufus scowled and took a step forward. "This son of a—!"

"Inspector Grayson!" Winterbourne snapped.

Rufus froze in his tracks, his knuckles white at his sides.

The commander watched Evander and Viggo with a hooded gaze.

Viggo's eyes bore cruelly into Evander.

"Well, mage?" he scoffed. "What is the precious line you told your Queen you would never cross?"

Evander took a shuddering breath and repeated the words he had told the woman who held his fate in her hands on the night he had informed her of his intentions to become a Special Arcane Investigator.

"There will not be another War of Subjugation. Not while I live and breathe."

Viggo recoiled as if physically struck, the shock flaring across his face draining the blood from his complexion.

Evander turned to Winterbourne, surprised his hands weren't trembling. His body felt hot and tight, as if it wanted to burst out of his skin.

"If you imprison Magnus Graveoak, the tensions between thralls and magic users will rise to fever pitch," he said in a hard voice. "All this city needs is one more conflict and the House of Lords will pounce on the opportunity to press the government and Her Majesty to remove the Arcane Division from the jurisdiction of the Met and place it under their control."

Rufus drew a sharp breath. Winterbourne went still.

"How did you—?" the commander started stiffly.

"I'm not a moron, sir," Evander snapped. "I don't attend all those balls and social functions for nothing. Lord Ashbrooke confirmed the motion is garnering favour in Parliament a few nights ago." He blew out a sigh and ran a hand through his hair. "Of course, the House of Commons will fight it, but if the House of Lords gets Her Majesty on their side, it might as well be a done deal."

Winterbourne cursed colourfully.

"What does that mean?" Viggo said tensely. "What does it mean if the Arcane Division is no longer under the authority of the Met?"

Evander pursed his lips at his anxious stare.

Well, at least he's no longer looking at me like I'm a piece of rotting excrement under his boot.

"It means the Arcane Division will become a tool

nobles will wield to rule over thralls. Whatever rights the magicless have fought for and won over the last decades will be overturned. You will become what you were before. Cattle to be used and abused at the will of those who possess magic."

Evander knew he was being needlessly cruel. The horror widening Viggo's eyes and the dread visibly tightening his body told him so. But he couldn't help it.

He wanted Viggo to know why he'd decided to join the Met despite being an Archmage. More than that, he wanted to hurt Viggo for not trusting him.

That realisation stopped Evander short and brought a lump to his throat.

What am I doing right now? He doesn't deserve this.

"Alright."

Evander's distracted gaze shifted to Winterbourne.

The commander was looking at him with a resigned expression. "I will release Magnus Graveoak." His tone hardened. "But you and Mr. Stonewall will bear full responsibility for him and his actions until this case is closed."

Relief made Evander giddy.

Viggo swallowed and closed his eyes briefly. "Thank you," he mumbled to Winterbourne after a short silence. He hesitated before turning to Evander. "And I apologise, your Grace. I should not have said those things to you." A trace of bitterness underscored his voice. "I may hate who you are and what you stand for. But you saved Magnus not just once, but twice. And for that, I will forever be grateful to you."

CHAPTER 21

"YOUR GRACE?" VINCENT BROWN said in a troubled voice. "Are you alright? You look a little pale."

"I'm fine, Mr. Brown."

Evander caught the worried look Rufus shot his way where they stood in the AFD's Alchemical Analysts' lab.

An array of brass and copper instruments gleamed on the benches and shelves around them, alongside dozens of bubbling retorts and alembics connected by networks of glass tubes. One wall of the room was occupied by an immense glass-fronted cabinet filled with hundreds of small vials and jars, each meticulously labelled and organised. A fume hood enchanted to safely disperse any dangerous vapours or magical emanations stood beside it.

Chained to a pedestal in the centre of the chamber was its most prized possession, a massive, leather-bound tome filled with several centuries of alchemical knowledge and enchanted to update itself with new discoveries and techniques. Magic hummed faintly around the Alchemist's

Codex, the numerous protective wards in place shimmering slightly as they caught the light.

Evander realised most of the staff had stopped what they were doing and were openly gawking at him. Brown scowled.

The men and women resumed their tasks guiltily.

"I apologise, your Grace," the alchemist grunted. "I'm afraid you'll be the subject of gossip for a while yet."

Evander hesitated. "Are you not curious? About why I hid the fact that I'm an Archmage?"

Brown met his steadfast stare. "I gathered you decided it would be too much trouble for it to become common knowledge, your Grace." The alchemist shrugged. "To be honest, I would have done the same if I were in your shoes. Many would no doubt relish the authority and prestige that come with that title, but anyone acquainted with yourself knows you are not that kind of man."

Relief lightened Evander's chest. The fact that his closest associates were not threatened by his secret and had chosen not to treat him any differently after discovering his hidden abilities filled him with more gratitude than he could ever express.

It had been the same with Ginny and Rufus too.

Viggo's face swam before his eyes. Evander couldn't help but go over what the Brute had said in Winterbourne's office, before they'd parted ways. His throat tightened. He doubted Viggo would ever treat him with more than just basic civility now that he'd learned exactly what he was.

"Are you certain about the nature of the powder Shaw found at the scene of the attack?" Rufus asked Brown.

Evander focused on what they were saying.

"Yes. I believe what Miss Shaw discovered at Hyde Park Corner is *Monk's Lilac*." Brown indicated the glass tube sitting inside a rack on his workstation.

Evander frowned at the purple dust coating the lining of the vessel.

"Isn't that a rare plant with magical properties?"

"It is indeed, your Grace." The alchemist lifted a small bottle containing a similar looking substance from the bench. "As luck would have it, I found a sample of it in our stores."

Rufus's face tightened. "Can this help us find the mages who attacked his Grace's carriage?"

"It might if it was actually *Monk's Lilac*," someone drawled.

They turned. Evander's shoulders knotted at the sight of Viggo.

Rufus drew himself to his full height. The inspector did not even bother to hide his hostility.

"What are you doing here?"

Something Evander couldn't read flashed in the Brute's gaze when their eyes met.

Viggo shrugged. "Magnus is still out, so I asked if I could tour the facilities."

His relaxed tone made Rufus's mouth flatten to a thin line.

"This isn't some goddamn museum, Stonewall!" the inspector snapped.

Shaw stepped out of the Brute's shadow.

"Commander Winterbourne gave his permission," the

mage piped up cheerfully. "Viggo was especially keen to see where our alchemists worked."

Rufus's face darkened.

"You should have started with the basement," he muttered. "And why are you calling him Viggo, like you're friends?"

Shaw's expression grew pinched. "He told me to." She crossed her arms and arched an arrogant eyebrow. "Why, are you jealous, sir?"

Rufus made a choked noise.

Evander swallowed a sigh as they started bickering. Though he wasn't entirely sure why the inspector had taken an instant dislike to Viggo, he suspected it had to do with the Brute's attitude towards him in Winterbourne's office. He became conscious of a rising din and looked around.

If his freshly revealed secret of being an Archmage had created something of a ruckus in the lab, Viggo's presence was about to cause a veritable uproar.

"What's the matter with you, folks?" Brown shouted over the brouhaha. "Ain't none of you seen a Brute before?!"

"But it's the Ironfist Brute, sir!" someone exclaimed.

"He's the leader of *Nightshade*, no less," another alchemist said.

Brown glowered. "And?"

The alchemists reluctantly returned to their tasks, though not without stealing covert glances at Viggo.

"I apologise about that," Brown said gruffly. His expression cleared and his mouth curved in a faint smile as he observed the Brute. "Vincent Brown. I'm an old drinking friend of your uncle." He gave Viggo his hand.

Surprise jolted Evander. Even Rufus looked astonished.

Viggo stared before slowly shaking the alchemist's hand. "You are?"

"Yes." Brown's smile faded. "Or at least I was before your aunt Mary died. I doubt you remember, but I was at the funeral."

"I don't," Viggo said quietly. "Thank you for coming."

Evander could tell the Brute truly meant his words.

Brown rocked back on his heels. "How's Jack?"

"He's well." Viggo's expression loosened a little. "I shall tell him we met."

"Please do. I really should catch up with him." Brown beamed. "Now, tell me why you think this isn't *Monk's Lilac*, young man." He slapped Viggo heartily on the back, only to wince and shake his hand.

"Do you mind?" Viggo gestured to the glass tube in the rack.

"Not at all."

Curiosity piqued Evander as Viggo picked up the vessel and held it up to the light streaming through the arched windows looking out over the river. Contrary to his expectations, the Brute appeared remarkably comfortable in the unusual milieu he found himself in.

Somehow, he suspected few situations would unnerve the man.

Viggo's eyes gleamed as he inspected the content of the tube. "*Monk's Lilac* produces a deep purple powder when dried and ground." He uncorked it and took a careful sniff. "It has a sweet musky aroma that intensifies when the powder is disturbed."

Brown nodded and rubbed his beard approvingly, like a professor pleased with a particularly excellent student.

Rufus scowled when Viggo dipped his index finger inside the vial and lifted specks of the dust onto his skin.

"You shouldn't be touching the evidence like that!" he snapped.

"It's alright, Inspector," Brown drawled with surprising benevolence. "That's not the only sample Miss Shaw found."

This earned the alchemist incredulous stares from several of his associates. Anyone else would have had their hand chopped off if they'd attempted the same.

Viggo ignored Rufus's interruption and rubbed the residue between his fingers.

"*Monk's Lilac* is extremely fine and clings to surfaces," he said thoughtfully. "It was correct of you to assume it would still be present at the crime scene."

Brown cocked his head to the side, his expression quizzical. "Then, why do think I'm wrong?"

The faint smile that tugged at Viggo's lips made Evander's stomach flip-flop. The intelligence and confidence in the Brute's gaze was a facet of his personality he was witnessing for the first time.

He found it positively breathtaking.

"You forgot to factor in the degradation process in the location where it was discovered."

Viggo's answer made Brown blink and Shaw suck in air.

"Cor blimey!" the forensic mage mumbled, earning herself a narrow-eyed look from Rufus.

"The temperature and humidity." Brown stared dazedly at Viggo before looking out the windows. "It's autumn!"

Viggo dipped his head. "Correct." He picked up the bottle containing *Monk's Lilac* and poured a small amount in a glass dish before holding it out to Evander. "Do you think you can lower the temperature in this dish to about twelve degrees centigrade and add, say, some eighty percent humidity?" he asked lightly.

Evander noted that the Brute didn't call him His Grace this time around.

"Sure."

His fingers grazed Viggo's hand as he took the receptacle off him.

The Brute's skin was hot and firm under his touch. Evander hoped he didn't notice the way his breath quickened and his pulse accelerated at the barest contact.

It took some effort to concentrate on his water magic. Coolness danced through his veins. A damp chill coiled around his hands.

Everyone stared as the *Monk's Lilac* faded to a greyish hue.

"Good grief!" Brown said hoarsely. "Then the powder Miss Shaw found is—!"

"*Noctis Bloom*," Viggo said gravely. "They share many similarities, including their smell and their consistency in powder form."

"But *Noctis Bloom* retains its deep, rich colour when

exposed to the elements for a considerable length of time." Brown gave Viggo a stunned look. "How did you know?!"

The Brute shrugged. "You could say I'm an amateur botanist."

Heat suffused Evander's body when their eyes met.

"There's nothing amateurish about your knowledge, my boy." Brown patted Viggo's shoulder gingerly, his face bright with admiration. "Why, I should get our commander to recruit you!"

Viggo grimaced. "I think I'll pass."

"Does *Noctis Bloom* have magical properties?" Rufus asked grudgingly.

"Yes. It's more potent than *Monk's Lilac*. And it only blooms at midnight during a new moon." The Brute furrowed his brow. "There is one other major difference between the two flowers. One many people remain unaware of to this day."

"And that is?" Rufus sounded genuinely intrigued for once, all animosity forgotten in this moment of revelation.

Even Brown and Shaw leaned forward expectantly.

Evander could relate. Unravelling mysteries was one of the most gratifying aspects of their job after all.

"*Noctis Bloom* is used by dark magic users in their rituals. In fact, there's even a rumour that dark mages use it to enhance their powers," Viggo said grimly.

CHAPTER 22

THE SETTING SUN WAS CASTING A GOLDEN GLOW OVER THE Thames when Evander's carriage turned up to collect him. He climbed inside distractedly and gazed at the grand silhouette and gothic spires of the House of Parliament etched against the vivid purple sky as they pulled away from Scotland Yard.

Magnus had woken up late that afternoon. Though still shaky, he had been in full possession of his faculties and did not appear to have suffered any repercussions from having the cursed gem removed so violently from his body. Viggo and Solomon had taken the Brute home after he was given the all clear by the healer who'd seen to him.

Evander wasn't sure what to make of Viggo's attitude. The Brute's expression had been cryptic when they'd parted ways. Solomon on the other hand hadn't been able to hide his relief at finally exiting the premises.

The clip-clop of horses' hooves on cobbles and the

rattle of carriage wheels soon escalated as Graham manoeuvred the vehicle through the busy thoroughfares of the capital, the din punctuated by the occasional whinny and the shouts of newsboys hawking the evening papers.

Evander leaned his head against the backrest and closed his eyes.

I wonder if reports of me being an Archmage has made the front pages yet.

He knew he should be more upset about the fact that his long-held secret had been revealed. He suspected Ginny would have a few sharp words to say about the matter when he next saw her. Never mind the grief he was going to get from Mrs. Sinclair and Hargrove once they found out.

But the simple fact was he would not have been able to hide his identity as an Archmage forever.

There were dark forces at work in the capital and the country.

People who shared the same views about magical supremacy as the Archmage who had decimated Viggo's village and destroyed the lives of thousands of thralls. Men and women who believed England would be better off without the magicless and who were hellbent on bringing about a second and more definitive War of Subjugation.

Evander had planned to reveal his true powers to oppose them when the right time came. Having to do so a few years earlier than anticipated was an inconvenience for sure but hardly the end of the world. Or so he was trying to convince himself.

Of course, someone won't see it that way.

Evander's shoulders slumped. He wondered when he would be summoned to the palace. His mouth twisted as he recalled Queen Victoria's stringent expression the last time they'd met.

She won't let this go. However much she harps on about what a fool I was for letting this happen, I don't regret what I did. Magnus's life was more important.

Viggo's face danced through his mind once more, the way he'd looked back at the lab seared in Evander's consciousness.

Chances are our paths won't cross again unless it has to do with Magnus's involvement in our investigation.

That thought made his chest grow tight. He could no longer deny what he felt towards Viggo.

He was attracted to the Brute. And not just sexually.

There was more to the owner of *Nightshade* than people realised. A depth to his character that was likely too often overlooked. And it drew Evander like few things could.

In Viggo, Evander felt he had found a kindred spirit. A man who shared the same values as him. Who was bright and quick-witted and just. Someone who would be loyal to those he loved and who would protect and defend them come what may.

The kind of man Evander wished he could spend the rest of his life with.

The fact that he was entertaining such thoughts about someone he'd met a mere day ago was frankly irrational. Yet, his instincts, and his heart, told him Viggo was everything he wanted and more.

A wave of lassitude washed over him, the events of the past three days and his own turbulent emotions finally catching up on him. Evander took a shaky breath and pinched the bridge of his nose.

I have to get over these unrealistic feelings. Nothing will ever come of them. He hates mages and he's made that fact crystal clear.

The distant toll of church bells marked the hour a moment later.

Evander opened his eyes and looked outside. He frowned.

They were passing Covent Garden.

Alastair Millbrook's atelier was located nearby, on King William Street.

I should visit the place with Rufus tomorrow.

Shaw had already processed the workshop and Millbrook's lodgings above it with the help of a team from the AFD. Though she hadn't picked up any clues as to the identity of Millbrook's murderer, her report indicated that someone had recently broken into the building.

Evander was pondering what Viggo had revealed about *Noctis Bloom* and its properties and what that said about *Nightshade's* ability to glean information no other guild could, when the bustling sounds of central London faded upon the carriage reaching Mayfair.

Graham soon pulled up in front of the townhouse.

Evander thanked Samuel and the coachman as he stepped outside.

The magical wards he'd erected around his home brushed against his skin when he climbed the stairs leading to the portico of the elegant Georgian residence.

157

The Portland stone and tall, multi-paned sashed windows making up the frontage gleamed in the light of the elegant lanterns flanking the heavy, black door with its brass knocker in the shape of a raven perched on a crescent moon.

Hargrove gave him a quizzical look when he took his coat in the foyer.

"Bad day at the office, my Lord?"

Evander took this as a sign that his recently revealed secret had yet to make it to the manservant's ears.

"You could say that. Please tell Cook to prepare a light supper and bring it to my private study. I shall retire early tonight."

The office adjacent to his bedchamber was a more intimate and functional space than the formal one downstairs. The walls were covered in a rich, forest green, textured paper with a subtle pattern of leaves and vines, and lined with bookshelves holding an extensive collection of arcane tomes and spell books. An enchanted map of London highlighting the current crime scenes in the capital took pride of place above the marble fireplace, the orange glow of the dots warm beneath the glass case protecting them.

It was a smaller replica of the one in Winterbourne's office, in Scotland Yard, and had cost Evander a pretty penny to commission.

Tucked in front of the window was an oakwood desk carved with magical symbols and runes to protect the private contents of its drawers. The desk was perfectly organised, with neat stacks of parchment and quills, and inkwells that Hargrove regularly topped up.

A door at the back led to a small laboratory equipped with a workbench, various alchemical tools, and shelves stocked with magical ingredients and components.

Evander was enjoying a drink in one of the velvet armchairs by the fire when Hargrove entered the room with a serving cart laden with a carefully curated selection of dishes. He set out a rich, steaming broth and an accompaniment of fine cheeses and sandwiches on the table beside Evander's chair.

Hargrove returned an hour later to clear the dishes.

"Would you like some tea, my Lord?"

"No, thank you. I prefer something stronger tonight."

Hargrove eyed the Scotch glass in Evander's hand. "Isn't that your third drink already?"

"It is." Evander narrowed his eyes slightly at the manservant's disapproving tone. "Why?"

Hargrove pursed his lips. "You have a day off this Sunday, do you not?"

"I do," Evander replied warily. "Where is this going, Jasper?"

Hargrove took on an aggrieved air. "Just go visit that poncy club, my Lord. That toy of yours is not doing you any good. You will feel much better after spending the night under a rugged, hairy-chested stud who will make you forget all your troubles."

Evander did his best to ignore the vision of one particular rugged, hairy-chested stud he would love to be under and pinned the manservant with a scowl.

"How about you mind your own private affairs and let me worry about mine?"

"But your private affairs are my concern, my Lord,"

Hargrove fairly whined. "Including your sexual gratifica—"

Evander threw a cushion at him. Hargrove caught it deftly, much to the mage's irritation.

"Shall I prepare your bath, my Lord?" Hargrove said sullenly as he finished clearing the table.

"Please do." Evander sniffed. "And stop looking inside my bedside drawer."

Hargrove hesitated by the door.

"What is it now?" Evander grunted.

The manservant's eyes gleamed with the spirit of curiosity.

"Is it true that you and the Ironfist Brute are working together, my Lord?"

Evander stiffened. "Who told you that?"

"A little bird I shall not name," Hargrove replied nonchalantly.

Evander scowled. "Is this little bird five foot three, with brown hair and eyes?"

Hargrove maintained a poker expression at Samuel's description. "I cannot say, my Lord."

"Jasper?"

"Yes, my Lord?"

"Get out."

Steam carrying the smell of herbs and rejuvenating potions greeted Evander when he entered his bathroom moments later. It was a luxurious space, with walls panelled in dark polished wood and a floor tiled in black and white mosaic marble. Tall windows made of frosted glass graced one wall of the chamber, the heavy velvet curtains framing them adding another layer of opulence.

The centrepiece of the room was the giant, freestanding copper bathtub, its burnished surface gleaming in the soft glow of the crystal chandelier suspended from the coffered ceiling and the enchanted ornate sconces.

Evander laid his enchanted cufflinks and folding cane on the marble-topped vanity and stripped out of his clothes. He turned and walked inside the magnificent, open shower opposite. Hot sprays burst from the multiple heads in the ceiling and walls as he twisted an array of taps.

Evander ran his fingers through his hair and lifted his face, his skin prickling pleasantly as the powerful jets cleansed the sweat and grime from his flesh. He washed up with a lavish, vetiver scented soap, rinsed himself off, and padded out to the copper tub.

Water sloshed as he climbed inside, stirring the concoctions Hargrove had poured. A sigh left him as he sank in the hot, fragrant vapour. Evander submerged himself to his neck and propped his elbows and head on the edge of the tub.

He closed his eyes and was just beginning to relax when the hairs lifted on the back of his neck. Magic flooded his bloodstream in a heartbeat. He twisted and cast the weapon in his fingers at the curtains behind him.

A figure caught the ice spear in his bare hand.

Evander's heart stuttered.

Viggo stepped out of the shadows and raised an eyebrow. "Is this how you greet all your guests?"

CHAPTER 23

IT TOOK ALL OF VIGGO'S WILLPOWER TO KEEP HIS VOICE steady as he observed Evander.

He hadn't meant to spy on the mage.

Having approached the back of the townhouse in Mayfair with a stealth borne of years of experience getting into places where he didn't belong, it had taken him but a moment to clear the rear fence, its impressive height posing little challenge to his strength as he'd vaulted over it in one deft move.

Viggo had waited to make sure the magic wards that had tickled his skin failed to raise an alarm before moving swiftly across the manicured lawns, the shadows cast by ornamental shrubs and statues aiding his furtive passage to the back of the house.

A quick scan of the rear facade revealed a trellis covered in climbing roses that offered a convenient route to a first floor window. The staff would no doubt be taking turns having their dinner in the kitchen below stairs at this hour, which meant the upper levels of the property would be clear of foot traffic.

He'd climbed the wooden frame with surprising silence for a man his size, his hands and feet finding secure holds among the lattice even in the dark. Viggo had paused and peered through the window to make sure the room beyond was empty before carefully jimmying the lock and slipping inside.

He'd found himself inside a dressing area. The place was meticulously organised, with racks and hanging frames holding an extensive collection of fine clothing, shoes, and accessories for a nobleman, and a couple of dressers and a masculine vanity unit.

The room smelled of Evander.

Viggo had caught a glimpse of his reflection in the full-length mirror next to the window and stilled at the contrast between his humble appearance and the wealth on display around him. His chest had tightened.

Once again, circumstances made it painfully clear how different his and Evander's worlds were.

The sound of approaching footsteps had jolted him into action before his mood took a complete downturn. Viggo had ducked through a door into the next chamber, only to discover that it was Evander's private bathroom. He'd cursed silently and sought refuge behind the curtains when the footsteps followed him.

A man in his forties with sharp angular features and a neatly trimmed beard had entered the bathroom. Though dressed in a manservant's outfit, the way he'd carried himself as he'd prepared the bath and laid out a bathrobe and towels told Viggo he was former military of some sort.

Evander's attendant had left after getting the place ready, oblivious to his presence to the end. Instead of vacating the room to try to figure out the best place to meet and talk to the mage discreetly in his own home, Viggo had found himself rooted to the spot.

Common sense had told him staying and watching Evander bathe would be the height of foolishness. But his heart hadn't listened to his head and he'd found himself biding his time for Evander to arrive, his stomach churning with anticipation.

He hadn't had to wait long.

Keeping still while Evander undressed had been the purest form of mental torture Viggo had ever endured. The intimacy and thrill of the moment had taken his breath away, squashing whatever guilt he felt at this stolen glimpse into the mage's private world.

He hadn't been able to tear his gaze away from Evander as he'd revealed every inch of his glorious body.

Viggo was already certain the mage possessed the handsomest face he'd ever laid eyes on. He'd assumed his figure would be slender and soft, like most nobles. But Evander's physique was graceful and athletic, his muscles defined and his flesh toned to perfection. Broad shoulders tapered to a narrow waist that gave way to svelte hips and firm, round buttocks Viggo itched to sink his fingers into. Bar a few moles, the mage's skin was free of scars and blemishes, the unexpected golden hue speaking of hours spent in the sun.

Viggo's groin had swelled uncomfortably at the sight

of Evander's manhood nestled amidst dark curls. His shaft was perfectly formed and ridged with delicate veins. It'd made Viggo wonder what he would taste like.

He'd stood in the shadows and shamelessly drunk in the intoxicating sight of the man he hadn't been able to get out of his mind for the past day while the latter had showered and climbed inside the opulent copper bathtub, blissfully unaware of Viggo where he'd skulked behind the curtains.

The Brute had realised then that what had guided his steps to Mayfair and Evander's home that night was something he could no longer fight. Because it wasn't just attraction he felt for Evander.

It was need. Pure, unadulterated, potent need.

It made no sense. He'd only met the man a day ago.

Yet, he wanted Evander with an urgency that shocked him. He wanted to touch him and kiss him and taste every inch of his bewitching body. He wanted to see what colour his eyes would take in the throes of passion. He wanted to sink inside the mage's body and experience his heat as he claimed him. He wanted to watch Evander climb the heights of pleasure and shatter beneath him.

He wanted to wreck him. To possess him.

To chain him to his side so he could never leave him.

The wealth of emotions stirring Viggo's heart and the fire burning in his veins had him unconsciously shifting where he stood.

The movement finally alerted Evander to his presence.

The speed at which the mage cast his magic had Viggo's stomach clenching as he grasped the icicle winging its way towards his shoulder.

Even naked and vulnerable, the mage possessed a strength of will and a composure few men in his acquaintance could demonstrate under the circumstances.

Viggo stepped out of the shadows, the weapon cooling his hand. "Is this how you greet all your guests?"

Evander's eyes flared. "What the devil are you doing here?" he spluttered. "And how did you get past my wards?!"

Viggo swallowed a smile.

Not so composed after all.

The colour rising in Evander's cheeks and the awareness darkening his eyes told the Brute the mage was as conscious of him as he was.

"I came to talk. And I'm a Brute. You of all people should know magic doesn't work on me."

He knew he'd said the wrong thing when Evander's mouth thinned.

"I'm an Archmage," he said icily. "My magic isn't exactly ordinary."

"Then, that must make me a very special Brute."

This answer seemed to irk Evander even more. The mage scowled.

"Do you make it a habit of spying on the people you wish to talk to when they bathe, Mr. Stonewall?" He rose without waiting for an answer, water cascading off his gleaming body.

Viggo nearly swallowed his tongue, the vision that was Evander in that moment threatening to unravel the last threads of his sanity.

The mage flushed at his hungry stare.

He climbed out and reached hastily for the towel robe

hanging on the free standing rack beside the tub, but not before Viggo glimpsed his swelling cock.

His arousal made Viggo conscious the only thing masking his own raging erection was his coat. And it confirmed what he'd suspected all along.

Evander felt the same beguiling pull he did. And he seemed just as helpless in the face of it as Viggo was.

"Not usually," Viggo finally managed. "I was hiding from your manservant."

Evander's hands stilled on the towel he was using to dry his face and hair. "How long have you been here?"

Viggo tried not to fidget at his suspicious tone. "A little while," he confessed sheepishly.

Evander drew a sharp breath. "So, you were—watching the whole time?! While I got undressed and showered?!" Indignation raised the pitch of his voice.

Viggo sighed and rubbed the back of his neck. "I know I should apologise but I don't want to."

Evander opened and closed his mouth silently.

"What?" he finally mumbled. "Why?!"

Viggo decided there and then that honesty was going to be the best policy when it came to dealing with this man.

"Because I want you," he said quietly. "I want you like I've never wanted another in my entire life."

CHAPTER 24

Evander's breath locked in his throat.

He could hardly believe Viggo was here in the flesh, in his home, and talking to him. Not just talking to him but looking at him with eyes that burned with barely suppressed desire instead of the rage he deserved.

"You—what?!" he stammered.

Evander knew he sounded like a blithering idiot, but he couldn't help it. The situation he currently found himself in was so surreal he wanted to pinch himself.

A smile tugged at Viggo's lips. It evidently amused him to see Evander all hot and flustered.

And not just flustered.

Evander's cock throbbed between his thighs, a painful reminder that it had been ages since he'd last relieved himself.

"I said I want you, Evander," Viggo repeated. He tipped his head to the side. "I take it you know what that means."

Evander swallowed and licked his lips. Even if he

didn't, the Brute's expression made it all too clear what it was he craved.

Viggo took a step towards him.

Evander backed away, unable to stop himself.

It was the instinct of prey in the presence of a predator.

Viggo's face took on a wolfish appearance. He closed the distance to Evander even as he continued retreating across the bathroom.

Evander's back struck the vanity unit.

Viggo placed his hands atop the marble surface on either side of him and crowded him in, effectively trapping him.

Evander panted as he stared into the Brute's stormy eyes, his heart racing and his stomach quivering at the incandescent attraction sparking the air between them.

"Don't run away from me," Viggo said gruffly. His scorching gaze roamed Evander's face before locking on his mouth. "I want to kiss you." He leaned down and brought his lips to Evander's ear. "May I, Evander? Kiss you?"

Evander shuddered at the titillating sensation.

Viggo straightened and stared hotly in his eyes, waiting for his answer.

Evander watched him dazedly.

He felt as if he were standing on a knife's edge, ready to fall on a blade not of his making.

On one side of the precipice was his comfortable if somewhat unconventional life, his career, his position as a noble, and his status as an Archmage.

On the other was the unpredictable future he could see in Viggo's gaze.

A future riddled with obstacles and turmoil, where they would both have to make choices they might one day regret. But also one where they could discover something few people ever would in their entire lifetime.

A love that would endure forever more.

A connection between souls that could not be broken, even by death itself.

A shiver raced through Evander.

This is absurd. We barely know one another!

Yet he could not look away from Viggo. Nor could he deny that he very much wanted to see the future the Brute's eyes promised.

Evander was conscious the choice he was about to make would change his entire existence. He could sense it in the air. Taste it on Viggo's hot breath where it tickled his face. See it in the depths of his passionate stare.

He could either push Viggo away, thereby denying what the Brute's ardent expression hinted at. Or he could take the first step towards their uncertain destiny.

Viggo stilled when Evander lifted a hesitant hand to his cheek. He shuddered at Evander's caress before grasping his fingers and pressing a featherlight kiss to his palm.

"Are you sure?" The Brute's voice shook a little.

Evander knew the question wasn't just about this moment. He nodded tremulously. Then Viggo's hands were on his face and he was crushing their mouths together and the whole world faded around Evander.

The Brute's lips were hot and firm as he explored

Evander's trembling flesh, his hooded gaze locked on Evander's eyes. He moulded their mouths together and sucked and gently bit Evander's lips for a timeless moment before sweeping his way inside. Evander trembled as their tongues met and began a heady mating dance.

He gasped when Viggo grabbed his waist and lifted him up onto the vanity unit. The Brute parted his knees and crowded the cradle of his thighs, his hands dancing up and down his legs as he worked them inside the bathrobe.

Evander's breath hitched at the first touch of Viggo's fingers on his manhood. He couldn't help but moan when the Brute closed his hand around his twitching shaft and began stroking him. Viggo undid the belt of the bathrobe and parted the lapels, exposing Evander and his own wicked ministrations.

He wrenched their mouths apart and nudged Evander's chin up so he could press torrid kisses down the column of his throat.

"Do you like that?" he growled, nipping at Evander's skin.

Evander moaned, barely able to put together a coherent thought.

Viggo was circling the head of his erection with his thumb and spreading the precum he found there so he could slick up his palm. He pinched Evander's tip playfully.

"Ah!" Evander squeezed his eyes shut and dropped his head back. "Yes! I like everything you do to me!"

His confession galvanised Viggo.

The Brute's blistering touch and kisses ignited all of Evander's senses and left scorching trails on his skin as he explored his body, making him lightheaded with pleasure. He knew it wouldn't be long before he climaxed. Not with the skilful way Viggo was working his aching manhood.

The sound of a buckle being undone registered dimly.

Something hot and hard brushed against Evander's cock.

He blinked and looked down. His breath caught.

Viggo had freed his erection and was rubbing both of them briskly, his face tight with passion.

Evander gulped.

The Brute's cock was long and thick, just like he'd hoped it would be.

He shuffled forward eagerly and wrapped his legs around Viggo's hips, making it easier for the Brute to hold them.

Viggo grunted his approval and took his mouth in another scalding kiss.

They shared a sultry stare as he locked their cocks in his hold and resumed stroking them both, the smell of sex thick between them.

Evander groaned and gasped at the heat flowing and ebbing down his spine and through his groin, Viggo's laboured breaths and throaty grunts echoing his growing ecstasy. His hips began rolling in a rhythm as old as time, his body seeking a release he was certain would shatter him.

Evander grabbed Viggo's shoulder with one hand and pressed the other atop the vanity behind him, securing his purchase. Viggo cursed and released their cocks so he could grasp the backs of Evander's knees and hitch his legs higher, tilting his body at a delicious angle. The unit rattled beneath them as they succumbed to their bodies' primal instincts, hips thrusting their swollen shafts together, Viggo stealing a hand around so he could work their sensitive flesh with his sinful touch once more.

Evander's orgasm raced through him like liquid fire.

They peaked together, their mouths meeting frantically so they could swallow each other's guttural shouts, their convulsions shuddering through them with sweet violence.

CHAPTER 25

It was a while before Viggo found the strength to move.

He lifted his face from the crook of Evander's neck and met the mage's languid blue gaze.

"That," Viggo panted and swallowed, "—was something else."

Evander smiled, his chest heaving. He squeezed Viggo's waist with his thighs. "I'm glad you found the experience satisfactory."

"Yes. It was extremely satisfactory." Viggo nipped at his lower lip. "Give me a minute and I'll be ready to go again."

Evander stilled, his smile fading a little. "Go? Go where?"

Viggo flashed him a sly look before slipping his fingers beneath his balls and lightly stroking his taint and hole. The mage's eyes almost rolled into the back of his head.

"I think you know exactly where I'm going to sink my

cock next time," he whispered seductively in Evander's ear.

The mage sucked in air, recoiled, and grasped his wrist. "No! You can't!" He shook his head vehemently to emphasise his words.

Viggo froze. He stared uncomprehendingly at Evander, unable to grasp his meaning at first. Confusion gave way to understanding as he watched the mage bite his own lip. He kissed him softly.

"Don't worry. I know I'm big, but I'll be gentle and make sure it doesn't hurt." He caressed Evander's opening again and was rewarded by a twitch and a low whimper.

The mage shuddered. "It's not your size I'm concerned about." He removed Viggo's hand where he was still exploring him and put it firmly on top of the vanity, his expression hardening. "We can't have sex until this case is solved. You're a witness and potential collaborator, Viggo. And I'm the investigating officer. Sleeping with one another is a conflict of interest."

Viggo's eyes rounded. "What?"

His shocked mumble did not move Evander one iota. The mage pushed him away, jumped down from the vanity unit, and rearranged his robe.

He looked remarkably composed for someone who was moaning and panting in Viggo's arms mere minutes ago.

Frustration churned the Brute's belly.

"You are jesting, right?!"

He was about to run his fingers through his hair when he realised they were still coated with the evidence of his and Evander's pleasure. Viggo scowled and washed them in the sink.

The mage had the decency to blush. He cleared his throat while Viggo dried his hands jerkily on a towel.

"What brought you here tonight? You said you wanted to talk."

Viggo pinned him with a sharp stare. "Are you changing the subject?"

"Yes." Evander sighed at Viggo's irritated expression. "Look, I don't like this either, but it's the right thing to do. I don't want our relationship to start on a bad note."

All of Viggo's protests came to a screeching, stomach-flopping halt.

"You—you want a relationship with me?!" he said numbly.

Evander stared. "Of course I do." Wariness crept into his face. "Don't tell me you're only after sex." His shoulders slumped. "I am not into that kind of—"

Viggo closed the distance to the mage and cut him off with his mouth.

"Of course I want a relationship with you," he whispered hotly against Evander's lips.

The mage swallowed, his hands trembling slightly where he clung to Viggo's chest. "You do?" He squinted a little, as if he didn't quite believe him.

Viggo kicked himself for being a fool. "Yes." He shuddered and pressed their foreheads together. "You've cast a spell on me, mage. I will gladly follow you into the fires of Hell itself if it means I can be with you."

Evander's eyes widened at his heartfelt confession. He took hold of Viggo's face and kissed him sweetly before wrapping his arms around his neck. They stayed like that for a moment, hearts thundering against one another.

"Let's go into my study," Evander murmured. "It will be more comfortable to talk there."

Viggo reluctantly let him go. "What about your manservant?"

Evander smiled. "Jasper won't come up to my chambers again tonight."

He grasped Viggo's hand and guided him through his dressing room and into his bedroom. It was a spacious and elegant space. A large, four-poster mahogany bed draped with heavy velvet curtains embroidered with a delicate pattern of silver and gold threads dominated it.

Evander stopped to get rid of his bathrobe.

A shiver danced through Viggo at the sight of his enticing naked form as he wrapped himself in a dark, silk dressing gown. The Brute directed a hopeful look at the bed.

"How about we just test the mattress?"

Evander chuckled at his fervent words and led him through another door and into a cozy room where a fire crackled. Viggo took the glass of whiskey the mage poured him before studying the enchanted map above the mantlepiece.

"Looks like you take your work home with you."

Evander shrugged. "The same could be said of you."

They exchanged a small, intimate smile.

"What did you have to tell me?" Evander indicated an armchair.

Viggo sat down and leaned his elbows on his knees. He stared into his glass and swirled the golden liquid inside, still amazed at where he found himself and all that had happened tonight. His stomach fluttered when he lifted his head and met Evander's inquisitive gaze.

I can't believe the Ice Mage who is known for being cold to anyone who approaches him is willing to be mine.

The enormity of what had passed between the two of them and the unspoken promise they'd made to one another made Viggo fairly lightheaded. He focused on what had brought him to Evander's townhouse.

"*Nightshade* is looking for sources of *Noctis Bloom*. And I wanted to apologise again. For how I treated you back in Winterbourne's office."

~

EVANDER'S THROAT CONSTRICTED AT VIGGO'S TORMENTED look.

It was clear his actions that morning had been weighing heavily on his mind.

"You had every right to say what you did, Viggo." Evander put their glasses on a side table and leaned forward to take the Brute's hands. "You are a thrall whose entire family was killed by mages. I would have been more surprised if you had forgiven us and embraced us."

Viggo shuddered and closed his eyes. "But I cannot keep blaming *all* mages. I realised that when I met you and the people you work with today." His dark eyes gleamed hotly when he opened them. "Your kind is not all evil. *You* are not evil."

Evander's mouth lifted in a lopsided smile. "I don't

know about that. I've done some pretty wicked things in my time. And you should see what Shaw gets up to."

Viggo laughed. "I like that about you. You don't take yourself too seriously. And you treat your subordinates with kindness."

Evander's stomach clenched. The Brute's face when he smiled from his heart was simply breathtaking.

Viggo's expression turned puzzled. "What?"

"You are magnificent."

Viggo startled at Evander's earnest words. His expression softened.

"I think the magnificent one here is you."

Evander shook his head, his chest full to bursting. "No. You truly are incredible, Viggo." He turned the Brute's hand over and kissed his knuckles. "You overcame so much pain and devastation to get where you are today. Not many men would have been able to conquer those obstacles and rise to a position of power." He squeezed Viggo's fingers and met his dazed stare unflinchingly. "Yet, somehow, those awful experiences did not corrupt your soul. You are kind and smart and just and generous to a fault. I only need to see how Magnus acts around you to know this."

Colour stained Viggo's cheekbones. "Evander," he mumbled thickly.

"I know what *Nightshade* means to the non-magical community, Viggo. I've spent enough time in the slums to see the effect your organisation's presence has had on the magicless." Resolve tightened Evander's face. "You are a beacon of hope for thralls in England and throughout the

Empire. And I am determined to see to it that your flame is never extinguished."

CHAPTER 26

Viggo's eyes widened. "What do you mean?"

"There are people in London and the wider magic community who wish to see another War of Subjugation. One that will take away the rights of thralls, permanently this time. And I have every intention of stopping them."

Viggo felt the blood drain from his face. He stared at where Evander held his hands in the tense silence that befell them, his pulse racing.

I always suspected there might be another war, but to hear him say it makes it all too painfully real.

Bloodied memories of the past flooded Viggo's mind. He suppressed them firmly and looked at Evander.

"Is that why you chose to work for the Met?"

Evander's shoulders visibly knotted at the question. "Why do you ask?"

"I've been wondering about it since I met you," Viggo confessed. "Even more so after I realised you were an Archmage."

It was Evander's turn to fall quiet. His voice when he spoke was underscored by regret.

"The day my father died, I realised the foolish dreams I had always entertained about the future of this country and the fate of thralls would forever remain a fantasy unless I stepped out in society and started taking serious action."

"Dreams?" Viggo repeated. "What kind of dreams?"

Evander met his gaze steadily.

"I want to set thralls on an equal footing with those who possess magic."

Shock jolted Viggo. "What?" He blinked rapidly, his heart pounding erratically against his ribs. "But—how?!"

"It won't happen overnight. The first thing is to stop the injustices perpetrated against the magicless community. The first War of Subjugation was triggered by a single terrible act of brutality, after all." Evander furrowed his brow. "The recent tensions in the East End make me suspect someone, likely a group of nobles, is determined to repeat the mistake of the past."

Viggo licked his lips. "So, by being an active officer in the Met, you hope to stop a similar incident?"

Evander did not take offence at his scepticism.

"Being in the Arcane Division means I can keep my finger on the pulse of the action." He looked at the enchanted map on the wall. "And I know the areas where I need to intervene before things go too far."

Viggo followed his gaze. Realisation dawned belatedly.

"Is that why you're the one who mediated all those disputes between the Met and the non-magical community?" He stared at Evander, bewildered.

"The officers involved were not terribly pleased by my intervention." Evander smiled faintly. "Being a Duke has its advantages."

Viggo let this all sink in.

"But surely, that won't be enough to bring about change for thralls." He furrowed his brow, his mind spinning. "Even if you are successful at stopping another war, the providence of the magicless would remain the same."

"That's where people like me and Ginny come in."

Confusion shot through Viggo all over again. "What does Lady Hartley have to do with any of this?"

Evander spoke of the work he, Ginny, and dozens of other nobles they'd brought to their side had been doing behind the scenes. Viggo grew positively dumbfounded as he enumerated the long list of philanthropic enterprises he, Ginny, and their associates had privately founded and supported over the last five years.

Employing thralls. Creating opportunities for them to rise out of the poverty their births had sentenced them to. Feeding them. Teaching them to understand the laws of the land and their rights. More importantly, providing them with education and healthcare and even a safe roof over their heads so they could thrive.

"The new hospital in Whitechapel? And the school in Spitalfields?" Viggo said hoarsely. "That was all *you*?!"

"Yes. Like I mentioned before, change won't come about overnight. It will take years for everyone to alter their way of thinking, including those without magic. We need to reform people's attitudes from the ground up."

Viggo swallowed heavily, still reeling from everything the mage had just revealed.

"What about the House of Lords and that petition?"

"Ah. Yes. The House of Lords." Evander sighed heavily. "My second option beside joining the Met was to take a proactive role in politics and enact policies for the fair treatment of thralls from the very heart of government." The mage grimaced. "Alas, that place is a nest of vipers that would have given me no end of headaches, so I decided to keep an eye out for the pro-subjugation faction from the fringes."

Viggo recalled what Evander had said in Winterbourne's office.

"By attending balls and functions?"

"Yes. It's surprising how much you can learn at those parties. Ginny and I often find business partners who share our convictions there."

~

"You and Lady Hartley seem very close," Viggo grunted.

Evander studied his pinched expression for a bewildered moment before bursting out laughing.

"Are you jealous?!" he chortled once he got his breath back.

Viggo scowled. "What if I am?"

"Ginny and I aren't like that." Evander chuckled and wiped his eyes. "Besides, she correctly guessed my sexual preference within an hour of meeting me."

Viggo appeared somewhat mollified by this. "Does that mean you've always been interested in men?"

"Yes." Evander cocked his head curiously. "And you?"

"I've slept with a few women," the Brute said with refreshing honesty. The smile he flashed at Evander made his stomach flutter. "But I don't think I will have eyes for anyone else but a certain Archmage with blue eyes from now on." He lifted Evander's hand to his lips and kissed his knuckles, his hooded gaze gleaming.

Heat rose in Evander's cheeks. He cleared his throat, his voice stern.

"Good. Because I'll probably rip out the eyes of any woman who catches your interest."

Viggo stared at him blankly. It was the Brute's turn to dissolve in raucous laughter.

"What—" he said in a strangled voice, "what if it's another man?!"

Evander jutted his chin out. "I'll crush his balls so hard he'll walk with a permanent lurch."

This had Viggo doubling over.

Evander waited until he'd regained his composure before voicing a final sliver of doubt.

"Am I the only one who thinks this whole situation is far-fetched?" A shaky laugh left him. "We met a day ago. We barely know anything about one another. And yet here we are, pledging—" He stopped and bit his lip.

Viggo sobered. He traced Evander's mouth with his thumb.

"Pledging our hearts to each other." He leaned over and kissed Evander gently. "No, you aren't the only one who believes what's happening between us is insane." The Brute's gaze roamed Evander's face, the light shining in their depths so intense Evander could not help but shiver. "None of this makes sense. But one thing I am confident about."

"And that is?" Evander mumbled.

"It feels right." Viggo took Evander's hand and pressed it to his chest. "My heart never lies to me. And it's telling me that what's growing between us is meant to be."

Evander's breath caught. Emotion clogged his throat. His eyes prickled.

"I think I'm falling in love with a hopeless romantic," he said tremulously.

Viggo smiled and wiped the tear trembling on his lash with a knuckle.

"I believe I shall very much enjoy courting you." The Brute's tone turned teasing. "Why, I'm even entertaining the idea of giving you flowers." He pasted a solemn expression across his face. "I've *never* given anyone flowers."

Evander snorted. "Jasper will keel over if you do."

Viggo chuckled.

"Don't worry about the House of Lords," Evander said on a more serious note. "Many of us will voice objections to their latest proposal. And no voice will be louder than mine and the current Commissioner."

Viggo stared. "You mean, Sir Ambrose?"

Evander dipped his head.

Sir Ambrose Watson, now Lord Watson after his royal appointment to the House of Lords, was the current Commissioner of the Metropolitan Police. A driving force for reform in Scotland Yard, he had worked relentlessly to improve relations between the magical and non-magical communities even before Evander had come on board. He'd always been a staunch advocate for the fairer treatment of thralls, often butting heads with more conservative elements in the government.

His nomination to the role of Commissioner after his retirement from the army was one of the reasons Evander had opted to enlist in the Arcane Division.

"That may not be enough." Viggo's expression grew troubled. "There are many unsavoury elements in Parliament. *Nightshade* has come across a fair few in the time the guild has been in operation."

"If all else fails, I can always threaten them. I'm an Archmage, after all."

Viggo's eyebrows drew together. "Don't jest. That will land you in Irongate Prison for sure."

"It doesn't have to be a physical threat." Evander met his concerned gaze steadily. "As an Archmage, I stand to play a key role in this country's defence. All I have to do is convince them I will leave England and the British Empire, and the Queen will have no choice but to cave in to my demands and intervene."

Viggo's eyes widened. "You would really do that?!"

Evander nodded.

"But—why?" Viggo swallowed convulsively. "I don't understand why you and nobles like Lady Hartley would go so far for thralls."

Evander gently caressed the Brute's face.

"Because we believe magic isn't meant to divide us," he said softly. "It exists to unite us." He pressed a soft kiss to Viggo's brow. "Your very existence is proof of this. It is

Nature trying to find a way to balance the scales before this entire world tips into chaos."

Viggo's breath shuddered out of him.

"You truly are remarkable," he mumbled against Evander's throat. "Then, I will help you." He straightened, determination hardening his voice. "I promise that I will use all the resources at my hand and do everything in my power to see your goals achieved."

Evander smiled at his resolute expression. "Alright."

Viggo wrapped his arms around him. Evander sighed and sank into his embrace.

The Brute drew back after a moment and tipped Evander's chin with his knuckles. He lowered his head and claimed Evander's mouth in a sensual kiss. Evander shivered, heat coiling through his veins.

It didn't take long for the kiss to turn passionate.

Viggo pulled Evander onto his lap. He went willingly, desire lighting up his senses with every stroke of Viggo's tongue. Viggo's gaze grew hooded as he kneaded Evander's back and dropped his hands to his backside where he straddled his thighs.

Evander shuddered when their erections bumped.

He indulged Viggo for another minute before wrenching their mouths apart and pinning him with a sharp look.

"We're not fucking, Viggo."

The Brute's shoulders slumped. "Oh, come now!"

"I said no and I mean it." Evander ignored his beleaguered stare, climbed off his lap, and rearranged his dressing gown. "Off you go." He waved briskly towards the door. "The hour is late and I need my sleep."

Viggo's jaw dropped open. "Are you kicking me out?!"

Evander bit his lip and just about managed to keep a straight face at the sight of the Brute's outraged expression.

"Yes, I am. Now, hurry up and leave."

Viggo groused as Evander herded him into the dressing room and out the window he'd used to enter the townhouse.

"My lover has a heart of stone," the Brute grumbled, taking hold of the trellis.

Evander couldn't resist dropping a kiss on his nose. "Goodnight, Viggo."

He closed the window in the glum Brute's face and drew the curtains closed. A wide grin split Evander's face as he made his way to the bedroom, his heart lighter than it had been in days.

CHAPTER 27

"DID SOMETHING HAPPEN?" RUFUS ASKED CURIOUSLY.

Evander gave his friend a puzzled look as they got off the carriage.

"Why do you ask?"

"You're positively glowing."

"Oh." Heat rose in Evander's face.

He could hardly tell Rufus that he'd spent a good hour relieving himself with the enchanted toy in his bedside drawer last night after Viggo had left, all while imagining it was the Brute's cock that was firmly wedged inside his body and wrecking him until he fairly shuddered with pleasure.

Evander had wanted to pinch himself when he'd woken up, certain he'd imagined everything that had happened between them. One look at the love bite Viggo had left on his neck made him realise it hadn't been a dream.

He still wasn't sure what a future with Viggo would look like. But he wanted to see it nevertheless.

Evander's chest tightened at the truth he had yet to reveal to the Brute.

It made him recall the scene that had met him when he'd gone downstairs that morning. He'd been greeted by a funereal atmosphere upon entering the foyer.

"My Lord," Mrs. Sinclair had murmured despondently.

Hargrove had stood beside the housekeeper, the morning papers in a white-knuckled grip. The manservant had looked about ready to spit nails.

Evander's shoulders had tightened. "How bad is it?"

"It's worse than bad, my Lord," Hargrove had grated out. "They're saying your position in Scotland Yard is untenable and you should be summarily dismissed."

Evander's stomach had sunk at that. He'd clenched his jaw.

"Looks like some nobles in the House of Lords are really keen to get rid of me."

It shouldn't have come as a surprise. He'd been a thorn in their side for years.

"What happened, my Lord?" Mrs. Sinclair had asked quietly.

Evander had met his former nanny's steady gaze unflinchingly. Unlike Hargrove, she knew *all* his secrets, including the one that would rock the entire British Empire if it were to be made public.

Though he could not reveal the exact details of what had taken place the day before at Scotland Yard, Evander had told them he'd used his powers to save a man's life.

His explanation had gone some way towards mollifying Hargrove.

Mrs. Sinclair had sighed. "I guess it couldn't be helped. Please, pay no heed to the papers, my Lord." She'd shot a narrow-eyed look at a scullery maid who'd slowed to gawk at Evander. "I shall ensure that our staff keeps their mouths shut."

The maid had flinched and hurried about her business.

Rufus's voice brought Evander back to the present.

"I saw the print rags this morning." The inspector was frowning.

"Come now," Evander said lightly. "You should know better than to believe everything you read in those gossip columns."

A muscle jumped in Rufus's cheek.

"How can you be so blasé about this? We're talking about your future, dammit!"

Guilt stabbed through Evander at his worried expression.

"Nothing will happen. I may jest about it, but I should count myself lucky my status as an Archmage never came to light before now."

Rufus swallowed heavily. His mouth flattened to a thin line a moment later.

"What of Winterbourne's threat yesterday? He said the Queen could strip you of your role as a Royal Arcane Liaison and force you to resign from the Met once he informed her of what happened."

"I have no doubt Her Majesty will be...*upset*." Evander did his best to keep his voice neutral as an array of conflicting emotions formed a tight knot in his chest. "But she won't make me relinquish my position."

Rufus looked unconvinced. "How can you be so certain?" he said doggedly.

"Let's just say Her Majesty and I go back a long way."

Alastair Millbrook's workshop bore an unassuming facade where it stood nestled amidst more opulent storefronts tucked between St. Martin's Lane and Adelaide Street. The exterior was weathered brick, with frosted windows covered in intricate, gold filigree that prevented passersby from peering inside. A brass plaque was affixed to a wooden door painted a dark green. It read *A. Millbrook, Artifice & Enchantments*.

Shaw was waiting for them in the small foyer with a couple of constables Evander recognised.

"Top o' the morning to ya, your Grace," Shaw greeted brightly.

Rufus narrowed his eyes. "You're being suspiciously cheerful, Shaw. What did you break this time?"

"It was some kind of clockwork device, Inspector," Constable Oliver Bartley snitched before Shaw could protest her innocence. The constable was short and round and wore a perpetually earnest expression on his ruddy face.

Shaw sucked in air, outraged at being ratted out. "How could you, Ollie?!"

Bartley's ears flushed. "It's not right to lie, Miss Shaw."

Rufus said a rude word. "I was jesting. Did she really destroy a piece of evidence?!"

"We tried to stop her, sir, but she said she needed to examine the device closely and then it just sort of went—

Poof!" Bartley made an elaborate exploding gesture with his hand.

"Turns out the thing wasn't meant to be treated like a maraca," the lanky figure beside him contributed drily.

Freddie Fitch was known for being observant and quick-witted.

Evander had high hopes he would make sergeant by the end of the year.

"Best go in and survey the damage, your Grace, Inspector." Fitch dipped his chin respectfully at Evander and Rufus. "We'll be out here, making sure no one else decides to come and play shake the priceless magical artefact."

Shaw gave the constables a dirty look and avoided meeting Rufus's eyes as she led them inside Millbrook's workshop.

A whispered exchange started behind Evander.

"Pssst!" Bartley hissed to Fitch. "We forgot to ask his Grace about that rumour! You know, the one saying he's an Archmage!"

"Ollie?" Fitch muttered.

"Yes, Freddie?"

"Remember how I often tell you there are times when it's best to keep mum?"

"Ah-huh?"

"Now's one of those times."

"Oh."

Shaw sneaked a look at Evander. Having refrained herself the day before, the mage appeared to be bursting with questions. To Evander's relief, she decided not to voice them in the face of Rufus's warning stare.

"I'm afraid there isn't much to see, your Grace." Shaw indicated the interior of the Charm Weaver's workshop.

It ran the entire length and almost the whole of the width of the building.

A bright autumnal sunlight filtered through a multi-paned, arched window overlooking a small courtyard and garden at the back. It illuminated the ornate workbench sitting beneath the wide stone ledge and the array of tools and mysterious objects cluttering its surface.

The rays danced off a large brass-and-crystal ornery suspended from the ceiling, the device intended to map magical ley lines instead of celestial bodies. Shelves lined a significant portion of the room, racks crammed with bottles and vials of every shape and size. A pair of tall, wooden apothecary cabinets with assorted drawers framed a library nook containing a well-stocked collection of arcane texts, engineering manuals, and ledgers. One corner of the workshop was dedicated to metalworking, the space dominated by a magically-enhanced forge. An anvil and a table holding trays full of hammers, tongs, and alchemically-treated pliers stood next to the furnace.

Evander's gaze landed on a wall covered in dozens of exquisite magical clocks. Each was a unique piece that would no doubt fetch several guineas on the current market. Their rhythmic ticking filled the atelier with an eerie susurration that made the hairs lift on the back of his neck.

Shaw's voice nearly made him jump.

CHAPTER 28

"LIKE I WROTE IN MY REPORT, THE PROTECTIVE WARDS around the building have recently been disturbed, which suggests forced entry," the forensic mage said. "Also, this place is more of a mess than I'd expect it to be, considering how neat Millbrook's lodgings are upstairs."

Evander noted the paperwork spilled across the floor and the various items that had been knocked off the bench and shelves as he crossed the room. Half-finished projects littered Millbrook's workstation. Amidst the enchanted gadgets was a pocket watch, its intricate engravings still glowing faintly.

A frown furrowed his brow when he recognised a set of engraving tools for carving precise magical runes and a rectangular device the size of a music box beside the watch.

"That's not something you'd normally expect to find in a Charm Weaver's workshop," Evander muttered.

"What is it?" Rufus joined him at the bench.

Shaw came over, curiosity sparking her eyes.

Evander carefully lifted the box. It was covered in dials and switches.

"It's a thaumic capacitor."

Rufus and Shaw levelled blank stares at him.

"It's a device made for storing and releasing magical energy." Evander wrinkled his brow. "Their use is restricted to government research labs. There are only a handful of these in the country."

Rufus's eyes bulged. His gaze switched from Evander to the device.

"Did Millbrook steal this?!"

Evander lifted the box to his eye and peered through a circular window at the complex arrangement of gears, crystals, and what appeared to be miniature lightning contained within the glass tubes visible inside. Glowing softly at the centre was a crystal pulsing with stored magical energy.

"No. I'm pretty certain Millbrook made this."

Evander put the box down, his thoughts lingering on why a Charm Weaver would need such a device.

I wonder if it has something to do with the crystal vial I found in the alley?

Shaw sucked air through her teeth and rocked back on her heels.

"Soooo, I've been meaning to ask something, your Grace."

Rufus narrowed his eyes at her innocent expression. "Shaw, this had better not be—"

"Is it true that the Commissioner is going to give you the old heave-ho?"

The mage stared avidly at Evander, all ears.

Rufus cursed and pinched the bridge of his nose.

"I trust Lord Watson has better things to do with his time than to read the gossip rags, Miss Shaw," Evander replied tactfully. He released a faint wave of elemental power as he began wandering around the room.

Shaw brightened. "So, the rumour that you're gonna get the sack isn't true?"

"Shaw!" Rufus snapped.

"What?" The mage shrugged, unrepentant. "There's a betting pool going on in the mess. I need to hedge my chances if I want to pay the cleaning bill for his Grace's boots."

Evander slowed when he reached the centre of the workshop. He could feel something in the room. A barely noticeable undercurrent that tickled his magic senses.

"Dare I ask what the odds look like?" he said distractedly, letting loose a stronger wave of power.

Shaw grimaced. "Fifteen to one says you'll be out on your ear come the end of the week, your Grace."

Rufus's face darkened.

Evander pulled up short and blinked. "That's quite a… decisive stand."

He stiffened in the next instant.

The air where he stood was thick with the smell of metal, oil, and various alchemical reagents. Underneath it all was a faint scent reminiscent of ozone.

It was the smell of raw magic.

Evander followed it to an easel holding a chalkboard covered in arcane formulae and engineering diagrams.

There were scorch marks on the floor behind it, a short distance from the fireplace. Goosebumps broke out on Evander's skin when a familiar coppery waft teased his sensitive nostrils.

"Blood was shed here," he said grimly.

"What?" Rufus hurried over, Shaw in his footsteps.

Evander squatted and focused his magic into his hand.

Coolness flowed through his veins and formed a mist above his palm. The droplets coalesced into a small, spinning whirlpool. He manifested his wind magic and merged the two to create a controlled jet of water with a precision few could manage.

Evander carefully directed the spray at the scorch marks.

It cleared them in seconds.

Shaw gasped. Rufus swore.

Evander clenched his jaw. The stone slabs were covered in a large blood stain.

"Miss Shaw, can you examine the fire irons?" Rufus asked stiffly.

Shaw removed a pair of examining gloves from her coat and pulled them on. She lifted the implements from the stand next to the fireplace and scrutinised them.

"The poker is clean, sir."

Their gazes swung to the thick layer of ash and soot in the hearth.

"Someone tidied up after themselves," Evander said thinly. "Mortimer said Millbrook suffered a blow to the head before his death. I guess this was where he was struck."

The trail of ozone led him from the fireplace to the furnace.

Evander stopped when he reached the area beyond the table. His scalp prickled. There was a lingering chill in that corner of the room that should not be there.

It hinted at the use of dark magic and death.

"I think Millbrook was killed here."

Rufus and Shaw exchanged a tense look. They knew better than to voice their doubts. This aspect of Evander's abilities was what had earned him the status of Special Arcane Investigator after all.

"Stay back," Evander warned in a hard voice. "I'm going to attempt something."

Rufus and Shaw retreated several steps.

Heat licked through Evander's bloodstream with his next inhale.

Shaw choked on her breath when sparks ignited the air around him.

Dark wisps flickered into view all around Evander, the strands roiling as if tossed by a gale as they clashed with his powers. The sinister residue he'd revealed settled on the floor around him under the influence of his fire magic, forming a fine layer of inky dust.

Acid burned the back of Evander's throat when he found himself standing on the outline of a body curled up on itself.

"Bloody hellfire!" Shaw croaked.

Rufus swallowed and cut his eyes to Evander. "Is that—?"

Evander nodded curtly. "A Shadow Imprint."

He could tell what Rufus and Shaw were thinking from their stunned expressions. The ability to manifest the location of a dead body—the place where a soul had recently departed this world—was the remit of the most powerful Archmages in the world.

"Miss Shaw, did you find a logbook on the premises? The one where Millbrook would have kept details of his recent projects and clients?"

Shaw gulped and shook her head. "No, your Grace. I found that surprising and made a note of it in my report."

Evander exchanged a troubled look with Rufus.

"Whoever killed Millbrook probably came back for the logbook," the inspector said darkly.

"That or they were looking for that crystal vial," Evander muttered.

Shaw scratched her head. "There's something I don't get. Why go to all that trouble? Why kill him here, then take his body to the East End and make it look like he was murdered there?"

"To throw us off." Evander's voice hardened. "Had we not found that crystal vial, we may never have discovered Millbrook's identity or the involvement of dark mages in his murder."

"And even if we had, it would have been weeks after the fact," Rufus added sourly. "The trail would have gone cold by then. And whatever their intentions were, they might already have achieved them."

Evander's stomach churned. Things were getting more dangerous with every passing day.

"We should talk to the Artificers and see if they've

figured out what that crystal vial is. It's a key component of those dark mages' plans." Evander clenched his jaw. "I am certain of it."

But all thoughts of visiting the Artificers fled Evander and Rufus's minds when they returned to Scotland Yard. An anonymous letter had been delivered to the Met in their absence. It claimed a dark magic cult was behind Alastair Millbrook's death.

CHAPTER 29

THE CHURCH LOOMED ON A LOW KNOLL BETWEEN MILE
End and Old Ford, a dark shape against the smog-filled
sky of London's East End. Viggo studied its weathered
stone walls and crumbling gargoyles from the vantage
point where he lurked with Solomon and Finn, in an alley
across the street.

The stench of the nearby slums hung heavily in the air,
the sickening mix of human waste, unwashed bodies, and
despair a stark reminder of the world they'd fought so
hard to escape. Underlying the stink was the faint scent of
Noctis Bloom that wafted towards Viggo on the occasional
muggy breeze.

They watched as several cloaked figures slipped inside
the church through a side door.

"Looks like our spy was right, boss," Finn murmured.
"That's the third lot we've seen enter in the last hour."

Viggo frowned.

The lead on *Noctis Bloom* had come from one of

Nightshade's most reliable informants. Still, seeing it confirmed made his stomach sink. This church, once a sanctuary for the downtrodden, had seemingly become a den of dark magic. That they were going about their wretched business so brazenly in broad daylight told Viggo whoever was behind the scheme was either foolhardy or powerful enough to overcome his adversaries.

"Bet they're all quaffing on purple powder in there," Finn said with morbid glee.

"*Noctis Bloom* is poisonous when absorbed in sufficient quantities," Solomon muttered. "I strongly hope they're not quaffing on it."

Viggo shot a surprised look his way.

Solomon caught his stare and shrugged. "I do pay attention to what you say. Also, remind me again why we're helping the bloody Met?" His voice carried a healthy dose of scepticism. "Since when do we stick our necks out for mages?"

Viggo clocked the troubled lines etched into his friend's face. He understood the thrall's wariness; trust didn't come easily to any of them, especially when it came to those with magic. Doubly so if they also wore a badge.

But things had changed.

"This is not just about the Met." Viggo's gaze found the church once more. "It's about Magnus and the others like him who might have fallen under those mages' control." He clenched his jaw. "You heard what those bastards did to him. How they made him do their bidding with that damn gem. We can't let that stand."

Finn bobbed his head. "The boss is right, Sly. Magnus

is one of us. And if someone messes with one of us, he messes with *all* of us."

"That's rich coming from the bloke who just stood there and watched me get slugged in that pub fight a month ago," Solomon said darkly.

"A wise man knows when to choose his battles," Finn quipped.

"It's thanks to Evander and the Met that Magnus is alive and a free man right now." Viggo remembered the relief he'd felt yesterday when Magnus had finally awakened, confused and shaken but himself again. "We owe them for that, at least."

"Fair point," Solomon admitted grudgingly. "But still, working with mages...All I'm saying is it's a slippery slope, Viggo."

"I know," the Brute admitted reluctantly. "But Evander is different."

The mage's name felt warm on his tongue, bringing with it memories of their encounter in the townhouse in Mayfair the night before.

The aching vulnerability in the mage's ice-blue eyes when Viggo had made him confront his own feelings. The passion in his touch and kisses when he'd finally surrendered to the desire burning between them and responded to Viggo's lovemaking. His sincerity as he'd spoken of his dreams of a better world for thralls.

Viggo's belly tightened as he relieved all of it for the umpteenth time.

Time and distance had not diminished his feelings for Evander. If anything, they had strengthened the attraction he felt for the mage, to the extent he was fairly certain he would embarrass himself the next time they met.

A scowl spread across Finn's face.

"I knew it! You have a thing for the Ice Mage!" He huffed. "Who would've thought you'd want to play hide the ol' bag of mystery with that—*ouch!*"

Solomon had smacked him on the back of the head.

Finn rubbed his skull and gave Solomon a hurt look. "What was that for?"

"You're being loud."

Viggo swallowed a sigh. "How about we focus on the task at hand? Whatever's happening in that church, it's hurting our people. The magicless. That's why we're here."

A low mumble left Finn.

"And because you want to have your little bit of fun with that smarmy—*ouch!*" He glared at Solomon. "Hey, go easy on the noggin! I can't afford to lose my charming wit!"

Solomon ignored him and studied the building across the street with a frown.

"What's our next move? Should we sneak in there and see what they're up to?"

The clatter of hooves and wheels on cobblestone drew their attention before Viggo could respond. The Brute stiffened when a sturdy police wagon appeared at the end of the road. It pulled up in front of the church a moment later.

A sleek black carriage materialised behind the wagon.

Viggo's stomach plummeted when he saw the man who stepped out of it.

"Speak of the devil," Solomon muttered.

The sight of Evander in his formal uniform sent an illicit jolt through Viggo. He could not help but revisit the vision that had been the mage half-naked in his bathroom last night, his beautiful face flushed and his eyes a vivid indigo as he'd writhed and panted with pleasure in Viggo's arms.

"What's the Ice Duke doing here?" Finn grunted.

Viggo curbed his errant thoughts. "I'm not sure."

Did the Met get a lead on Noctis Bloom *too?*

Evander was joined by Inspector Grayson.

A dozen constables emerged from the wagon. They were led by the gruff-looking sergeant Viggo recognised from his visit to Scotland Yard the day before. Over half of the officers fanned out, creating a perimeter around the church fence. Evander and Rufus entered the churchyard with Griffiths and the rest of the constables.

A figure wearing a cassock emerged from the building and came swiftly down the path to meet them.

Evander and Rufus stopped and exchanged words with the priest. The man nodded jerkily and gestured towards the church entrance.

They followed him inside.

"Time to move." Viggo pushed away from the wall a couple of minutes later. "We should take a look at the back and—"

His words were cut off by a deafening explosion that shook the very ground beneath their feet. The windows of the church exploded outward in a shower of flames and broken glass.

Horror squeezed Viggo's heart.

"Evander!"

He sprinted towards the burning building, all semblance of stealth forgotten.

～

EVANDER FROWNED AT THE NEIGHBOURHOOD THE CARRIAGE navigated on their approach to the church. The warren of filthy streets and their overcrowded, crumbling tenements spoke volumes about the desperate conditions in this part of London.

It was a sobering contrast to the world he and Rufus had just left.

"I wonder who sent that letter," Rufus said distractedly opposite him.

The constable who'd taken delivery of the anonymous missive outside the entrance to Scotland Yard reported it'd been brought by a messenger boy. The chances of finding the lad amidst the hustle and bustle of London was virtually non-existent.

Though they'd left the letter with Shaw and the alchemists of the AFD in the hope they might be able to trace the item back to its source, Evander suspected they would reach a dead end.

Something about the whole affair troubled him.

The timing of the letter seemed preordained at best and dubious at worse. Still, they could hardly ignore it.

The church appeared around the corner of a slope. It straddled a low bank, its grounds sparse but for crowded gravestones and an oak tree with bare branches. The police wagon they were following stopped outside the gated fence a moment later. Sergeant Griffiths rallied the constables as Evander exited the carriage with Rufus.

He ignored the burning and, in some cases, frankly reverential glances several of the officers stole at him. Griffiths quelled the men's gawking with a stern frown.

"Leave some of our officers out here as lookout," Evander instructed the sergeant. "The rest can come with us." He paused. "And Griffiths?"

"Yes, your Grace?"

"Have your truncheons at the ready." Evander studied the building atop the rise warily. "We don't know what we'll find inside."

The sergeant cut his eyes to the church. He dipped his head.

"Alright, your Grace."

They started up the path, only to be met halfway by a small wiry man with thinning grey hair and watery blue eyes.

"Hello." The priest's gaze flitted curiously to the constables at the bottom of the hill before focusing on Evander and Rufus. "How may I help you, gentlemen?"

"Good morning, Father…" Rufus started.

"Smith." The man smiled pleasantly. "It's Father Smith."

"We have cause to believe dark magic is being used on these premises," Evander said. "We would like to examine the church and the outbuildings."

The priest gasped and blinked rapidly.

"Oh! How terrible!" He pressed a hand to his chest, his voice flustered. "I have no idea where such awful rumours came from, but I can assure you that they are untrue!"

"Still, it would be in everyone's best interests if you

allowed us to take a look around the place." Rufus's face was a mask of professional detachment.

"Of course," the priest mumbled, contrite. "Please, come this way."

It took Evander a moment to fathom why something felt off about the man as they headed for the church entrance.

His eyes never quite met theirs and his smile seemed too wide and forced.

Evander wondered if Rufus had picked up on the faint, sickly sweet odour coming from the priest. He was almost certain it was the scent of *Noctis Bloom* he'd smelled in Brown's lab yesterday.

The officers looked around uneasily when they entered the church, eyes darting to murky corners and hands hovering near their weapons. Even Griffiths looked nervous as he studied the layout of the building.

Evander shared their disquiet. The church's interior was even more depressing than its exterior, the faded pews and windows covered in a layer of filth that seemed to absorb whatever light illuminated the inside.

"Evander," Rufus said quietly, his tone laced with fresh tension.

Evander followed his gaze. His pulse quickened.

"I see them."

CHAPTER 30

A GROUP OF CLOAKED FIGURES LOITERED IN THE SHADOWS at the far end, their faces obscured by their hoods. Evander counted a dozen men at least. Though they stood still, their posture projected an alertness they failed to mask.

"Griffiths," Rufus muttered warningly.

The sergeant gave a silent signal to the constables. They removed their truncheons from their waists, the runes on the wood glowing faintly as they engaged the defensive magic contained within.

"Oh, don't worry about those men," Father Smith said hastily when he noticed their weapons. "They are student priests joining me for prayer this evening."

Evander reluctantly entered the nave and headed after him with Rufus and the other officers, the unease coiling inside him intensifying with every step he took.

Father Smith was already halfway towards the chancel, the priest moving as if the devil himself was on his tail.

They were twenty feet inside the building when he shot a glance at Evander over his shoulder. A smirk twisted his mouth.

Evander stiffened, the dark mage from the alley where Millbrook's body had been found coming immediately to mind. The man had worn a similar expression when Evander had chased him on the rooftop.

He barely had time to fathom the priest's strange expression and its uncanny resemblance to Millbrook's murderer when his senses were assaulted by a wrongness that made his scalp prickle.

The air inside the church suddenly felt thick and oppressive, as if trying to smother him. A bitter taste coated his tongue at the same time an ominous buzzing filled his ears. But worst of all was the bone-deep chill that seemed to emanate from the very walls, a cold that had nothing to do with the autumn weather outside.

Dark magic!

Every instinct screamed at Evander that something terrible was about to happen. There was a malevolent energy growing around them, like a storm about to break.

Power blossomed in his chest and raced through his veins.

"Get out! *Now!*" he barked at Rufus and Griffiths.

The inspector and the sergeant startled and froze.

Before Evander could say more, the sinister energy drenching the inside of the church surged. A sixth sense had him erecting a barrier of wind and ice around them a heartbeat before the world exploded in a violent flash of searing light and sound.

The force of the blast sent Evander staggering

backward even behind the magic shield. He shot an alarmed glance at Rufus and the officers. Relief rendered him weak for a brief instant when he saw they were unharmed. Motion captured his gaze.

His ice magic had begun to melt, revealing the shadowy figures emerging from the smoke and debris.

A vile power bloomed around several of the men. Tendrils of darkness reached for Evander through the wind barrier, hungry and cold. He deflected them with his magic, his heart slamming erratically against his ribs.

It took him a moment to register that Father Smith was leading their assailants. The priest's face was contorted in an evil expression.

Except he no longer looked like the man Evander and Rufus had just met.

The figure leering at him was the principal suspect in Millbrook's murder.

Standing amidst the group poised to attack them were the men who'd been with Magnus when Evander's carriage had been ambushed.

Evander's chest tightened as he studied the dark mage who'd worn the disguise of a priest. He was tall and lean, with blond hair slicked back above his sharp, angular features, and cruel grey eyes that made him look older than his thirties.

He must have an Illusion Amulet on him!

Light from the flames licking through the church gleamed off a silver locket hanging from the mage's neck. The edge was engraved in minute arcane symbols, their intent to alter the wearer's appearance to the extent where they would be unrecognisable, including changing their age, height, and even their gender.

It could not however mask their scent.

"We meet again, Ice Mage," Millbrook's murderer sneered, the smell of dark magic and *Noctis Bloom* rising thickly off him amidst the smoke.

Evander swallowed down bile.

The letter had been a trap meant to lure him to the church.

Rufus appeared beside him. The inspector was unscathed save for a cut on his forehead. He wiped the blood away with the back of his hand.

"Do you know this bastard?!"

"Yes." Evander clenched his jaw. "He's the dark mage who attacked us in the alley where Millbrook's body was discovered. The one I chased on the rooftop."

Rufus's eyes grew flinty.

"Your Grace, Inspector Grayson," Griffiths said stiffly, "the exit is blocked."

Evander's shoulders knotted when they looked behind the sergeant.

Rufus swore.

A wall of flames sealed off the entrance to the church.

Evander knew there was no point trying to douse the fire burning through the building. It was too heavily tainted with dark magic and would be resistant to water for some time. His gaze swept the interior of the building.

Dark mages stood in the path of the remaining escape routes at the side and the back of the building.

Dread curdled Evander's blood as their dire situation sank in.

It had taken a single dark mage to incapacitate Shaw and Brown in Bethnal Green.

Rufus and our officers won't be able to withstand a sustained attack from this many of them. They're only casters! Even channelling their magic into their weapons will barely scratch these men!

Though Rufus and Griffiths were doing their best not to show their nervousness, Evander could see panic growing in some of the younger officers' faces.

The dark mage's eyes shrank to slits. "Oh my. Are we boring you?"

His gaze flicked to the right.

A strangled shout had Evander's head snapping around. His throat closed up at the sight of the constable writhing on the floor.

One of their attackers had managed to pierce his barrier.

Bands of wind magic trapped the officer's body in a cage that cut straight through his uniform and lacerated his flesh, the wards in his truncheon and clothes helpless in the face of a power polluted with dark magic. Griffiths rushed towards the screaming constable, only to fall back when an inky bolt cracked the stone at his feet. The sergeant cursed.

Evander's stomach sank when he saw the crimson light brightening the wind mage's pupils. The man's face was unnaturally blank.

It's just like what happened with Magnus!

He looked jerkily around and realised half the cloaked figures had eyes glowing a similar uncanny red beneath their hoods. The rest wore rings bearing the dark stone that had robbed the senseless mages of their will, including their leader.

"Dammit!" Evander bit out. "They're being manipulated!"

Understanding tightened Rufus's face.

Evander's nails dug into his palms. Unleashing his magic fully inside the crumbling church risked bringing the building down on all their heads and hurting not just the officers, but the innocent men whose minds the dark mage and his followers had ravaged with their corrupt magic.

His gaze found the loathsome figure heading the group, conscious their enemy had picked this location for that very reason.

"What the hell do you want?!" Evander growled.

"It's simple, really. We're going to capture your friends and hold them hostage until you bring that vial to us. If you refuse, we'll kill them. Then we'll go find some more Met officers and kill them too." The dark mage shrugged, his expression growing disinterested. "And so on and so forth, until we get what we want."

Rage narrowed Evander's vision.

It was at this point that a voice shouted his name.

Evander whirled around. There was movement at the church entrance.

His heart leapt when he recognised the imposing figure barrelling through the smoke and flames.

Viggo?!

Their eyes met across the chaotic space.

"Sorry I'm late!"

CHAPTER 31

Viggo's heart pounded as he raced towards the burning church, Solomon and Finn hot on his heels. The acrid smell of smoke filled his nostrils, mingling with the ever-present stench of the ghettos and the sickly-sweet scent of burning *Noctis Bloom*.

He jerked to a stop when he reached the constables frozen around the building.

"What are you waiting for?!" Viggo roared. "Use your goddamn whistles and go get help!"

The officers jumped, pale faces turning towards them. One frowned and began reaching for his truncheon.

"Now's not the time to be messing about, you pillock!" Solomon snarled. "Can any of you use water magic?!"

The constables exchanged fearful looks and shook their heads.

Frustration churned Viggo's stomach. He looked hurriedly at Finn.

"Find the nearest Soot Squad and water pumps! This fire is going to spread if we don't stop it right now!"

Debris from the explosion had already set alight one of the branches of the oak tree and clumps of dry grass in the graveyard. As if to prove him right, the thatched roof of a house next to the church ignited with a *whoomph* that sent birds lifting towards the sky in a mad flight.

Finn nodded jerkily and dashed off towards the slums. People had already begun trickling out of alleyways and were gathering in the street. Confusion gave way to fear when they saw the blaze.

A fire in the slums could decimate buildings and kill dozens in a matter of minutes.

The church soared above Viggo as he and Solomon pelted up the path, the blasts of the Met's enchanted whistles splitting the air behind them. The weathered stone walls were already black with soot.

His chest tightened at the sight of the bright flames shooting out of the broken windows. The fire burned too intensely, too eagerly, to be anything but magical in origin.

"Sly," Viggo barked as they closed in on the doorway where flames crackled and spit. "You know what to do!"

Solomon nodded grimly. He reached inside his coat and withdrew a small leather pouch before darting around the side of the building. Viggo felt the weight of his own bag against his chest, filled with the magical countermeasures that had saved their lives more than once.

There was no time for finesse.

He barrelled through the church entrance while yelling

out Evander's name, ignoring the searing heat of the fire and the alarmed shouts of the constables outside. Smoke stung his eyes as he tumbled to a halt in the narthex and squinted at the chaos within.

There, in the midst of it all, stood Evander.

Their eyes collided across the burning nave.

Surprise widened the mage's gaze.

"Sorry I'm late!" Viggo called out, a grin tugging at his lips despite the dire situation.

Relief danced across Evander's face.

"Your timing could use some work!" he shot back, voice tight with tension. "But I'm damn glad to see you!"

Before Viggo could respond, a bolt of sinister energy cracked the air towards him.

Instinct had him diving to the side.

He rolled behind a fallen pew as more attacks pelted the slabs around him.

Though he was immune to most threats of a magical nature, there was no point taking any chances, especially in the face of magic he had not encountered before.

Viggo's pulse raced as he came up in a low crouch behind a cracked pillar. He peered around the column and took stock of the situation from his new vantage point.

A group of cloaked figures were advancing on Evander and the Met officers. Though the casters were doing their best to defend themselves with the wards in their weapons, they did not stand a chance against dark magic.

Viggo stiffened.

Some of the mages moved with eerie synchronicity, their pupils glowing an unnatural red. Realisation dawned, drawing a muffled curse from his lips.

He knew from Evander and Ginny's accounts that Magnus had looked that way when he'd been trying to hurt them.

Those mages are being controlled, just like Magnus was!

There was movement at the back of the church. Solomon was darting stealthily from pew to pew. Their eyes met through the smoke-filled air. Viggo gave a sharp nod. Solomon dipped his head and reached into his pouch. He withdrew a handful of small, glass marbles.

Viggo's breath misted in front of his face. A chill was spreading through the church. His startled gaze found Evander.

His heart stuttered.

Ice and wind swirled around the mage in a furious dance as he defended the casters at his side from their enemy's strikes, his handsome face set in a fierce mask. A wall of frigid air blasted outward from him, knocking back his nearest foe and briefly extinguishing some of the flames ripping through the church.

Viggo swallowed.

The power and control Evander demonstrated as he shielded his associates was a far cry from the cruel, capricious magic he'd grown up fearing.

This was magic wielded with the intent to protect.

A dark mage broke through Evander's defences and bore down on a young constable. Rufus moved to intercept the man, Evander too focused on the battle before him to notice the incursion.

Viggo surged to his feet and crossed the distance to the mage in a few long strides. Evander's magic proved a temporary obstruction, one he had to grit his teeth and force his body through, losing a precious couple of seconds.

He caught the mage's arm just as he was about to deliver a deadly spell to the inspector and wrenched it backward with brutal force.

The man howled in pain and fury. He twisted to face him. But Viggo was already moving, his fist connecting with the mage's jaw in a bone-jarring punch. The man crumpled, unconscious before he hit the ground.

"Watch out!" Rufus shouted.

Viggo dropped and rolled, the heat of a spell warming his skin as it passed over him. He rose on one knee on the far side of the nave and found another mage in his path. This one's eyes glowed the sickly red of possession, his face a veneer of inhuman focus.

"Now, Sly!" Viggo bellowed.

Solomon leapt atop a pew and tossed the marbles into the air.

They shattered amidst the dark mages, filling the space between them with a brief shower of glittering shards. Thick, silver fog billowed from the magical devices, the enchanted mist obscuring the vision of the enemy and causing several to stumble in confusion.

Griffiths and the constables took advantage of the chaos to attack, the runes on their glowing truncheons changing colour as they shifted from defensive to offensive magic.

Viggo jumped up and closed in on the controlled mage. He grappled the man and used his superior strength to force him to the ground before knocking him out with a blow to the head.

Solomon appeared on his right.

"Where the hell did they learn to fight like that?!" he mumbled.

Viggo looked around. His jaw nearly dropped.

Evander had engaged a pair of half-blinded mages, his attacks fluid and brutal as he delivered a series of strikes that rapidly incapacitated them. Two more figures closed in on him. He kneed one in the crotch, slammed the sides of his palms in the other one's ears, perforating his drums, and booted the first man in the belly with a powerful side kick.

Rufus similarly had his hands full with another mage. He ducked nimbly to avoid a blow to his temple and elbowed his assailant viciously in the nose as he straightened. Bone crunched. The man howled.

It was clear from the practiced way Evander and the inspector moved that they were used to defending themselves in a physical brawl.

"Well, aren't they full of surprises," Viggo muttered.

Power detonated around Evander a moment later, rapidly engulfing him in a whirlwind of elemental fury that made the Brute's breath catch all over again.

Ice lanced from the mage's fingertips, pinning one attacker to the wall. He gestured sharply with his other hand and sent a man flying across several pews with a violent gust of wind.

But for every foe Evander felled, two more took their place.

Viggo scowled, aware they were still badly outnumbered.

They needed to even the odds.

"Can you herd them to the chancel?!" he yelled.

Evander glanced his way and nodded grimly.

Viggo took out a short metal stick from the pouch inside his coat as the mage used wind and ice to drive their enemy to the back of the church. He hesitated for a split second, old instincts warring with necessity.

Using any kind of magic, even defensively, went against everything he'd believed for so long.

A pained cry from one of the constables made the decision for him.

Viggo activated the disruptor rod. It hummed to life in his hand.

He drew his arm back and hurled it towards the dark mages.

A ripple of energy pulsed outward from the device as it dropped towards the cloaked figures. The mages cursed, their spells fizzling out as the disruptor's field interfered with their casting.

Evander's eyes widened as he registered what Viggo had done.

But there was no time for explanations.

Viggo charged forward, taking advantage of the mages' momentary weakness to engage them directly before the effects of the anti-magic device faded.

CHAPTER 32

Viggo moved on instinct, his fists blurring and smacking into flesh as he ducked and weaved. Evander stood at his back, the ice and wind he'd manifested fending off dangerous spells as the mages least affected by the disruptor rod resumed their attacks.

They fell into a rhythm, moving together as if they'd fought side by side for years. When a spell slipped past Viggo's guard, Evander was there to deflect it. When a mage got too close to Evander, Viggo was there to put them down hard.

Even in the heat of battle, that fact thrilled Viggo like little else could.

Still, he couldn't shake a niggling sense of unease even as they fought.

This felt all too convenient. Too perfectly set up. His gaze swept the chaos, searching for the puppet master behind it all.

A mage crouched behind the altar a short distance away. He was watching the melee with calculated interest.

Unlike some of the others, his eyes didn't glow red.

He must be the leader!

"Evander!" Viggo jerked his head towards the altar.

Evander followed his gaze. "That's the man suspected of killing Millbrook." His expression hardened. "Cover me!"

Viggo shifted closer to Evander and used his bulk to shield the mage as they advanced across the church. Solomon, Rufus, and the officers still conscious noticed their movement and adjusted their own positions to provide additional protection.

The dark mage's lips curved in a cruel smile when Viggo and Evander neared the altar. He seemed undaunted by their approach.

"The Ice Mage and his pet Brute. How touching."

Viggo ground his teeth and took a threatening step forward. Evander's hand on his arm held him back.

"It's over." Evander's voice was cold and steely as he addressed the dark mage. "Release your hold on those mages and surrender."

The man's laughter sent a chill down Viggo's spine.

"Oh, I don't think so. In fact, I think you'll find this is only the beginning."

He raised his hand, the ring on his finger pulsing with a surge of malevolent energy.

Viggo tensed, ready to push Evander out of the way of whatever spell was coming. But instead of attacking, the mage snapped his fingers.

Dark magic bloomed from the inky gemstone atop the

ring, wrapping the man in thick billows that quickly concealed his form.

Viggo's eyes rounded. "What the—?!"

Startled shouts rose behind him and Evander. They spun around.

The dark mages were fading within identical black clouds, the ones they held sway over dragged passively into the sinister miasma.

Their leader's mocking voice echoed around the church.

"Until next time, Ice Mage."

He melted into the shadows faster than Viggo's eye could follow.

"No!" Evander rushed forward with an outstretched hand.

His fingers closed on fading wisps.

Evander's chest heaved as he stood there, his expression glassy with disbelief.

"We need to go after them!" Viggo was already moving towards the door at the side of the church. "They can't have gone far!"

Evander shuddered and grabbed his wrist. "We can't." He met Viggo's confused gaze and shook his head, frustration thickening his voice. "We need to stop the fire from spreading!"

The screams and shouts rising from outside finally registered in Viggo's hearing. His heart sank.

He followed Evander as the mage moved swiftly towards the main exit.

The magical fire in the building had started to abate.

Evander created a tunnel of wind for their safe passage nonetheless.

Viggo's throat closed up when they emerged from the church.

His worse fears had come to pass.

The blaze had spread and was engulfing the surrounding area. Flames leapt from building to building, fed by dry wood and thatch and fuelled by dark magic.

Viggo spotted Finn where he stood in a bucket chain at the bottom of the hill, his red hair bright against the billowing smoke and his face covered in soot as he and the volunteer brigade that formed the fire squad in this part of the slums shouted directions at the petrified locals. Solomon joined him, the thrall having slipped out of the side of the church to avoid the Met officers inside.

Evander's face set in grim lines at the sight of the chaos gripping the ghetto.

"I have to stop this fire. Or this entire neighbourhood will burn!"

Viggo's heart thundered against his ribs, all thoughts of pursuing the escaping mages gone from his mind in the face of the destruction being wreaked around them.

"*Can* you stop it?"

Evander clenched his jaw at the question before starting down the hill.

"I have to try at least. It'll be too late by the time the Phoenix Brigade and the Salamander Corps get here."

In contrast to the Soot Squads of the East End, the Phoenix Brigade and the Salamander Corps were elite fire services that employed highly trained mages and utilised advanced magical artefacts, the Salamander Corps specialising in magical and alchemical fires.

Viggo had often expressed his disgust at the irony of those two squads mainly serving the richer suburbs of the capital. The chances of a large-scale fire breaking out was higher in the slums, where non-magical means of lighting and heating were still extensively used.

He curbed his bleak thoughts and fell in step beside Evander.

"What do you need?"

Gratitude flashed in Evander's eyes as he glanced his way.

"Just...stay close."

Emotion tightened Viggo's chest. That Evander was calling on him for support made him incredibly happy despite the awful circumstances.

To his surprise, Evander stopped halfway down the slope. He took a deep breath and widened his stance.

Viggo realised he needed the vantage point to see where to direct his magic.

The air around them grew heavy with power as the mage raised his hands.

Water coalesced out of thin air above the burning buildings, forming swirling streams that danced at Evander's command. He guided them to the flames, dousing fire after fire from the furthermost blazes and working his way inward.

Goosebumps broke out across Viggo's skin as he watched him work.

This was what it truly meant to be a mage. Not just raw

power, but the ability to shape the very elements to one's will.

He could see the toll it was taking on Evander however. Perspiration began beading the mage's brow and his breathing grew increasingly laboured as he fought to control the massive amounts of water he was conjuring.

The closest conflagrations resisted his power, still tainted with dark magic.

"Dammit!" Evander cursed.

He retracted his powers and shuddered as he pressed his hands to his knees.

The water drenching the air dissipated.

Viggo's stomach churned. They were going to need the Salamander Corps after all.

Evander wiped rivulets of sweat from his face with the back of his hand, brow furrowed and gaze dark with resolve.

"Viggo?"

"Yes?"

"Brace yourself."

Viggo blinked at the warning, confused.

The mage straightened, his jaw clenched tight. He spread his arms a little and closed his eyes.

A different kind of magic imbued the air, strong and thick with the rich smell of fresh earth. The ground started shaking beneath Viggo. He stumbled and widened his stance, startled.

Movement drew his eyes. His breath froze.

Soil was lifting off the ground, tiny particles that moved against gravity as they rose in the air. Viggo looked around jerkily as the tombstones in the graveyard began trembling.

Evander's eyes snapped open.

"If you can't douse a fire with water, you can choke it with earth!" he growled.

The muscles in his neck bunched. He grunted, his face red.

Viggo stepped closer without thinking and placed a hand on his back. A tremor ran through the mage's body at his touch. But Evander's concentration never wavered.

Then the topsoil on the entire hill heaved, causing grave markers to tilt precariously and smash into one another, and the church building to creak.

Viggo and Evander were left standing on a narrow hump of intact dirt.

CHAPTER 33

VIGGO COULD ONLY WATCH IN HEART-POUNDING AWE AS Evander's magic blanketed the sky above the entire neighbourhood with a mantle of earth. Frightened screams rent the air as it swallowed the sun.

Wind magic swelled protectively around them a moment before Evander released the blanket of soil. It crashed down with the thunderous sound, smothering the magical fires and putting out the errant flames springing back to life here and there.

Viggo stared, his pulse racing so fast he felt fairly dizzy at the overwhelming power the mage was displaying.

Evander swayed.

Viggo caught him before he collapsed. "I've got you!"

Evander managed a weak smile and clutched his arm.

"Thanks." He straightened on trembling legs. "I think I might have overdone it a bit."

Viggo swallowed, his mouth dry. "Just a bit."

His gaze roamed the shocking scene around them. Though smoke still clouded the air, the fire that had threatened to engulf the slums had died out.

He chuckled.

"What?" Evander said, puzzled.

"I think we'll have to call this one the Great Mud Bath of the 1800s."

The dirt Evander had used to put out the blaze had mixed with the water still soaking people, buildings, and the ground alike, turning everything to sludge.

Finn was cursing and spitting mud out of his mouth down below.

Strangled laughter left Evander.

With the immediate danger passed, the reality of what had just happened began to sink in. Viggo observed the scorched buildings before focusing a frown at the church.

This had been no random attack.

"It was a trap," Evander said quietly, reading his mind. "An anonymous letter was sent to the Met this afternoon. It was a setup to lure us here. To lure *me* here."

Viggo clenched his jaw as he met the mage's gaze.

"Why? What were they after?"

"The vial."

Viggo stared, nonplussed. "What vial?"

Evander grimaced. "Oh. I didn't tell you about the vial." He paused. "To be fair, it's evidence in an active murder case, so it's not as if I could talk openly about it anyway."

Viggo sighed at his defensive tone.

"I'm not going to blame you for doing your job, Evander."

Relief brightened Evander's eyes. Viggo wanted to kiss him then.

Evander faltered and chewed his lip.

"Those devices you used. The fog and that thing that disrupted their magic. Where did you get them?"

Viggo tensed, acutely aware of the weight of the pouch against his chest. He'd known this conversation was coming, but that didn't make it any easier.

"*Nightshade* has—connections," he said carefully. "Ways of acquiring things most people can't get their hands on."

Evander narrowed his eyes. "They're illegal," he said.

It wasn't a question.

Viggo met his gaze steadily. "Yes and no," he admitted. "They're not officially classed as criminal artefacts under the laws of this land." He paused. "Let's just say they've saved the lives of *Nightshade* agents more times than I can count. In our line of work, we can't afford to be defenceless against magic."

He expected anger or at least disappointment. But Evander just looked tired.

"I understand," the mage said softly. "I may not like it, but...I understand."

Viggo felt something in his chest loosen at those words. He cupped Evander's face gently.

"Thank you."

Their tender moment was interrupted by the arrival of Rufus, looking harried and smoke-stained as he stomped down a path that was no longer there. The inspector froze in his tracks at the sight of the mud-stained slums.

"Did you use your earth magic?!" His shocked gaze

moved to Evander and Viggo. He stiffened, eyes shrinking to accusing slits. "Why is he holding you?"

Evander flushed and moved out of Viggo's arms. Viggo released him reluctantly and frowned at the inspector.

"Thanks for coming to help, Viggo," he said sarcastically. "I really appreciate you saving my ass back there."

"What?" Confusion wrinkled Rufus's brow.

Evander sighed.

The inspector finally understood Viggo's jibe and had the grace to look contrite.

"Oh. Yes, er, thanks." Suspicion clouded Rufus's face all over again. "Why *are* you here anyway?"

Viggo cursed under his breath.

Evander intervened. "What's our status?"

"Most of the mages escaped," Rufus said grimly. "But we managed to capture two of the ones they were controlling."

Surprise jolted Viggo. "You did?"

Evander stared. "How?"

"Their shadow manipulation wasn't enough to make all of them vanish. The pair we've taken into custody reappeared after you left the building. They're unconscious, but alive."

Viggo's scalp prickled at the name of the dark magic ability the mages had used. It was clear Evander and Rufus had come across it before in their line of work.

"What of our men?" Evander asked tensely.

"There are no serious injuries among them, thank God." The inspector blew out a sigh and ran a hand through his hair.

"And Constable Weir?"

Rufus's expression softened a little at the concern clouding Evander's face.

"He'll be fine once he sees a healer. Those cuts might leave scars though."

"Better he lives with scars than be six feet under," Evander muttered. "Have Griffiths take the mages back to headquarters." A muscle twitched in his cheek. "And make sure no one touches the cursed gems on their neck. I want Mrs. Scarborough to examine those devices as soon as possible."

A heavy silence fell between them as the sun began to set over the scarred buildings of the slum, casting their shadows across the church yard.

Viggo could almost see the wheels turning in Evander's mind, piecing together the puzzle of what had happened here.

"We need to regroup," Evander said in a preoccupied tone. "This incident changes everything. We're dealing with something far more dangerous and coordinated than we initially thought."

Unease tightened Viggo's gut at his words.

"You suspect there's an organisation behind this?"

Evander hesitated before bobbing his head, his expression troubled.

"Possibly. Or someone extremely determined who has a definite objective in mind. One that goes well beyond murdering a Charm Weaver." Frustration underscored his voice. "What that goal is we don't yet know."

"I'll have our men secure the area and take statements

from witnesses who might know what went on in that church," Rufus grunted.

Viggo frowned. "What's your next move?"

"We go back to the beginning." Evander looked from Viggo to Rufus, his jaw setting in a hard line. "Alastair Millbrook's workshop. There has to be something we missed there, some clue as to what that vial is and why they want it so badly."

The mage hesitated a moment before squaring his shoulders and turning to Viggo.

"We'll need all the help we can get. If you're willing, I'd like to bring *Nightshade* in on this officially."

Viggo's pulse quickened. Evander's plan suited his objectives of finding out who had hurt Magnus.

Still, he was surprised by the offer.

"Are you sure?" he asked quietly.

Evander nodded solemnly. "I'm sure." A faint smile curved his lips. "Whatever's coming, I want you and *Nightshade* on our side."

Viggo's stomach flip-flopped at his words. In that moment, he felt a fierce surge of...something. Pride. Affection. Desire.

Whatever it was, it made him want to pull Evander close and never let go.

Instead, he settled for a small nod.

Rufus's gaze danced between Evander and Viggo, evidently picking up on the cozy vibe and not liking it one bit from the scowl that quickly darkened his face.

A commotion at the end of the street had them turning.

Viggo grimaced. "Looks like the cavalry is finally here."

The dying light glinted off the shiny brass and copper tanks atop the Phoenix Brigade's horse-drawn, magically-enhanced, steam fire engine, the runes and symbols on the body of the vehicle glowing and humming with arcane energy. The Salamander Corps' smaller Special Unit carriage was behind it, along with a slew of police wagons.

Evander rubbed the back of his neck and sighed ruefully.

"Want to ride to the Met with us?" he asked Viggo. "We're going to need a statement from you and Solomon."

"Alright." To his everlasting surprise, Viggo realised the prospect of visiting Scotland Yard again did not fill him with apprehension, unlike yesterday.

He spoke briefly to Finn before he and Solomon climbed in the carriage that had brought Evander and Rufus to the church.

Viggo was entertaining the idea of asking Evander if he wanted to have supper later as they approached Scotland Yard, when the mage leaned forward jerkily and let loose a string of curse words so colourful it made Rufus suck in air and Solomon's eyes bulge.

"What is it?" Viggo said tensely, senses on alert once more.

Evander did not reply.

Viggo followed the mage's gaze and saw what had captured his dismayed stare. Coldness gripped him.

A carriage stood outside the entrance of the Met.

It was a grand, state landau painted a deep blue, with a gilt trim and elegant wheels with spokes picked out in gold leaf. Four white horses with manes and tails braided with blue and gold ribbons stood at the front, their leather harnesses adorned with brass fittings polished to a mirror shine.

Even though Viggo had never seen the likes of it before, he recognised the coat of arms emblazoned on the vehicle's doors.

It was a carriage belonging to the royal family.

CHAPTER 34

EVANDER PACED THE LENGTH OF THE OPULENT ANTEROOM, each step leaving a faint smudge of soot on the pristine marble floor. The royal mages guarding the entrance to the Queen's private chambers watched him warily, some with awe, most with disapproval.

He knew he looked a sight. His once-immaculate uniform was torn and stained with smoke and mud, his hair wild and matted with sweat and ash. The events at the church had left their mark on him, both physically and mentally.

He'd barely had time to see to it that Viggo and the others were safely inside the Arcane Division's wing before the harried palace messenger who'd been looking all over Scotland Yard for him had found him and delivered the royal summons.

The terse note had made it clear that his presence was required immediately, regardless of his current state.

Dammit. They should at least let me clean up!

He'd asked if he could wash his face before the audience. The stony-faced mage who'd escorted him to the Queen's quarters had flatly refused.

"Her Majesty's orders were quite clear, your Grace." His tone had made it transparent that Evander's ducal title meant little here. "You are to be brought directly to her presence as you are."

Evander had sat there for a good hour before getting up and treading the stylish marble floor in front of the Queen's private chambers, blatantly ignoring the guards whose stares said they wished he'd sit back down quietly.

He knew the Queen was deliberately leaving him to stew.

The irony of the situation wasn't lost on Evander. He, who could level this entire wing of the palace with magic if he so wished, had been reduced to anxiously awaiting the Queen's pleasure.

A clock on the mantelpiece chimed the hour, its delicate tones seeming to mock Evander's impatience all while adding another knot to his shoulders. He turned, ready to demand entry once more, only to find the doors to the Queen's chambers swinging open of their own accord.

One of the Queen's attendants stepped out.

"Her Majesty will see you now," he intoned sombrely.

Evander squared his shoulders and strode past him, chin held high. Whatever the Queen had to say, he would face it with the dignity befitting his station.

The private sitting room he entered was a study in

understated elegance. Delicate floral wallpaper interspersed with priceless paintings, some new from the last time he'd visited the place, adorned the walls. A fire crackled merrily in the hearth, keeping away the cold seeping through the windows and casting a warm glow over the rich furnishings.

Evander did not bother inspecting the rest of the chamber.

Because there, seated in a high-backed chair that might as well have been a throne, her posture impeccable despite her small stature, was Queen Victoria.

Her round face was framed by dark hair pulled back severely under a delicate lace cap and bore the lines of age and responsibility. She wore her usual black silk dress, its colour a testament to her perpetual grieving for Prince Albert, and a plethora of dark mourning jewellery.

Despite her advanced years, there was an undeniable air of authority about her, a strength that seemed to fill the room. The weight of her crown, though not physically present, was palpable in her stare.

Evander bowed low, years of training taking over.

"Your Majesty," he murmured.

"Good God, Evander!" Victoria's voice was sharp with shock and disapproval. "What on earth happened to you?"

Evander schooled his face into a neutral expression as he straightened and met the Queen's piercing gaze.

"There was an incident in the slums, Your Majesty. A trap set by dark mages. I—"

Victoria cut him off with a wave of her hand. "Spare me the details." Her cold gaze raked him over, taking in every smudge and tear. "I can see well enough what sort of 'incident' it must have been. Really, Evander, presenting yourself to your Queen in such a state! What would your father say?"

The mention of his father sent a sharp pang through Evander's chest. It took every ounce of his willpower to stay impassive in the face of this unjust accusation.

"I apologise for my unseemly appearance, Your Majesty. I came as soon as I received your summons." He couldn't fully mask the bitterness lacing his tone. "I did request I be given access to a bathroom to—"

"Yes, well." Victoria sniffed, pretending to be oblivious to the fact that it was her orders that had kept him in a filthy state for God knows how long. "I suppose we must make allowances for the nature of your work." The way she said it made it clear exactly what she thought of his chosen profession. "Though that is precisely what we need to discuss."

Evander's stomach tightened. He'd known this conversation was coming from the moment his Archmage abilities had been revealed, but that didn't make the situation any less challenging.

"You made me a promise, Evander," Victoria said, her voice low and hard. "You swore to me that you would keep your abilities hidden. That you would not draw attention to yourself or your," she waved a hand angrily, "—unique position."

"Your Majesty, I—"

"I'm not finished!" The Queen's voice cracked like a whip, making her attendants jump. "Do you have any idea of the position you've put me in? Rumours are already flying! There have been whispers in the Court about your lineage for years, about why a Duke with your pedigree would lower himself to common police work. And now this! An Archmage in the ranks of the Metropolitan Police. It's unprecedented, Evander. It's reckless."

Evander clenched his jaw, forcing himself to remain silent as Victoria continued her tirade.

"I've had quite enough of your fanciful aspirations," she stated bitingly. "This game of cops and robbers has gone on long enough. It's time for you to embrace your true role. You will resign from the Metropolitan Police with immediate effect. You will take up your proper place as the Duke of Ravenwood. And," her eyes shrank to slits, "you will find a suitable wife from high society and settle down, as befits a man of your station."

Something inside Evander finally snapped, the careful control he'd been maintaining crumbling in the face of Victoria's cruel demands.

"Everyone out," he growled, his voice quaking with barely suppressed power.

The attendants hesitated, looking to the Queen.

Magic surged through Evander. "*Now!*"

The room temperature plummeted. The attendants fled, the doors slamming shut behind them.

"How dare you—" Victoria began.

Evander cut her off.

"No, how dare *you!*" he roared. "You sit here in your gilded cage, passing judgment on a world you barely understand. Do you have any idea what's really happening out there? The suffering? The inequality? The injustice that festers in the very heart of your precious Empire?!"

Victoria's face flushed with anger. "Mind your tone, young man. I am still your Queen."

"And I am still a Prince of this realm," Evander shot back. "Royal blood runs through my veins! Or have you forgotten that inconvenient truth?" He fisted his hands. "The secret you're so desperate to keep hidden?!"

CHAPTER 35

Victoria almost vibrated with fury as she glared at him.

"I haven't forgotten anything," the Queen hissed. "I remember all too well the day your father came to me, begging me to overlook the fact that his son, the forgotten Prince, was a magical prodigy, the youngest Archmage this Empire had ever seen. Convincing me you would never become a hazard to the throne despite your powers." Victoria took a shuddering breath. "The threat you pose to the stability of the royal succession if your true nature and identity came to be known is something that has often preoccupied my thoughts since that day, child."

Evander's chest tightened even as he laughed bitterly.

"Stability? Is that what you call this farce of a society we've built? Where men and women are treated as less than human simply because they lack magic? Where corruption runs rampant and the powerful prey on the weak?!"

"You go too far, Evander," Victoria warned.

Evander was beyond caring at this point.

"I don't think I go far enough," he said icily. "You want me to quit the Met? To turn my back on the only real good I've ever done? To ignore the rot that's eating away at the foundations of this Empire?" He jutted his chin. "I won't do it. I *cannot* do it."

"It is not your place to question the natural order of things!" Victoria shouted, rising to her feet. "You have a duty to your bloodline, to your title—"

"*My duty is to justice!*" Evander bellowed. "To the people of this country, magical and non-magical alike. And if you can't see that, then perhaps it is time for a new perspective on the throne!"

The words hung in the air between them, sharp and dangerous.

Victoria's face went white, then red with wrath.

"You would threaten me? Your own flesh and blood?!"

"It's not a threat," Evander said, suddenly weary. His voice grew more composed. "It's the truth. The world is changing, Victoria. The old ways, the old prejudices. They can't last. And if the Crown doesn't change with them, it will be left behind."

Silence reigned for a long moment.

Evander could hear his own heart pounding in his ears, could feel the magic churning beneath his skin, eager for release. He took a deep breath, forcing it back down.

When Victoria spoke again, her voice was calm.

"You truly believe in this cause of yours, don't you?"

Evander nodded. "With every fibre of my being."

Victoria sank back into her chair, looking every one of her years.

"You remind me so much of your father sometimes," she murmured. "He had the same fire in his eyes when he believed in something."

The fight drained out of Evander at the mention of his father. He slumped into the chair across from Victoria, the heat of their argument fading and leaving him with a bitter aftertaste.

"I'm sorry. I was out of line. I shouldn't have said those things." He pinched the bridge of his nose. "Not like that, at least."

Victoria's mouth quirked in a small, sad smile. "Perhaps we both said things we regret." She sighed and reached out to pat Evander's hand. "Oh, my dear boy. What am I to do with you?"

Evander met her gaze squarely then, seeing not the strict monarch, but the woman who had been like an aunt to him growing up.

"Let me do my work," he said quietly. "Let me try to make a difference, in whatever way I can."

Victoria was silent for some time. She finally nodded, resignation etched in her face.

"Very well. I won't force you to resign from the Metropolitan Police. But," she held up a warning finger, "you must be more careful. The secret of your identity, of your place in the line of succession—it must remain hidden. For all our sakes."

"I understand," Evander said. "I'll do my best to be more discreet."

"See that you do." Though Victoria's tone was stern, there was a warmth in her eyes that belied her words. "I worry about you, you know. More than I perhaps should, given our complicated relationship."

A lump formed in Evander's throat.

"I know," he said softly. "And I'm grateful for it, truly."

Victoria cupped Evander's cheek in a gesture of surprising tenderness.

"We are blood, you and I," she said. "Never forget that, my dear. Whatever else may come between us, that bond will always remain."

Evander leaned into her touch, feeling some of the tension of the past few days begin to ease.

"I won't forget," he promised.

He left the Queen's chambers a short while later, his heart and mind ablaze with a storm of emotions.

Relief at having weathered Victoria's anger. Determination to continue his work with the Met. A lingering warmth from a rare moment of familial affection.

Underlying it all was a growing sense of dread. The attack at the church, the dark mages' mysterious agenda, and now this confrontation with Victoria.

It all pointed to a larger turmoil brewing on the horizon. One that could threaten not just Evander's carefully constructed life, but likely the very foundations of the society he'd sworn to protect.

Viggo's face rose before him. His belly tightened.

There was zero doubt in his mind that he'd be dragged kicking and screaming for an audience with the Queen if their burgeoning relationship ever came to light.

He'd long suspected Victoria had an inkling where his sexual interests lay. It was not a topic she would ever broach willingly. The fact that she'd re-iterated she wanted him to wed suggested she would rather forget about it.

One thing Evander was absolutely certain of.

He would never put a ring on a woman's finger and bind them to a marriage that would cage them both.

The guards at the palace gates snapped to attention as Evander approached, no doubt startled by his dishevelled appearance. He'd come inside the grounds in the landau after all. Evander nodded briskly to them, his mind racing ahead to what needed to be done next.

Graham and Samuel were standing outside by his carriage, their expressions betraying their concern in the light of the enchanted lamps lining the road. Rufus was with them.

The inspector's eyes widened at the sight of Evander.

"Good God!" he gasped, appalled. "They let you in there like that?!"

Evander shrugged. "The Queen insisted."

He glanced past Rufus to the interior of the carriage, a little hopeful.

It was empty.

Evander squashed his chagrin. "Did Viggo and Solomon go home?"

"Yes. I took their statements. *Nightshade* will keep looking into *Noctis Bloom* and start hunting for information on those dark mages. We've received the official approval from Winterbourne and my commander to bring Viggo's guild in."

Relief loosened Evander's shoulders. "Thanks, Rufus."

Rufus's sombre expression eased a little. "I'm only doing my job."

The inspector's gaze flitted to the imposing palace as they climbed inside the carriage.

"How did things go? Did Her Majesty rake you over the coals?" He hesitated, his face strained. "You're still a Special Arcane Investigator, right?"

Evander smiled faintly. "Yes, I am." He glanced at the Queen's official residence one last time as they pulled away from the pavement. "Our conversation was—enlightening."

Rufus watched him for a moment before sighing. "Ginny was right."

Evander shot a puzzled look at him. "About what?"

"You have cryptic down to an art form."

Evander stared at his irritated mien before snorting. "I'm not that bad."

"You are, really. We should call you the Sphinx."

They gazed fondly at one another.

"I'm glad you were there today, old friend," Evander murmured on a more serious note.

"And I you." Rufus looked out at the busy streets, a muscle jumping in his cheek. "I daresay Griffiths and I may not have made it out of that church alive had you not been with us."

Evander ran his fingers through his hair and grimaced at the soot coating his skin.

"I'll freshen up before we go take another look at Millbrook's workshop."

Rufus pinned him with a disbelieving stare before scowling.

"Like hell we are! You're going home, taking a bath, eating a hot meal, and going to bed, young man."

Evander blinked. "What are you, my mother?"

"And don't you forget it." Rufus crossed his arms and huffed. "You'll get a spanking if you misbehave."

Silence fell between them.

"Rufus?"

"Yes?"

"I feel I should make it clear that I'm not into spanking, in or out of the bedroom."

"Shut up, Evander."

CHAPTER 36

THE EVENTS OF THE PREVIOUS DAY WEIGHED HEAVILY ON Evander's mind as he and Rufus crossed Covent Garden on their way to Millbrook's workshop, Shaw scampering ahead of them.

He'd spent the morning compiling his report for Commander Winterbourne, each word carefully chosen to convey the gravity of the situation without revealing too much about how he'd used his Archmage powers to accomplish a feat that would likely go down into the annals of the capital's history as the strangest way a fire was ever put out.

As for the mages who'd been captured at the church, they were still unconscious. Mrs. Scarborough was in the process of examining the cursed gems on their necks to determined what kind of magic the dark mages had used to control their minds.

Evander had met briefly with the curse-breaker to apologise for what had happened the last time they'd met.

Mrs. Scarborough had brushed aside his apologies with an embarrassed expression.

"It is I who should be asking for your forgiveness, your Grace," the curse-breaker had said with a grimace. "Had you not used your Archmage powers when you did, I would have been in serious trouble and Mr. Graveoak would have died for certain."

The afternoon sun struggled to pierce the perpetual haze hanging over London as they turned into the street where the Charm Weaver's atelier was located. Evander got a taste of the unwelcome fame his future might hold when they approached the unassuming facade of the establishment.

Two familiar figures stood guard outside.

"Constable Fitch, Constable Bartley," Evander greeted lightly with a dip of his head. "I see you've drawn this assignment again."

Fitch snapped to attention.

"Yes, your Grace!" he barked, his gaze gleaming with reverence.

Bartley practically vibrated with excitement beside him.

"Is it true, your Grace?" the constable burst out, unable to contain himself. "About what happened at the church yesterday? They're saying you summoned a tidal wave out of thin air!"

Evander stared. "I'm afraid the reports have been somewhat exaggerated."

Rufus cut his eyes to Shaw. The forensic mage avoided his gaze and began inspecting her boots with questionable eagerness.

Fitch elbowed his partner.

"Don't be daft, Ollie," he hissed. "It wasn't a tidal wave. I heard his Grace called down lightning from a clear sky!"

Evander swallowed a groan. The rumours were getting worse by the minute.

Rufus scowled at Shaw.

The mage shrugged innocently. "You'd think they'd never seen magic before."

"I'm pretty certain you were the first to hound his Grace this morning about it when he arrived at Scotland Yard," Rufus said scathingly.

Shaw sucked air between her teeth. "Hound is a strong word, sir. I prefer expressing healthy curiosity."

Evander sighed at their habitual bickering and proceeded inside the building without waiting for them. The familiar scent of metal, oil, and chemicals lingered in the air when he entered Millbrook's workshop.

Rufus and Shaw soon joined him.

"Let's go through everything again." Evander swept the room with a sharp gaze. "We must have missed something yesterday."

They spent the next hour meticulously combing through the workshop. Evander examined Millbrook's magical artefacts and equipment while Rufus pored over the Charm Weaver's ledgers and papers. Shaw scrutinised every nook and cranny with the specialised forensic tools she carried in her bag.

Evander was studying the half-finished pocket watch he'd spotted the previous day when Shaw mumbled to herself.

"I wonder why everything happened here."

Rufus looked up from a stack of invoices. "What's that?"

Evander turned from Millbrook's workbench.

Shaw squatted at the other end of the room. She was staring at the blood stain Evander had exposed the previous day.

"Millbrook was struck here." Her brooding gaze moved to the furnace and the area next to the table where Evander's Shadow Imprint had revealed the spot the Charm Weaver met his dire end. "He likely stumbled or was dragged over there."

Rufus frowned. "And?"

"Millbrook put some pretty clever wards on this workshop to alert him to intruders." Shaw chewed her lip. "He must have known when that mage broke into the building. So why was he still standing here? Why didn't he try to leave?"

Evander's scalp prickled.

"Maybe he didn't know whoever broke in intended to kill him. Or maybe he got distracted by a formula or one of those engineering diagrams." Rufus indicated the chalkboard.

The Artificers at the AFD had already examined Millbrook's work and concluded there was nothing sinister about what he was doing in his workshop.

Still, Evander had a feeling Shaw was on to something.

It was in moments like these that the forensic mage demonstrated exactly why she was a rising star in the Arcane Division.

He watched as she rose, her focused gaze scanning the

area around her. She took a step here and there, her fingers occasionally brushing against surfaces.

A sudden stillness came over her in front of the hearth.

"Your Grace, I think Millbrook was surprised here."

Evander and Rufus joined her in a few quick steps.

Shaw pointed to a barely visible scuff mark on the floor.

"It looks like he might have struggled with his assailant before he was struck on the head. There's a faint impact mark on the mantle, just here." Her finger traced a fresh chip in the stone. "The poker probably missed him the first time. I'd wager Millbrook was standing here when his attacker arrived. But he wasn't just standing idle." The forensic mage narrowed her eyes. "He was doing something. Something that had his whole attention."

Evander followed her stare to the hearth. His pulse quickened.

"Rufus, did Mortimer mention anything about soot on Millbrook's body?"

Rufus lowered his brows as he thought back to the physical examiner's report. "Now that you mention it, yes. There was some soot under his fingernails. We assumed it was from his work, but—"

"But what if it wasn't?" Evander finished.

They stared at one another, the thrill of being close to uncovering another clue brightening their gazes.

Evander crouched in front of the fireplace and called on his wind magic. He wielded his powers and carefully lifted away the layers of soot and ash filling the hearth, only to stiffen a moment later.

Rufus frowned and leaned in closer. "What is that?"

Blood pounded in Evander's veins as he studied what he'd unearthed. He carefully lifted the object in a handkerchief.

It was a small wooden cylinder about the length of his palm, looked to made like a piece of kindling.

He could feel magic humming faintly from it.

"It's enchanted." Surprise jolted Evander when he recognised the power tickling his skin. "Some kind of fireproofing spell."

His gaze swung to the hearth. The reason he hadn't sensed its presence yesterday was likely because Millbrook had concealed it deep beneath the ash.

Shaw shifted from one foot to the other. "Go on, your Grace. Open it!"

Evander twisted the top of the cylinder with delicate precision, Rufus and Shaw watching with bated breath. Something rattled as he upended the contents in his hand.

It was a key wrapped in a blank piece of paper.

Evander held the metal up to the meagre sunlight seeping through the window, his heart racing.

It was too small to be intended for a regular door lock.

A safe, perhaps? Or some kind of box?!

Whatever the key represented, it was their first solid lead to Millbrook's murderer.

"Why put it in that?" Shaw said.

She pointed at the scrap of paper in Evander's hand with a puzzled expression. The edges were torn, indicating Millbrook has hastily ripped it from a page.

The hairs lifted off Evander's nape, warning him they were on the cusp of another discovery.

"Maybe he wrote something on it in invisible ink,"

Rufus suggested. He flinched at Evander and Shaw's stares. "What? It could happen."

"You're a genius, sir!" Shaw blurted out. She fixed Evander with an excited look. "I bet it's enchanted, your Grace."

Evander nodded, the thrill shining in the forensic mage's eyes dancing through him. He focused his powers and rubbed the paper carefully between his fingers, trying to gauge the magic it contained.

His belly clenched at what he sensed.

Fire Magic? Again?! But—how? Millbrook wasn't a fire—!

Realisation struck him like a bolt of thunder. His gaze landed on the engraving tools next to the half-finished pocket watch.

"Of course," Evander mumbled numbly.

"What is it your Grace?" Shaw asked tensely.

"I was wondering how Millbrook was able to cast Fire Magic," Evander explained. "He didn't. He used his engraving tools to carve out fire magic spells."

Rufus and Shaw stared wide-eyed at the items on the workbench.

Evander couldn't help but experience a deep sense of admiration for the dead Charm Weaver.

Alastair Millbrook had been a genius.

"So, you're saying he used Fire Magic to enchant that paper?" Rufus said, his tone still sceptical.

"Yes."

Shaw's expression grew determined. "I hate to sound like an arsonist, your Grace, but there's only one thing for it."

Rufus's eyes rounded.

"Wait! You surely don't mean he should—!"

A hard smile curved Shaw's mouth. "Too late."

The air was shimmering around Evander's fingertips, fire magic pulsing in his blood stream in a controlled flow.

Rufus sucked in air when sparks lifted off his skin and ignited the letters hidden in the paper, scorching out a word.

Rosa.

They stared at it breathlessly.

"Is that his wife's name?" Rufus said.

Shaw shook her head. "His wife is called Martha." Concern wrinkled her brow. "We still don't know her whereabouts or that of their son William. Their family home in Finsbury was empty when we last called there two days ago. Neighbours reported they hadn't seen a soul on the premises in well over a week."

Evander's mind raced.

Does that mean Millbrook knew he was in danger and had his family go into hiding?!

"Millbrook's family might be able to tell us who Rosa is and what this key opens." Evander turned to Rufus. "We should send a message to *Nightshade*. Viggo and his people can help us track them down."

Rufus nodded reluctantly. "I'll get Fitch onto it."

It was late afternoon by the time they finished checking the workshop for further clues and finding none. Bartley was snoring softly where he leaned against the wall when they exited the building.

The constable woke up with a guilty start when Rufus shut the door sharply.

"It's a good thing we weren't attacked by dark mages, Bartley," the inspector said sourly.

"I'm sorry, sir," the constable mumbled, cheeks growing a more ruddy colour than usual. "My ma says I have the constitution of a sloth."

"Why don't you two take the evidence back to Scotland Yard before you sign off for the day?" Evander suggested to Shaw and Rufus. "We should give that cylinder and the key to the Artificers to analyse."

Rufus frowned. "Won't Graham be waiting for you at the Met?"

"I told him I wish to walk home today."

"Alright," the inspector said reluctantly. "Be careful."

CHAPTER 37

THE SETTING SUN WAS PAINTING COLOURFUL STREAKS across the sky as Evander set off towards Mayfair. The streets grew busier, the shadows lengthening as people hurried home from work while others ventured out for evening entertainments.

He almost missed the figure that detached itself from an alley when he passed Piccadilly Circus and entered Regent Street, so engrossed was he in his thoughts.

The man moved with purposeful stealth towards him.

Magic coiled beneath Evander's skin. Though he was reluctant to showcase his powers in the middle of one of London's most glamorous shopping districts, he would defend himself if he had to.

A familiar voice reached his ears before he could act.

"Fancy seeing you here, your Grace."

Evander's shoulders loosened at the sight of Solomon.

"Mr. Barden," he acknowledged with a smidgen of caution. "I wasn't expecting company."

"Please, call me Sly. I owe you that much after what you did yesterday."

"Alright." Evander met the thrall's gaze steadily. "And you can address me as Evander."

Solomon grimaced. "How about we take it one day at a time?"

They fell into step.

"Why are you here?" Evander said curiously. "You can't have found Millbrook's family already."

"Viggo thought it would be prudent to keep an eye on things, given recent events."

Evander's eyes widened. "He sent you to guard me?"

Solomon sighed. "I know. You, the Archmage, being protected by me, a thrall. I told him it was ridiculous, but he was having none of it."

Evander found himself suppressing a foolish smile. He forced himself to focus on the business at hand.

"Has *Nightshade* uncovered anything about the city's dark mage problem?"

"Yes." Solomon tucked his hands in his pockets, his brow furrowing. "The *Noctis Bloom* business is booming." He glanced at Evander. "Looks like someone is intending to use a boatload of dark magic soon."

Evander's brief reprieve faded as the thrall filled him in on *Nightshade's* most recent findings, including whispers in the underworld hinting at some kind of large-scale sinister plot on the horizon.

The mage sensed there was something else on Solomon's mind from the brooding looks the thrall occasionally stole at him as they walked.

Solomon finally spoke when they neared Mayfair.

"Your Grace, may I be frank?"

"Of course."

Solomon hesitated, like he was choosing his words carefully.

"This thing between you and Viggo. I have concerns."

Evander stiffened, conscious the thrall was overstepping the mark. What he and Viggo chose to do was their personal business. Still, he was curious to know what was troubling the Brute's right-hand man.

"What sort of concerns?"

Solomon didn't answer straight away.

"Viggo has been through a lot," the thrall finally said, his voice uncharacteristically soft. "He doesn't trust people easily, especially not mages. But he trusts you." Solomon glanced at him. "If that trust ends up being misplaced, I don't know what it will do to him."

Understanding dawned on Evander. Solomon's apprehension wasn't based on prejudice or disapproval.

"You're worried I'll hurt him," he said quietly.

A muscle twitched in Solomon's cheek.

"Viggo is more than just my boss. He's one of my dearest friends. I've seen him weather storms that would break most men. But this? If this goes wrong…" The thrall trailed off. "He has never looked at another man or woman the way he looks at you."

Evander swallowed, thrilled in part by Solomon's words and equally nervous by their gravity. It wasn't as if he hadn't had similar worries, particularly in view of the secret he had yet to reveal to Viggo.

"I understand your disquiet. And I appreciate your loyalty to Viggo. But I want you to know that my feelings for him are genuine. I would never intentionally hurt him. I—" Evander stopped and clenched his fists. "Viggo means a lot to me."

Solomon studied him intently, as if trying to read the truth in his eyes. Whatever he saw there seemed to satisfy him, at least for now.

"See to it that you don't," he grunted. "Viggo deserves happiness." He hesitated. "And for what it's worth, I think you might be good for him."

Evander's townhouse came into view.

"See you soon, your Grace." Solomon slowed and melted into the shadows.

Evander climbed the steps to his front door, his mind full of the exchange he'd just had with Viggo's right-hand man. He was barely inside when Hargrove appeared, a strange look on his face.

"You have a visitor, my Lord," the manservant said as Evander gave him his coat. "The Ironfist—I mean, Mr. Stonewall is here to see you. I've shown him to your study."

Evander's heart skipped a beat. "Thank you, Hargrove. I'll see to him now."

He made his way swiftly to the study and paused outside for a moment to collect himself before twisting the doorknob.

Viggo was standing by the fireplace, his broad frame silhouetted against the light of the dancing flames. He turned when Evander entered. His dark eyes scanned the mage from head to toe, as if checking for injuries.

"You're late."

Evander registered the concern underlying his gruff

note. A mixture of emotions clogged his throat at the sight of the Brute, his composure rattled once more.

"My apologies." He forced a small smile. "The investigation took longer than any of us expected."

Viggo relaxed. "As long as you're safe."

Evander crossed the floor and indicated the damask sofa opposite the fireplace.

"Did you find anything?" the Brute said, sitting beside him.

Evander filled him in on the discoveries at Millbrook's workshop; the hidden cylinder, the key, and the mysterious *Rosa*.

"The Met has no leads as to the whereabouts of Millbrook's family," the mage finished. "I hope your guild can help us track them down. I'm certain they're pivotal to unravelling this mystery."

"We'll do what we can. *Nightshade* has contacts all over the country."

"Thank you," Evander said softly. He hesitated. "And thank you for sending Solomon to keep an eye on me. It wasn't necessary, but I appreciate the thought."

Something flickered in Viggo's gaze, an emotion Evander couldn't quite name. The Brute shifted closer, close enough that his knee brushed Evander's leg and his intoxicating heat wrapped around him.

"I'm aware you're a powerful Archmage, but I can't stop worrying about you." He took Evander's chin in a gentle hold and traced his lips with his thumb, his gaze so intense Evander's toes almost curled. "I doubt this fear of mine will ever go away, however long this lasts." Viggo paused, his eyes glittering with heat. "I, for one, hope it lasts a long, long time."

The admission, so plainly stated, sent a shiver down Evander's spine and roused his heart. The air between them ignited with an attraction that threatened to rob him of his senses.

"Viggo—"

Whatever Evander had been about to say was lost in the Brute's searing kiss. He melted into his embrace with a soft groan, his hands rising to tangle in Viggo's hair.

The kiss was everything Evander had imagined and more. Passionate, savage, with an underlying tenderness that made his heart ache. He lost himself in the sensation. In the feel of Viggo's strong arms around him. In the heady taste of him on his tongue.

They broke apart only when the need for air became too great, both of them panting and trembling. Evander tugged Viggo down for another hungry kiss, only to freeze when a strangled sound came from the doorway.

Mrs. Sinclair stood there, a tea tray in her hands and an expression of utter shock on her face.

Hargrove popped his head around the door.

"I knew it!" the manservant hissed with undisguised glee. "He's shagging the Ironfist Brute!"

Viggo's jaw dropped open. He snorted in the next instant.

Mrs. Sinclair's face turned an unhealthy hue as she cut her eyes to Hargrove.

The manservant sobered.

"I beg your pardon, my Lord," the housekeeper said

stiffly, her gaze flitting to Viggo. "I didn't mean to interrupt."

Evander flushed, wishing a hole would appear in the floor and swallow him whole.

"It's quite alright, Mrs. Sinclair," he managed. "You can leave the tea and go."

Mrs. Sinclair came in and set the tray down next to the sofa. She dipped her head courteously at Viggo.

"It's a pleasure to meet you, Mr. Stonewall. Our young Samuel is very much enamoured with your achievements." Her expression grew cautious. "I hope you and his Grace continue to get along."

"It's a pleasure to meet you too." Viggo smiled faintly. "And yes, I fully intend to do so."

Whatever the housekeeper saw in the Brute's face made relief gleam in her eyes. She exited the study with Hargrove, but not before the manservant released a parting shot under his breath.

"Well, I suppose that's one way to blow off steam. Ride the biggest one-eyed snake in London."

"Mr. Hargrove!" Mrs. Sinclair snapped.

The door closed on the housekeeper berating the manservant in a low voice full of ire.

Evander groaned.

"I like them," Viggo said with a chuckle.

His laughter vibrated under Evander's hand.

Evander spread his fingers unconsciously, marvelling at the hardness of the Brute's chest, only to freeze when Viggo's breath caught.

He snatched his hand away, his cheeks burning. "I'm sorry."

Viggo captured his fingers and pressed them to his heart.

"Don't be," the Brute said gruffly. "I like it when you touch me." He hesitated, a hint of vulnerability swirling in the depths of his eyes. "To be honest, I was concerned about how your servants might receive me."

Evander felt a sudden rush of affection for Viggo. That this fierce, strong Brute could face down dark mages without flinching but worried about the opinion of his household staff humbled him. It made him grateful once more to whatever Fate had made their paths cross.

"They'll accept you wholeheartedly," he assured Viggo, reaching up to cup his cheek. "They're loyal to me and they want me to be happy. And you," Evander's voice dropped to a near whisper, "you make me very happy."

Viggo's face softened. He leaned in for another kiss, this one sweeter than the ones they'd already shared.

It turned heated all too soon.

Viggo wrenched their mouths apart a moment later, his fingers digging possessively in Evander's back and his face hard with desire.

"Evander?"

"Yes?" Evander panted, his cock throbbing between his thighs.

"I want to see you ride the biggest one-eyed snake in London." Viggo's gaze darted feverishly to the Persian rug in front of the fire.

Evander's stomach clenched at that illicit vision. He narrowed his eyes.

"We talked about this."

"But—" Viggo protested.

Evander pressed a finger to his mouth, his tone firm. "No buts. We can't do anything more than kiss until this case is over."

Viggo frowned. "Mark my words, mage. We're going to fornicate over this entire room when that happens."

Evander looked at him blankly before chortling, much to Viggo's annoyance.

CHAPTER 38

THE HALLS OF THE ARCANE FORENSICS DIVISION HUMMED with activity around Evander as he navigated them with Rufus the next day. Mages and alchemists hurried past, arms laden with scrolls, artefacts, and mysterious bottles.

A few startled and stumbled at the sight of Evander.

He resigned himself to their gawking stares.

The rumours about him being an Archmage were now firmly rooted in London society following more articles detailing the impossible feat he'd achieved at the church two days past. Not only were they claiming he'd saved hundreds of lives, police officers and thralls alike, they also incorrectly stated he'd been summoned to the palace to be congratulated by the Queen.

Evander swallowed a sigh.

I bet Victoria choked on her crumpet when she read that.

He'd pondered Viggo's silence on the matter of his visit to the palace before the Brute had left his home last night.

"I gather there are some things you can't tell me yet," Viggo had said in response to his question, a faint smile hovering on his lips where he'd stood on the doorstep of the townhouse. "I'll wait until you're ready."

The Brute's confident expression had almost made Evander throw caution to the wind and pull him back inside the study so they could play out his filthy promise.

Ginny had made an impromptu visit later that night, on her way back from dinner with Lord Fairfax. Evander had related all that had passed since their last meeting while they'd enjoyed a nightcap, being careful to omit his visit to the palace. To his relief, Ginny hadn't probed him on the subject.

"*Nightshade* is officially working with Scotland Yard?" she'd said, wide-eyed.

"Yes."

She'd stared out the window of his study then.

Evander had followed her gaze, puzzled. "What are you looking at?"

Ginny had pursed her lips. "I'm checking for flying pigs."

"Har-har," Evander had grumbled.

He and Rufus approached the Occult Research department presently.

A harried-looking man in his sixties nearly collided with them outside it, his arms full of ancient tomes.

"Ah! Your Grace, Inspector." Quentin Inkwell brightened, his owlish eyes huge behind his enchanted spectacles. "I was just coming to see you."

"We received your message," Evander said cautiously.

"Have you discovered what the symbols on Millbrook's body mean?" Rufus asked without preamble.

Inkwell beamed. "Indeed I have. Please, follow me to my office."

Surprise jolted Evander. He'd been certain the symbols had meant nothing.

The interior of Inkwell's room was exactly what one might expect of an occult researcher's workplace. A labyrinth of towering bookshelves, arcane symbols scrawled on paperwork scattered upon every available surface, and the perpetual scent of old parchment and magic runes.

"Come." Inkwell dumped the tomes he'd been holding on a chair already creaking under some dozen grimoires and headed briskly for his desk in the alcove next to a window. "Let me show you my findings."

Evander traded a wary look with Rufus. It seemed they might be about to unearth another clue that could lead them to Millbrook's murderer.

Inkwell sat down and spread the documents on the surface of the table.

Evander studied the occult researcher's packed handwriting. Beside them were the transcription of the runes found on the victim.

"It's quite remarkable, really," Inkwell said. "After extensive research and cross-referencing with no less than seventeen obscure grimoires, I can say with utmost certainty that these symbols are—"

Rufus leaned forward expectantly, his hand finding the back of Inkwell's chair. Evander moved closer, his interest equally piqued.

"—complete and utter nonsense."

Rufus's hand slipped, almost sending him tumbling to the ground.

Evander blinked while the inspector cursed softly under his breath.

"I beg your pardon?"

Inkwell beamed. "Gobbledygook, your Grace. Gibberish. A magical wild goose chase, if you will." He waved his hand at the paperwork, almost gleeful at the revelation. "Whoever carved those symbols was either woefully ignorant of true arcane script or—"

"—deliberately trying to mislead us," Evander finished. His tone turned flinty. "So, it was a diversion after all."

Inkwell nodded. "Precisely, your Grace. A most cunning deception, I must say. It's rare to see such intricate fabrication of arcane symbology. Why, if I hadn't spent the last three decades studying obscure magical alphabets, I might never have—"

"Thank you, Mr. Inkwell," Evander cut in, sensing the start of a lengthy tangent. "Your insights are invaluable as always."

The mage's mind raced as they left the occult researcher's office and made their way to the Artificers' lab.

"That Millbrook's killer went to such lengths to misdirect us tells me time is of the essence in finding out what their goals are."

"I agree," Rufus said grimly. "Let's hope that bunch of lunatics has better news for us."

The Artificers' lab was a stark contrast to Quentin's cluttered office. Here, everything was meticulously organised, from the gleaming instruments and machines atop the surfaces, to the carefully labelled artefacts lining shelves and cabinets against the walls.

Alas, the environment did not reflect the personalities of the people who worked there. The reputation of the AFD's artificers for being crazed eccentrics had even reached the continent, much to the Commissioner's ire.

Evander was surprised to see Brown when they entered the room.

The alchemist wore goggles as he stood beside a man in his fifties fiddling with the knobs of a machine that was sending lightning through a convoluted glass and metal mechanism to a clear, cylindrical chamber. The crystal vial pulsed with a faint blue light inside it where it was held between two clamps.

The hairs on the back of Evander's neck stood on end at the magic crackling the air around the object.

Brown noticed them first. He removed his goggles, his expression brightening.

"Your Grace, Inspector. I assume you're here about the vial?"

The gleam in the alchemist's eyes told Evander they'd found something.

"Have you discovered what it is?"

Elias McAndrew, the chief Artificer, turned off the device he'd been manipulating. The cloud of magic around the crystal vial dissipated.

"Long time no see, your Grace." McAndrew removed his protective glasses and pinned them with an excited stare. "I must say, whoever made this thing is a prodigy."

"How about you tell us what it actually is, first?" Rufus asked impatiently.

McAndrew grinned and opened the compartment holding the vial. He removed it from the brackets and handed it to Evander.

"As near as we can tell, it's some kind of conduit for raw energy."

A chill danced down Evander's spine as he stared at the object warming his palm.

The artificer and the alchemist continued speaking, oblivious to his growing dread.

"The liquid inside is a stabilising agent of some sort," Brown explained. "What it's meant for won't be clear until we see the device it's intended for."

"Device?" Rufus repeated.

McAndrew nodded. "This vial is a component of something larger."

Evander's pulse quickened. "Some kind of artefact?"

McAndrew and Brown shared a glance.

"That's our best guess, yes," Brown said.

A troubled light darkened McAndrew's eyes for a moment.

Evander lowered his brows. "What is it you're not telling us?"

McAndrew hesitated, his gaze flitting to the vial. "I suspect whatever the device is, it can potentially harness massive amounts of energy."

The coldness gripping Evander intensified.

"What kind of energy?" Rufus said warily.

McAndrew's face turned chagrined. "That I do not yet know."

Frustration gnawed at Evander. He thanked the artificer and the alchemist and left the lab with Rufus, his mind spinning with a dozen thoughts. He didn't notice Rufus was talking to him until the inspector laid a hand on his arm.

"Evander? Did you hear me?"

Evander startled distractedly. "Sorry, what?"

Rufus's brow furrowed with concern. "I said we should tell Winterbourne. We can't just sit on this information."

Evander hesitated. "Alright."

The idea taking root inside him solidified as they made their way through the west wing of Scotland Yard. Of all the options he was weighing up, it was their quickest alternative to drawing out their enemy. Evander waited until they reached Winterbourne's office before putting his plan forward.

Rufus gaped at him as if he'd proposed they parade naked in front of the Queen.

"You can't be serious!" he spluttered.

"I agree with Inspector Grayson," Winterbourne said grimly. "Spreading the rumour that you possess the vial on your person is too dangerous."

"It's time we stopped reacting and started acting," Evander argued. "Doing this means we draw them out on our terms."

"It's too risky," Rufus protested. "You'll be painting a target on your back!"

"The target's already there, Rufus," Evander snapped "They've been after me ever since we found Millbrook's body. At least this way, we get to choose the battlefield."

He fisted his hands. "I won't have them endanger more innocent officers just to get to me."

They were still arguing when a commotion rose outside the commander's office. The door burst open, revealing Winterbourne's flustered secretary scurrying behind a determined Viggo.

CHAPTER 39

"I'm sorry, sir," the secretary stammered. "He insisted on—"

"It's alright," Winterbourne said gruffly. "Mr. Stonewall is working with us on this case."

The secretary nodded jerkily and left.

Evander couldn't help the butterflies that swarmed his stomach at the sight of the Brute.

Heat flashed in Viggo's eyes before he schooled his face in a neutral expression.

"I apologise for the interruption. I have information about Millbrook's family."

Evander's pulse accelerated. "You do?"

Viggo nodded curtly. "One of our agents talked to someone yesterday who'd spotted a woman and a young man fitting Martha and William Millbrook's description at a train station in Hertfordshire, about a week ago." Lines wrinkled his brow. "But it was Lady Hartley's information that guided us to their hiding place."

Rufus frowned in confusion. "Lady Hartley?"

Evander blinked. "Ginny helped you out?!"

"Yes. She contacted us this morning. She said she'd thought the name Millbrook sounded familiar. She had her staff scour her various business ledgers and found that someone by the name of Martha Millbrook had ordered several household items and furniture from one of her shops. Except the address given for the purchases made under that name wasn't for the property in Finsbury."

Gratitude loosened Evander's chest.

I must thank Ginny when I see her next!

The Brute related the rest of what *Nightshade* had uncovered, which coincided with Ginny's tip. Millbrook's wife and son had fled London shortly before his death and taken refuge close to the village of Harpenden.

A heavy silence fell over the room in the wake of this news.

"Whatever Millbrook was involved in, it terrified him enough that he forced his family to abandon their lives in London and go into hiding." Evander met Viggo's gaze, feeling energised at this fresh clue. "We should go meet them."

Viggo glanced at the light leeching out of the sky beyond the windows. "It'll be nighttime when we get there. Tomorrow would be better."

Evander heaved a sigh and ran a hand through his hair. "You're right, of course."

Winterbourne narrowed his eyes. "You appear to have conveniently forgotten what we were just discussing, Ravenwood."

Evander's mouth pressed to an irritated line.

Viggo's puzzled gaze swung between them. "Did something happen?"

"We've discovered what the crystal vial Evander found at the murder scene may be intended for," Rufus said grimly. "Evander wants word put out that he has it on his person. He intends to act as bait and draw the dark mages out."

Viggo narrowed his eyes dangerously. "What?"

His stormy expression almost had Evander squirming as he fixed him with a deadly stare.

"It's a good idea," Evander said, unable to mask the defensive note creeping into his voice.

"It's a stupid idea is what it is!" Viggo snarled.

The Brute's vehemence startled Winterbourne and drew a weary exhale from Rufus.

"But—" Evander started.

"Absolutely not!" the Brute growled. "It's suicide."

"That's what I said!" Rufus exclaimed, vindicated.

Evander's face tightened. "It's our best chance to ensnare them. We can't keep waiting for them to make the next move."

"So you're offering yourself up as a sacrificial lamb?" Viggo's voice dropped, low and dangerous. "I won't allow it."

Evander scowled. "*You* won't allow it?!"

The temperature in the room dropped noticeably as his magic responded to his agitation.

Viggo stood his ground, unfazed by the display of power.

"Hmm, Evander—" Rufus murmured.

Evander cut his eyes to him. "Stay out of this, Rufus!"

The inspector sagged.

Winterbourne stared, confounded. The commander regained his composure.

"Gentlemen, perhaps we should all take a moment to—"

"No," Evander said bitingly, his eyes locked on Viggo. "This needs to be settled now." He jutted his chin. "I'm not asking for permission, Viggo. I'm telling you what I intend to do."

If Winterbourne was shocked at the fact they were on a first name basis, he didn't indicate it.

Viggo and Evander stared at one another, the air between them practically crackling with tension.

Viggo looked away first.

"Fine," he said gruffly. "But I'm not letting you do this alone. Wherever you go, I go." He pinned Evander with an unrelenting look. "You want to use yourself as bait? Then you get me as your personal bodyguard."

Evander blinked, as taken aback by the sudden capitulation as he was by the bold suggestion that immediately followed it.

"I...that's not necessary. I'm perfectly capable of—"

"I know you are," Viggo interrupted. His eyes darkened. "But you don't *have* to do everything alone. Let me help."

The look on the Brute's face made Evander's chest tighten.

He swallowed hard, acutely aware of Rufus and Winterbourne's presence.

It was the only reason he didn't close the distance to Viggo and embrace him.

"Alright," Evander murmured.

Relief brightened Viggo's gaze.

Winterbourne leaned towards the inspector.

"Is there something going on between those two?" he hissed.

Rufus pursed his lips. "They're just friends, sir."

"I forgot to mention." Viggo frowned. "A name cropped up during *Nightshade*'s investigations of *Noctis Bloom* and those dark mages. Caine Renwick."

〜

THE NEXT MORNING DAWNED CLEAR AND COLD, A RARITY IN smog-choked London. Viggo took in the sights and sounds around him where he stood on a platform at Charing Cross station.

A vaulted iron and glass ceiling soared overhead, the magical lamps suspended beneath it supplementing the natural light streaming inside the building. Porters scurried about, weaving carts laden with trunks and valises expertly between the milling passengers. The air was thick with the smell of coal smoke and ozone, the latter a byproduct of the enchantments that powered the trains.

His shoulders tensed fractionally as he studied the hulking steam engine a little down the way from where he stood.

The locomotive was a marvel of modern engineering and magic, its brass fittings gleaming in the weak sunlight and the runes etched along its dark body pulsing with arcane energy.

Despite its impressive appearance, Viggo couldn't shake the unease that settled in his gut at the thought of boarding it. This would be his sixth time on a train and he remained as cautious as he'd been during his first journey a few years ago. He was recalling a particularly nasty incident in Strasbourg involving a locomotive when a voice came behind him.

"Everything alright?" Evander asked curiously.

Viggo turned.

The mage and his inspector friend were coming towards him, having collected the first class passes Scotland Yard had booked for their passage to Harpenden from the ticket office.

Viggo was briefly distracted by Evander's striking face and his alluring physique beneath the uniform he wore.

Damn, he's a handsome fellow. He couldn't wait to peel off the mage's clothes and explore his delectable, naked body. *One day. Soon.*

He wasn't the only one staring at Evander. Scores of passengers were shooting covetous looks at the oblivious mage.

"Viggo?" Evander asked, puzzled.

Viggo curbed his feverish imagination.

"I was thinking I don't trust this beast of a machine." He indicated the train. "Give me a damn horse any day."

Amusement sparkled in Evander's eyes at his crotchety tone.

"I never thought I'd see the great Viggo Stonewall intimidated by a means of transportation."

"I'm not intimidated," Viggo grumbled. "I'm cautious. There's a difference."

"Of course there is," Evander chuckled.

Rufus's face grew pinched at their flirting. "We should board soon. The train leaves in ten minutes."

Viggo couldn't help but notice the uneasy glances his presence earned as they made their way down the platform. Charing Cross was a hub of activity, with mostly magical folks hurrying to and fro. Yet, the crowd seemed to part instinctively around him, as if he carried a contagious disease. He caught snatches of whispered conversations.

"Is that…?!"

"My God, it's the Ironfist Brute, I'm sure of it!"

"What's he doing *here*?!"

Viggo set his jaw, determined to ignore the stares and murmurs.

He realised Evander was glaring at the people ogling him. That fact alone loosened his shoulders and had him keeping his chin up.

Viggo had to duck to avoid hitting his head on the doorframe when they boarded their carriage. The interior was plush, all polished wood and velvet upholstery, and more luxury than a thrall could ever afford in their lifetime.

It was a far cry from the cabins where commoners travelled.

"Hertfordshire isn't far," Evander said as they settled into their seats. "We'll be there before you know it."

Viggo couldn't help but stiffen when the station master blew his enchanted whistle. The train lurched into motion.

Evander gave him an encouraging look from across the way.

The mage had elected to sit beside Rufus.

Viggo wasn't sure if it was because he was choosing to maintain a professional distance or he'd sensed the Brute's hidden intent to jump him.

The journey passed in a blur of green fields and small villages, the landscape rushing by at a speed that amazed and troubled Viggo in equal measure. He couldn't help but drum a nervous rhythm on his knee as the train carried them to their destination.

He'd faced down mages and fought battles that would make most men quake with fear, but something about hurtling through the countryside in a metal box made his skin crawl.

Soon, they were pulling into Harpenden station.

A man was waiting for them on the platform, his nondescript clothing belying the alertness in his gaze. He strolled up to them as they got off their carriage.

"All clear, boss," he told Viggo in a low voice. "There've been no signs of mages around these parts since yesterday."

"Good work." Viggo introduced the man to Evander and Rufus. "This is Hawk, one of *Nightshade*'s undercover agents. He's been keeping an eye on things."

Hawk dipped his flat cap at the two Met officers and escorted them out of the station.

CHAPTER 40

VIGGO COULDN'T HELP BUT NOTICE THE CHANGES THAT HAD come with the arrival of the railway as they made their way through the sun-lit village. What had once been a quiet farming community was now a bustling parish, with new shops and houses springing up alongside traditional cottages.

A horse-drawn cart driven by a weathered old farmer waited for them at the edge of the settlement.

"I'm afraid this is our ride for the next leg of our journey," Hawk said, a hint of apology in his voice. "It's less conspicuous than a carriage."

Evander eyed the cart dubiously, his nose wrinkling a little at the distinct aroma of manure that clung to the wooden slats. Rufus looked no more enthused, his aloof composure slipping as he climbed gingerly aboard.

Viggo felt a grin tugging at his lips as he and Hawk settled on the rough bench behind the driver.

"What's the matter?" the Brute asked innocently.

"Don't tell me you prefer that fancy steam contraption to good old-fashioned horsepower?"

Evander shot him a narrow-eyed look.

"I think I liked you better when you were nervous about the train."

Viggo chuckled.

The cart started moving jerkily. Evander and Rufus clung to the sides, their faces a study in barely concealed discomfort.

As they trundled along country lanes and through dense coppices, Viggo found himself relaxing for the first time since they'd left London. He felt more at ease out here, away from the crowded streets and prying eyes of the city. The scent of earth and growing things filled his lungs, a welcome change from the ever-present smog and stink of the capital.

After what felt like hours of bone-jarring travel but was only some forty minutes in reality, they arrived at a small hamlet. The farmer guided the cart past a pond where ducks swam and into what passed for a main street overlooked by a cluster of downtrodden buildings.

Viggo's throat constricted at the sight of the destitute thralls trying to carve a meagre living from the land under the blazing sun. It reminded him painfully that this was still the fate of his kind through most of the country.

Evander's troubled expression lingered on the figures toiling the fields as they left the hamlet behind.

The farmer dropped them off at the edge of heavy woodland some two miles later. Hawk handed him some pennies. The man slipped the coins into his pocket, tilted his straw hat at them, and continued down the lane.

Hawk waited until the cart disappeared around a bend before leading them into the shadows beneath the trees, the path he took barely a trail.

The smell of smoke soon tickled Viggo's nostrils.

A cottage appeared, nestled in a clearing with a well and a small vegetable garden. Lazy trails curled up from a red brick chimney. The faint clucks of chickens and the sound of wood being chopped rose close by.

A curtain twitched at their approach.

The axe stopped a moment later.

A young, stocky man with dark hair and suspicious brown eyes rounded the side of the cottage, the steel blade at the end of the tool he held glinting as he clasped the wooden handle in a solid, two-handed grip.

≈

EVANDER STOPPED, CERTAIN HE WAS LOOKING AT WILLIAM Millbrook.

The young man bore an uncanny resemblance to his father.

"What business do you have here?" William called out, making no effort to hide his hostility.

"My name is Duke Ravenwood. I'm a Special Arcane Investigator in Scotland Yard," Evander said calmly. He indicated Rufus. "This is Inspector Grayson." He met William's gaze steadily. "We're investigating your father's murder."

William's eyes rounded for a split second. His face grew shuttered in the next instant.

"I have no idea what you're talking about. Please leave. This is private property."

"Come lad, they only want to help," Viggo said gruffly.

William clenched his jaw. "And who the devil are you?"

"I'm Viggo Stonewall, the head of *Nightshade*."

William flinched. "The information guild?"

"Yes, the very one."

Fear drained the blood from William's face. He stepped back, his gaze jerkily scanning the edge of the clearing and the pools of darkness between the trees.

"You're with them, aren't you?" His voice grew shrill, his fingers twitching jumpily on the handle of the axe. "You're with the bastards who killed my father!"

"Enough, William," someone said harshly.

A woman stood in the doorway of the cottage. She tugged the ends of her shawl closer and studied Evander and his companions with a dull look.

"What do you want, your Grace?"

"We would like your help finding your husband's killer," Evander replied.

Something sparked in the depths of Martha Millbrook's deadened eyes then.

A flash of fear. Despair. And an emotion he couldn't identify.

"It's too late," she muttered. "Alastair is dead and there's no bringing him back. We just want to be left alone."

Viggo took a step forward. "Mrs. Millbrook, will you listen to my story?"

Confusion clouded Martha Millbrook's expression.

"It won't take long, I assure you," the Brute continued,

his tone gentle. "We don't have to go inside your home either."

Evander stared at Viggo, curious as to what he intended.

Martha hesitated. "Alright," she murmured reluctantly.

William watched them sullenly.

"Twenty-eight years ago, on the night I turned six years old, a group of mages arrived at my village just as my family sat down for supper," Viggo said. "By midnight, I was the only person left alive in a community of two hundred souls."

Evander stilled, his frozen gaze on Viggo's calm countenance. Rufus looked equally stunned as he stared at the Brute.

Hawk listened with an impassive face.

"I had four brothers and two sisters, the youngest barely a year old," Viggo continued steadily, as if talking about the weather. "By the time the mages finished with them, their corpses were unrecognisable. My father and my mother tried to fight them, but what could thralls who'd lived their entire lives pretending the rest of the world didn't exist do in the face of evil they could never comprehend?"

Grief constricted Evander's chest until he could barely breathe.

Even Martha paled at the Brute's ghastly confession.

"They hung my mother from the apple tree next to our house until her neck snapped. As for my father, they cut off his legs and tossed him to the hunting hounds they'd brought along to hunt us. Not a woman, man, or child was spared that night except for me." A muscle jumped in

Viggo's cheek, the first sign of emotion he'd demonstrated since he'd begun his dark tale. "You see, I was the lucky one. I was...the *chosen* one." The Brute's eyes gleamed. "They always left one alive. One thrall who would bear witness to their horrifying acts of violence and who would carry that awful burden to his grave. But not before he spread tales of their deeds and instilled fear in the heart of every one of his kind he met. A child who they deemed would not lose his mind and become a gibbering fool rendered insane by terror." He faltered. "A child the mage who led the massacre inevitably branded with his signet ring."

Viggo shrugged his left shoulder out of his coat and pulled down the neckline of his shirt. An ugly scar in the form of the letter A wrinkled his inked skin beneath his left clavicle, the mark inches from his heart.

Evander shuddered and gulped down air, his entire body trembling and his legs weak. Rufus clenched his teeth, brow furrowed in an angry scowl.

William dropped the axe and covered his mouth with his hands, his cheeks drained of blood.

Viggo pulled his clothes back up, his voice brittle.

"What you're feeling right now? I felt it too. For a long, long time. Terror. Desperation." A bitter sound left him. "There were nights when I hardly slept. When I was afraid to close my eyes for fear of what I would see in my nightmares. But after a while, after I fled to London and found myself living on the streets of the capital, struggling to stay alive each day that passed, I met others like me. Children cast aside by their own terrible circumstances. Orphans who could only count on themselves as they navigated a world full of cruelty and devoid of compassion. And I realised that we had one thing in common."

"What was that?" Martha said breathlessly.

"Rage." Viggo's voice grew flinty. "We were full of rage. At the world. At the unfairness of our plight. At *everything*." He took a shaky breath. "We wanted retribution. Revenge. We wanted the people who'd thrown us in the pits of Hell to burn and suffer eternal torment." He met Martha's frozen gaze unflinchingly. "And I see you want that too." Viggo glanced at William. "That you *both* want that. I promise you this. If you help us, we will make certain to deliver justice for your husband."

The silence that fell across the clearing was heavy and fraught with tension.

"Come in," Martha said, her voice barely above a whisper.

CHAPTER 41

THE INTERIOR OF THE COTTAGE WAS COZY BUT SPARSE, signs of a hasty relocation evident in the half-unpacked trunks visible in the rooms they passed. Millbrook's widow led them to the sunlit kitchen at the back, William bringing up their rear.

Hawk stayed on guard duty outside.

Porcelain tinkled as Martha placed crockery on a tray and brought it to the table. She served them freshly bake scones and poured them tea from the kettle on the fire.

"Thank you," Evander murmured. He clasped his steaming cup in his hands and took a sip of the hot, sweet drink.

It did little to warm his body.

He couldn't stop reliving the harrowing tale Viggo had just told them. The rumours he'd heard about the Brute's childhood paled in comparison to the reality of the horrors he'd just painted with the bold strokes of his recollection from the eyes of the child he had been at the time his life changed forever.

Evander found himself unable to look at Viggo, too ashamed of the magic that ran through his veins and defined him as a mage.

Rufus cast a worried glance his way before addressing Martha Millbrook.

"Can you tell us what Alastair was working on before his murder?"

She exchanged a glance with her son.

"He rarely talked about the commissions he accepted," she told them guardedly. "Many of the projects he undertook were under strict confidence. It isn't as if he could tell us about them even if he wanted to."

"But we knew something was wrong." William frowned. "We could see it in his face when he came home." Frustration underscored his voice. "Not that he visited Finsbury much in the two months before his murder. Father spent most of his time in Covent Garden. He slept in the lodgings above his workshop."

Evander took a shallow breath. He couldn't just sit there wallowing in his emotions. Not when there was work to be done.

"What prompted you to leave Finsbury?" he asked Martha.

The widow twisted her hands in her dress. Her reply confirmed what Evander had suspected.

"Alastair came home just under a fortnight ago." Martha's expression grew haggard. "I have never seen my husband so afraid. He told us we had to leave London, for our own safety." A shudder shook her as she squeezed her eyes shut. "I wish I had asked him to come with us. Not a day passes that I do not regret my decision to stay silent on the matter."

Her voice broke. She pressed a hand to her mouth.

William's chin trembled as he clasped his mother's shoulder. Martha touched his hand, her throat working convulsively.

"We found out about my father's death in the papers." William's gaze burned with barely contained anger despite his tears. "Do you know who killed him?!"

"It was a dark mage."

William recoiled at Evander's quiet words.

Martha's eyes widened.

"A dark mage?" she mumbled. "But—Alastair would never have anything to do with—!"

"I doubt he knew," Viggo cut in. His stiff gaze flitted briefly to Evander before focusing on the Millbrooks. "The reason he became scared was likely because he'd realised what he'd gotten himself involved in."

"Mr. Stonewall is correct," Evander said levelly. "We suspect your husband didn't know what he'd signed himself up for when he took on the commission that led to his murder."

William's expression darkened.

"Are you saying the people who hired him intended to kill him?"

The fire crackled noisily in the tense lull that ensued.

"That I cannot tell you for certain." Evander met the younger man's glare unflinchingly. "But, yes. There's a high probability that they planned to get rid of him after he completed the project they'd assigned him."

Martha paled. William cursed.

"Alastair knew this," Evander said. "That's why he took measures to foil their plans and left clues that could lead to his killer."

Confusion clouded Martha and William's faces when he removed a small pouch from inside his coat and placed it on the table. Evander pushed it towards them.

"We found this hidden in his workshop."

Martha's hands shook as she opened the bag and removed the key they'd discovered. Her breath caught at the name his fire magic had scorched upon the scrap of paper that came with it.

The blood drained from William's face.

"Who's Rosa?" Evander asked softly.

Tears bloomed in Martha's eyes.

"She was my daughter," she choked out when she could speak.

William wiped the wet trails coursing down his cheeks with a jerky movement.

"Rosa was my baby sister," he croaked, his voice thick with sorrow. "She died from scarlet fever when she was two."

"Does the key mean anything to you?" Rufus said tensely.

William shook his head.

"No," Martha mumbled.

Evander's gut knotted. They'd banked on the Millbrooks telling them what the key was for.

A strange expression dawned on Viggo's face. His tone when he spoke carried a hint of hope.

"Where is Rosa buried?"

Confusion wrinkled William's brow. "In the woods, not far from here."

Evander's pulse spiked.

"This cottage belonged to my family," Martha explained at their stares. "We often come here during autumn and winter."

"Can you take us to Rosa's grave?" Evander asked William.

~

UNEASE COILED THROUGH VIGGO AS THEY FOLLOWED Millbrook's son out of the cottage and into the woods. He could tell Evander was avoiding looking at him.

He moved closer to the mage while William led them along a barely visible path.

"What's wrong?"

Evander glanced at him, his expression brittle. "Nothing's wrong."

Viggo frowned. "You're lying."

Evander closed his eyes briefly and shuddered.

"If you really want to know, I—kind of hate myself right now."

Surprise jolted Viggo. "Whatever for?"

A muscle jumped in Evander's jawline.

"Because I was born with magic," he said bitterly. "The same magic that runs through the veins of the devils who killed your family and destroyed your village."

Viggo's throat tightened at the remorse thickening his voice. His hand brushed the back of Evander's.

"It's not your fault. You were only what, three at the time?"

Evander shook his head. "I was two years old."

Viggo hooked their little fingers together for a moment.

"There you go then," he said lightly. "I could hardly expect an Archmage in diapers to come to my aid."

An involuntary snort escaped Evander. He regained his composure and pursed his lips at the Brute.

"This is no laughing matter, Viggo."

"It isn't." He bumped shoulders with the mage. "But I can't keep blaming all mages for the work of a small group of evildoers. You've shown me that these past few days."

Evander swallowed, gratitude bringing a flush of colour to his cheeks.

They soon came upon a small, secluded grove. In the centre of the clearing stood a simple stone marker inscribed with the name Rosa Millbrook and her year of birth and death.

William stopped before it, his shoulders slumping a little.

"Hello, Rosa," he said softly. "It's been a while."

The young man squatted and tidied the weeds encroaching the grave.

"Let's take a look around," Evander suggested to Viggo and Rufus.

They fanned out across the glade.

"What are you doing?" William asked curiously after a moment.

"Your father's clues led us here." Evander glanced his way. "My guess is there's something he wanted us to find."

William's pupils widened. His gaze swept the area around the grave. He rose, determination hardening his face.

"I'll help."

It was William who discovered what Alastair Millbrook had hidden in the vicinity of his dead daughter's remains.

"Here." He crouched in front of a beech tree whose branches and leaves shielded the grove. "The ground looks disturbed!"

CHAPTER 42

EVANDER'S PULSE QUICKENED AS THEY JOINED THE YOUNG man. He hunched down and carefully brushed away the loose soil. A hint of magic grazed his senses.

His fingers struck something solid a moment later.

"Rufus, Viggo, give me a hand."

Together, they unearthed the ornate box Millbrook had buried at the edge of the grove. It was made of polished wood inlaid with mother-of-pearl.

Evander cleared the dirt clinging to the surface before carefully inserting the key they'd found in the Charm Weaver's workshop in the lock, his heart thundering against his ribs.

It was a perfect fit.

Inside the box were a leather-bound journal, a logbook, a stack of notes, and a small, cloth-wrapped bundle.

Evander checked the logbook with Viggo and Rufus while William began going through his father's notes.

The name of Millbrook's last client was one Caine Renwick. The object he had commissioned the Charm Weaver to make was a pocket watch.

Evander's scalp prickled at the address Renwick had provided.

It was the place where he'd spent his formative years as a mage.

"What in the blazes?!" Rufus mumbled.

Viggo scowled. "That dark mage works at the Royal Institute for the Arcane?"

Evander opened the journal next, Viggo and Rufus peering over his shoulder.

It was a record of Alastair Millbrook's days as a Charm Weaver. His neat handwriting danced across the pages, etching out his thoughts, emotions, and the humdrum that sometimes defined his occupation. He'd even hastily jotted down random ideas that came to him at the edges of the paper, as if he couldn't find the patience to write them elsewhere or was fearful he might forget them.

The tone of his journal changed in the last fifteen pages or so. His penmanship grew more shoddy, ink blots darkening the sheets here and there, the language he began using hasty and blunt.

Sentences jumped out at Evander, the words betraying the Charm Weaver's growing dread.

I am beginning to question the purpose of this commission. I fear R hasn't been completely honest with me.

R came to the workshop again today. He grows impatient.

The hairs lifted on the back of Evander's neck when he turned a page.

What have I done? Dear God, could this be what I think it is?!

R is a dark mage. I am certain of it now.

Viggo shifted closer, his knee brushing Evander's thigh, the tension roiling off him reflected in Evander's whitening knuckles.

I have to get Martha and William out of London. I curse the day I ever accepted R's offer. This is the devil's work and I shall be part of it no longer!

The journal rustled when Evander flipped the paper.

Millbrook's final entry made him freeze and drew a curse from Rufus.

I am sure he will come to kill me tonight. I have done my best to foil his plans. To anyone who finds this, please, forgive me. I hope you find a skilled artificer to complete the countermeasure I'd begun to make. Give my love to my wife and son. And may God pardon me my sins!

Evander clenched his jaw so hard his teeth hurt.

The fact that Millbrook had not sought help meant he was either fearful for his family or things had happened too quickly near the end for him to do so.

Or maybe he thought Renwick was too powerful a foe to be stopped by Scotland Yard.

That thought chilled his blood.

"Your Grace."

William's dazed tone had them looking over at him.

The young man was kneeling in the dirt, his father's notes spread out before him.

"If I'm reading this correctly, my father created a device called the *Blood Siphon*," he mumbled. "Its purpose is to capture and store vast amounts of energy."

The pieces of the puzzle slotted into place like death knolls inside Evander's mind.

"The crystal vial." Rufus met Evander's shocked gaze. "McAndrew and Brown said it was some kind of energy conduit!"

Evander swallowed and nodded. "That explains the thaumic capacitor we found in Millbrook's workshop."

William's eyes rounded. "My father has a *thaumic capacitor*? No, before that. You said something about a vial!" His gaze roamed a series of drawings on the ground. He grabbed a page and thrust it in their faces. "Do you mean this?!"

Goosebumps erupted on Evander's skin.

Penned elaborately on the paper was a perfect representation of the object he'd found near Millbrook's body.

Evander touched the drawing with trembling fingers.

"Yes. I found something like this next to your father!"

Viggo stiffened beside him. "What the—there's a second one?!"

Evander followed his gaze to a sketch on the ground next to William.

It showed an object in the shape of a pocket watch, its edges covered in intricate engravings that made up complex runes. Two vials sat in the centre of the device, amidst a web of delicate gears and springs.

A buzzing sounded in Evander's ears.

"William, did your father write down the design of those two vials and the purpose of the artefact?" he heard himself say from a distance.

"Yes, I think I saw something scribbled down

somewhere in his latest notes." William searched his father's paperwork. "Here it is!" He snatched up a page. "Father wrote *'I believe they intend to use the red vial to absorb and store the raw life force...of...magicless individuals.'*" He faltered, face turning ashen. *"'The blue vial—'"* He stopped and swallowed hard.

Evander's heart thumped painfully against his ribs as he took the note from William's shaking hand and finished reading out what he could not.

"'The blue vial, being a stabiliser and refiner of energy, will turn the accumulated life force into a more potent, stable form,'" he quoted numbly. *"'I think their true purpose is to make the device act as a reservoir of life energy that can fuel and augment magic. This would theoretically allow mages to grow their powers and have an almost infinite source of magic at hand to draw upon.'"*

Rufus finished reading the rest as Evander lapsed into silence.

"'The device is fashioned in such a way that both the absorbing and the stabilising components are essential for it to function as it should,'" the inspector mumbled in a voice full of horror. *"'Without the stabiliser, the* Blood Siphon *will be dangerously unstable and prone to exploding.'"*

The curse that left Viggo turned the air blue and made them jump.

"That bastard Renwick is planning to use this thing on thralls?!" he snarled, face dark with fury.

Evander clenched his jaw. Considering dark mages' agenda as a whole, that fact did not surprise him.

Still, a crime of this magnitude would go beyond what the War of Subjugation intended to accomplish. This won't just be genocide. This will be the mass extermination of an entire race of humans!

He stared at the note in his hand, blood pounding dully in his skull.

Alastair Millbrook's final actions on the night he died had just become blindingly apparent. The blue vial had not ended up in the alley accidentally. He'd removed it from the *Blood Siphon* likely moments before Caine Renwick had broken into his workshop to collect the device and kill him.

William sagged, his face slack with disbelief. "Did my father really make such an awful invention?!" He stared unseeingly at Evander and his companions, as if begging for anyone to tell him he was wrong.

Evander faltered. "I don't think that was his intention. I believe once he realised what it was he'd created, it was already too late."

Rufus placed a gentle hand on William's shoulder. "Part of his motives for completing this project may very well have been to protect you and your mother."

Evander dipped his head in agreement. "Besides, he said he'd started making a countermeasure."

"Is this it?" Viggo said in a hard voice.

They turned.

The Brute had uncovered the cloth-wrapped bundle in the box. A half-finished pocket watch sat in his palm, metal gleaming in the bright rays piercing the overhead canopy.

The pocket watch on Millbrook's workbench flashed before Evander's eyes.

Was that one a prototype?!

William unfroze and hastily shuffled the diagrams and notes scattered around him. His expression turned triumphant.

"This is it." He showed them another schematic, this one a mirror image of the incomplete artefact Viggo held. "This is what he was making." His fingers traced the diagram and the matching notes, his lips moving silently as he deciphered the complex engineering language. His face brightened, relief rendering him weak. "It says here this artefact could cancel out the effects of the *Blood Siphon*."

The ramifications of everything they had uncovered in the glade made Evander's head fairly spin.

"By the way, how come you can read those drawings?" Viggo asked William.

"I'm an apprentice Charm Weaver." William's ears reddened. "I want to follow in my father's footsteps."

"There's nothing wrong with that," the Brute grunted. "If it hadn't been for what happened to my family and those bastard mages, I would have ended up a potato farmer like my pa."

The incongruity of his statement compared to his reputation as the Ironfist Brute had William's jaw dropping and Evander biting his lip hard.

"A potato farmer," Rufus managed in a strangled voice. "It suits you."

A smile tugged at Viggo's lips.

The brief moment of levity lightened their sombre moods.

"We should return to London," Evander said. "This

changes things. We have to take this all the way to the top of Scotland Yard and the Ministry of Arcane Affairs."

Rufus nodded briskly. "We should inform the War Office and the Mage Council too."

They returned to the cottage with the box and its contents.

Evander filled Martha Millbrook in on their findings, carefully omitting the more gory details of the objective of her dead husband's last commission.

"Alastair was a good man caught up in something terrible. We'll do our very best to find and punish his murderer."

Martha nodded, her eyes gleaming with gratitude.

"Hawk will stick around and keep an eye on things," Viggo told William. "I'll send more men as reinforcements to relieve him."

"We'll have undercover officers from the Met come guard you too," Rufus promised.

William squeezed Evander's fingers as they shook hands at the door.

"Thank you." He glanced over his shoulder, the sound of his mother in the kitchen faint. "It would have broken her heart if she'd been told what father accidentally created." His jaw set in a hard line as he looked at them. "I hope you stop that bastard Renwick before he causes more harm."

They bade him goodnight and made their way out of the woods.

It didn't require too much persuasion to convince a farmer in the hamlet to take them into Harpenden.

The journey back to London was tense, the gravity of

their discovery weighing heavily on all of them. Evander spent most of the trip poring over Millbrook's notes and journal, a growing sense of unease eating at him with every mile that brought them closer to the city.

How and where is Renwick intending to use this device?

It wasn't long before their train pulled into Charing Cross. As they stepped out on the platform, a figure caught Evander's eye. The man disappeared in the bustling crowd, but not before Evander recognised the mocking sneer he shot his way. His pulse stuttered.

Renwick?!

CHAPTER 43

Dark magic surged across the platform before Evander could react, sucking all the warmth and oxygen from the surroundings and bringing a vile stench and taste to his nose and tongue. His ears popped as the pressure dropped.

Choked gurgles sounded around him. People began collapsing like flies.

Viggo cursed and caught Rufus as he swayed.

"What the hell is going on?!"

"They're here!" Evander said thickly.

Shadowy trails were absorbing the light pouring through the station's glass ceiling and emanating from enchanted lamps. Evander froze when the darkness coalesced on a tidal wave of sinister magic that bore down on them.

"Get down! *Now!*" Viggo barked.

He tackled Evander to the ground, Rufus in his hold.

The dark swell tore through the train carriage like it

was made of paper, smashing metal and shattering glass in a deafening cacophony that seemed to go on forever. Debris rained down on them, Viggo doing his best to shield them with his giant frame.

There was a moment of breathless stillness when the echoes of the detonation faded.

The world exploded into chaos.

Screams rent the air as passengers who'd escaped the initial attack scrambled to flee, their panicked cries mixing with the groans of those less fortunate than them.

Evander's skull fairly rang as Viggo climbed off him and pulled him to his feet. He stared, stomach churning.

Half of Charing Cross station resembled a war zone. Smoke billowed from the wrecked train beside them, mixing with the acrid stink of dark magic that hung heavily in the air.

Evander's alarmed gaze found Rufus. "How is he?!"

"Alive, but out like a light," Viggo said grimly.

Relief made Evander weak. The fact that Viggo was still standing gave him the strength he needed to do what he must. He clenched his jaw and reached for his magic.

Pulsing heat came to life inside his chest, clearing his mind and sharpening his senses. Flames blossomed around him, the incandescent sparks moving under his will. Evander moulded the blaze until it formed a rippling, roaring cloud and sent it soaring above the platform and the comatose passengers.

Fire magic purified the air of the dark energy choking it.

Audible gasps and wheezes sounded as people started coming around.

Rufus stirred and moaned. The inspector blinked his eyes dazedly, a thin trail of blood trickling from a cut on his head. Viggo helped sit him up.

"What in the blazes just happened?!" Rufus gasped, leaning heavily on the Brute.

"Renwick's here," Evander said grimly. "I saw him when I got off the train." He scanned their surroundings with a heavy frown. "It's not just him. I can sense several sources of dark magic close by."

As if summoned by his words, a group of robed figures emerged from the billowing smoke. There were sixteen of them. A third wore the blank faces and crimson pupils that signalled them as victims of the cursed gems being used to control their minds. Leading the mages was Renwick, his grey eyes chilling.

Evander's blood ran cold.

The malevolent aura surrounding the dark mage was worse than when he'd last seen him. It was a discordant, jarring presence, at odds with the natural harmony of the world.

His every sense reacted viscerally to it.

"Duke Ravenwood." Renwick's voice was smooth, almost pleasant. It betrayed none of the evil Evander knew lurked beneath. "I must say, I'm impressed. Not many could have survived that blast."

Evander's nails dug into his palms. His gaze flitted to the figures accompanying the dark mage.

"I should have known you'd be too much of a coward to face us alone."

A flinty smile played on Renwick's lips. "Coward? No,

your Grace. Merely practical. I can't afford to take chances. Not when the stakes are this high."

"Stakes?" Viggo bit out, body tense and ready to spring into action. "You mean stealing the life force of innocent people?!"

Surprise flickered in Renwick's eyes. It was replaced by cool calculation.

"I see you've discovered the true purpose of the artefact I had Millbrook build for us." He cocked his head mockingly. "It changes nothing. You're too late to stop what's already been set in motion."

Evander's mind raced.

Us? Someone else is involved in this? And what does he mean, set in motion?!

Viggo shifted protectively in front of Evander and Rufus.

Amusement gleamed in Renwick's eyes. "What are they paying you, Stonewall? I'll double it, whatever it is."

"You can't afford me," Viggo growled. "Even if you could, I would never work with the likes of you!"

Renwick's expression turned ugly.

"A worthless thrall will always remain a worthless thrall, I see."

He signalled to his followers.

Shadows came to life around the mages, writhing and reaching out with grasping tendrils. Horror gripped Evander's chest in a vice when Renwick's followers directed their attacks at the passengers in the station, their intent to maim and destroy all too clear.

A woman screamed and fell, her body twisted at a strange angle.

A man dropped to his knees, air rasping through his throat as he clutched desperately at the dark bands throttling him.

Power rolled through Evander on a wave of fury, the elements answering his call as if waiting for this very moment. The wind and fire that sprang up at his command deflected the sinister wisps seeking fresh targets. Ice and earth sprouted from the ground, sharp spikes shooting towards the enemy.

A couple of mages let out gurgled shouts when the elemental spears found them.

"Rufus!" Evander shouted over the howl of wind and magic. "Get everyone out of here and evacuate the station!"

The inspector nodded jerkily before disappearing into the billowing smoke. His enchanted whistle soon rose above the pandemonium gripping Charing Cross. An answering sound echoed in the distance scant seconds later.

This close to Scotland Yard, reinforcements would come quickly and in large numbers.

Evander fisted his hands.

We just have to hang in there until they arrive!

He stiffened when dark magic bubbled around Renwick's hands. The temperature plummeted. Frost crystallised on the platform as the dark mage's powers leeched the warmth from the air.

Fear squeezed Evander's heart when he grasped Renwick's intent.

"*No!*"

Heat flashed through his blood as he stepped in front

of Viggo. A wall of fire burst into life around them, the flames so intense sweat immediately beaded the Brute's brow.

The elemental barrier absorbed most of Renwick's deadly attack.

A dark bolt slipped through, its power still potent despite being dampened by Evander's fire magic.

Viggo yanked Evander behind him and blocked it with his forearms, a grunt of pain leaving him as the magic scalded his skin.

Evander braced his hands against the Brute's back and grounded them with earth magic as the impact shoved them some half a dozen feet.

Viggo dug his heels in and brought them to a halt.

The fire faded, revealing Renwick and his followers.

The Brute bared his teeth. "My turn."

He drew his arm back and slammed his fist into the ground with a roar.

Evander gasped when the platform shuddered violently beneath them.

A crack split the surface. It spread as it snaked towards the dark mages.

Renwick scowled and moved nimbly out of the way of the rupture. Two of his associates weren't as lucky. Their feet got jammed into the break, snapping their ankles.

Viggo smiled viciously at their screams.

The rest of the mages brought forth bolts of sickening shadows as they encircled them, Renwick hanging back with a contemptuous smirk.

Evander reached for his elemental powers, his heart

thundering against his ribs. He'd never faced so many dark magic users at once.

The corruption wafting off them made his skin crawl.

Viggo's back brushed against his as he spun to defend their rear.

"Together!" the Brute barked over his shoulder.

Evander dipped his head. "Be careful!"

Wind and fire rippled into life between them and the dark mages, keeping the worst of their attacks at bay.

Evander and Viggo pushed back as they had done in the church, their movements fluid and synchronised, as if they'd performed this deadly dance a hundred times before. What got past Viggo was deflected by Evander. What escaped Evander's magic was physically punched aside by Viggo.

Evander's heart sang as they fought side by side, the expression he occasionally glimpsed on Viggo's face telling him the Brute found the way they matched one another on the battlefield as exhilarating as he did.

He felt like he could take on the whole world in that moment of mutual affinity.

A quick glance around revealed civilians still trapped in the station, their escape route blocked by the fierce battle taking place on the platform. Evander subdued his magic slightly, conscious he could bring the entire structure down on their heads if he went at full power.

A scream cut through the din of battle.

His head snapped around.

A young woman had been cornered by one of the dark mages. Shadows were creeping up her legs.

Evander moved without thinking, his wind and earth

magic snatching her from danger and depositing her safely some distance away.

The momentary distraction cost him.

A bolt of corrupt energy slipped past his defences and penetrated his shoulder. Pain lanced through Evander, hot and sharp. He cried out, his flesh burning as black magic began seeping into his body like poison.

"Evander!" Viggo shouted.

The Brute cursed when he found his way obstructed by dark mages.

Evander's vision blurred as the corruption bled into his veins and headed for his heart.

CHAPTER 44

"WHERE'S THE CRYSTAL VIAL, ICE MAGE?!" RENWICK barked. "I know you have it on you! Give it to me and I will spare these people!"

Sweat dripped down Evander's face. He shook his head and sought the dark mage with his desperate gaze, only to freeze.

Renwick towered over a group of cowering passengers. A volley of dark magic bolts whined in the air close to the terrified men and women's faces, ready to pierce their flesh and blind them.

Evander blinked and forced himself to focus. He couldn't falter now. Not with so many lives at stake and Viggo fighting desperately to overcome their enemy and reach him. Blood pounded thickly in his veins as he gritted his teeth against the agonising pain threatening to rob him of his senses.

There was only one thing he could do to save himself

and the innocent bystanders who'd found themselves in the midst of this battle.

I hope the building can withstand it!

Evander's laboured breaths rattled in and out of his chest as he closed his eyes.

The first time he'd tried this during a private lesson at the Royal Institute, he'd almost destroyed a wing of the building.

He blocked out the chaos around him and looked deep within, to where his magic dwelled. The four elements flickered and grew in his mind's eye, a riot of blue, crimson, green, and gold energy bubbling and swirling where they twined around one another, hungering to be let loose.

Evander lifted the lid on them a fraction more.

Elemental power rushed thorough him on a wave that made him gasp and invigorated his senses. The station trembled, metal whining and glass vibrating in the face of the violent energies bursting forth from his flesh.

The fire magic racing through Evander's bloodstream obliterated the dark power seeking to weaken and kill him. Air entered his starving lungs, cold and blissful.

He opened his eyes to find a veritable wall of ice spears and fire lances encircling him, each as thick as his arm. Spikes made of rock and compacted earth levitated amidst them. Above his head, spinning in a growing funnel that swept debris up from the ground, was a storm of wind magic, the currents ruffling the flames crowning his head.

Renwick recoiled at this devastating display of power, his pale eyes widening with a flash of fear.

The air crackled with energy as Evander unleashed a

barrage of elemental attacks throughout the station. His magic swept across the interior of Charing Cross like a hurricane, absorbing the sinister tendrils thickening the air, smashing shadow bolts to smithereens, and sending mages flying into walls and pillars. The ground buckled and heaved, opening fissures that entrapped many of Renwick's followers.

For a moment, Evander dared to hope the tide was turning.

Then he heard it. The screech of metal on metal. The hiss of steam. The rumble of an engine pushed far beyond its limits.

He pivoted on his heels, his pulse racing.

Renwick had abandoned the passengers he'd been holding prisoner and jumped down on the tracks so he could cross over to the other side.

Evander realised why when he saw the train barrelling towards Charing Cross. It was wreathed in dark magic and would jump the tracks and crash inside the station the second it hit the bend, killing all that stood in its path.

Evander's heart thudded painfully in his chest as he fleetingly met Renwick's triumphant, snake-like gaze where the dark mage had reached the opposite platform.

It was clear the locomotive had been rigged in advance, likely in anticipation of the fight he would put up.

Time seemed to slow.

The train, a juggernaut of steel and corrupt magic, would crush the people frozen in terror in a matter of seconds.

And Viggo was too far away to help.

Evander's body moved before the decision had fully formed in his mind.

He jumped down on the tracks and sprinted towards the oncoming train.

"Noooo!" Viggo howled in horror. "Evander, stop!"

Magic surged through Evander, more power than he'd ever channelled before as he lifted the lid on his magic. The elements responded with a boom that shook the station and enveloped him in a maelstrom of energy.

Ice spread across the tracks and raced towards the train in a desperate bid to slow its progress. Wind roared, pushing against the unstoppable force of the engine. Earth rumbled and heaved as it tried to derail the massive vehicle. Fire took hold of the motor and wheels, melting metal to destroy its moving parts.

Still, the train kept coming, the dark magic and man-made machinery powering it smashing through the obstacles Evander erected in its path, a screaming demon hungry for destruction.

Evander planted his feet and stretched his arms out before him, his heart drumming a violent tempo against his ribs. He grunted as he poured everything he had into one last, desperate stand.

Walls of elemental energy given physical form sprang up before him, ice, earth, fire, and wind forming barrier after barrier the height of ten men and the thickness of a tree.

The train struck them with a noise like the world ending.

Metal shrieked. Magic flared.

The locomotive began to slow some thirty feet from the bend.

Evander's vision flickered.

It's too late. It won't stop in time!

He swayed, the taste of blood on his tongue as he felt himself nearing the limits of his powers. A crimson trickle flowed out of his left nostril.

Evander closed his eyes, his shoulders slumping and his last thought directed towards the man who had come to mean the world to him in the past few days.

I'm sorry, Viggo!

The shadow of the approaching train engulfed Evander. Just as he prepared for the crushing impact, something large and solid slammed into him from the side. He went flying out of the path of the train, landed hard on the ground, and tumbled across the divide between the tracks in a tangle of limbs.

Evander rolled to a stop onto his front, dazed and ears ringing.

The sight that met his eyes when he looked up made him freeze, just as it did everyone in the train station.

Viggo had braced his hands against the front of the train and was slowly, impossibly, bringing the massive engine to a halt.

The Brute bellowed, his face a rictus of effort. Tendons stood out on his neck. Muscles strained and veins bulged in his arms. His boots dug furrows in the ground as he relentlessly shoved against a machine that should have crushed him.

The train ground to a stop mere feet from the bend in

a final, tortured screech of metal. For a moment, silence reigned.

Loud cheers erupted, the sound deafening as people cried and embraced each other in relief and disbelief.

Viggo stumbled back from the train, his chest heaving. His eyes found Evander's, his expression a mix of relief and fury.

"You damn fool!" He stormed over to Evander and yanked him to his feet, his gaze wild and his voice trembling with lingering fear at what almost came to past. "What were you thinking?!" He shook Evander's shoulders before hugging him tightly to his chest, his body fairly vibrating with the after rush of adrenaline.

Evander shuddered and clung to him, heedless of who might be looking their way.

"I'm sorry," he mumbled in the crook of Viggo's neck. "I was thinking I couldn't let those people die." He pulled back slightly and squinted at Viggo. "The rumours were true. You stopped a train with your bare hands before."

Viggo cupped his face. "This was worse than Strasbourg. Seeing you standing in the path of that damn thing almost made my heart stop." He pressed his brow to Evander's, his hands shaking where he clasped his cheeks.

Evander opened his mouth to speak when he was cut off by Rufus's shout.

"*Evander! Viggo!* Renwick's getting away!"

CHAPTER 45

Evander and Viggo twisted on their heels.

Shadows danced around Renwick as he fled towards the other end of the station. The dark mage had unleashed his wind magic to aid his escape.

"Shit!" Viggo cursed.

He moved, his long strides eating up the distance to the opposite platform.

Evander willed his battered body to life and bolted after the Brute, wind magic lightening his steps. Behind them, Rufus started shouting orders at the Met officers who'd just turned up.

Evander caught up with Viggo seconds later.

"Don't fight this!" he barked.

The Brute shot a puzzled glance at him when he drew level.

"What do you—?! *Bloody hellfire!*"

Viggo's eyes rounded as the power of the wind buffeted his body and propelled him forward. They burst out of the station onto Villiers Street and looked around wildly.

Viggo pointed. "There!"

Renwick was on the footpath of the railway bridge, heading for the south side of the river. They sprinted after him, Evander's lungs burning with each gasping breath despite the elemental wind carrying him.

He'd nearly exhausted his reserves of magic trying to stop the runaway train.

Barges and boats moved sluggishly in the currents below them as they pounded the walkway after Renwick. The dark mage reached the south embankment, jumped down, and vanished in the warren of alleyways connecting the factories and mills crowding the riverfront.

Evander wondered briefly if they were being led into another ambush.

Trap or not, we have no choice but to go after him!

From Viggo's tight face, the Brute had had the same thought.

Letting Renwick escape wasn't an option.

"Don't slow down!" Evander yelled.

Viggo nodded grimly.

Magic surged through Evander as he manipulated the wind and brought them safely to the ground when they leapt. They took off in the direction Renwick had vanished, boots striking packed dirt and cobblestones.

Buildings pressed in on either side of them as they navigated a labyrinth of passages, the walls shutting out most of the late afternoon sunlight and casting them in ominous twilight.

"Can you sense him?!" Viggo shouted as startled figures cursed and jumped out of their way.

Evander narrowed his eyes. "I can!"

He accelerated and took the lead, following the scent of dark magic Renwick had left in his wake. It brought them to a section of the embankment lined with wharves and warehouses.

Evander slowed as they neared a deserted junction. The wisps of sinister power he'd been tracking had faded on a breeze blowing from the south. He stopped, his heart racing and his chest heaving with his breaths as he spun on himself and scrutinised the alleyways.

"Did you lose his trail?" Viggo asked guardedly.

"Yes." Frustration knotted Evander's belly. "Let me try something!"

Viggo watched tensely as he called on his fire magic and sent sparks dancing through the air. Evander stiffened when one of the streams of elemental power he'd cast out reacted to dark magic a moment later.

"This way!"

He twisted and bolted down the passage on his left, Viggo on his heels.

Their footsteps echoed against grimy walls as they approached a warehouse on the edge of the water. The building soared before them, cast iron windows catching the setting sun and smokestacks etched against an orange sky.

The oppressive weight of corruption hanging in the air pressed in on Evander like a suffocating shroud.

"Be careful," he warned Viggo as they reached the entrance. "This place reeks of dark magic."

A muscle jumped in the Brute's jawline.

They slipped through a gap in the heavy doors.

It took a moment for Evander's eyes to adjust to the gloom inside the warehouse. The interior was a maze of towering shelves packed with boxes and crates arranged over three floors, all connected by a central staircase and two goods lifts. Dim light filtered through the grimy windows beneath the roofline, the rays barely piercing the shadows in the eaves and between the murky aisles.

The air was thick with dust and the cloying scent of dark magic.

Evander's scalp prickled as they moved deeper into the building. They cleared the ground floor before proceeding to the south-facing stairs, Viggo in the lead.

Every creak of the wooden steps they climbed set Evander's teeth on edge. Renwick had to know they were in the building by now.

There were no signs of their foe on the first floor.

A pulse of malevolent energy washed across Evander's skin when he and Viggo reached the landing to the second floor. His heart thumped painfully as he brought forth a barrier of defensive wind magic, ready to repel whatever attack Renwick might send their way.

Every instinct he possessed told him they were likely walking right into the dark mage's trap.

They reached the top of the staircase and moved quietly towards the closest aisle, only to freeze when a low chuckle echoed through the cavernous space. They whirled around, trying to pinpoint its source.

"Welcome, gentlemen." Renwick's voice seemed to

come from nowhere and everywhere at once. "I'm glad you could join me for this momentous occasion."

Evander fisted his hands.

"He's using shadow manipulation to mask his location," he told Viggo in a low voice.

Viggo scowled.

"Stop hiding and show yourself, you cowardly bastard!" he shouted.

"Ah, but where would be the fun in that, Brute?" Another chuckle, closer this time. "Besides, I'm rather busy at the moment. Perhaps you and the Ice Mage would like to see what I'm working on?"

Evander's pulse stuttered when dark magic surged around them.

Crates and boxes exploded before he could react, showering him and Viggo with splinters. A violent storm swept through the building, raising a whirlwind of dust and debris that obstructed their sight.

Evander's gut twisted when dark shapes lunged at them from the turbulent currents.

Viggo cursed and stumbled backwards. "What the devil are those?!"

Evander's blood ran cold as he studied the apparitions from behind the shield of wind and ice he'd raised. Made of pure darkness, they were vaguely humanoid in shape and carried a stench that made his stomach roil.

"They're shadow creatures."

Viggo shot a taut glance his way. "Is this another kind of shadow manipulation?"

Evander nodded stiffly. He'd read about shadow creatures in arcane texts, but had yet to see them in real life. He realised then that he'd severely underestimated Renwick.

Only someone whose powers were nearly equal to that of an Archmage could bring shadow creatures to life.

One of the monsters dove for Viggo.

The Brute reacted instinctively as it breached Evander's barrier, his fist connecting with its face in a split second. To his shock and horror, his blow passed right through the apparition's dissipating form. The shadow creature rematerialised a moment later.

Evander released the shield and called on his fire magic. Globes of dazzling flames exploded into life around them. The creatures recoiled, their shapes flickering in the radiance.

"Viggo, we may be in over our heads," Evander said in a fraught voice. "If I'm right, Renwick could make scores of these creatures before we get to him!"

The Brute's face hardened with determination. "Then we'll just have to fight harder and find the bastard, won't we?"

Viggo's grit tempered the worst of Evander's fears. He took a deep breath and allowed elemental power to rush through him. Static sparked on his skin and hair.

Lassos made of wind and fire formed in his hands.

The shadow creatures shrieked and attacked.

Evander grounded his legs with earth magic and spun the elemental weapons around his head. The whips tore through the monsters, shredding them until they were nothing more than fading wisps of darkness. Viggo guarded his back, his immunity to magic a physical barrier even if his attacks proved useless against the creatures.

Sweat beaded Evander's forehead as the battle took them deeper into the warehouse, the shadow creatures coming at them on an endless tide of darkness just as he had feared. They rounded a corner and found themselves in an open area.

What Evander saw made him stop short in horror and had Viggo cursing out loud.

In the centre of the space stood a massive contraption. It was a nightmarish fusion of magic and metal some twenty feet tall. Tubes and wires snaked across the floor and connected to a circle of dark, pulsing crystals.

Evander's breath locked in his throat when his gaze found the source of the sinister magic powering the device. There, suspended inside a web of crackling dark energy above the monstrous machine, was Renwick.

The dark mage's eyes were closed, his face a mask of concentration as he levitated on a buffer of wind magic. Power poured from his body, feeding the machine below.

"What in the blazes is that thing?!" Viggo snarled, his fists clenching at his sides.

"It's an explosive device." Evander's pulse hammered in his veins. "With this, he could level half the southern embankment!"

CHAPTER 46

Renwick's eyes snapped open at Evander's words. They glowed with an unholy light that made him flinch.

The dark mage's voice resonated with power when he spoke.

"Very good, your Grace." A cruel smile twisted Renwick's features. "I'm glad to see your reputation for intelligence is well-deserved."

Evander steeled himself. "This madness ends today, Renwick!"

He gathered his magic around him like a cloak.

Renwick's smile widened. "Oh, I don't think so. You're a tad too late, your Grace. You see, the process has already begun. Soon, this part of London will be nothing but a graveyard for the thralls who live here."

Rage narrowed Evander's vision.

Viggo took a step towards Renwick, his eyes burning with hate.

They startled when the floorboards began vibrating under their feet.

The machine beneath the dark mage had hummed into life. An ominous energy crackled along its surface, filling the air with malevolent power.

Evander moved in front of Viggo and thrust his hands forward, sending a barrage of ice shards hurtling towards the device. He scowled when a wall of darkness sprang up before they could connect, absorbing the attack.

The shadow creatures had retreated to their master's side and merged to form a shield around the machine.

Renwick laughed, the sound echoing unnaturally around them.

"Did you really think you could stop me, Ice Mage?!"

He sent a wave of corrupt energy surging towards them with a flick of his hand. Evander barely had time to throw up a barrier of wind and ice before it struck. The force of the impact sent him skidding backward into Viggo, his boots leaving furrows in the dusty floor.

Viggo steadied him before charging forward with inhuman speed. He leapt, his massive frame soaring impossibly through the air towards Renwick's suspended form. His fingers were about to close around the dark mage's ankle when the black wall rose and solidified.

He slammed into the barrier and went flying backwards, crashing into a stack of crates.

"Viggo!" Evander cried out in alarm.

The Brute shook off splinters and dust and climbed to his feet. "I'm alright."

Evander's mind raced as his gaze found Renwick and his evil contraption. There had to be a way to stop it, to shut down the device before the dark mage could unleash its devastating power.

This can't be what the crystal vial was intended for! It's too big! Is this just another part of their plans to rid this city of thralls?! He clenched his jaw. *None of that matters right now.*

"Viggo, we have to destroy that machine! I'll create a path for us!"

The Brute dipped his head briskly.

Magic exploded around Evander as he unleashed his elemental powers.

Renwick scowled. Bolts of evil energy bloomed around the dark mage, along with another horde of shadow creatures.

Wind, ice, and fire swirled around Evander in a furious maelstrom as he deflected Renwick's attacks and mowed down the monsters, Viggo at his side. They advanced step by gruelling step, the Brute smashing aside the dark magic projectiles that got through his elemental defence.

The vile power crackling around Renwick intensified.

Evander's stomach dropped.

How the devil is he doing that?! It's almost like he's tapping into an endless well of dark magic!

The warehouse began trembling from the force of the battle, sending dust spiralling down on them.

Evander felt his strength begin to flag when they got within a few feet of the barrier. Sweat poured down his face. His breaths started coming in ragged gasps. Behind him, Viggo's movements were also slowing, the countless impacts he'd endured finally taking their toll.

Dread chilled Evander to the bone as he cut his eyes to the tiring Brute.

We're running out of time!

Renwick took advantage of his momentary distraction to strike.

Shadow creatures surged from the dark wall, faster than Evander could react. They wrapped around Viggo, pinning his arms to his sides and lifting him off his feet as they snatched him away. The Brute roared in fury, face reddening and muscles bulging as he struggled against their insubstantial yet unbreakable grip.

"Viggo!" Evander shouted, his throat thick with fear.

Renwick blocked his path as he floated down to the floor. He approached Evander, a vile energy swirling around him.

"Stand still if you don't want my shadow creatures to choke your dog, Ice Mage," the dark mage sneered.

Evander ground his teeth so hard his jaw ached.

Corrupt bands were coiling around Viggo's throat.

Their eyes met, their frantic gazes reflecting their dread and desperation.

Evander forced himself to remain motionless when Renwick stopped in front of him. The stench of corruption coming off the dark mage was so dense it almost made him gag.

"I must thank you, your Grace." Renwick reached inside Evander's coat. "I would never have found this had it not been for your presence in that alley."

He pulled out the crystal vial Evander had recovered from the scene of Millbrook's murder.

Evander cursed.

Renwick ignored him. He held the object between two

fingers and examined it with an evil smile, his grey eyes gleaming with triumph.

"The final piece of the puzzle," he murmured. "With this, my master's device will be complete."

Evander's pulse stuttered. *His master?!*

The suspicion he'd harboured solidified into certainty. Renwick wasn't working alone. There was someone else, someone even more powerful pulling the strings from the shadows.

Renwick slipped the vial inside his coat and twisted on his heels. He paused on his way to the machine rumbling menacingly a short distance away.

"Oh. I almost forgot." He turned and closed the distance to Viggo, an evil expression distorting his features. "Here's a parting gift."

Evander's chest tightened, his body fairly vibrating as he vacillated between the urge to rush to Viggo's side and not moving for fear Renwick would order his monsters to hurt the Brute.

"What are you doing?!" he demanded harshly.

His breath froze in the next instant.

Viggo's eyes widened at the sight of the dark gemstone Renwick had just extracted from his coat. The Brute cursed and began struggling even more fiercely against the monsters restraining him.

"Don't," Renwick warned coldly when Evander finally gave in to his instincts and moved.

The shadow creatures tightened their grip on Viggo's windpipe.

Evander skidded to a stop as the Brute choked and

wheezed, his nails digging so hard into his palms he drew blood.

"Please," he mumbled, despair a living thing eating at his soul. "Stop this! I beg of you!"

Tears sprung to Viggo's eyes. His face turned purple as he locked gazes with Evander, as if he wished to see him and him only in his final moments.

Renwick stared between the two of them. Understanding had him drawing a sharp breath.

"Oh." Stunned laughter left the dark mage on a bark. "Oh my! You and the Brute are lovers!"

His ecstatic tone as he bent over and laughed made Evander want to rip his heart out of his chest with his bare hands.

"I shall enjoy watching this even more!" Renwick said gleefully.

He straightened, walked over to Viggo, and rammed the gem into the back of his neck with a burst of dark magic.

Viggo's scream shattered Evander's world.

Renwick removed a ring from his pocket and slipped it on his finger. The dark stone atop it glowed crimson when he poured his magic into it.

Evander watched numbly as the shadow creatures under Renwick's command released Viggo.

The Brute landed on the floor with a soft thud. He looked up slowly.

A fresh wave of agony twisted Evander's heart as he gazed into Viggo's red pupils and impassive face.

No.

"Kill him," Renwick ordered callously.

Viggo moved, each step he took impossibly loud in Evander's ears.

Evander stared up at the Brute when he stopped in front of him, the fight draining out of him. He didn't realise he was crying until his vision blurred.

His name on Viggo's lips made him flinch.

"Evander," the Brute whispered in a strained voice. "Do you trust me?"

Evander swallowed convulsively, Viggo's expression clearing as he blinked rapidly.

The scarlet flare in the Brute's eyes was dimming. His jaw set in a hard line.

Evander went weak-kneed with relief.

Viggo was fighting Renwick's magic and the cursed gem. And by the looks of it, the Brute was winning.

Renwick made an angry sound behind Viggo and took a couple of steps towards them.

"I said, kill him, dammit!" he snarled.

Evander looked from the dark mage to the Brute and finally answered his question.

"With every beat of my heart."

Viggo smiled grimly. His hand flew to the back of his neck.

Evander's eyes rounded when the Brute ripped the cursed gem out of his flesh with a grunt of pain. Viggo turned and hurled the stone at the explosive contraption behind Renwick, along with the pouch he'd yanked out of his coat.

Renwick whirled around, hand outstretched and face contorting with rage.

"*No!*"

But he was too late. The gem had embedded itself in the machine, along with the Brute's bag of anti-magic tricks. Dark energy crackled and surged inside the device. It began to shake ominously.

Viggo lunged for Evander.

Evander gasped as the Brute barrelled into him and lifted him off his feet as he ran for the wall facing the river. Viggo smashed a window with an elbow and tossed him outside with all his might.

CHAPTER 47

THE WORLD SPUN DIZZYINGLY AROUND EVANDER AS HE FELL backward from the building.

No! Viggo!

Cool air chilled his flesh and ruffled his hair as his stunned gaze met the Brute's fleetingly.

"I love you," Viggo mouthed with a sad smile.

Then the dark waters of the Thames were rushing up to meet Evander. He plunged into the river, the cold driving the breath from his lungs.

Evander floundered as he sank, disoriented for a moment. Desperation squeezed his chest, sharpening his senses and allaying the panic threatening to overwhelm him.

I have to get back! I have to help him!

Water magic bloomed around Evander, creating an air pocket in which he could breathe. He swung his arms and kicked towards the surface, wind forming currents that aided his ascent from the icy embrace of the river.

He emerged with a gasp and spun around where he bobbed in the water.

The current had carried him a short way downriver.

He could see the warehouse some hundred feet ahead and to his left, the building dark and ominous against the twilight sky.

It disappeared in a violent flash that scorched Evander's vision.

The *whoomph* that accompanied the detonation made the air tremble and the surrounding buildings quake in their foundations.

The shockwave hit Evander like a physical blow, driving him back under the water. By the time he surfaced again, the warehouse was nothing more than a smouldering wreck.

"No," Evander mumbled.

His heart felt like it might burst from his chest as he swam desperately for the shore, wind and water magic carrying him there faster than his limbs could.

His feet touched the muddy bottom of the river after what felt like an eternity.

Evander staggered onto the embankment, his legs threatening to give out beneath him. He stumbled towards the burning wreckage of the warehouse, ears ringing and blood pounding in his skull.

"Viggo!" he shouted. "Viggo, where are you?!"

Smoke and dust choked the air as Evander picked his way through the debris, heedless of the flames still licking at the ruins and the sour stink of corrupt magic lingering in the air. He came to his senses and invoked his water magic to create a shower that rapidly doused the pockets of fire.

The Met's enchanted whistles echoed shrilly in the distance. A horde of officers were running along the footbridge towards the south bank.

Evander ignored them and wielded his wind and earth magic in a desperate search for the man who had come to mean the world to him, carefully lifting beams and sections of collapsed brickwork.

He has to be alive! Dear God, please make it so that he survived this!

Evander's eyes stung, whether from the smoke or unshed tears, he couldn't say. A sound made him freeze a moment later. His head snapped up.

A beam groaned as it was heaved from underneath, some fifteen feet ahead.

Evander nearly swallowed his tongue when he saw the large hands pushing it up.

"Viggo!"

He was at the Brute's side in a heartbeat and used magic to move the debris trapping him.

Viggo looked up at him from what remained of one of the chimneys. His face was covered in dust and soot and his hair was a mess, but he was otherwise miraculously unscathed.

The smile the Brute gave Evander was the most beautiful thing the mage had ever seen in his entire life.

"Well, now I know where to hide if a building explodes around me," Viggo said wryly.

"Viggo," Evander mumbled. His legs collapsed under him.

Viggo caught him as he fell to his knees.

"You idiot," Evander said thickly, tears streaming down his face.

Viggo gently embraced him.

"I know," he whispered in Evander's hair, his voice trembling.

"You ginormous buffoon." Evander's tone hardened.

Viggo sighed. "Alright, I deserved that one too."

Evander pushed him away and punched him in the chest. "You utter knucklehead! Why, I ought to—!"

The rest of his protest was swallowed by Viggo's lips.

Evander stiffened before shuddering and melting into the Brute's embrace, emotion choking his breath.

It was some time before they came up for air.

Evander cradled Viggo's face and stared into his eyes, his anger and grief all but forgotten.

"How did you know that would work?"

Viggo grimaced. "I didn't. I remembered what Millbrook's notes said about the device he'd made for Renwick becoming unstable if it was used under the wrong circumstances. I just hoped the gem and the disruptor rods in my possession would overload that bastard's machine." He glanced around, his expression sobering. "Looks like they performed better than I expected."

Evander frowned as he followed Viggo's gaze. "Renwick?"

"He's not a Brute, so I'm pretty sure he's dead."

They discovered the dark mage's body moments before Rufus arrived with a team of Met officers.

Renwick had been close to his diabolical machine

when it'd exploded. The detonation had ripped through most of his left side and blown away half his skull. He stared at them from his remaining eye, pupil blown and unseeing.

A glint in the rubble next to the dead mage caught Viggo's eye.

He crouched and picked up a fragment of the crystal vial.

"Damn." The Brute's jaw tightened. "I was hoping we could use this to track down Renwick's master."

Evander squatted beside him, his troubled gaze on Renwick's slack face as he recalled all they had learned that day.

"That vial is a fake."

Viggo's head whipped around. "What?"

Evander met his stunned stare and shrugged. "I was hardly going to go around with the real thing once we discovered what they were after."

"You crafty mage," Viggo murmured, admiration underscoring his voice.

Evander smiled faintly. "This crafty mage is all yours now, Brute."

Viggo blinked before visibly brightening. "So, the case is over?"

Evander swallowed a chuckle at his eager expression. "For now."

Viggo's gaze turned scorching. He clasped Evander's shoulders and leaned in for another kiss. Evander tilted his head, as eager to surrender to the man who had captured his heart as Viggo was to claim him.

They were interrupted by a shout.

"Evander!"

Rufus was clumsily climbing a mound of debris towards them, his eyes shining with relief.

"Damn it all to hell," Viggo groaned against Evander's brow.

Evander sighed and pulled away. "We have all night," he murmured soothingly.

Viggo scowled. "No, we don't. You'll probably be stuck writing up reports in Scotland Yard for the next couple of days at least."

Evander's heart sank. "Blast it. You're right."

They rose to their feet as Rufus reached them.

The inspector surprised Evander by yanking him into a bone-crushing hug in front of the Met officers who'd turned up with him.

"Are you alright?!" Rufus pulled back, his worried gaze roaming Evander's face before taking in the destroyed warehouse and the smoking debris. "What happened? What was that explosion? Where's Ren—?! Oh." The inspector sobered.

He'd spotted the dark mage.

"He's dead," Rufus mumbled numbly.

"We'll make a copper out of you yet," Viggo muttered nastily.

Rufus looked over with a frown. "I forgot you were still here."

Evander narrowed his eyes.

Viggo ignored his warning look.

"I swear, if it wasn't for the fact that you're Evander's friend, I would throw you in the river right now," he growled at Rufus.

Evander's mouth pressed to a thin line.

Rufus bristled and squared his shoulders. "Oh really? I'd like to see you—!"

They both gasped when cold water splashed down on their heads.

Evander retracted his magic and glared at them.

"What was that for?" Viggo muttered.

Rufus looked equally hurt.

"It's common practice to throw water on fighting dogs," Evander said in clipped tones.

"You tell them, your Grace!" someone shouted.

They turned.

Shaw was beaming at them from the bottom of the rubble.

"What are you doing here, Miss Shaw?" Rufus said sharply.

"I'm a forensic mage, sir," Shaw replied brightly. "I'm forensicing."

CHAPTER 48

EVANDER PINCHED THE BRIDGE OF HIS NOSE AND SAT BACK in his chair.

It was his fourth day writing up reports concerning the investigation into Alastair Millbrook's murder and its unexpected outcome. Not only had he had to submit the official paperwork due to Winterbourne, he'd also been asked to pen an account for the Ministry of Arcane Affairs and the War Office.

Viggo's going to be furious.

He'd met the Brute in his official capacity as the lead investigating officer on the case two days ago, when he and Rufus had taken his statement. Though Viggo had acted out his role as the head of *Nightshade* superbly, he'd been unable to mask his desire for Evander at times, something which Rufus had noted with a pinched expression.

Evander's crotch grew uncomfortably tight as he recalled the way Viggo's leg had brushed tantalisingly against his thigh under the table. Heat warmed his cheeks at the memory of the erection he'd sported throughout most of their meeting.

Thank goodness Rufus didn't notice.

Evander worked for another hour before putting his quill down and pushing away from his desk. He walked over to the window of his office in Scotland Yard and looked broodingly out over the Thames. His gaze found the blackened ruins downriver, as it had done many a time these past few days.

The events that had led to Renwick's death played through his mind like scenes from a nightmare. The battle at Charing Cross Station. The chase across the Thames and the southern embankment. And their final confrontation in that ill-fated warehouse.

Sleep had not come easily to him since that day. Every time he closed his eyes, he recalled the searing light of the explosion and the heart-stopping moment when he thought he'd lost Viggo.

They were still no closer to finding out the identity of Renwick's master, the true architect of the ghastly plan behind the *Blood Siphon*. In that respect at least, the dark mage's death was something Evander had come to regret. Still, there was no guarantee Renwick would have revealed his secrets even under the influence of a powerful enchanter.

A knock at the door drew him back to the present. He turned from the window.

"Come in."

Rufus entered, looking as weary as Evander felt. Dark

circles shadowed his eyes and his usually immaculate uniform was rumpled from hours of work.

"The report's in." The inspector dropped a thick folder on the desk and sat down heavily in the chair opposite. "You're not going to like this. Caine Renwick was a professor at the Royal Institute for the Arcane."

Evander's pulse quickened. He moved to the desk and opened the folder.

The Royal Institute was his alma mater, the place where he'd learned to hone his magical abilities and control his immense power. The thought of someone like Renwick teaching there made him sick to the stomach.

"He specialised in advanced Elemental Magic?" Evander said tightly as he read the file.

"Yes, with a focus on wind magic." Rufus sighed. "He was quite respected in his field, apparently. His colleagues describe him as brilliant, if a bit intense." He rubbed the back of his neck. "There's more. It seems there were a few rumours involving Renwick and some of his students. They were apparently brushed under the carpet by the higher-ups in the institute. Word on the street is money may have changed hands to silence the students' families."

Evander straightened. "What kind of rumours?"

Rufus hesitated. "The kind involving dark magic. Wind magic may not be the only thing he taught at the institute."

Evander stared blindly at the report, his mind racing.

How many young mages did Renwick influence with his twisted ideologies? And how deep does the corruption run?

"This is worse than we thought." Evander sat down heavily. "If Renwick was able to hide in plain sight at the institute, who knows how many others might be doing the same."

Before Rufus could respond, another knock sounded at the door. This time, it was Elias McAndrew and Vincent Brown. Both men could barely contain their excitement as they entered the room.

Philippa Scarborough trailed in behind them, concern etched across her normally serene face.

Surprise jolted Evander. He and Rufus rose hastily.

"Mrs. Scarborough," Evander greeted. "It's good to see you again."

"It's good to see you too, your Grace, Inspector." The curse-breaker dipped her head. "I wish my visit was taking place under better circumstances."

Unease pooled in Evander's belly at her grim tone.

"I shall let Mr. McAndrew and Mr. Brown talk first," Mrs. Scarborough said crisply.

"Your Grace," McAndrew started without preamble. "We've completed our preliminary analysis of the wreckage of the device recovered from the warehouse."

"It's absolutely fascinating, your Grace." Brown's eyes gleamed. "The level of magical engineering involved in that contraption is—well, it's beyond anything either of us have seen before. Whoever designed it is a genius."

"Get to the point," Rufus said impatiently.

McAndrew cleared his throat. "Renwick's device was designed not just to produce a powerful explosion the likes of which we've probably never seen before, it also acted as a channel to focus vast amounts of magical energy. It's how he was able to manifest abilities normally reserved for Archmages, just as you described in your account of the incident at the station and in the warehouse, your Grace."

Evander's heart thrummed heavily.

"How is that possible?" he said numbly.

"*Midnight Obsidian*," Brown said animatedly, oblivious to the dread chilling Evander's blood.

Confusion clouded Rufus's face.

"What's *Midnight Obsidian?*"

It was Mrs. Scarborough who replied.

"It's an incredibly rare and dangerous substance. Most magic users go their entire lives without ever laying eyes on it. It has the unique property of absorbing and amplifying magical energy."

McAndrew nodded vigorously. "It's like the mythical *Philosopher's stone.* Rumour has it you can only find *Midnight Obsidian* in remote caves in Western Siberia."

"The stone in Renwick's ring and the crystals powering his machine were made from the stuff," Brown added. He glanced at Mrs. Scarborough. "As were the cursed gems used to control Magnus Graveoak and the mages taken into the custody of Scotland Yard at the church in the East End."

Tension knotted Evander's shoulders as he processed these disturbing revelations.

"So, Renwick wasn't actually as powerful as he appeared. He was using *Midnight Obsidian* to boost his abilities?"

"Precisely," McAndrew confirmed. The artificer hesitated, his expression awkward. "Make no mistake, your Grace. Even without *Midnight Obsidian*, Renwick was a formidable mage. To control that much power without being consumed by it—" He shared an uneasy look with Brown. "Well, it speaks to his considerable skill."

Brown bobbed his head in agreement.

Evander clenched his jaw as he recalled the overwhelming dark energy that had emanated from Renwick during their final confrontation.

His master taught him well.

"There's more, your Grace," McAndrew continued reluctantly. "It appears what Mr. Stonewall did indeed stop the machine before it was fully activated. Had the two of you been unsuccessful in your attempts to stop Renwick…" The artificer trailed off.

"The explosion might have levelled half of London," Evander finished grimly.

A tense hush befell them at the thought of the dire fate they'd narrowly avoided.

"I fear I bring worse news, your Grace," Mrs. Scarborough said quietly.

Evander met her steady stare warily.

"The power used to control Magnus Graveoak and those mages is a form of *Blood Magic* known as *Sanguine Subjugation.*"

Evander went deathly still.

Brown cursed. McAndrew's eyes rounded.

Rufus blanched.

"*Blood Magic?*" The inspector glanced at Evander. "But that's—!"

"Forbidden magic," Evander said in a hard voice.

Mrs. Scarborough nodded gravely. "It's one of the darkest forms of magic known to exist. The ability to manipulate life force and vitality. To use blood to fuel powerful spells and even control the bodies of others. *Blood Magic* was considered taboo since it was often associated with dark rituals and sacrifices. There has been no known practitioner of the art in the last two hundred years."

Rufus swallowed. "And this—*Sanguine Subjugation* is similar?!"

"Yes." Mrs. Scarborough's jaw tightened. "*Sanguine Subjugation* allows the caster to completely dominate the will of another person, turning them into nothing more than a puppet. It requires a drop of the victim's blood, which is magically bound into the cursed gem used to control them. Just forcibly inserting the gemstone in someone's flesh would be enough to achieve that."

Rufus swore under his breath.

"That's—barbaric," Brown muttered.

Evander's chest tightened as he relived the moment Renwick had buried the gem in Viggo's flesh. The wound on the Brute's neck had already healed, courtesy of his powers of recovery and the Met's healers.

"As long as the cursed gem is intact and the matching stone is in the possession of the caster, they have complete control over their victim's actions." Mrs. Scarborough frowned. "The fact that Mr. Stonewall was able to resist the power of *Sanguine Subjugation* and break Caine Renwick's control over his mind is nothing short of miraculous."

Evander's mouth went dry. Not for the first time, he experienced a sense of profound relief and gratitude that Viggo had been born a powerful Brute.

"I hear he achieved more than one miracle that day,"

Brown grunted with a proud smile. "He stopped a runaway train with his bare hands *and* he survived that explosion."

"Yes, well, I'm sure Mr. Stonewall will get a medal for all his ridiculous achievements," Rufus said irritably.

Everyone stared at him, Evander with a scowl.

Evander suppressed an annoyed sigh and turned to Mrs. Scarborough.

"Is there any way to protect against this magic?"

The curse-breaker shook her head. "Not that I know of, your Grace." She met Evander's stare steadily. "The best defence is to never allow your blood to fall into the wrong hands."

CHAPTER 49

Evander's mind was still reeling from all he had learned that afternoon when he returned to his townhouse in Mayfair.

"Would you like dinner now, my Lord?" Hargrove said.

"Yes," Evander replied distractedly. "I shall freshen up first." He crossed the foyer and paused, one foot on the staircase. "Has there been any news from Mr. Stonewall?"

Hargrove's expression made him immediately regret the question.

"I'm afraid not, my Lord," the manservant said in a saccharine voice. "You shall be the first to know when he sends a missive."

Evander sighed. "Jasper?"

"Yes, my Lord?"

"Stop smiling like that. It's making me want to punch you in the face."

"That's cold, my Lord."

Evander took a shower and changed into comfortable

day wear before making his way to the dining room. Hargrove's stare turned disapproving as he watched Evander wolf down his meal.

"You'll get indigestion if you eat that fast, my Lord."

"And you'll be right there to nurse me back to health," Evander quipped, rising from the table.

"Har-har, my Lord," the manservant grumbled. "Shall I bring you some coffee?"

"Please do. And make sure no one disturbs me. I shall be working late."

Evander retired to the formal study on the ground floor and picked up several tomes on dark and rare magic from his bookshelves before sitting at his desk. They were exclusive editions rarely available outside the Royal Institute. Some he'd picked out personally from little known shops in Europe when he'd toured the continent.

The clock on the mantelpiece had just chimed ten o'clock when a mild breeze rustled the pages he was poring over. He frowned, so immersed in what he was reading it took him a couple of seconds to realise he'd not opened the windows.

Magic ignited his chest and warmed his blood as he jumped to his feet and whirled around.

"Good evening," Viggo said.

The Brute stood watching him with a quiet intensity where he leaned against the wall, his ankles and arms crossed. Curtains moved gently next to him, letting in the night air through the window he'd pushed open.

Evander's body grew light with relief. He retracted his magic and smiled tiredly.

"How long have you been standing there?"

"A good few minutes." Viggo's eyes glittered. "I like watching you work."

Evander's mouth went dry at the predatory light in the Brute's stare. He swallowed.

"I wish you'd use the door, like everyone else."

Viggo's lips curved in a smile that quickened his pulse.

"And miss surprising you? That would be utterly boring."

He straightened and closed the distance to Evander.

Heat coiled through Evander, as it always did in Viggo's presence.

Viggo stopped in front of him. His gaze searched Evander's face before he gently cradled his cheek.

"You look worn out."

Evander's flesh tingled where the Brute caressed him. He leaned into his touch.

"It's been a difficult few days."

Viggo's gaze moved past him to the books on the desk. He wrinkled his brow.

"Your nighttime reading appears to be on a somewhat serious topic."

Evander hesitated before relating what he and Rufus had learned that afternoon. A troubled silence befell them when he finished.

"So, this isn't over yet," Viggo said in a hard voice.

"It isn't." Evander ran a hand through his hair and sighed heavily. "But the murder case is closed, for now."

Viggo's gaze dropped to Evander's mouth. Evander's breath caught when the Brute brushed his lower lip with a thumb, his eyes darkening with an emotion that made his blood sing and his cock spring to attention.

"Really?"

Desire licked through every inch of Evander's body. He nodded tremulously.

"Good," Viggo growled. "Because I'm about to fulfil the promise I made to you the last time we were in this room."

Evander barely had time to draw a breath before Viggo's mouth landed on his.

The kiss seared his senses. Lit up his heart. Made him weak to the bones.

Evander could only moan and cling to Viggo as he claimed his lips with passionate savagery. The Brute danced his large hands over Evander's body, stroking him, kneading him, rousing his nerves until his skin sparked all over.

Evander gasped when Viggo walked him backwards to his desk and lifted him so he could set him on the edge.

"I want to fuck you so badly I'm pretty certain I'm going to embarrass myself the moment I enter you," Viggo confessed roughly.

He hastily unbuttoned Evander's shirt and shrugged it off his shoulders before dropping it on the floor.

Evander looped his arms around Viggo's neck as he nipped at his swollen lips, the Brute's tongue snaking out to lave the wounds he made while his hands found Evander's nipples. Evander hissed and dropped his head back when Viggo pinched and rubbed the hard nubs, pleasure spearing him with every clever move of Viggo's fingers.

Viggo took advantage and pressed torrid kisses down the column of his neck. He paused to feast on the pulse beating frantically at the base of Evander's throat before exploring his chest with his lips and tongue.

Evander cried out when Viggo bit his nipples and sucked them inside his mouth. Then Viggo's hands were on the buckle of his trousers and he was freeing Evander's weeping erection.

"I swear, your cock is the prettiest thing I've ever seen," Viggo groaned.

He trailed his fingers up and down Evander's naked manhood.

Evander twitched and bit his lip to stifle a lustful moan, his chest heaving with shuddering pants as he watched Viggo caress his shaft.

"Don't." Viggo tipped his chin up and tugged his flesh free from his teeth. He pierced Evander with a scorching stare. "I want to hear the sounds you make when I make love to you, mage."

Evander almost swallowed his tongue when the Brute dropped to his knees. Then his lips and tongue were on Evander's aching erection and Evander lost himself to the dizzying pleasure that was Viggo performing fellatio on him.

He grabbed fistfuls of the Brute's hair as the latter worked him thoroughly with his mouth, his hips rocking to and fro and his heels digging into the larger man's back. The sounds he made would have made him blush had he been in possession of his senses. But Evander could only close his eyes and feel.

Every clever lick and suck. Every heated breath that danced across his sensitive nerve endings. Every groan the Brute made as he ate him to his heart's content.

Brightness seared Evander's sight when he came. He bucked and convulsed, his mouth open on lustful cries as he emptied himself on Viggo's eager tongue, his head spinning from the ecstasy of it all.

He came to after a fathomless moment and found Viggo gazing at him hotly, his lips grazing his inner thigh with soft kisses.

"Was that good?"

Evander gulped, still shuddering with aftershocks of pleasure.

"Do you even have to ask?!" he panted.

A wicked grin lit Viggo's face. He rose to his feet, pulled Evander off the desk, and tugged his trousers and shoes off.

Evander's hole twitched as he watched Viggo strip, exposing the beautiful ink decorating his toned skin. His gaze roamed the Brute's brawny physique hungrily before landing on his impressive manhood. He swallowed, his insides quivering at the thought of being penetrated by Viggo.

The Brute took Evander in his arms and kissed him, his rock-hard shaft digging into Evander's belly as he worked his hands down his back and palmed his buttocks.

Evander clutched Viggo's shoulders and closed his eyes on a ragged gasp as he parted his crack and rubbed the pad of a finger up and down his entrance.

Viggo's whisper tickled Evander's ear. "Do you have something for—?"

"Second drawer on the right," Evander mumbled.

Viggo froze and straightened.

Evander blinked as he met his guarded stare.

"Should I be worried about the fact that you have that in your desk?"

Evander flushed. "I—I don't do that kind of thing in here. It was just—" He stopped and chewed his lip, his gaze lowering. "I remembered your promise, is all."

Viggo drew a sharp breath.

Evander sneaked a look at him from under his lashes. His toes curled at the sight of the Brute's feverish expression.

Viggo hastily opened the drawer and removed the vial of intimate oil Evander had tucked in there.

"Evander?" the Brute mumbled as he uncorked the bottle with his teeth.

"Yes?" Evander hummed and closed his eyes, his senses focusing on the delicious feel of Viggo's finger circling his hole.

"I don't think I can be gentle right now."

The Brute twisted him around, knelt behind him, and spread his buttocks.

Evander's mouth rounded on a shocked gasp as Viggo exposed him to the cool night air before flicking him with his tongue. He grasped the edge of the desk with a white-knuckled grip and moaned and cursed as the Brute used his mouth on him for a long, torturous moment.

Viggo climbed to his feet, his breathing loud and fast.

The musky smell of the oil hit Evander's nostrils as the Brute poured a generous amount in his hand. He shivered when cool drops anointed his entrance. Then Viggo's fingers were warming him, rubbing and circling with brisk motions before slipping inside.

Evander arched his spine and dropped his head back on a guttural moan as Viggo worked him open.

It wasn't long before the Brute crowded his back and pressed his cock to Evander's opening. They both groaned when he pushed inside, Evander shivering at the delicious penetration.

Sweat dripped off his nose as Viggo slowly filled him up, the sensation of fullness so exquisite Evander almost came there and then. He hissed when Viggo reached the tightest part of him, the sting and burn making him stiffen.

Viggo pressed soft kisses to his nape and worked his hand around his body.

Evander whimpered as the Brute started working his aching manhood.

Viggo waited until Evander was writhing and rocking his hips in pleasure before punching all the way to the hilt in a single thrust.

They both stilled, their pants echoing around the room.

CHAPTER 50

"Fuck!" Viggo growled. "You feel so good!"

He sank his teeth in Evander's shoulder, withdrew, and plunged back in.

Stars exploded in front of Evander's eyes as Viggo's cock hit the pleasure spot inside him. He came with sweet violence in Viggo's hand, his body convulsing and twitching uncontrollably, his breaths hiccupping through his throat.

Viggo swore as Evander's climax squeezed his shaft.

Then he was moving, one hand locked tight on Evander's hip so he could control the angle of penetration while the other cupped Evander's balls and teased his dripping manhood.

Evander moaned and groaned as he swayed under the Brute's powerful thrusts, the sting of his ardent possession lost in the mind-numbing pleasure he was delivering with every slick move of his cock. He knew he would be sore tomorrow but he was past caring right now.

Viggo waited until Evander came again before pulling out and turning him so he could push him down on the desk. He hooked Evander's legs around his waist and punched back inside his body with a curse.

Evander bit his lip as the new position allowed their eyes to meet.

Viggo watched him with fierce intensity as he made love to him, as if he were imprinting every second of this moment in his mind.

Evander squeezed his insides and laughed shakily when Viggo grimaced and let rip a particularly foul curse. His breath caught as Viggo grabbed the underside of his right knee and straightened his leg so he could drop his ankle on his shoulder.

Heat scorched Evander's cheeks, the new position exposing him to Viggo's hungry stare. He trembled when Viggo caressed his stretched rim with a thumb.

"I could stay inside you all day," Viggo whispered reverently.

He turned his head and kissed Evander's calf, his face flushed with passion as he stared into his eyes.

Evander lost track of time as Viggo made love to him, the desk shaking and rocking beneath them.

The way Viggo's neck muscles corded and his face took on a glazed expression as he finally neared his climax had Evander's breath catching. The Brute's fingers tightened painfully on Evander's waist, fixing him to the table so he could ram his swollen cock inside him with erratic thrusts.

Viggo exploded inside Evander with an animal sound of satisfaction that made his heart throb and his soul sing.

The Brute's orgasm tipped him over the edge once more, his insides contracting and his body convulsing jerkily until he was limp and loose-limbed with pleasure in the Brute's strong arms.

Evander's eyes fluttered open when Viggo pulled out gently. He bit his lip as the Brute stared at the place he'd thoroughly ravaged. A shiver shook him when he touched him there.

"Do you think you can go again?" Viggo asked, his fervent gaze finding Evander's.

Evander blinked. "Huh?"

His pulse stuttered when he looked down and saw the Brute's cock.

Viggo was still rock hard.

Evander didn't know whether to cry or lick his lips.

It seemed the rumour that Brutes had an insatiable appetite in the bedroom had not been exaggerated.

The decision was taken out of his hands when Viggo kissed him. He melted in his embrace, barely aware of the Brute picking him off the desk.

Evander found himself on his feet and facing the wall a moment later.

Viggo nibbled on his left ear. "I've fantasised about fucking you against these bookshelves ever since I first saw them."

Evander's cock instantly hardened at that. "You did?" He tilted his head to the side, giving Viggo access to his neck.

"Ah-huh." Viggo kissed and bit his flesh.

He nudged Evander's ankles wide apart, spread his buttocks, and impaled him with a ragged sigh.

Evander's eyes almost rolled into the back of his head as the Brute filled him to the hilt, the new angle providing a different kind of stimulation to his pleasantly used insides.

"Viggo?"

"Yes?"

Evander gave the Brute a hooded look over his shoulder. "I fantasised about this too."

Viggo blinked. Then his hands were on Evander's hips and he coaxed Evander's willing body into a wicked dance that had him moaning and gasping and cursing until he painted the floor with his seed, the bookshelves rattling under the force of their frenzied love making.

They moved to the rug in front of the fire next.

Viggo's eyes widened a little when Evander pushed him on his back and took control. The Brute surrendered willingly, his groans and breathless gasps soon filling the room. The sounds Viggo made echoed sweetly in Evander's ears as he used his fingers and mouth and tongue to explore the Brute's body the way he'd wanted to for days, learning what brought him the most pleasure.

Viggo licked his lips when Evander stopped suckling his cock and straddled him.

He stared breathlessly as Evander squatted above his rigid shaft and sank down slowly, hips rocking and a teasing smile playing on his lips as he took him in inch by slow inch. Viggo raised his hands to hasten the process, only to have his arms pinned above his head by Evander's wind magic.

"No touching," Evander hummed, his insides stretching deliciously around Viggo's cock.

"You're such a tease," the Brute groaned.

Evander panted as he seated himself fully on Viggo's manhood. He pressed his hands to Viggo's chest and began rising and falling, his body finding a rhythm he knew would drive them both wild.

Viggo cursed as Evander repeatedly impaled himself on his rigid erection. Evander shuddered, sweat dripping off his chin and splashing on Viggo's belly, his moans and cries ringing in his ears.

Viggo took over when he finally released his arms. He locked his hands on Evander's hips and thrust up powerfully until they both climaxed with loud shouts, his expression feral.

It was some time before Evander's awareness returned.

He realised he'd passed out from the pleasure of his last orgasm.

Viggo had fetched a bowl and towel from the small bathroom adjoining the study and was cleaning him up. They gazed silently at one another as he wiped his own body down and took a blanket and cushions from a sofa.

There was no need for words.

The affection shining in Viggo's eyes settled over Evander like a warm balm as they made themselves comfortable in front of the dying fire.

"I love you," he said quietly, his head on Viggo's chest.

"I love you too." Viggo pressed a soft kiss to his brow. "Now, sleep."

And sleep Evander did, the powerful beat of the Brute's heart lulling him into a dreamless state.

It felt like only minutes had passed when a shrill female scream awakened both of them with a start.

"What the—?!" Viggo sat up abruptly.

Evander looked around. He cursed at the sight of the wide-eyed and red-faced maid standing in the doorway of the study, a log basket in her hands. Chunks of wood clattered noisily to the floor when she dropped the receptacle and dashed out of sight.

"Did you forget to lock the door?" Viggo said.

"I told Hargrove I was not to be disturbed." Evander pushed up on his elbows, mortified. He froze and winced before carefully lowering himself back down. "That was last night though," he groaned.

Viggo stared. "That bad huh?"

Evander squinted at him. "Are you laughing?"

"I am not," Viggo protested in a strangled voice.

Evander gave him as haughty a look as he could summon considering they were both stark naked under the blanket.

"Well, you're not the one who's had a battering ram inserted inside his behind all night, sir."

Viggo guffawed.

Evander punched his thigh and groaned when the movement made his back and his intimate parts twinge even more. Viggo doubled over.

He was still laughing when the voices of Evander's housekeeper and manservant echoed down the hallway.

"What do you mean, his Grace has been eaten by a beast?!" Mrs. Sinclair said in an irritated voice as she drew closer.

Evander yanked the blanket up to his neck.

"I bet I know what kind of beast it is," Hargrove piped up in a devilish tone.

"I swear it, Mrs. Sinclair, Mr. Hargrove!" the maid whined. "His Grace was as naked as a fresh born lamb—"

"Lamb," Viggo snorted, tears streaming down his face.

Evander pinched his back, to no avail.

"—and the beast! Why the beast made such terrible impressions on his pristine skin! It must have hurt his Grace! It's—oh, it's *awful*, Mrs. Sinclair!" the maid fairly sobbed.

"I was right," Hargrove inserted gleefully into the conversation. "It was that kind of beast."

Evander looked down at his body under the blanket and sucked in air at the sight of the dozens of love bites Viggo had left on him. He scowled at the Brute.

Viggo chortled, unrepentant.

Mrs. Sinclair and Hargrove appeared in the doorway, the tearful maid hovering behind them.

"Oh." Mrs. Sinclair froze and blinked.

Hargrove's face split in a know-it-all grin that made Evander swallow a curse.

"Good morning, Mrs. Sinclair, Mr. Hargrove." Viggo smiled pleasantly, not in the least bit embarrassed by his nakedness. "It appears we are to be blessed with another wonderful day."

Mrs. Sinclair glanced at the sunlight streaming through the windows and the birds chirping merrily in the trees outside, as if wondering what the weather had to do with the depraved sight before her.

The housekeeper swiftly regained her composure and squared her shoulders.

"Good morning, Mr. Stonewall." She turned to the

confused maid. "Rosie, this is Mr. Stonewall. He is his Grace's friend—"

"Lover," Viggo interjected smoothly.

"—lover," Mrs. Sinclair corrected without losing a beat.

"I can see why Rosie thought his Grace had been eaten by a beast, Mrs. S." Hargrove arched an eyebrow. "It seems our Lord and Mr. Stonewall spent the whole of last night indulging in some rather wicked—"

Mrs. Sinclair stomped on Hargrove's foot.

The manservant grunted.

"Shall I serve a meal for two in the breakfast room, my Lord?" the housekeeper said serenely after shooing Hargrove and the maid away. "Say half an hour?"

Evander sighed. "Make it an hour."

The whole household will be talking about this for days.

That thought did not bother him as much as it should have. And that had everything to do with the man he'd just spent an unforgettable night with.

Evander realised Mrs. Sinclair was still standing in the doorway.

The housekeeper fidgeted. "Would you like a salve, my Lord?"

Horror widened Evander's eyes.

Viggo turned his head and bit his knuckles, shoulders quaking.

"No!" Evander yelped. He swallowed, his tone growing more composed. "I mean, no, thank you, Mrs. Sinclair."

Mrs. Sinclair wrung her hands. "My Lord, I can also heal your—" She faltered, her gaze dropping pointedly to the blanket. "I have changed your diapers after all."

Viggo strangled another snort at that.

Evander's face went even hotter. "I am quite alright, Mrs. Sinclair. Away with you."

Relief washed over Mrs. Sinclair's face. "As you wish, my Lord."

She left, closing the door quietly behind her.

Viggo began howling with laughter.

"You're a dead man, Viggo Stonewall," Evander hissed at the Brute. "Just you wait until I can move again!"

Viggo kissed him.

CHAPTER 51

THE LETTER ARRIVED ON A DISMAL MORNING, INSIDE A cream envelope that gave no indication as to its unsettling content. Penned in red ink, the polished cursive script was as elegant as it was cold.

"My dear Duke Ravenwood,

I must commend you on your impressive defeat of Caine Renwick. He was a talented pawn, but a pawn nonetheless. You and your Brute have piqued my interest. Rest assured, our paths will cross again. This game is far from over.

Until then, my worthy adversary.

I."

The thick, cream paper crumpled at the edges as Evander's grip tightened on it.

It had been a week since he'd received the chilling missive. The forensic mages at the AFD were still no closer to figuring out its origin or the identity of the man who'd written it. There were no magical traces on the letter, nothing to indicate its source or even a single clue as to where the paper and ink had come from.

Rufus and Shaw had wondered briefly if it was a bluff.

Evander had pointed out that Renwick's identity as the criminal responsible for the incident at Charing Cross had still not been made public. Whoever 'I' was, he was real.

A sigh distracted him.

"That's the third time you've read that letter in the past fifteen minutes," Viggo muttered, his large frame filling the plush seat beside Evander.

Their carriage rattled over cobblestones on the way to Belgravia, the enchanted interior dampening the jostling they would have otherwise experienced.

"Forgive me," Evander murmured apologetically.

He put the correspondence back in its envelope and tucked it inside his coat. They were on their way for afternoon tea with Ginny, following an enigmatic summons that had come the week before.

"There's nothing to forgive." Viggo clasped his fist where he'd rested it on his knee. "I share your frustration." His voice hardened. "We'll find him, don't worry." He uncurled Evander's hand and slipped his fingers through his.

Evander slowly relaxed, the Brute's warmth seeping into him. He leaned against his lover.

"Have I told you lately how much I like you?"

Viggo grinned. "You screamed it pretty loudly last night."

It was Evander's turn to let out a sigh. "Is your mind perpetually in the gutter?"

"When it comes to you, yes," Viggo said bluntly.

Evander pursed his lips, not sure whether to be annoyed or pleased. There was no denying that they were perfectly matched in the bedroom.

"I still can't believe you convinced William Millbrook to join the Charm Weavers Guild," Viggo said thoughtfully.

"It wasn't that difficult." Evander glanced outside the window. "He has his father's talent and passion for the craft. He just needed a gentle push in the right direction."

It had taken him a few days to convince Martha Millbrook and her son to return to London. With William now officially a guild member, their future in the capital was assured. Still, there was a risk their presence in the city would endanger them once more. Both *Nightshade* and the Met had assigned men to guard them for the time being.

Evander frowned.

Whoever I is, no one in this city will be safe until we get to the bottom of what he's after.

Viggo's troubled voice pulled Evander from his dark thoughts.

"Do you think he can do it? Complete his father's work and make the countermeasure to the *Blood Siphon?*"

The box they had uncovered in the woods outside Harpenden had miraculously survived the train explosion in Charing Cross, thanks in no small part to the protective charms Alastair Millbrook had built into it.

Evander hesitated. "All we can do is trust in him. I know the head of the Charm Weavers Guild. He'll keep an eye on William and offer him his support."

Viggo met his gaze steadily. "You believe we'll need it, don't you?"

Evander's jaw tightened. "I hope not. But after everything we've seen, everything we've learned—we need to be prepared for the worst."

The carriage turned onto Eaton Square and soon delivered them to Ginny's townhouse. Viggo eyed the white stucco residence warily as they climbed the steps to the front doors. Though the Brute had gotten used to spending his nights in Evander's home, the mage could tell he was still uncomfortable when it came to visiting other nobles' houses.

Viggo tugged his cravat uncomfortably.

"How can you wear this day in, day out?" he grumbled. "I feel like I'm being perpetually throttled."

Evander perused the Brute critically from his head to his toes, taking in his crisp shirt, royal blue waistcoat, the elegant, brown double-breasted frock coat highlighting his powerful frame, and his polished dress shoes.

He'd taken Viggo to his tailor in Savile Row a few days ago. Viggo had insisted on paying for the outfits Evander had ordered for him, this despite the mage's protests that he wanted to gift them to the Brute. Evander had surrendered in the end.

Viggo was a proud man after all and *Nightshade* didn't exactly lack the funds.

I definitely should avoid taking him to balls. All the ladies will swoon the minute he walks through the doors.

He wrinkled his nose at the thought of the men who might also entertain the idea of taking the Brute for an intimate ride.

"What's wrong?" Viggo said anxiously. He stared down at himself. "Do I look that bad?"

Evander kicked himself and brushed his hand against the Brute's knuckles. "Not at all," he soothed. "I'm just thinking I might have a pest problem if I take you out like this all the time."

Viggo stared, nonplussed. "What?"

Ginny's butler answered the door before Evander could elaborate. Viggo tensed.

"Don't worry," Evander murmured as they entered the townhouse. "Ginny doesn't bite."

"I've heard evidence to the contrary," Viggo grunted. "I'm pretty certain there's a gentleman in the city missing a chunk of his left ear because of Lady Hartley."

The butler didn't bat an eyelid as he ushered them across a grand foyer.

Evander knew the man had seen far worse. Some of Ginny's visitors struggled to maintain decorum in the face of her charms.

They were escorted into a sumptuous drawing room overlooking a garden.

Sunlight streamed through the large windows, the golden rays highlighting plush, velvet-upholstered furniture in various jewel tones and glinting off the silk threads in the rich, forest green, damask wallpaper.

Ginny rose from the sofa, her eyes sparkling above her cream-coloured day dress.

Ophelia Miller shot to her feet beside her, her expression stilted. The brunette was impeccably dressed, her outfit and accessories matching her blue eyes and highlighting her fair skin.

Ginny touched her hand reassuringly before crossing the room to greet Evander and Viggo.

"Evander." She smiled and kissed Evander's cheek warmly before bobbing her head at Viggo with a guarded stare. "Mr. Stonewall, it's a pleasure to have you in my home."

"The pleasure is mine," the Brute said. "And please, call me Viggo."

Ginny watched him for a beat. Her face relaxed. She grinned and looped one arm through a surprised Viggo's elbow and the other through a resigned Evander's.

"I can tell we shall all be great friends," she said confidently as she guided them to the other side of the room.

"Miss Miller," Evander greeted with a dip of his chin.

Ophelia bobbed stiffly. "Your Grace."

"Have you met Miss Miller?" Ginny asked Viggo.

Viggo met Ophelia's curious stare steadily.

"I'm afraid I haven't had the pleasure."

Ophelia's eyes rounded when Ginny made the introductions.

"You're the Ironfist Brute?!" she squealed, instantly casting aside her perfect image of a demure, well-bred young lady.

Viggo blinked, startled. "I am."

To everyone's shock, Ophelia grabbed her reticule from the sofa and reached frantically inside. She turned and waved a piece of paper and a magic quill under Viggo's nose.

"I would like your autograph, please."

Viggo opened and closed his mouth soundlessly.

"What?" the Brute finally mumbled in a dazed voice.

Ginny turned slightly, shoulders quaking on unlady-like snorts. Evander smiled.

Viggo cut his eyes to him beseechingly.

The mage made little effort to mask his delight and amusement.

Ophelia's jaw set in a determined line as she glanced between them.

"I know full well that you gave Duke Ravenwood's footman your autograph, Mr. Stonewall," she said doggedly. "It won't hurt to give me one too." She paused and blushed a little. "I am an ardent fan of yours, after all."

Viggo squinted owlishly. "You are?"

Ophelia ignored his incredulous tone and nodded vigorously.

"I am. It is my long-held wish to visit *Nightshade* one day and immerse myself in the atmosphere of your guild."

Viggo's eyes glazed over a little. Evander exchanged a startled glance with Ginny.

The effect Ophelia would have if she ever stepped foot inside *Nightshade* made all three of them shudder.

"Let's revisit that idea another day, shall we?" Ginny said brightly. "How about you give the lady what she wants, Viggo?" She dug an elbow in his ribs.

The Brute hesitated before gingerly signing the note.

Ophelia stared at it like it was treasure before carefully tucking it inside her reticule.

A knock sounded at the door. The butler announced Rufus.

The inspector entered the room. He wore a smart

double-breasted frock coat and was fussing with the cufflinks of his dress shirt as he walked in.

"I swear, these things are the devil's work," he muttered under his breath. He looked up and arched an irritated eyebrow at Ginny. "So, what's the momentous occasion that made you invite me here for afternoon—?" He trailed off as his gaze landed on Ophelia.

Rufus froze, his eyes rounding.

Ophelia stared unblinkingly back at the inspector, a delicate blush creeping into her cheeks.

A hush descended on the room as the pair gazed breathlessly at one another.

"Should we leave the two of them alone?" Viggo hissed, sotto voce.

Evander and Ginny surreptitiously stepped on his feet.

The Brute didn't even wince.

CHAPTER 52

Rufus finally regained his senses. "My apologies." He bowed his head stiffly at Ophelia. "I didn't know Lady Hartley had company."

Ginny introduced them to one another.

"It's a pleasure to make your acquaintance, Miss Miller," the inspector said, his Adam Apple bobbing nervously.

Ophelia curtsied shyly. "The pleasure is mine."

The butler had the maids serve them afternoon tea before closing the drawing door.

"Ginny told me you wanted to see us?" Evander asked Ophelia lightly after they'd helped themselves to tea and cake.

Ophelia exchanged a tense glance with Ginny. Ginny nodded wordlessly.

Evander was pleased to see the exchange despite the evident gravity of the situation. It seemed the two women had become firm friends, just as he'd hoped.

Ophelia took a deep breath and met Evander's gaze unflinchingly.

"I gather you know what I am, your Grace?"

"Please, call me, Evander," he murmured. "I have a feeling the five of us will become more than just friends today."

Rufus and Viggo gave Evander a puzzled look. Ginny frowned faintly.

"As to your question, yes, I know what you are," Evander told Ophelia quietly. "You're a light mage. And an incredibly powerful one at that."

Viggo stiffened. Rufus's eyes bulged.

Ginny cursed. "So I was right! That night at the ball, when you warned Evander. It was because you had a vision?!"

Ophelia bobbed her head. She sagged on the sofa, as if a great weight had been lifted off her shoulders.

"Vision?" Viggo said, puzzled.

Rufus frowned. "What vision?"

Evander gave them a cursory account of what had transpired at the Ashbrookes' ball. So much had happened since that night he'd utterly forgotten to tell them about the incident.

He studied a pale-faced Ophelia with a mix of wonder and concern in the hush that followed.

Wonder because light mages were incredibly rare and possessed powers that easily humbled most other forms of magic, chief among their talents being the ability to foretell the future. Concern because of the immense responsibility and danger that came with that status.

Light mages were considered on a par with Archmages

and could easily become targets for those who sought to exploit or destroy them.

Evander recalled the uproar that had accompanied the revelation of his Archmage status.

I understand why she chose to remain silent about her powers. Her family must have helped her.

"I appreciate your discretion in this matter." Ophelia's gaze searched Evander's face before flicking nervously to the others. "I hope you can all keep my secret for longer. It's not something I'm ready to reveal yet."

"Of course, we'll keep your secret." Ginny squeezed Ophelia's hand, her voice gentle. "We are friends, are we not?"

Ophelia sniffed and nodded, her chin wobbling. Ginny passed her a handkerchief.

"Thank you." She dabbed at her eyes before steeling herself and meeting Evander and Viggo's gazes. "The reason I wished to see you is because I had another vision last week."

Evander's pulse quickened. He leaned forward. "What was it about?"

Ophelia swallowed hard. "Before I tell you, I must say something. I cannot control my foresight, nor can I force it. The fleeting glimpses I receive of the future are often so vague I cannot fathom their meaning until the events are unfolding before my very eyes." Her gaze swung between Evander and Viggo. "I'm glad you heeded my advice about *Nightshade*. The two of you will need each other's strength to fight what's coming."

Tension radiated off Viggo in waves. Evander held his breath.

"Tell us what you saw, Ophelia," Ginny urged gently.

Ophelia closed her eyes, as if trying to block out the memory even as she recalled it. "I saw London." She swallowed, her voice barely above a whisper. "But not as it is now. It was frozen. Decimated by an ice storm."

Ginny sucked in air. Rufus cursed.

Evander's hand found Viggo's fingers, his heart thundering in his chest.

"The Thames was a solid white," Ophelia continued. She opened her eyes and fixed Evander with a look of desperation. "Buildings were encased in ice and frost, windows shattered by the cold, pipes buckled. And the people—" She stopped and shuddered. "Those who hadn't fled were frozen where they stood. It was like a city of statues, preserved in a moment of terror."

A chill that had nothing to do with Ophelia's vision shook Evander to the core at these words. His mind raced, possibilities and fears tumbling over each other in a dizzying whirl.

"I don't know when this will happen," Ophelia mumbled, oblivious to the sick feeling twisting Evander's stomach. "But it will, that I'm certain of."

"Evander? What's wrong?"

Viggo's concerned voice jolted Evander from his horrified daze.

Perspiration beaded Evander's brow as he stared at Ophelia. He could see the truth she had yet to reveal in her troubled gaze.

"It was me, wasn't it?" Evander said numbly. "It was my power that froze London in your vision."

Ginny gasped, hand rising to cover her mouth.

"What?" Rufus mumbled.

Ophelia fisted her hands on her lap. But she did not deny his statement.

Viggo unfroze and shifted closer to Evander, as if to protect him from what she would say next.

"That was part of it," Ophelia confessed reluctantly. She met Evander's stare unflinchingly. "But I am certain it was not the whole picture."

A heavy silence fell over the room.

"But—how?!" Rufus looked at Evander beseechingly, silently pleading him to deny the very possibility of such a future.

Evander could barely breathe, his chest was so tight.

"It's happened before," he said in a brittle voice. "Not to me, but to other Archmages. Losing control of our powers. It's rare, but when it happens, the results are invariably catastrophic." His tone turned bitter. "The only reason this is not widely known is because the authorities invariably mask the incident as a natural disaster."

Viggo's voice was unusually quiet when he spoke.

"Evander, you're the most controlled mage I've ever met."

Evander's heart thumped painfully as he met the Brute's steadfast gaze.

"I say this as someone who has seen what an Archmage can do, not just when I was a child but barely two weeks ago, in Charing Cross. The idea that you'd ever lose control like that is—" He trailed off and took Evander's hands. "I refuse to believe you could do that."

Evander shuddered, grateful for Viggo's words and his unshakable trust.

Ophelia drew a sharp breath, her stunned gaze shifting from their interlocked fingers to their faces.

"I'll tell you about it later," Ginny whispered conspiratorially in her ear.

Ophelia flushed and nodded jerkily.

"I can." Evander touched the Brute's face lightly. "If someone were to threaten you," he paused and glanced at Rufus and the two women in the room, "—threaten those I cherish, I would burn the world to save you."

Tears glittered in Ginny's eyes. Rufus gulped convulsively.

Ophelia wiped her wet cheeks. Her eyes bulged and a muffled squeak left her when Viggo took Evander in his arms and pressed a kiss to his hot brow.

"Then, we will stop you. We will stay by your side and make sure that doesn't happen," the Brute said in a voice that would brook no argument.

It was late by the time they left Ginny's home.

As their carriage rolled through the darkening streets of London, Evander's mind began to churn again. The anonymous letter, the lingering threat of what was still to come, and now Ophelia's vision. All of it threatened to drag him down into a dark mire from which he feared he would never escape.

He flinched when Viggo reached out and took his hand, engulfing it in his much larger one.

"Stop fretting."

Evander's shoulders loosened a little. He squeezed Viggo's hand. "You should know by now how much of a worry wart I am."

"I do," the Brute grunted. "I also know a way to distract you."

Evander gasped when the Brute picked him up and sat him on his lap so he straddled his muscular thighs.

"Viggo!" Evander yelped. "People can see." He glanced nervously out of the windows.

"No, they can't," the Brute said.

Evander's mouth flattened to a thin line.

Viggo sighed and pressed the button that rendered the glass opaque.

"How did you know about that button?" Evander asked.

He shivered as Viggo ran his hands down his back and cupped his buttocks.

"I had an informative chat with young Samuel about the special fittings of this carriage," the Brute muttered, nudging Evander's chin up with his nose so he could nibble on his throat.

Heat danced through Evander and pooled in his belly. His cock came to life.

"Viggo," he moaned.

The Brute tugged him closer and ground their erections as he continued kissing his neck. "What is it, your Grace?"

Evander twitched.

Viggo paused and straightened, a knowing smile lighting his face.

"I knew it. You like it when I call you your Grace when we're making love, don't you? I noticed the other night, when I was inside you." He leaned closer and whispered in

Evander's ear. "You squeezed me so tightly, I thought you were going to castrate me."

Evander shuddered, Viggo's breath on the shell of his ear driving him wild.

"No, I didn't," he denied weakly.

Viggo's voice turned gravelly. "Yes, you did—*my Lord.*"

Evander's cock jerked. Viggo's low chuckle echoed around the carriage.

Evander cursed, tugged the Brute closer, and silenced him with a blistering kiss.

THE END

~

AFTERWORD

Dear Reader

Thank you for joining Evander and Viggo on their first adventure through the magical streets of Victorian London.

Writing "Arcane Entanglement" has been an incredible journey, allowing me to explore a genre I have never written and a world where magic and romance intertwine in the most unexpected ways.

Bringing these characters to life and weaving their story amidst the backdrop of a London both familiar and fantastical has been an immensely satisfying experience. I've loved every moment of crafting this tale, from the intricate magical systems to the simmering tension between our male leads.

If you enjoyed your time in this arcane realm, I would be deeply grateful if you could leave a review. Your words not only help other readers discover this magical world but also fuel my inspiration as I continue to write the next books in "The Mage and His Brute" series.

As always, I thank you for your support. I hope you'll join me for the next chapter in Evander and Viggo's story soon.

With my most heartfelt gratitude,

Ava Marie Salinger.

BOOKS BY AVA MARIE SALINGER

FALLEN MESSENGERS

Fractured Souls - 1

Spellbound - 2

Edge Lines - 3

Oathbreaker - 4

Harbinger - 5

Crimson Skies - 6

Wicked - Fallen Messengers Short Story Collection

THE MAGE AND HIS BRUTE

Arcane Entanglement - 1

∾

CONTEMPORARY ROMANCE WRITTEN
AS A.M. SALINGER

NIGHTS

One Night - 1

The Escort - 2

Tokyo Heat - 3

Sweet Obsession - 4

Sweet Possession - 5

The Proposition - 6

TWILIGHT FALLS

ABOUT THE AUTHOR

Ava Marie Salinger is the pen name of an Amazon bestselling urban fantasy author who has always wanted to write MM urban fantasy romance. When she's not dreaming up hotties to write about, you'll find Ava creating kickass music playlists to write to, spying on the wildlife in her garden, drooling over gadgets, and eating Chinese food. She also writes contemporary MM romance as A.M. Salinger.

Visit Shop AD Starrling and buy all of Ava's ebooks, paperbacks, hardbacks, and exclusive special edition print books direct.

Click the link below to discover where you can connect with Ava:
Linktr.ee

Milton Keynes UK
Ingram Content Group UK Ltd.
UKHW020350211124
451507UK00015B/197/J

9 781912 834488